THE DEATH COLLECTOR

THE DEATH COLLECTOR

by

Neil White

Magna Large Print Books
Long Preston, North Yorkshire,
BD23 4ND, England.

British Library Cataloguing in Publication Data.

White, Neil
    The death collector.

    A catalogue record of this book is
    available from the British Library

    ISBN   978-0-7505-4033-9

First published in Great Britain in 2014 by Sphere

Copyright © Neil White 2014

Cover illustration © David Wall by arrangement with Arcangel Images

The moral right of the author has been asserted

Published in Large Print 2015 by arrangement with
Little, Brown Book Group

Magna Large Print is an imprint of Library Magna Books Ltd.

Printed and bound in Great Britain by
T.J. (International) Ltd., Cornwall, PL28 8RW

Acknowledgements

Being a writer is a solitary pursuit most of the time, but that is only part of the story, because my efforts would amount to nothing were it not for the patience and hard work of others. For every bad idea and muddled thought my editor and desk editor at Sphere, Jade Chandler and Thalia Proctor, are always there, to guide and advise, and it is their hard work that turns my first draft into something capable of sitting on a bookshelf.

A special thank you goes to my agent, as always, the wonderful Sonia Land from Sheil Land Associates, who made it possible for me to work with the people at Sphere, and has been a constant source of sound advice. Long may that continue.

Outside of the publishing world, I need to be grateful for the patience shown by my family, my wife and three sons, who tolerate me being the man who locks himself away for hours, quiet and moody. Writing can be as hard for them as it is sometimes for me. As for everyone else, it's the people I meet who inspire me, the source for ideas or characters or those little asides or quirks that somehow make it into the story. They might not know it, and it is often best that they don't, but I enjoy a secret smile at the knowledge of where they appear.

One

He sank back into the shadows as they stepped out of the car.

There were two of them. The car was parked right up against the wooden garage door, so that they had to walk round the back to go towards the house. There was a man he had seen before – the reason he was there – tall and slender in a grey wool jacket and a silk scarf slung over his shoulder, his shoes pointed brown leather, trendy and smart. The woman next to him was smaller, in high blue heels and a navy skirt that fell just below her knees, elegant and poised. Her heels made loud clicks that echoed as she walked.

He closed his eyes for a moment, steeled himself, not wanting to be caught. Although concealed by the darkness of a house opposite, along someone's garden path and in the space where the night still had its grip, he couldn't take any chances with a stray glance. The streetlights would bathe his face in orange light if he leaned out too far.

He listened out for any other movement but the street was silent apart from their footsteps. He tried to be patient, to wait until they got into the house, but the need to know was too much. He leaned out.

It was past midnight, most of the windows along the street were in darkness, with just the blue flicker of televisions visible in some. They were tall Victorian houses, three floors, with stone bay windows and small peaked eaves above attic rooms, cars parked along the street or crammed into the driveways.

The man fumbled with a key and said something that made the woman laugh, but only briefly and politely, so that his smile lasted longer than hers. She hoisted her handbag onto her shoulder and looked to the floor. Nothing more was said. There was an atmosphere. He was trying too hard. She didn't look interested. The door opened and they went inside.

He waited for the door to close and then emerged from his hiding place, his eyes sweeping the street, checking to see if he was being watched. It looked clear. He tried to walk normally to avoid suspicion, but his footsteps seemed like loud crunches that snapped in the night air, making him jumpy.

At the front of the house he paused, one hand on the gate, small and wooden and painted green. He took a last look around; still no one watching. He pushed and went through.

The garden was small, with just enough space for a rectangle of grass and flowerbeds. A line of concrete running to the front of the house served as a path. He crouched down as he went, stopping before the door. It matched the gate, wooden and green, with a stained-glass circle in the centre. He leaned forward and then craned his neck to see through, ready to duck back if he saw anything. The hallway was long and led to a kitchen at the rear, lined by polished oak floorboards and deep red wallpaper, the lights shielded by purple shades.

The main room was to the side, the light turned on. The curtains had been a canvas of dancing lights earlier – a real fire was his guess, left burning when the man went out – but the light was on now and had cancelled it out, turning the dark curtains into a bright red.

He moved quickly towards the window, to listen out, but then he saw a gap in the curtains. It wasn't much more than a crack, but it was enough for him to see through.

He ducked down, took one more look around, and then crept forward. He stopped at the gap and raised his head slowly above the sill, waiting to be seen. His heart hammered in his chest, his throat tight with nerves, as the room came slowly into view.

It was as he expected. There was a sofa and two chairs grouped around a fireplace, the man putting on more coal, bending over. Then he straightened and went to the woman, taking her coat from her shoulders, playing the host, the gentleman. She held her right elbow with her left hand so that her left arm acted as a shield. She looked nervous, and the short bursts of laughter that drifted through the window came only from him.

The man removed his jacket and scarf and put them on one of the chairs as she sat down on another, and then he went over to a table in the corner. As he removed the top from a bottle, she looked round the room as if it was her first time there, stiff and uncomfortable.

He passed her a glass but she didn't drink from

13

it. Instead, she held the glass in one hand as her other arm remained across her. He walked over to another part of the room, where there was something on a table. He lifted a lid to reveal a record turntable. It was dated, the colours faded. The man flicked through some albums stacked against the wall, and when he made his selection he took out the black vinyl and surveyed it against the light from the fire. He wiped it with a cloth, handling it only by the edges, and then placed it delicately on the centre spindle of the record player. He clicked a switch and there was a pause before the needle arm moved slowly through the air. As it landed, there was a crackle, and then the opening bars of a song he recognised but didn't really know burst from the speakers, loud and distorted. He had expected some modern smooch music, some kind of serenade designed to get his guest in the mood, but instead it was old-fashioned, something from decades before.

He ducked down as the man turned around. He was directly in line, so he waited as the song acquired its rhythm. Crazy, the voice sang, her tone deep and rich, the words distorted by the crackles from the speaker.

His breaths had got shorter, nerves making his fingers tremble, but still he wanted to watch. It was as if the rest of the street had faded; all he could think of was what was going on in the house.

He raised his head slowly. The man and woman were closer now, the man holding out his hand, inviting her to dance, his head cocked, expectant. She hesitated, as if embarrassed, awkward and stiff, but then her manners got the better of her.

She shrugged and put her glass on a small table nearby before going to him.

They moved together slowly, one of her hands on the back of his neck, her other loosely behind him, her head rested against his chest. He murmured to her as he swayed from side to side. The flickering light from the fire made her dark curls move and shift, just shadows in the gloom.

He became engrossed in watching them, their movement hypnotic. He didn't hear the footsteps behind him, heavy soles on the concrete path. He just felt the strong arm reach around his neck and then he gasped as he was pulled down to the ground.

Two

Joe Parker rubbed his eyes and rang the buzzer outside the police station entrance. It was a modern block of concrete and white windows on one of the roads out of Manchester, protected by high blue railings that were littered with take-away wrappers and crisp packets, blown against them by the passing traffic.

Summer was a couple of months away, so the spring nights still held some of the chill of winter. Joe shivered and pulled his jacket up to his chin. Lost sleep was one of the downsides of being a defence lawyer, he knew that, but that knowledge never compensated for the fatigue that he knew would pull at him the following day.

The intercom sparked into life and a bored voice said, 'Hello, can I help you?' It was loud along the empty street.

'It's Joe Parker from Honeywells,' he said. 'You've got someone in the cells for me.'

The intercom buzzed and then the door clicked open.

Joe checked his watch before he pushed his way inside: two thirty a.m. He hoped the visit would be quick; he might just grab a couple of hours sleep before he had to collect his thoughts and make some sense in the courtroom.

There had been a time when a visit to a police station was exciting, the fun of seeing the wilder side of life, like living out every police drama he had ever seen, but that was in the early days of his legal career. Ten years on, it was just part of the job, an unpleasant intrusion.

Some of the law firms in Manchester had their own army of clerks and police station runners, wages propped up by overtime, so the qualified lawyers avoided most of the late calls, doing just the duty solicitor roster to stay on the list. Honeywells didn't have that luxury. It was just Joe with his phone in his apartment, hoping that when he went to sleep the next sound he heard would be his alarm. He was helped out sometimes by Gina Ross, a retired detective who worked his cases, but Gina didn't like going to the police station. It was too much like her old job but from the other side of the table.

Joe always turned out, because sometimes that unexpected call turned out to be a big case that would keep the department in profit for another year, which was quite an achievement for a criminal defence lawyer.

So it was Joe's footsteps that echoed as he walked along a short tiled corridor towards another locked door, the buzzer sounding as he got there, the custody sergeant noticing him as he put his face to the reinforced glass pane.

The sergeant gave Joe a bored look as he entered the custody suite, a high-ceilinged space with no windows. Just a desk and the walls lined by noticeboards and pigeonholes, posters pinned to any spare space, informing prisoners of their rights in numerous languages or telling solicitors that phones weren't allowed. Joe dug into his pocket to hand his over but the sergeant shook his head.

'You won't be here long.'

Joe smiled. 'Good. There are better places to be at two-thirty in the morning.'

The sergeant considered him for a moment, and then said, 'Do you want a coffee?'

Joe was pleased that he had hit on one of the friendlier sergeants. 'Yes, thanks. Just milk.'

The sergeant went towards a small room at the back of the custody suite and the air was filled with the rumble of a boiling kettle. Joe didn't envy the man his job, responsible for every person who gets dragged through the doors, some quiet and compliant, others kicking and screaming – but they all have to be treated the same, the sergeant accountable for every bad thing that can happen. Some kept a quiet distance, sick of hearing every excuse and piece of abuse they got, and others saw themselves as hosts. It was a good sign, coffee in the middle of the night.

There were three custody records mounted on battered wooden clipboards hanging from hooks, each one bearing the scribbled records of a prisoner's time in the police station. The sergeant came back through, holding two white mugs. Joe pointed to the clipboards. 'One of those my guy?'

The sergeant put the mugs on the counter and then reached behind. He plucked one of the clipboards from the hook and handed it to Joe. 'Yes, if you could call him a guy. Just some quiet kid. Something going on though. He didn't want his mother here, so we've got the YOT lady instead.' And he gestured towards a holding cell, really just a glass box, where those queuing to be booked in sat until their space at the desk came free.

As Joe looked, he saw a young woman in there, the unlucky one from the Youth Offending Team, playing with her phone, in jeans and a big jumper. Hastily thrown on, was Joe's guess.

'So what do you know about this kid, then?' Joe said.

'Nothing. Never seen him before and he hasn't said much.'

'Why's he here?'

'He was snooping around a house, staring through a window. Wouldn't say why he was there but he looks like a peeper. A bit young for it though. If this is how he's starting out, well...' And the sergeant let the sentence hang so that they both knew what he meant. Bad habits only ever get worse.

'Okay, give me ten minutes with him and I'll get his story,' Joe said. 'If he's got a good excuse, he'll tell you and then I can go home.'

'And if he hasn't?'

Joe groaned. 'I'll tell him to keep his mouth shut and I suppose my night will get longer.'

The sergeant smiled. 'You'll make someone happy. There's a young copper on this job who doesn't fancy going back out into the night. Processing your boy keeps him warm in here until his shift ends.'

Joe pulled a business card from his pocket and slotted it into the clip on the board. He guessed at why he had been called out. Budget cuts had reduced overtime, so most officers went home when their shift ended, the prisoners left to stew on a plastic mattress with only the promise of a breakfast in a plastic tray ahead. The next day, a team of detectives would work their way through those locked up. Joe reckoned that they knew already they didn't have much of a case this time, so they wanted the prisoner in and out quickly. Just enough to arrest him, but everyone knew the case wasn't going to amount to much. They wanted him back on the street before they were obliged to feed him.

The details on the custody record were unfamiliar. Carl Jex — not a regular client. Joe flicked the pages and saw that he'd been arrested for voyeurism. Fifteen years old, his list of possessions amounted to a mobile phone, house keys, a bus ticket and some loose change.

Joe thanked him and went over to the holding area. As he went in, the YOT worker looked up. She didn't smile.

'How long are we going to be?' she said.

Joe could hear the tiredness in her voice. 'As

long as it takes,' he said. It was the only promise he could make.

She sighed and swept her long hair back. She didn't want to be there any more than Joe did.

As Joe took his seat, he looked to the rear of the custody area. Two officers were loitering near the pigeonholes at the back, where the property bags and police station slippers were kept, just nylon slip-ons in red or blue. They looked like detectives – the suits gave them away – but they were dishevelled, as though they had also been dragged out of bed. The older of the two, beyond fifty and tall, seemed familiar. He had a good tan and hair that was dark and swept back, so that it looked too high and slick. The other man was shorter and greyer, wearing his years less well, in a light blue jacket and white shirt that strained at the buttons.

Joe drank the coffee; he needed it. The day had been long, with a court appearance and a desk-full of correspondence. The one that lay ahead was unlikely to be any different. He couldn't escape the impression that the two detectives were interested in him but doing their best not to give it away. They kept glancing at the holding cell and didn't appear to be doing much else.

'Do you know anything about this lad?' Joe said.

She looked up from her phone. 'No. Not one of ours. His mother should be here really, not us.'

'Well, you're here now,' Joe said, as the door opened. A skinny kid with scruffy brown hair was escorted in by a white-shirted civilian gaoler. His eyes darted around as he came in, glancing through the glass wall towards the two suited men. Once they were alone, Joe said, 'Hi. I'm Joe

Parker, from Honeywells, and this is...'

'Susie, from the Youth Offending Team,' she said.

The young man kept his eyes on the two men in suits for a few seconds longer before turning to Joe. 'I'm Carl.' His voice was quiet and nervous.

'So tell me your story, Carl,' Joe said, as he rooted through his folder to find the sheets of paper he was obliged to fill out so that he could get paid for leaving his bed.

Carl sat down and said nothing. His knees turned inwards and he looked down at his feet.

'Don't be ashamed of anything,' Joe said, his voice low. 'Whatever you were doing, I've heard worse.'

Carl didn't look like a typical criminal, casually dressed in a checked shirt, jeans and blue trainers, although Joe reminded himself that the boy had been arrested for voyeurism. Sex offenders were hard to spot, driven by whatever lurks deep inside rather than by the kicks given them by life, even more so when they were this young. Carl's skin was pale, with a dark shadow on his top lip, his features awkward, part-man, part-boy.

'If you've called me out, you've got to talk to me,' Joe said.

Carl leaned forward, his arms on his knees. He spoke quietly. 'Is this room bugged?' he said. 'Why are we in here, in this room?'

Joe looked around and then back towards the custody sergeant, who was reading a newspaper, just filling time between his regular checks on his prisoners. 'They want you out quickly is my guess.'

When Carl didn't respond, Joe tried to stop his

irritation building. He could do without this. It was too late.

'Okay, I'll humour you,' Joe said. 'Why do you think it might be bugged?'

'Because they chose this room to put us in.'

'What do you mean?'

'These places have interview rooms, but they've put us in here. Why?'

Joe looked at his new client. He was used to dealing with people whose wires just didn't connect right, but there was nothing about Carl that stood out. Just some kid, looking a bit tired and like he would rather be somewhere else.

'Like I said, I get the impression they aren't planning on keeping you long,' Joe said. 'So talk to me.'

'Not in here, if you can't guarantee there are no microphones,' Carl said, his voice sulky.

Joe looked out of the room. The sergeant had stopped reading and was talking in whispers to the two detectives who had been hanging around at the back of the suite. No one seemed particularly interested in the holding area.

But he couldn't offer Carl any guarantees. He had heard of cases where the interview rooms were miked up, to pick up on conversations between crooks waiting for interview. It couldn't be used in court, but it might help to steer an investigation.

Joe sighed. 'Okay, I can't promise there are no microphones.'

'So we don't talk until later.'

'How can I advise you in your interview if you aren't going to tell me anything?'

'You don't have to,' Carl said. 'I was going to stay quiet anyway.'

All of Joe's fatigue rushed back at him. He could taste it in the staleness of his breath and feel it in the slow drag of his skin.

'If you're going to stay silent anyway and not tell me anything, why the hell have you dragged me out of bed?'

'I needed someone from Honeywells to be here. I didn't know it was going to be you. I'm sorry.'

Joe frowned. 'You could have just called the office if you wanted a chat.'

'I was going to at some point, but...' He shrugged. 'I can tell you all about it outside, but not in here.'

'Why is it so bad in here?'

'It's too dangerous,' Carl said.

Joe was too tired for games, but when he looked at Carl he saw a determination in his eyes that said that he wasn't playing. Whatever was on his mind, he was deadly serious.

And Joe couldn't deny that he was curious to know what it was all about. He smiled wearily. 'Okay, let's get this done and get out of here.'

Carl returned the smile. 'Thank you.'

Three

It was the comedown he hated.

The fire had maintained him through the night, kept loaded with coal to keep their heat and make it intimate, the flames casting moving shadows as they lay together. One last time.

His head was against her breast, his arm across her, keeping her close. He remembered their times together, those nights in his car in secluded lanes, or reaching for her hand in quiet restaurants far away from home so that no one would see them. Their secret, close and intense.

He opened his eyes and the scene had altered somehow. Gone was the warmth of before. The flames were dying down and the mood was different. Now, it felt empty.

Things had changed. The police had been outside earlier and someone had been at his window. That changed everything. It could be the end. How did he feel about that? He searched his mind for that gentle flicker of fear, but there was nothing. Just an acceptance. He had always known it was coming. The end.

He raised himself up on his elbows and looked at the fire. It kept him warm but it cheated him too. The heat would make her stiffen up too quickly, the rigor mortis setting in before the full rush of sunrise. All of a sudden she would feel alien and unreal against his skin.

He clenched and unclenched his right hand. Once tight round her throat, it was now cramping from the effort. He'd held her hands high above her head, stretched out across the floor, because she hadn't drunk anything. He'd relied on pure force, and it had made it different, not how he'd expected it. Normally they drift away before he takes them. This one hadn't worked out that way. He had looked into her eyes as he squeezed, tried to see her final thoughts in them, and they'd been there. Confusion at first, then fear, before he saw what he had been chasing. Realisation: the knowledge of what she should have always known.

No one leaves.

He'd seen that truth reflected in her tears. Her final view of the world had been his face screwed up in effort, brows furrowed, eyes narrowed, teeth gritted. If she'd mistaken that for passion she had been wrong. It was exertion, nothing more.

But it wasn't about her death. It never had been. He didn't fantasise about killing anyone. This was no pursuit of a rush he had felt once but couldn't recapture. As her skin puckered under the grip of his hand and he heard the fast rhythm of her heels on the wooden floorboards, the spittle landing on his cheeks as she fought, it was something else that gave him pleasure.

For now though, all he had was the waiting.

Her hair had fallen over her face, so he brushed it to one side, making it neat again. He looked at her. Where did all the excitement go? He had changed everything for her, brought some brightness into her routine. It had made her feel alive, so she said. So why end it, to finish up just the way she had started?

The clothes were always the difficult part. Her weight was too much now, but still he had to do it.

He reached for her blouse, flicking at the buttons before lifting her, gasping with exertion, pulling her blouse from one arm and then wrestling her so that he could do the same with the other until it dropped from her shoulders. Her bra came off next, before he lowered her gently back to the floor. Her skirt was easier, once he had undone the zip at the back, then her knickers.

He lifted her blouse to his face and buried himself in it. It bore traces of her, the orange blossom and spicy ginger from her perfume mixed in with her own soft traces, something unique to her.

It was important to know perfumes. Scents evoke memories and he needed to retain them. If he wanted to remind himself when he was out, he would go to the free samples, pick a small white strip and just wave it under his nose as he walked around.

He put the blouse and skirt onto a hanger and zipped them into a suit carrier. When he needed them, the smells would come flooding out, taking him back to when she had been his for a moment.

More music was needed.

He thumbed through his record collection and selected a Sinatra album. He went through the same routine. The careful removal of the vinyl. The gentle wipe with the anti-static cloth. The click of the record player – an old Dansette in pale green with a matt grey turntable. And then the pause before the needle landed with a fizz. Only when the first notes crackled through the

26

speaker did he go back to her.

He moved her left knee so that it was over her right and closed her legs, preserving her modesty. He took off his shirt, his skin glowing red from the effort of lifting her and the warmth from the fire, and lay next to her. He kissed her gently on the shoulder. Her skin still had some warmth but she would lose it soon. He put his arm across her and rested his head on her breasts once more. He closed his eyes. For a short while he would still have her, before she was gone for ever.

Four

The first light of morning was still an hour away when Joe left the police station. Carl Jex was behind him, yawning, and Susie followed.

Joe wondered whether he should just say good-bye and let the boy find his own way home. There wasn't much criminal work to be had out of Carl Jex. He was too clean cut and Joe hated being relegated to a chauffeur once he was out of the station, but Carl was young.

Susie said, 'I'm going the opposite way.'

'It's all right, I'll take him,' Joe said, taking the hint that Susie thought she had done enough. He wanted his bed, but he had to admit that he was curious about Carl's story.

'Where do you need to be?' he asked Carl, pressing the fob to unlock his car as Susie walked to her own. 'I can take you there.'

The police interview had been short, once it was obvious that Carl was going to stay quiet. He was released and told to return two weeks later, to allow someone to look at the evidence and decide there was no case.

'Are you sure you don't mind?' Carl said.

'You're too young to walk, and let's just say I'm still curious.'

Carl paused, looking back at the station, and then said, 'Okay, thank you. Can I go home?'

Joe remembered his address. He didn't know the street but he knew the area and it was the opposite way from his own home. His night had been long enough already, but the journey would give him a chance to find out more. He glanced towards the hills in the distance as he climbed into his car, the brooding shadows of Saddleworth Moor just silhouettes against the faintest glow of a lighter blue, the stars fading into the slow spread of daybreak.

The moors made him shudder. Even on the sunniest days they seemed to drag the mood downwards. They were devoid of high vegetation, just a long spread of heather and moorland grass, sometimes undulating gently and at other times rising and falling in sheer drops. It was as though a dark grassy blanket of sour mood had been thrown over the Pennines, the long stretch of hills that divide the north, the bleakness broken only by the glimmer of reservoirs fashioned out of the valleys.

Joe turned away. Even though he had lived in Manchester all of his life, the moors never failed to remind him of murdered children. They had

28

been used as a burial ground by an evil couple, the shifting ground of peat and soil making sure that one poor boy remained unfound, left for ever under the rough grass, his family in a never-ending search for his body. Myra Hindley and Ian Brady had stained those moors.

He didn't want to think of murdered children. He had endured similar pain in his own life, when his sister, Ellie, was murdered sixteen years earlier. She was attacked on his eighteenth birthday as she took a shortcut from school along a wooded path. The pain never went away. Ellie's death had defined Joe's adult life and her shadow was always with him as he went about his day job knowing that what he did helped bad people, some of whom had done similar things to whoever had killed Ellie. Yet it was the career he had chosen.

Ellie's killer was still out there, and Joe looked for him constantly. Every time he went to the police station he hoped to see the face of the man who had taken her away. Joe had seen him, a skulking figure who had turned to follow Ellie as she headed down the path, and he had done nothing. It was this secret that tortured him and had driven him to become a lawyer. He dreamed of seeing the man again, never letting that glimpse leave his memory. He had promised himself, and Ellie, that when he found the man, he would kill him.

Carl looked around before he got into the car, his eyes darting towards the murky corners of the car park.

'You look nervous,' Joe said, trying to shut away the brief memories of Ellie.

Carl was about to say something, his mouth

29

was open and the words almost formed, but then he shook his head. 'It's too early. I need to find out more.'

'What about? I thought you wanted to talk to me?'

'I do, but not here, and I'm tired.'

Joe nodded. Carl was right. 'Come and see me tomorrow, if you need to, after school.'

'I will.'

Carl stayed silent as Joe set off. The roads were quiet and, apart from the occasional wait at empty traffic lights, they were soon heading uphill and towards the small towns and villages that spread themselves along the foot of the Pennines, the last stop before the quick rise and the bleak plateau. Carl was constantly in motion, looking ahead and then behind through the car windows, only relaxing as they got further away from the police station.

They passed a bowling alley. Carl pointed to a turning off the main road. 'I was arrested a couple of streets further down there,' he said.

Joe looked to where Carl had pointed as he passed the junction, but saw just houses, nothing specific. He turned to him. 'Curiosity is getting the better of me,' he said. 'At least give me a clue: what's this all about?'

'Just watching two people dance in front of the fire,' Carl said.

'Oh, come on, there's more to this than just some cosy night in.'

Carl paused, as if he was thinking of what to say. He turned towards Joe and said, 'Have you ever heard of Aidan Molloy?'

Joe frowned. The name was familiar. 'You're going to have to help me out.'

'He's in prison, for a murder he didn't commit.'

Joe raised his eyebrows and gave Carl a wry smile. 'You're too young to understand this, but every murderer I've represented didn't do it, or so they said. But they all did.'

'Aidan Molloy might be the one telling the truth. Honeywells represented him.'

Joe was surprised. The name was familiar but it wasn't someone he had represented. 'It must have been before my time,' he said, and then something occurred to him. 'Is that why you wanted Honeywells, because of Aidan Molloy?'

Carl nodded. 'Your firm was the first one that came into my head.'

'So was this connected to Aidan Molloy, whatever you were doing tonight?'

'It's too complicated,' Carl said, putting his head back against the headrest. 'Like you said, I'll tell you tomorrow.' He glanced towards the brightening sky. 'Today, really.'

They drove in silence for a while longer, until Carl pointed to a small country lane marked out by trees that hung over its entrance. They cast growing shadows that twisted away from the streetlights that lined the main road. 'I live just down there.'

Joe was about to turn into the lane when Carl said, 'Here is fine. Otherwise you'll have to turn your car around and it'll wake everyone up.'

As the car came to a halt and Carl climbed out, Joe leaned across and said, 'I knew the name was familiar. Aidan Molloy. It's come back to me now. There's a woman in Crown Square most days. She has placards. She doesn't say anything, doesn't shout. Just gets his name out there, runs something like a one-woman campaign.'

'That's Aidan's mother, Mary,' Carl said. 'I've seen her there. I tried to speak to her once, but she didn't seem interested.'

'Who are you, Carl, and why does Aidan's case involve you?'

'I don't know if I can trust you.'

'I'm your lawyer,' Joe said. 'If I pass on what you tell me, you can get me struck off.'

Again, more silence as Carl considered that, until he said, 'If you're really interested, I'll show you later.'

'Why can't you tell me now?'

'Honest answer? I'm tired. I need to think.'

Joe smiled. 'Okay,' he said, and then gave a wave as Carl clunked the door closed. He watched the boy as he walked along the lane, just a shadow of awkward teenage limbs until eventually he disappeared altogether.

Joe shook his head. Carl was so young but there was something more worldly about him, as if he bore a burden that was beyond his years. Joe was intrigued, but it was late. He needed some sleep.

He set off again, heading back into the city to let the orange spread of Manchester take over his life once more.

The steady crunch of Carl's footsteps mingled with the early-morning birdsong as he walked down the lane to his family home. Trees overhung the road and blocked out some of the glow from the lone streetlamp at the end.

He rounded the corner and then he stopped. His mouth felt dry and his heart began to pound. He thought there was someone up ahead but there was nothing tangible. It was a sensation, or perhaps his mind working things out too slowly in that strange place that existed between awake and asleep, where dreams interject into the waking world. They hadn't been followed from the station, he had kept watch all the way home and there had been no car. So had someone got there ahead of them to lie in wait?

Carl listened, trying to hear something, nervous breaths or sticks snapping underfoot. He stood still straining for a sound, not breathing, but there was nothing, he was sure of it. He moved forward again, more slowly this time, his feet inching ahead, always ready to run, his footsteps silent so that he would hear any sudden movement. The lane didn't help, all shadows, just the spreading glow of the sun over the hills providing some relief.

He stopped, startled. There it was again, something ahead. Some movement, he was sure of it, like someone darting into the cover of a hedgerow. He closed his eyes for a moment. It might be his imagination, nothing more. He took some deep breaths before opening his eyes and setting off again.

The light from the streetlight disappeared completely. His house was further along, one of the first on the left, part of a row of houses built in the seventies, semi-detached houses clad in pebbledash. He thought he could make it there, but he could be trapped as he fumbled for his key. His hand reached out for the hedge that lined one side of the lane, so that nothing could jump out from the shadows without him feeling it first.

He stopped again. There was another noise, like the hiss of suppressed conversation, someone lying in wait. He looked back and shrieked. There was someone there, an outline of a man walking towards him, just a faint silhouette. Carl faced forward, looking around, panicking, and then there were noises, fast feet running at him.

Carl bolted for a gate that he knew was close by, his hands grabbing at the five bars, hauling himself over, panting and scared. He landed hard and started running, not looking back any more. His feet stumbled over uneven ground, molehills and raised clumps of grass under his feet. The quick thump of his footsteps gave away his position but he knew he had to keep going. They were coming after him.

The sun was rising ahead so his outline would be visible, but he gambled on his youth and local knowledge helping him. He aimed for a small copse of trees ahead, scrambling over a small stile, his breaths getting faster as he ran. The morning air was cold in his eyes, streaming tears along his cheeks, but he didn't stop until he reached the first shadow of the trees, his legs brushing against the longer grass, fallen twigs snapping under his foot-fall.

He leaned against a tall sycamore and looked back, his chest aching, sweat breaking out on his forehead. There was movement in the field. Two people. They were still coming.

Five

Joe Parker let the morning sun wake him as he walked to his office, the few hours' sleep since he'd returned from the police station not enough to rejuvenate him.

The Honeywells office was just a short stroll from Joe's canal-side apartment in Castlefield. It was the place where the railways and the canals all joined and created a busy triangle of bridges, where the electric screeches of the trams drowned out the calm lap of the water and the gentle putter of narrow barges. Their red and green paintwork was reflected perfectly in the dark water as two willow trees trailed their branches against the surface, the nearby streets nose-to-tail with cars and the clamour of the start of another working day.

He needed to feel the pleasure of his walk. He had tried a morning jog and a large pot of coffee to give his day some kind of a kick-start, but he felt the late night in the sag of his cheeks and heaviness around his eyes.

It made him think back to Carl Jex.

It had been an unusual police station visit. Some are like that – the demons that lurk inside some people can make them act strangely, made worse by the bare walls and the stamp of authority inside a cell complex. But it had been more than that, Joe was sure. Young criminals can be sullen and quiet, often hostile, but Carl was different.

Or perhaps it had been more ordinary than he realised. He didn't do as many late-night visits these days and the early hours can make minds wander and nerves fray. Only the serious cases kept going through the night. The smoking ban had made the visits easier; when he first started out as a lawyer, clients would call him out just in the hope that he had a cigarette. If he had forgotten to stock up, the meeting would soon get fraught and the person in front of him wouldn't care that Joe had given up on sleep to be there.

Carl Jex. A quiet and nervous teenager who wasn't willing to give up his secret, although it had been obvious that he'd wanted Joe to hear it. It all centred on Aidan Molloy, though.

The walk took Joe under railway arches and through a small public garden, created on the site of the church that had given the area its name: St John's. The streets that led away from it were lined with grand old Georgian houses, occupied through the decades by the professions, doctors and lawyers and accountants. Back then, it had been nothing more than a façade. Despite the air of gentility at the front, the streets behind had been crammed with workers' dwellings, front-street grandeur hiding the tough northern grind further back. The workers' dwellings were gone now, but the grand entrances of the main street with their lattice sash windows and Tuscan doors were still sought after.

The double white pillars in front of Joe's office building were visible through the rhododendron bushes that crowded out the exit gate with pink flowers, almost too pretty for a criminal law

36

practice. Joe was carrying on a tradition. Honey-wells maintained its criminal department out of habit; there wasn't much money in criminal law but it had lucrative offshoots. Childcare law, family cases, immigration disputes, prison law, because those who get on the wrong side of the police tend to get on the wrong side of many things. Criminal law wasn't yet a loss-leader, but it wasn't far from it.

Joe paused for a moment before he walked in through the side entrance, to the separate reception area reserved for the criminal clients. The thought of the grind ahead made him weary. He took a deep breath and went inside, smiling at Marion, the fifty-something receptionist who ruled the clients like a headmistress.

'Good morning, Mr Parker.'

He had told her often enough that he preferred just Joe, but the other departments felt it was more corporate to be addressed formally. Joe didn't care for any of that, and neither did his clients, but Marion seemed to enjoy the brief brush with respectability before she spent the day dealing with people whose lives ran along a different track.

'Morning. All quiet so far?'

'Seems that way,' she said, although as Joe walked up the stairs that curved to the first floor Marion shouted after him, 'Mr Newman was looking for you.'

That made him pause. Tom Newman, the senior partner. Joe gripped the handrail and peered back into the reception area. 'Did he say what it was about?'

'No, but he seemed keen to find you.'

Joe grimaced. He had been avoiding Tom for a while now because Tom just wanted to talk money. He tried to dress it up as targets and figures, but the truth was that the crime department did not put enough cash into the partners' pockets. Honeywells was a business. It was about the money, nothing else. There had been a partners' meeting over the weekend, a two-day event, where they drank and planned and developed the strategy for the future. If Tom was looking for him, Joe guessed that the criminal department had been discussed.

'Thank you, Marion,' Joe said, more subdued now, and then carried along the narrow corridor to his office, a small square room dominated by a leather-topped desk and with views to the gardens outside. It was decorated to look like a drawing room, with striped wallpaper and law books along one wall. The building was originally two grand old houses but long ago they had been knocked through into a small labyrinth of tight corridors and small rooms.

He savoured the quiet. Soon it would be time for the daily calls to the various police stations – checking whether there was any work to be had, keeping his name on the lips of the custody sergeants – and then he would have to focus on his existing clients and the day ahead in court. Another day of people who leave everything too late, who turn up at court expecting Joe to be ready even though they never bothered to turn up at the office to tell him their own stories. They were his constituency, those people whose lives had somehow been left behind. This was a moment of calm and he should enjoy it.

He looked at his desk, expecting to see the files for the day ahead, but there were none. He put his bag there instead, a small leather one that held the papers from the visit to the police station, and went looking for Karen, his secretary.

The secretaries worked from a small room down a flight of stairs, six of them serving all the departments. When he walked in, they were in a huddle, whispering to each other. When someone noticed him, they broke up and went to their seats behind their desks.

'It's all right, carry on,' he said, trying to be jocular, but when no one said anything he asked, 'What's going on?'

It was Karen who spoke. She was small and quiet with straight mousy hair.

'Mr Newman came in before,' she said. There was a tremble to her voice, and she looked at the other women in the room.

'What did he say?'

'He warned us that some departments might be closing, that we might have to look for new jobs.' A tear appeared in her eye. 'I can't lose this job. My husband's just been laid off, and well... I'm sorry, but it's hard.'

Joe sighed. This wasn't a good way to start the day. 'I'll speak to him,' he said.

Karen got to her feet and used the heel of her palm to wipe her eyes. 'I'll get you your files.'

'No, leave them,' he said, putting his hand on her arm. 'Bring them when you're ready.'

She looked at him and Joe felt the weight of responsibility. These people needed their jobs and it was Joe's job to bring in the money, which he wasn't doing. He gave her a smile of reassurance, but she must have seen the effort in it as she merely nodded and sat down again. Nothing was said. The smile wasn't returned.

He went to the kitchen to make a drink, needing the caffeine, the snatched couple of hours of sleep making it hard to concentrate. By the time he got back to his own room, Tom Newman was waiting for him.

Joe exhaled loudly. He didn't need this.

Tom was tall and trim and hawk-like, his hair receding and his nose in the air, standing in the doorway in straight pinstriped trousers and a well-pressed shirt, no pocket, with white cuffs and collar.

'Tom, good to see you,' Joe said, faking it.

'We need to talk about the fees,' Tom said. He grinned nervously when he said it, knowing there was conflict ahead.

Joe sat down in his chair, not ready for the discussion. 'I know how it looks, Tom.'

'No, don't,' Tom said, cutting him off, his hand in the air. He stepped into Joe's office and closed the door, leaning back against it. 'We know the reasons, Joe, and no one blames you. It's the cutbacks, we know that, and the way the police work, but that doesn't make you any more profitable.'

Joe took a sip of his coffee. 'So what do you need me to do?'

Tom looked down.

'Are you thinking of closing the department?'

Tom didn't answer.

Joe raised his eyebrows. 'Are you?'

'Not yet,' he said, 'but you need to find ways to make savings. We've all been hit by the recession, and businesses aren't buying and selling like they used to. It's all about consolidation, you know how it is. We kept the criminal department because of a promise to old man Honeywell, but now we have to look at breaking promises. I'm sorry, but the firm comes first.' He held out his hands in apology. 'Just make a profit, that's all. It doesn't have to be big; it's useful having you here, with all the spin-off family work.'

'And what about the civil side?' Joe said. 'How much profit have you made from my clients coming to you with beefed-up personal injury claims, or actions against the police?' Tom didn't answer. 'You'll lose all of that if I go somewhere else.'

Tom paused and then said, 'We can't carry any more losses. Take a look at your staff, see if you've got more than you need.'

'What, sack someone?'

'If you want the department to survive, you've got to make it pay,' Tom said. 'We need your proposals by the weekend. If you can't come up with a way of cutting costs without hurting fee-earning, we'll close it down, and then you'll be out. We can use your secretary and clerk in an expanded commercial department, but you won't fit there.'

And with that, Tom left the room.

Joe put his head back. So that was it. *Cutting costs* meant sack someone or walk away. Sacrifice himself to let his secretary keep her job.

The ring of his phone interrupted his thoughts.

'Hello, Joe Parker,' he said, always formal. Sometimes he gave out his direct number to clients.

It was Marion.

'Mr Parker, there's a woman here to see you.'

He checked his watch. He needed to be in court soon and he hadn't read the files yet. 'What's it about?'

'Carl Jex, your client from last night. It's his mother. She says it's urgent.'

He groaned to himself. It was hardly *last night*. The scent of the custody suite – stale sweat and disinfectant – was still on him.

He rubbed his eyes. He had no interest in seeing her. He didn't think Carl was going to be prosecuted and if there's no court appearance, there's no money. But if something was so urgent, she would only come back. He might as well bring an end to it now.

'Okay, send her up, thank you,' he said, and put the phone down.

He went to his office door and looked along the corridor. He could hear Marion giving directions – up the stairs and along the corridor and last door on the right – and he smiled politely when a small woman appeared further along. She didn't return it. She just stared ahead as if steeling herself for something.

Joe showed her in to his office. She sat in the chair on the other side of his desk, her knees tight together, her hands toying with a handkerchief, knotting it around her fingers. Joe recognised some of Carl in her small pointy chin and pursed lips.

As Joe sat down in his chair he smiled again, to put her at ease, and said, 'What can I do for you?'

'I'm Carl's mother.'

Joe didn't respond.

'From last night. Carl Jex. I'm Lorna, Carl's mother.'

'I know, my receptionist said, but I'm sorry, I can't discuss anything about the case, not without Carl being here.'

'I'm his mother.'

'The same applies.'

'It's not about the case,' she said, and her chin trembled as she looked up to the ceiling, tears brimming onto her lashes. 'Well, not really.'

Joe held up his hands. 'Okay. What is it?'

He knew something was coming. He remembered Carl's nervousness at the police station, his worry about being overheard, and although he was expecting something bad, the words still hit him like a punch when he heard them.

'Carl is missing, and I'm scared that he might be dead,' she said, her efforts to control her tears giving way to deep sobs. 'You've got to help me. You were the last person to see him alive.'

Six

Sam Parker straightened his tie as he arrived at the prosecution office. He signed in at the lobby and then headed into the small lift, his police identification swinging from his neck.

These visits had become more routine for Sam since he'd joined the Murder Squad, or the Major Incident Team, as it was more properly

43

called, although those on the team still preferred the old moniker. It carried more of a buzz when dropped in pubs and clubs, some of the younger detectives using the title like a pick-up line. Sam had been there for a year, drafted in after a few years working on the financial crimes unit.

Murder cases brought the prosecution and police closer together. Someone had died, in this case it was a gang killing, and the only way for justice to be served was for the killer to be found and put away. Everyone involved had different views on the case, but they all shared the same goal: to lock up the person who took a life and hope that he never saw daylight again.

This visit was an important one though, because it was an attempt to rescue the case. The trial was the following week and they were having trouble with witnesses. It wasn't unusual with a gang killing, a senior man in one gang murdered by a junior man from another – some young wannabe on the way up – but it was so important to keep going. There would still be reprisals, but there would be even more if the killer walked away: one gang would be angry and the other would think it had become untouchable. A conviction would at least keep one more participant off the streets.

But the witnesses weren't from that world: they were people at a bus stop who saw the murder, the taxi driver who unknowingly drove the killer away from the scene. They were decent people, appalled, happy to stand up for what was right, but eventually the revulsion started to fade and was replaced by fear, especially when their homes were visited by large men in suits, the scars on their knuckles showing their real occupation, thugs and enforcers.

There had been no direct threats, of course, just polite offers of lifts to and from court or entreaties not to worry about giving evidence. But the message they conveyed – delivered with smiles and good manners – filled the witnesses with fear: *we know who you are and we know where you live.*

As the lift door opened, Sam straightened his tie and identification badge. He took a deep breath. He was nervous about the outcome. He would have to report back, and if he didn't get what he wanted people would remember that, not the reason.

The prosecutor was waiting for him as he emerged from the lift. Kim Reader. He was pleased to see her. Tall and elegant, she was just what he wanted from a lawyer. Kim was smart and assertive with a good legal brain, but she also had enough wit to beguile a jury. She wasn't the lead prosecutor, a QC would handle the main parts of the trial, but Kim would keep everything turning over just fine.

Sam knew this was a tough case for her. She'd started to use hire cars for her journey to her office. It was every prosecutor's fear, that the next case might be one they can't leave behind in the office, the sanctity of their home shattered by a shotgun blast through a window, or worse. Kim didn't want to be followed, and changing her car reduced that threat, although Sam guessed that her home address wouldn't be hard to find out. The unwritten code – that those who work in the law are left alone when at home – is obeyed by most, but not every criminal sticks to the rules.

'Hello, Sam,' Kim said, smiling as he approached her. 'This shouldn't take long.'

She turned to walk back into the office, which was made up of narrow white corridors. The once larger building had been subdivided into small rooms, although some areas were designed for open-plan use. Sam could see heads just above computer monitors along the length of a room, mostly quiet, either admin staff dealing with the day-to-day processing work or lawyers working on active cases.

Kim pointed into a room as she walked along. There was a table with papers separated into piles.

'I was just going through the case,' she said, as she walked on. 'Coffee?'

'Yes, thanks,' he said, and followed her into the office kitchen.

As Kim filled the kettle, she said, 'How's Joe?' She didn't look at Sam as she said it, as if it was just a casual enquiry.

'My brother?'

'Yes.'

Then Sam remembered. 'Oh, that's right. You were at college together.' He gave a small laugh. 'He seems just the same as ever.'

'Does he?' Kim said.

'What do you mean?'

She frowned. 'I saw him a couple of weeks ago, in court, and he didn't have that same bounce. He's always been serious, but now he just seems a bit ... I don't know, like flat.'

Sam shook his head. 'He's not said anything to me, but he wouldn't, I suppose. Actually, I'm seeing him tonight so I'll speak to him. We have to eat at my mother's at least once a week – part of a new routine. Our little sister is getting out of control, so the plan is to go round and keep her in check somehow.'

'Ruby? How old is she now?'

'Fourteen, but she acts older.'

'They grow out of it,' Kim said, as she passed Sam a cup. 'All you can do is guide her so that she comes out of it intact.' She took a sip from her own cup and then sounded nonchalant when she asked, 'So Joe hasn't found himself a woman yet?'

Sam smiled, guessing that this was the question she had wanted to ask at the outset. When she blushed, he said, 'If he has, he hasn't told me.'

'Let's go and look at those papers,' she said, and walked past him, her cheeks glowing red.

Seven

'Carl, missing?' Joe said, confused, looking at Lorna Jex. 'I only dropped him off a few hours ago. Why would he be anything other than alive?'

'He went out last night and he hasn't come home,' Lorna said, her jaw clenched, her hands gripping a handkerchief, tears brimming onto her eyelashes. 'I called the police this morning when he hadn't got back, and they told me that he'd been let out a few hours earlier, and that he was with you, but I know he wouldn't have stayed with you. He doesn't know you.'

47

'I dropped him near to your house. I watched him walk up the lane.'

'What time?'

'About half past four this morning.'

'You let a child walk alone down a dark lane?' she said, incredulous.

'He said he wanted it that way,' Joe said, suddenly defensive. 'He might have just gone for a walk. He'd spent a few hours in a cell. It can make you want the open spaces.'

'No, it's not that, I know it. He would have come home, to tell me what had happened.'

Joe rubbed his eyes, fatigue sweeping over him. 'I understand your concern, but what do you want me to do? It should be the police you're talking to, not me.'

Lorna shook her head. 'I can't.'

'Why not?'

'I just can't, and I'm scared.' She started to cry again. 'I'm worried about what the police might have done to him.'

Joe tried not to roll his eyes. He was used to dealing with people who were paranoid about the police. He knew now why Carl thought like he did – his paranoia came from his parents.

'The police let him go, that's all,' he said. 'You really have to speak to them about it.'

'Did Carl mention the Aidan Molloy case?'

He paused, and then said, 'I'm sorry, I can't say anything about what Carl told me.'

'Was Hunter there?'

'Hunter?'

'Yes. DCI Hunter.'

The images from the night before rushed at

48

him. The two detectives at the back of the custody suite. One of them looked familiar and now he knew why. Andrew Hunter, although Joe knew he preferred Drew. He was the force ego, ever-present at press conferences, but with a reputation for the ruthless pursuit of criminals. Joe had come across him occasionally, had even gone nose to nose with him once, when Joe had told him that his client wasn't going to answer any questions. Yes, Hunter had been there, but Joe shook his head. 'I'm sorry; I can't say anything, not without Carl's permission.'

Lorna looked down and nodded. 'I understand. Thank you. I'm sorry for wasting your time.'

She stood to go, and Joe rose with her, ready to show her out, when she turned and said, 'If he gets in touch, will you ask him to call home?'

Joe smiled. 'I can do that for you.'

She was silent as he showed her out of the building, her shoulders slumped, heavy with worry. When he got back to his room, Joe sat down in his chair and then swivelled to look out of the window. He watched as Lorna emerged onto the street. She looked around as she walked quickly away, as if she expected someone to be following her, although the street was quiet. No cars started up. There was no one on the opposite pavement watching where she went.

Joe turned away and looked at his desk again. The room felt too quiet. He reached for the papers from the night before. Carl's details were written in Joe's shaky writing, scruffy from the late hour, and Carl's signature was the same, just a scribble.

Joe exhaled loudly. His room seemed too dark, the day did, so he got out of his chair and headed for the door. He needed to feel the sun on his face as some kind of reassurance that this was just a normal day, not one bound up in conspiracies or the threat of redundancy.

He skipped down the stairs, ignoring Marion's curious glance, and emerged, blinking, into the sunlight. He knew where he was going.

The gardens were quiet now, in that lull after the morning rush of take-out lattes and last-minute smokes, but before the throng of lunch-time sandwiches. He wandered to a bench on one side of the gardens, secluded and quiet. It stood out from the rest. It was new, the varnish on the wood still gleaming, the brass memorial plaque glinting in the sun.

As he sat down, he put his head in his hands. He had to fight to keep the tiredness away, but it was hard. He could hear the movement of people on the nearby pavements, mainly lawyers heading towards the courthouses, spilling out of the law firms and barristers' chambers. Joe didn't want to look up because he knew what he would see: confidence, smugness, smartness. He hadn't become a lawyer to join that crowd, and each day that he saw it, he felt more removed from it. Joe wanted out; it was as simple as that.

He stayed like that for five minutes until he heard the steady click of heels. He looked up. It was Gina.

She had joined the firm after retiring from the police. She knew all the tricks used in interview and was able to spot when the police had got something wrong and were trying to cover it up. Defending people is often just about creating doubt, and Gina could spot a botched investigation.

'What are you doing, Joe?' she said.

He sat back and squinted into the sun. Gina was silhouetted against it, her hair gleaming, her figure slender. She was just starting her journey through her fifties and she was wearing it well, regular trips to the gym and never having the worry of children keeping her looks and her figure.

'I don't know how much longer I can do this,' he said.

She sat down next to him. She was holding two files in her hand. 'What's wrong? You're not yourself lately. You've lost your smile.'

He looked at the plaque again, wiped it with his hands to take away some of the dust and dirt that had blown onto it.

'Death,' he said. 'It never leaves us. Everyone dies, I know that, so I'm supposed to shake these things off, but that's not how it should be. I should care, because what kind of person have I become when death doesn't get to me? So what do I do? Worry when it gets to me and drains me, or worry when it doesn't?'

'Who is it, Joe?'

'It's nothing, really. You don't know him. I didn't until last night. Just some kid at the police station. An early-morning visit.' He sighed. 'He's not even dead. He just never made it home.'

Gina looked surprised. 'How come?'

'I don't know. I dropped him off near his house, just yards away, but he didn't make it there. I've

51

just had a visit from his mother. What if she's right and something's happened to him?'

'Should it have done?'

'No, of course not, but it's bothering me. He's only fifteen.'

'You're talking about a client, though. Since when do clients do anything normal? That's why they're clients, Joe; they do crazy things and get into trouble.'

'No, this was different,' Joe said. '*He* was different. Carl, he wasn't like a regular.'

'What had he been doing?'

'Looking into windows at the front of a house.'

'Burglar or voyeur?'

'The police don't know. The householder didn't want to get involved so it'll fizzle out.'

'Whose house was it?'

'The police wouldn't say. They mentioned the street but I can't remember it now. I don't even know if I made a note of it. If he's charged, I'll find out then.'

'What did Carl say?'

'Nothing, and that's the point. The only hint he gave was that it was somehow connected to Aidan Molloy.'

'Aidan Molloy?' Gina said, her eyebrows raised. 'I haven't heard that name for a while.'

'So you know about the case?'

'All coppers did at the time. The assistant chief constable's daughter was found dead on the moors, dumped like old rubbish. There was pressure to find her killer, believe me.'

'I see his mother sometimes, campaigning in Crown Square.'

52

'She won't accept what was obvious, that her baby boy killed that girl. She'll get no favours from the Force.' She frowned. 'So Carl didn't elaborate at all?'

Joe shook his head. 'He said he would tell me when he came into the office, as if he was nervous about saying anything at the police station.'

Gina sighed. 'You met this Carl once, in a police station, in the middle of the night. I did thirty years in the Force. Manchester is full of people who think the police are involved in some evil conspiracy. Don't read too much into it.'

'Yeah, maybe you're right,' he said. 'We see too much death, that's all.'

Gina didn't answer. Her gaze drifted to the brass plaque on the bench. *In loving memory of Monica Taylor. A beautiful daughter.* Nothing more needed to be said. The bench had been put there as a memorial to someone who had worked at Honeywells, a trainee who'd died a year earlier when helping Joe with a case. The firm had paid for the bench, although her parents chose the wording.

Gina put her hand on his, following Joe's gaze to the plaque. 'The point is that you care. Don't lose that.'

He paused, and then, 'Yes, maybe you're right.'

'I don't mean to be brutal, Joe, but you can't spend any time on this boy's case now.'

'What do you mean?'

'Have the police charged him?'

'No.'

'So until they do, he won't earn any money for the firm.'

'You've changed,' Joe said. 'When you first joined, you were all about justice. Don't become like them.' And he flicked a hand towards the people in dark suits heading towards the court-houses.

'I still am about justice, deep down, but I've heard the whispers just like you have,' Gina said. 'The department doesn't make enough for the firm and they want the rooms to do something else. If we don't start billing more, we're in trouble.'

'I know that, and the whispers are getting louder.'

'What do you mean?'

'I saw Tom earlier. He laid it out pretty bluntly.'

'So try to forget about the boy,' she said. 'If he turns up, what's the problem? If he never does, where's the profit?'

Joe thought about that, and tried to read more into his memories of Carl, but all he could remember was nervousness about a secret he wanted to share only with Joe. 'Thank you, Gina.'

She let go of his hand and passed him the two files. 'You need to be in court in thirty minutes. You better get walking.'

He took the files from her and looked at the covers. Routine cases. An assault. A shoplifter. The daily drudge. Sometimes amusing, some-times repetitive, but often fun. It was the court-room he would miss if he gave it up. The little dramas and the insights into people's lives that he wouldn't get otherwise. And it wasn't just the gritty stuff, the everyday gutter tales. Life behind respectable curtains often carried as many dark hues as those played out at the more embattled ends of the city. The scams carried out to repay gambling debts, or the never-ending neighbour wars over foot-sized strips of land.

'Okay, I'll forget about Carl,' Joe said. 'I'll do the paperwork and close the file.'

Gina smiled as he creaked to his feet. 'It doesn't mean that we forget about these people,' she said. 'I think about Monica all the time. I sit here sometimes, like you do, but you're the only criminal lawyer in the firm. You've got to keep it going for everyone. We've all got bills to pay, and that's why we do the job.'

'I hear you, I'm going,' he said, raising his hand in submission, smiling now.

As he walked out of the gardens, Gina was still sitting on the bench. He knew she was right. Honeywells was a business. Carl Jex had been a customer, for the briefest of times, and he would gain nothing by thinking about him.

Except it was all he could think about as he walked towards the court, the files under his arm. Carl Jex had wanted someone from Honeywells, as if that was some link to whatever secret he had. His mind went back to the dark outline of Carl as he walked along the shadowy lane to his house, the place at which he never arrived.

For all Joe had said about closing the file, he knew he couldn't leave it alone.

Eight

He sat back in his chair with one leg crossed over the other, and raised his glass to his forehead, the chink of ice cubes cooling the film of sweat, the light amber of the single malt a warm glow in the room. He could see her through the liquid, her body distorted by the glass. The pressure in his head was a constant pounding, his tension almost too much to bear.

She was cold now. Her limbs had become stiff with rigor mortis. It had set in as he lay across her but he hadn't left her until he felt all the life in her body slip away, like a slow release, a long hiss.

This was the risky time, the waiting, with her still on the floor; but he always left them like this. He had to see the change from who they were, so that nothing was left of the person he'd known. It was the only way he could deal with the come-down, dehumanising them in order to keep away the darkness that threatened to swamp him.

It was different this time though. The police had been to his house. He'd sent them away, told them he wasn't interested, a shrug, boys will be boys, a peep through the curtains, but that didn't mean they wouldn't come back. And what of the young man he had seen being taken away? Why had he been looking through his window? Who was he?

No, things were different and he had to act differently. He couldn't afford to wait for the rigor

56

mortis to slacken before he disposed of her.

He smoothed down his trousers, sleek grey mohair with a sharp crease, Italian styling, and tapped his lips with his fingers in a fast rhythm.

He was distracted by the chime of the large and ornate silver carriage clock on the mantelpiece. She would be along in a moment. He looked towards the window and out at the view along a curving suburban street of bay fronts and mock-Tudor peaks, with grass verges that separated the pavement from the road.

She was a few minutes late, and he saw the flush of her cheeks as she walked quickly. She was always alone, so he guessed that she was new to the area. Her hair was pulled back into a pony-tail and her body was hidden under a drab jumper and jogging pants, her arms folded across her chest, heading to work at a small warehouse a few streets away

He closed his eyes with frustration. He would never get to know her. This was it, the beginning of the end. He'd always known it would come one day. That's just the way. He had no escape planned. Where could he go? No one stays on the run for ever, and this was his home. Wherever he looked he could see the memories his parents had left behind. Their furniture. Their paintings. Photographs of them on the bureau in the corner of the room. Their laughter, their talking. And their screaming. He remembered the screaming.

He clenched his jaw and closed his eyes as he was transported back to their regular Sunday ritual. The music on the record player, the crackle of the fire, both his parents enjoying a whisky from the decanter, the treat before the grind of the working week started. His father the builder, hardworking and tough, hands scarred by his job.

He shook his head. Nothing good comes from memories. They're not around any more. He had to deal with the present. With her.

So what now? He could do the usual thing, but he remembered the face at the window, the flashing lights as they took him away. It was over, he knew it, unless he could get some protection.

Then it came to him. The plan. He wouldn't enjoy this, but there was no choice.

Joe was distracted by the steady tick of the second hand on the clock at the side of the court-room. The chairman of the Bench, a red-faced man whose neck was spilling over his shirt collar, was berating his client, a shoplifter whose plea of innocence had been ignored. It was the same old collection of last chances and warnings of dire consequences if he should steal again. Joe knew they would be ignored.

The trial had been brief. Kai Redburn had tried to claim that he was just showing the radio to his friend outside, the plausibility of which had been destroyed when the prosecution used his previous convictions for shoplifting – thirty-eight of them – and the wide-eyed innocent explanation had been seen for what it was: bullshit.

Joe had tried to warn him, but Kai had summed it up better than Joe had by proclaiming that he had nothing to lose, because who goes to prison now that they're all full? Kai expected another minor sentence, another warning not to do it again, and that's what he was getting. His life would drag on for another year of unheeded warnings as he got through each day by hawking stolen items around the pubs near the estates. Razor blades and coffee used to sell well, but with the economy gone to shit, his client did better with cheese and bacon and baby wipes.

The case was over before Joe realised. There was a noise behind him as Kai left the courtroom. Joe looked up to the Bench; the chairman was leaning back now and talking to the two magistrates on either side. His outrage had all been for show.

Joe gathered his papers and looked across to the prosecutor, who was scrolling through her laptop as she tried to find the details of the next case.

She looked up briefly and said, 'He keeps us all in work.'

Joe looked towards the court door, which was closing slowly. 'Some of us, I suppose,' he said, and then followed Kai out of the courtroom.

Kai was waiting for him outside, pacing up and down the corridor and then holding out his hand to shake. 'Thanks, man,' he said, grinning, and then he went, heading for another day that he hadn't yet worked out how to get through. Whatever occurred to him, Joe doubted it would be legal. The prosecutor had been right – the system ticks over with people like Kai, who was simply one of the small ripples between the bigger cases.

Joe went to the window and waited for Kai to emerge onto the street, and then watched him as he strolled past the designer shops just off Deansgate. Kai didn't even glance at them. Those shops would be safe because Kai would be spotted. They were as out of reach for him as a thief as they were for most people with jobs. It was the discount shops where Kai succeeded; although the rewards were smaller, the chances of being caught were lower. He went for safety first, no gambles. Like an easy-access saver account, it was low risk but low return.

So went his own life, doing this for Kai because he had his own bills to pay, a slog through the low end of the law just to get through another day. He wasn't sure he was much different to Kai, except that he coated his life in respectability, in a suit, in a profession. Like Gina said, they were all just trying to pay the bills.

He ran his free hand over his face. His cheeks felt warm and tired, and too little sleep made him feel maudlin.

It wasn't just tiredness, though. A lot of the enjoyment had been knocked out of his career when Monica was killed, a sweet young trainee who died because of her connection with the firm, at the hands of a dangerous client Joe should have protected her from. Before then, the job had been fun, but Joe had felt guilty about enjoying it ever since. A memorial bench in a small park wasn't enough. And now Carl Jex was missing.

He doubted whether any harm had come to Carl. He was a kid and had spent the night in a police station. The wide-open spaces must have held greater appeal than facing his mother, but her concern niggled at him. Carl was worried about something, and now his mother was too. It was all connected to the Aidan Molloy case, or so it seemed.

As Joe walked away from the court, he knew where he was going, and why.

He sidestepped through the lunchtime set, the suits and bustle and busy clicks of heels, and into Crown Square, peering through the tables of the Swiss Restaurant and towards the modern concrete blight of the Crown Court.

She was there.

It was like a vigil. A small wooden stand, like a newsagent's A-board, with AIDAN MOLLOY IS INNOCENT printed on the front like a headline. A woman stood next to it. Her hair was long and dark and she was wearing a bright yellow T-shirt with *Free Aidan Molloy* written across her chest. She was giving out leaflets, although most people ignored her. Not through ignorance, Joe guessed, as many smiled an apology, but because they'd had the leaflet before. Aidan's mother was a regular feature outside the court.

Joe walked towards her, slowly, not sure whether it was the right thing to do. As Gina said, his job was to make money to ensure that everyone's wages got paid. But he remembered Carl Jex from the night before and his curiosity pulled at him.

Aidan's mother looked up as he got closer, her face brightening at the thought of an interested person. He held out his hand for a leaflet and she smiled as she passed it over, her hazel eyes shining.

'He's innocent,' she said. Her voice carried a faint Irish lilt, as if it had been a long time since she had lived there.

He held up the leaflet and said, 'I'll read all

61

about it,' before walking on.

He looked back at her as he went. Her smile had gone, her face reset into a mask of determination. He was going to go back and ask if she knew anything about Carl Jex, but he knew that it would lead to questions that he had refused to answer for Carl's own mother.

Joe looked at the leaflet.

It was glossy and double-sided. One side was filled with a picture of Aidan Molloy, an awkward-looking young man with too much weight around his cheeks and a thin smile, along with the shouted proclamation of innocence that adorned the A-board behind Aidan's mother. He turned it over to read the other side.

I am Mary Molloy and I am the mother of Aidan Molloy.

Five years ago, Rebecca Scarfield was murdered and taken to Saddleworth Moor. It was a lonely place to be left, an act almost as cruel as the one that killed her. My son is not capable of something like that.

Aidan is a gentle man, guilty only of having few friends who could speak up for him, but I can. I am his mother, the person who knows him best of all.

Witnesses lied about my son. They lied about where he had been. They lied about the things he had done. The people telling the lies included not only people who barely knew Aidan, but the police too, the very ones who should be finding the real killer. Those lies were believed by a jury and now my son spends every night in a prison cell, wondering why he is there, wondering when someone will attack him for what they think he did.

My son is innocent. Campaign for his innocence and help catch the real killer, who is still out there, amongst you.

God bless my son, and God bless Rebecca Scarfield, for her killer has not yet faced justice.

It was long on passion but short on facts, an impassioned plea from a desperate mother. It could all be true, but Joe knew too well from his own court experiences that it could be nothing more than disbelief, that clinging onto the idea of injustice was preferable to the reality that her son had murdered someone.

He had to forget about it. Gina was right. Forget about Carl. Forget about Aidan Molloy. Do the paperwork and move on.

He stopped as he heard his name being called, and as he looked up he saw his brother, Sam, walking towards him. Kim Reader was just behind him, smiling.

Joe returned the smile. Sam thought it was meant for him, so he smiled along too, and then said, 'We were talking about you earlier, and here you are.'

'This is my area of the city,' Joe said. 'What are you doing here?'

'Just a case that needed to go before a judge, to get some witness summonses.'

'Hope it's not one of my cases,' Joe said. 'I don't want you making them any stronger,' and then to Kim, 'How are you?'

'I'm fine,' she said, and she moved her bag to her left shoulder, her hand on the strap. She was blushing, glancing at Sam.

Sam saw the exchange and said to Kim, 'I'll let you two talk. Catch me up.'

Once Sam had walked on a few yards, she said, 'How are you, Joe?'

'You know, the usual.'

'I haven't seen much of you.'

'I've thought the same of you.'

'You know where to find me,' she said.

'And you me,' he said.

He wanted to say more but didn't know what. He and Kim had been intimate in the past, a few drunken nights at college, a little flirting across the courtroom, but their timing had always been out. They were never single at the same time, and Joe didn't do infidelity.

Instead, he smiled at her dopily until Kim pointed to the leaflet in his hand and asked, 'You taking the case on?'

Joe looked back towards Aidan's mother, who had resumed her position, trying to interest passers-by. 'I was just interested in what she had to say.'

Kim followed his gaze. 'She used to come to our office, asking us to look again at the case, but it's been gone through so many times. So she started going more public.'

'Those closest to offenders often see things the least clearly,' Joe said.

'That was my line,' Kim said, and then smiled ruefully. 'It's sad, though. I'm sure she means well, but she needs to move on and accept what he did.'

'Would you, in her shoes?'

'I don't know. Perhaps when I've children of my

own, I'll see things differently.'

'Or less clearly,' Joe said.

She moved as if to go, but then hesitated, placing her left hand on his arm and giving it a squeeze. 'It's good to see you again, Joe.'

'Yeah, you too.'

Then he noticed her hand as he looked down. Something wasn't right. There was a half-smile on her lips. She wasn't wearing an engagement ring any more.

Kim let go and started to walk after Sam. Joe was going to say something, but for a moment he couldn't think of the right words. So he watched her go, talking to Sam as they walked back towards the prosecution offices.

Joe's walk back to his own office had more bounce than before. Seeing Kim had given him a spark that had been missing.

He read the leaflet again. His thoughts returned to Carl Jex and the secrets he had promised to reveal, somehow related to Aidan Molloy. And now, just a few hours later, Carl was missing.

Then Joe realised something else: for the first time in a while he was interested in his job.

Nine

Sam Parker arrived back at the police station, an old redbrick building that was due to be sold, part of the drive to find savings in the budget. It was crumbling slowly, but the Murder Squad occupied the first floor, using the rooms at the furthest end. It had no front desk, nowhere for the public to make any complaints. The squad just provided a reason to heat the building to stop it getting damp.

The walk down the corridor was along a ragged blue carpet worn thin over the years and past rooms filled mostly with boxes, the walls decorated with old posters, some faded and stuck fast to the walls, others hanging from one corner so that they flapped in whatever draughts blew through the building.

He put his head round the doorway of DI Evans's office. She was working her way through some kind of noodle dish that had been brought to life by the kettle.

'I've got the witness summonses,' he said, waving the pieces of paper.

She looked up, her trouser suit grey, her hair grey and short, her face tired-looking. 'Good. Get them served.'

'I thought I'd get a uniform to do it.'

Evans raised one eyebrow and shook her head slowly. 'In a murder case, where we need those witnesses so much? I don't think so. Start this afternoon.'

Sam stifled his sigh. 'Yes, ma'am,' he said, and went into the main squad room, heading for his usual seat in the corner, closest to the windows, so that his computer screen was often bleached out by the sun. In summer, the heat through the window made his shirt cling to his back and in winter the wind blew in around the old sash frames and made his neck ache from the cold. It was all the fun of being the newest on the team.

Charlotte looked up from behind the screen opposite and smiled, her white teeth and light brown skin framed by black curls that tumbled down to the light blue of her suit. 'How was your trip to the courtroom?'

Sam shrugged. 'It was okay. Got a grilling from the judge about what we had done to persuade the witnesses to go to the trial, but Kim said he was always going to issue the summonses. He wouldn't let nervous witnesses derail a case.'

'So now these decent people, who were just there when it all happened, have the threat of prison if they don't get in the witness box against violent gangsters?'

'That's the way it has to be,' Sam said. 'Do you want them to get away with it?'

'Honest opinion?' Charlotte said, her eyebrows raised, tweezed to a thin arch. 'It doesn't matter whether we convict the killer or not. There's one dead gangster and another one will replace him. Sometimes a jostle for power makes it worse. For some of these lads, it's the only prospect they have. Some money. Some status.'

'And some prison, and some danger.'

'That's just part of their life, but these witnesses will spend a large part of their lives scared now, just for doing the right thing.'

'It's a civic duty,' Sam said. 'That's what the judge said, and he's right.'

'Okay, okay, I give in,' Charlotte said, grinning.

Sam pointed towards a small pile of papers on her desk. 'Anything new here?'

She shook her head. 'Couple of missing person

reports. They've been mentioned to us but not getting any attention just yet. Been told to be aware of them, that's all, in case they escalate. One of them has got Hunter twitching, though.'

Sam looked over her shoulder to the DCI in the other corner of the room, who was tapping a pen on the desk and staring at a screen. 'How come?'

'Do you remember David Jex?'

Sam frowned, and then he remembered. 'The detective who went missing?'

'That's the one,' Charlotte said. 'I worked on the same team as him when I first started out. He worked with Hunter until about a year ago, when he requested a transfer and ended up on community policing. Then six months ago, he just went missing.'

'Breakdown?'

'So they reckon. Some rumours about becoming withdrawn, as if something was on his mind. I don't know what his wife puts in their food, but she called in earlier saying that now her son has gone missing.'

'That's unusual,' Sam said, intrigue creasing his forehead.

'Not really. He was arrested last night for being a peeping Tom. Just a kid and probably too ashamed to go home.'

'Yeah, maybe. What's the other?'

'Some married woman who went out all dolled up and never came home.'

Sam gave a wry smile at that. 'Someone slept in and too scared to go home to her husband?'

'That's my guess. That's at the bottom of the list. So what now for you?'

Sam held the witness summonses in the air. 'Going to spoil a few people's evenings and drop these on the witnesses.'

'Beats sitting in here. Why did you come back?'

'I was hoping to get a uniform to do it. Evans said no. And anyway, my sandwiches are in the fridge.'

'How very rock 'n' roll,' she said, laughing.

He grinned. 'I eat, and then it's back on the mean streets, playing at postman.'

Ten

Joe saw out the day by answering correspondence and going through his filing cabinet, writing chase-up letters to clients, reminding them of appointments they wouldn't keep and court dates they would forget. He had to keep the paper trail going to make sure they couldn't blame him, because when they got lifted on a fail-to-appear warrant they would try to do just that; their need to get free was always stronger than the desire to protect Joe. He visited their lives in brief patches and he was forgotten about as quickly as he had been needed.

He tried not to think too much about what the senior partner, Tom, had said about thinning the workforce. He would make his decision when he was forced, and a big case might yet rescue him – something like a large fraud, which would keep Tom from carrying out his threat for a while.

Joe didn't move as he listened to the office wind to a close, the secretaries saying their goodbyes, the clerks not far behind. He could go, he knew that, and he was too tired to do much more, but he was waiting to be alone.

So he drank coffee to keep himself awake and listened as the main door closed and the final farewells were said. He turned in his chair to watch them head back to the home lives that Joe hoped he wouldn't wreck. When all he had left was the tick of the clock in his office and the noise of the traffic that filtered through his window, he moved the mouse on his computer to bring up the screen again.

He opened the client search facility. He went to the archive section, just a drop-down tab, and typed in 'Molloy'. There were a few, but only one Aidan. He had a file number and a location.

The archive files were kept in the basement for three years before being stored off site until they received their destruction date another three years after that. Except for the murder files, because murder files never go quiet. Aidan Molloy's file was in the cellar.

As Joe went down the stairs that swept into the reception area, the office was quiet apart from the faint chatter of one of the family lawyers working late; there was always someone willing to put in the hours, and it was better for a career to do it late than do it early. No one spots the early starters.

The way to the cellar was down a set of stairs just off the reception. It was a well-worn stairway as it was also the route to the staff toilets and a small kitchen. Beyond that there were rows of shelving that stored the files that shuffled their way along until they reached the date when they were shipped out to the external storage.

Joe rarely went into that part of the cellar; there were other people who located old files if ever there was a need. He clicked on the light, a pull switch that turned on a dusty yellow bulb, a cobweb arching to the ceiling. The room smelled of damp paper and it made his nose itch.

As he went through the room, he tried to make sense of the system. The archive number was different to the client number, and seemed to be based on the destruction date. Only murder cases were kept separate. Unlike the victims, murder cases never died. A prisoner always wanted to proclaim his innocence, and for as long as they did, they would stay in prison. It was a high-risk strategy, that an eventual finding of innocence would set them free, but people wanted to leave prison without a stain and with no life-licence hanging over them, as if they couldn't trust themselves not to do it again. The murder files were kept in the cellar so that no slim chance of a quashed conviction was given up to the shredder.

Joe found the file eventually. It had its own box. He sneezed as he lifted it down and removed the dusty lid, just to check the contents. Five black files: the prosecution statements, defence statements, exhibits, correspondence and unused material. It was usually in the unused material that appeals were won, that collection of papers the prosecution decided not to use but often led to inquiries that should have been followed. There were some scraps of papers, receipts and legal aid forms, and a wrapped-up bundle of papers tied up in pink ribbon, the barrister's brief.

He carried it up the two flights of stairs and was breathing heavily by the time he thumped it onto his desk. More coffee was needed, and once he had filled his cup and returned to his desk, he flipped the lid open again and lifted out the file containing the witness statements. With all cases like these, there were a lot of statements that didn't say much. They exhibited the paper trail, like search records and small pieces of evidence found in bedrooms, or bus tickets and train receipts. The crucial ones were the direct eye witnesses and the forensic statements.

As he read, Joe saw that the case against Aidan Molloy was good. It had stayed in the public conscience because of the identity of the victim's father and the casual way in which the body was discarded.

A young couple had driven to Saddleworth Moor, to do whatever it is young people get up to in cars in the darkness. As they pulled into a small track they often used, someone ran to a car ahead and drove off at speed, but they saw enough to get a glimpse, and even managed a partial registration: the letters 'DDA'.

Once the car had gone, their headlights caught something pale in the distance. They were curious, and when they went over to look, they wished they hadn't. They found a woman, Rebecca Scarfield, twenty-nine years old, naked and dead.

The police were under pressure right from the start. Her father was Desmond Archer, the assistant chief constable, and she was a respectable woman, married to a local car salesman, two children. They wondered if it was a revenge attack connected to her father, but then attention turned to Rebecca's love life. That was when the case turned against Aidan Molloy.

Rebecca's marriage was in trouble. She had craved attention, and when her husband stopped giving it to her she went looking for it elsewhere. Her phone logs showed one regular caller: Aidan Molloy. So the police visited and the case started coming together.

Rebecca had been seeing Aidan, an impressionable young man caught in the glare of an attractive older woman. But when the police visited him, he lied. About whether he knew her and about where he had been that night. Once the lies started, he became a man with something to hide.

When the police ran the partial vehicle registration through the computer, 'DDA', there were a few matches, and one of the local ones was Aidan Molloy's car.

There was no DNA on Rebecca. There was no sign of a sexual assault. It was just circumstantial and Aidan's failure to nail an alibi made him a major suspect. When his mother was first spoken to, she told the police he had got in at two thirty in the morning, but Aidan had said it was half-past midnight. None of the neighbours remembered him coming home. The only thing Aidan could say was that it wasn't him.

And then there were the threats. Three young women gave statements claiming that Aidan had threatened Rebecca, saying he would kill her if she ever tried to leave him.

The spade was the clincher, in the boot of his car. Brand new, with a wooden handle and clods of peat stuck to the blade, the same sort of soil found on the moors near to where she had been found. The prosecution's case was that he had been caught in the act of burying her and when the young couple came along, he panicked.

Joe put the file down. The case was a good one. Aidan had made his protestations of innocence to the jury, and they had looked him in the eyes and not believed him.

He put his head back and closed his eyes, suddenly tired, aware that he had given some of his evening to satisfy his curiosity and it had come to nothing.

But it was more than that. He was trying to salvage something from his job, a spark to relight the fire that had dimmed after Monica's death and the guilt he felt because of it. It was as if he wasn't allowed to enjoy it any more. He was looking for a cause to inspire him.

It was time to go home. He stood up to put the file back into the box, just flicking through it one more time, the names and typed paragraphs merging into one spool of grey and white.

Then he saw it.

He stopped, went back through the statements, trying to see what had attracted his attention, his eyes skimming over the words. He saw it again. A single word. A name: Jex. Detective Sergeant David Jex.

It was an unusual name, an unlikely coincidence. Carl's father, or uncle? Brother?

That made Joe pause, his mind suddenly started to whirl, the gears clanking together. There was something else going on. Someone related to Carl Jex had been a detective on Aidan's case and now Carl had become interested in it. But Carl had been wary of the police whilst Lorna, his mother, was worried that the police might have done something to him. But why hadn't either Carl or Lorna mentioned the involvement of David Jex? And why would either of them be worried about the police?

Joe carried on flicking through the file, turning the pages faster, looking for anything else that seemed familiar. Then he saw something that surprised him. It was another name: DCI Hunter. He had been at the police station the night before. Lorna had mentioned him.

Joe allowed himself a small smile. Now he was interested.

Eleven

Carl Jex hid behind the leaves of a large laurel bush as he waited in the back garden of the house he had looked at the night before. There was just a long rectangle of neat lawn between him and a stone patio at the back. He was hungry and tired, having spent the day lying low, trying not to be seen by anyone.

He had been holding out for darkness and observing from afar, trying to see what was going on inside. Carl knew that he would be visible to anyone who looked out of the window, as his pale face gleamed in the fading sun, but he had to get closer, to keep watching. He had come this far and he wasn't going to stop now.

Carl could see the man inside, just walking around, cleaning up. All Carl could do was sit on the cold ground, his knees drawn up to his chest, and wait.

A light dimmed at the back of the house. Carl sat upright, more attentive, his hand moving the branch to one side. Something was changing. He listened out, heard a door closing and then the clunk of a car door being unlocked, the flash of the orange lights noticeable in the gloom. He waited and then there was the sound of an engine. The man was going out.

Carl waited for the engine noise to fade and then moved out of his hiding place slowly, crouching, wary that it was a trap.

It all seemed quiet, though, and when he was sure that he wasn't being watched he straightened and ran across the lawn, his soles squeaking on the damp grass, seeking the shadow of the house, unsure if a security light would light up when he got against the wall. It stayed in darkness.

He closed his eyes and waited for the thumping in his chest to calm down. The bricks were jagged against his cheeks, his stomach turning nervous loops. After a few minutes, he bent down to the small flowerpot by the back door. He had been watching the house for long enough to know that there was a key hidden underneath.

The door opened slowly onto the empty house.

Carl paused and listened out for a burglar alarm, but all he heard was the steady drip of a tap. He stepped inside and closed the door, the click of the latch loud.

Carl pulled out a torch from his pocket and shone it around. He gasped. Even in the moving shadows of the torch beam the house was like a museum piece. The kitchen in front of him was old-fashioned, with a deep ceramic sink that was riddled with veins and a free-standing kitchen with units in light blue. The hallway was further ahead, towards the wooden front door under a small arched porch, the door handle low and old, the brass plating long since worn away. The wallpaper was deep red, making the hallway seem dark, even with the streetlight shining orange from outside.

He twitched his nose. The house smelled of aftershave, rich and spicy, as if its owner had sprayed himself before he went out.

He shone his torch to the ground as he went towards the stairs, so that the flickering light didn't alert any neighbours. There was stained glass in the door, with panels alongside, so the beam would be visible from outside. Upstairs seemed like the place to begin. Carl guessed that was where most people kept their secrets.

The stairs creaked as he crept upwards, moving slowly, not wanting to trip and break something. He swallowed as he went, nervous, his tongue flicking to his lip. He wasn't a criminal and wasn't used to this mixture of fear and excitement, the adrenalin making him light-headed.

The stairs opened onto a small square landing, with five doors leading off it. He pushed open the first one. There was a bath and a sink, old and large, with limescale covering the brass taps. The toilet was next door, the door coated with decades of paint. The whole place had never had an update.

There were three bedrooms. The first door opened onto a small room filled with boxes. The curtains were open and there was enough street-light to let him see what was inside. He opened the first box. It was old newspapers. In the next, engineering magazines from the seventies.

Carl stepped out of the room. There was nothing in there for him.

The curtains were closed in the next room. They were thick and heavy and blocked out the streetlight, so he felt confident enough to turn on his torch.

The beam hit an old double bed with a solid iron frame and springs that sagged towards the floor, the cover a patchwork quilt, the mattress deep and heavy. The room looked like it wasn't used any more. There were ornaments and photographs scattered around, although they looked faded, as if from another decade, maybe longer, but there were none of the other signs of everyday living. No hairdryer on the floor or creams on a dresser or an open jewellery box. The alarm clock next to the bed was an old black-faced Westclox, the numbers painted in that faint green that maintained a moment's glow as he moved his beam away. He noticed the time. Five twenty. It had stopped.

Carl went to a wardrobe and looked in. The clothes smelled fusty, the hangers filled with dark heavy coats and blouses with frills.

He stepped away. It intrigued him, but it wasn't what he was looking for.

The next room was different. He could tell it was being used from the scent of stale sleep and deodorant. There was a double bed in the middle of the room, the cover red and silky, like a parody of something sensual. There were clothes piled neatly on one side of the floor, ready for the wash but still folded. Men's clothes.

He went to the wardrobe again, and there were women's clothes, like the other room, except these were different. They were more modern, slinkier, silkier. Skirts and blouses and scarves. Each set was covered in a clear plastic cover, like the sort his mum brought home from the dry-cleaner's. He flicked through them. Seven sets. One of them looked familiar, like the one he had seen the woman wearing the night before.

He closed the wardrobe door and went back onto the landing. He listened. It was still quiet. The man hadn't returned.

The living room was the next place to look, because that was where he had seen them together. He moved quickly down the stairs and went in through the door closest to the front door.

The heat hit him straight away. There was a coal fire glowing and it gave the room that sleepy heat, as well as enough light to let him look around. The torch went into his pocket.

The look of the room was dated. The fireplace was low and fronted by old green tiles. The chairs and sofa sagged in the middle and the standard lamp in the corner had a dark red fringe. Carl walked over to the record player, fascinated. He

79

had never seen one before, only those turntables used by DJs. This was a faded pastel green box with a dirty brown speaker grille, the word *Dansette* emblazoned on the front like a chrome badge on a classic car.

There were photographs on the wall. Carl looked at them. They were of a woman, about his mother's age, was Carl's guess, in her forties, although they were dated, the dirty colours of the seventies showing in the clothes. There was a young boy in some of them, but no men.

He sat down, disappointed. He wasn't sure what he had expected to find, but it all seemed so ordinary. It was time to get out and start looking again.

Then he saw it.

He had been looking towards the doorway and the stairs. There was an alcove under the stairs, filled with coats and umbrellas and boots. And there was a door handle too.

Carl went to it and twisted the handle. It was locked.

He looked for a key but he couldn't see anything at first, the walls too dark, making everything gloomy. Then he saw a gleam. There was a hook behind the coats, and swinging from it was a key.

It fitted. Carl swung open the door.

There was a flight of stairs going down, a solid wall on one side. He had expected a blast of cold air and the damp smell of a cellar, but instead it felt warm. He went down slowly, his torch on again, looking out for hazards. He took the key with him. He wasn't going to be locked in.

The stones were smooth and worn and narrow. He turned a corner at the bottom, into what would once have been the storage for the coal poured through the small opening at the top of the cellar space, long since bricked up. The floor was tiled, and there was a desk against a wall. As the torch flashed around, he saw some shelves along one wall holding garden things, like fertilisers and wood stain. It was used as a storage room, nothing more.

He turned to go back up the stairs when his torch flashed upon something else in the room. It was in the corner, hidden underneath some tarpaulin. He walked over and shone his torch on it. Why would something need to be covered up in a cellar?

He pulled back the tarpaulin and then dropped his torch in shock, casting him into darkness, but he had seen enough. He sat down, his hand over his mouth, worried he was going to vomit.

On the cellar floor was a woman. Naked and dead.

Twelve

Joe sat in his car and looked up at his mother's house, a small semi on an ordinary street, with a low brick garden wall and short concrete drive. The day at work had been long and he didn't have the energy for a family gathering, but it's what they did, the Parkers, some effort to hold together what was overshadowed by the darkness of Ellie's murder.

They had become more regular as the year had gone on, Joe and his older brother Sam worried that their mother couldn't cope with Ruby, a headstrong teenager born in the wake of Ellie's death, in the hope that the joy of a new life could somehow make up for the loss. Everyone knew that Ruby was a replacement and it seemed like she always struggled to live up to the billing. Joe's mother found it hard to cope, spending most days in a fog of vodka-fuelled unhappiness, so Sam had taken it upon himself to be there more for Ruby.

Their mother's life had been made even worse by the loss of their father a few years after Ellie, a heart attack bringing an end to his grief. Joe knew that visiting was a good idea, but he found himself pulling away from his family more and more. He had promised that he would make more of an effort, desperate to make up for the part he felt he had played in Ellie's death. It was his shadow, the dark cloak that surrounded him and stopped others getting close.

Sam was already at the house, his grey saloon parked on the drive, and Joe knew there was no way of avoiding it. Sam was made head of the family by their father's death and he bore that title like a duty. Even his choice of career had been motivated by their sister's murder, driven by the need somehow to make it right. But how could you make up for something like that?

Joe got out of his car and walked up the short drive. He knocked on the door, to announce his arrival before going inside. There were shouts from the living room and then two little blonde girls ran towards him, one jumping and grinning, the other running more chaotically, her arms raised in the air as if she was about to crash into the walls.

Erin and Amy, Sam's daughters. He bent down to kiss them on their heads as they clung onto his legs, laughing.

'Can you find your daddy for me?' Joe whispered to them, and they ran off, shouting.

When he looked up, Sam's wife Alice was there, wearily pretty, the humdrum of motherhood showing in her tired eyes. She smiled and then looked beyond his shoulder.

'What's wrong?' Joe said, turning round.

'I just wondered whether you were bringing someone with you,' she said, and Joe noticed a glint in her eye. 'A new girlfriend or someone. We keep hoping.'

Joe smiled. 'You know me better than that. If I ever meet someone, you'll find out when you get the wedding invitation.'

She leaned in and kissed him on the cheek. 'You should find someone, Joe. You're too good-looking to be single.'

'Thank you,' he said, laughing. 'But I'm thirty-four. All the good ones are taken now.'

Alice set off down the hallway, Joe following. 'So apart from being the most eligible bachelor in Manchester, how are you?' she said.

'Oh, just the same. You?'

'Married to your brother,' she said. 'So just blissful.'

It was meant as a joke, but there was an edge to her voice. 'Everything all right, Alice?' Joe said.

Before she could answer, Sam appeared at the end of the hallway, pulled along by his daughters, who were screaming, 'Uncle Joe, Uncle Joe.'

'I thought you weren't coming,' Sam said, a hint of complaint in his tone.

'I'd never miss it. How's Mum?'

'Just the same. On her way to drunk.'

'And Ruby?'

'She's not here.'

Joe sighed. Every week he wondered when he would get the call to say that Ruby had been arrested for something, dragged into stupidity by those kids who hang around in black hoodies, all dressed the same so that no one would be able to identify them properly. Joe appreciated the irony; he would stay out all night to help those in the hoods if he got the call.

'You've left it late,' Sam said.

'Yes, I know. Something came up at work.'

'Why do they always come first?'

'What, the crooks, the thieves and worse?' Joe said. 'Don't. I'm sick of the same argument. I'm too tired, and it wasn't like that.'

'So what was it?'

Joe thought about what he could say when Sam spotted the earnest look in his eyes and said, 'Something more than the usual?'

Joe shrugged.

'Anything you want to share?'

'Am I making it that obvious?'

'Come on, talk to me,' Sam said, and nodded towards the back of the house.

Joe followed Sam through the living room, towards a small conservatory at the back, where Joe knew his mother sat on her own when Ruby was at school.

Sam closed the door behind him, the warmth still there from a day of the sun streaming through the window and roof. He sat down with a sigh on the sofa, the cane supports creaking.

Joe had noticed that Sam had become quieter since joining the Murder Squad. It was harder to raise a laugh from him these days, and he wondered whether his brother was going through the same as him, if he too felt surrounded by death.

'I can tell you want to say something,' Sam said.

Joe sat down opposite. 'Times are hard at the office, that's all. I know you think we're all rich in law, but what you see from the police station runners is just show. The pinstripes, the flash cars. They feel the need to look the part, but the firm has had enough. I've got to work out who to sack, or else sack myself.'

'That's not good.'

'Yeah, but you know what, I might go for option two. I've had enough.'

'Come on, it can't be that bad?'

Joe rubbed his eyes. 'Yeah, maybe just a long day. I was at the station last night. Well, more like this morning.'

'Anything decent?'

'Not really,' Joe said. 'A strange one though. The client wouldn't tell me anything about it, and then I got a visit from his mother today, who told me that he had gone missing. It seems like I

85

was the last person to see him.'

Sam raised his eyebrows. 'How come?'

'I don't know. I dropped him off near his house but he never made it home. He's only a kid. Fifteen. They might blame me. I should have watched him all the way.'

Sam pulled at his lip and looked back towards the house, to where Erin and Amy were playing on the floor with Alice.

'You look as though you've got a secret to share now,' Joe said.

'Was it Carl Jex?'

Joe was surprised. 'How did you know?'

'His mother reported him missing,' Sam said. 'Some of us knew his father.'

'David Jex?' Joe said, and when Sam nodded, Joe knew that the coincidences were drawing together. But then something struck him. 'You said *knew*.'

'Well, know, I suppose, but he went missing around six months ago. Just vanished. People were talking about him today, after his wife called in about Carl. He was under a lot of stress so we're expecting him to turn up dead somewhere. I didn't know him but it's still pretty sad. The job can make people like that sometimes.'

Joe was surprised about that, his brow creased into a frown. Neither Carl nor his mother had said anything about David Jex going missing. 'So what are you doing about Carl?' he said.

'At the moment, not much. I heard that when someone offered to go round, his mother refused.' Sam leaned forward. 'Tell me about him. I might be able to get someone to do something.'

'A bit intense and awkward but he seemed pretty well-balanced for a teenager. No police record but he was pulled in for being a peeping Tom. He asked for Honeywells but wouldn't tell me anything about his defence. Nothing. He just wanted to know whether the cells were bugged. So he stayed quiet, because I couldn't advise him if I didn't know what he was going to say. He was interviewed, released, and I drove him home. Except that I didn't drive him all the way home. He walked the last part, once he was happy there was no one following. His mother said that he never made it, but I had watched him walk towards his house, so how can that be right? It's strange that his mother shared his paranoia about the police, as if it was some kind of family disease. It doesn't fit with being married to a detective.'

'Being married to a copper doesn't stop the crazies,' Sam said. 'And you should see some of the letters we get from people who think we're all part of some conspiracy, some state machine. The sort of people who think the Royal Family are lizards.'

'I know, I've met a few myself; but this seemed different.'

'How different?'

Joe thought about that, and whether he should mention the Aidan Molloy connection. Sam was his brother, but he was also a police officer.

'If I tell you something, I want you to keep it to yourself,' Joe said. 'I'm talking brother to brother here.'

Sam shook his head. 'You might switch off your morals when you go into work, but I have mine

87

with me all the time. I'm not keeping a criminal's secrets for you.'

'Can't you just switch off from being a copper for just five minutes?'

'You're not speaking to me because I'm your brother. It's because I'm a police officer.'

Joe sighed. 'Okay, I understand.' He leaned forward and spoke quietly. 'When we left, he told me that whatever he had been doing was connected to the Aidan Molloy case.'

'What, the miscarriage case?' Sam said.

'That's what Aidan's mother calls it.'

'Saying it often enough doesn't make it any truer.'

'I know that well enough,' Joe said, 'but David Jex was involved in the Aidan Molloy case, which makes me curious.'

'So what do you think?'

Joe thought about that for a few moments before he said, 'I don't know, but there's something going on. DCI Hunter was floating around the station last night, and he was David Jex's boss on the Molloy case.'

Sam looked surprised. 'Drew Hunter?'

'Yes.'

'Glory Hunter?' Sam smiled. 'Everyone's favourite cop. Whenever *Crimewatch* turn up, he's the one who likes to do the "to camera" pieces. It's a bit of a joke, his vanity, but he's lucky that he's got a reputation to match it. A good copper.'

'But you think it's a coincidence.'

'You're seeing shadows that don't exist. Aidan Molloy was a murder case, so they had a murder DCI on it. If David Jex was on his team, perhaps

Hunter feels protective towards his son.'

Joe put his head back against the chair and the cane arms creaked. Of course it made sense.

'Are you all right, Joe?'

He took too long to reply.

'You need a break,' Sam said.

'I can't afford to take a break.'

'Everyone needs a holiday.'

Joe shook his head. 'Do you know how stretched everything is in my world? I'm the only criminal lawyer in the firm, and we've got the other departments screaming at us to make more money. The recession is affecting how much commercial work there is and everyone wants lower fees. If I take any time off, the figures will suffer, and then my job will suffer. The way things are in criminal work, if I lose my job, I won't find another one, so I'll end up trying to stretch road traffic injuries into something worth paying out.'

Sam paused, and then said, his voice soft, 'You were never the one to feel the pressure. That was me. I'm worried that you've got cracks showing. You look tired. I mean, really tired.'

'I'm fine, Sam, don't worry about me.'

'And what about Carl Jex and Aidan Molloy?'

As Joe thought about what Sam said, he remembered Gina's advice and realised that there was only one answer.

'I'm going to forget about it.'

Thirteen

Carl leaned against the wall, his eyes closed, not wanting to open them again or to see what was in front of him. He felt dizzy. But he had to look, he knew that.

He steeled himself, the air filled with the fast drum of his heartbeat and the nervous rasp of his breath. He could do this. He scrabbled around on the floor for his torch, clicking it on when he found it and then opened his eyes.

His stomach rolled.

She was lying on her back, her head to one side, her dark hair fanned over the floor. She was much older than he was. In her thirties, he guessed, and pretty, but her face had lost all personality. He looked for injuries, like bumps and bruises, a cut, dried blood, some kind of hint as to how she had ended up in the cellar. All he could see were small brownish bruises around her neck, like spots. Her face was turned to one side, expressionless, her legs jutted out, stiff, so that she was like a mannequin thrown to the floor, the tarpaulin loose over her body.

He stepped closer, nervous, even though he knew she wasn't about to grab him. Her clothes weren't there, but then Carl remembered the clothes in the wardrobe, how one set looked familiar. From the night before.

He reached out, even though he knew he didn't

want to, but it was like a compulsion, just to re-assure himself that it was real. As his hand touched cold flesh, like something fat-coated from the butcher's window, he recoiled. He wanted to cover her up, make her decent, even though he knew it was pointless.

There was a noise. It was barely audible but something about it warned Carl that danger was heading his way. He stopped and listened out. Then he recognised it as the rumble of a car en-gine. The man was back. There was the crunch of tyres on the short driveway, followed by the open and close of a car door and then the slow click of footsteps.

Carl faltered. He might be caught if he left the cellar. Perhaps he ought to wait it out and sneak out in the dead of night. But what was the man going to do with the body? He would have to come into the cellar to dispose of her, and then he would be trapped.

He ran for the stairs, his torch off now and back in his pocket, needing both hands free, feeling his way along the walls. He had left the back door unlocked; he could make a dash for that. He didn't care about the noise. It was all about get-ting out. The front door opened as he ran up-wards, his footsteps echoing in the cellar space.

As Carl burst through the door and into the hallway the man was already running forward, shouting. Carl put out his hands, ready for the impact.

Carl was winded as the man's shoulder caught him under his ribs. He was knocked backwards, but the man kept on pumping his legs, so that

Carl was propelled backwards, his arms knocking against the walls, his feet struggling to keep his balance. He was pushed back towards the cellar, and his hands reached out for the doorframe but there was too much momentum against him. The man gave a final hard shove and then Carl was falling backwards, his arms out.

Carl knew the impact was coming, but it seemed to take an age. All he saw was the glare in the man's eyes as he braced himself for the collision. When it came, it was just a crack and then a bright light of pain. He heard someone scream as he carried onto the bottom of the stairs, rolling, jarring as he hit each step, realising belatedly that he was the one screaming.

When he hit the bottom, as his head hit the wall, the hot fire of pain was blotted out by the quick merciful descent into darkness.

Fourteen

Sam was eating his breakfast of buttery toast and hot coffee when he got the call. The morning sun was bright, adding extra gleam to his daughters' blonde hair. Alice was overseeing the routine of sugary cereal that seemed to decorate most of the table and the glasses of milk that painted white horns onto the corners of their mouths.

He put down his cup and took his phone from his pocket. It was Charlotte. She had been Sam's first real ally when he moved there from the financial crimes unit and they'd become their own little team, watching out for each other. Sam didn't play office politics. He caught crooks.

He felt a jolt of anticipation as he clicked the answer button, but it was taken away by immediate guilt. If you're on the Murder Squad and you get a call when you're off duty, someone has died and it's serious. But he couldn't avoid that feeling of excitement about what lay ahead, or the trepidation about what it might involve.

'Hi, Charlotte. I take it this isn't a friendly wake-up call?'

'Sorry, Sam, but they've found a body on the moors.'

'The moors? Saddleworth?' His mind raced with the potential press clamour, knowing the infamy of the location. Alice paused to look at him.

'Yes,' Charlotte said, but then added quickly, 'It's not what you think. Nothing to do with Hindley and Brady, but we need to get there.'

'Where are you now?'

'Just leaving home.'

'Can you pick me up on the way? No point in taking two cars up there.'

'No problem. I'll be ten minutes.'

Sam threw his phone onto the table and drank his coffee quickly to shake himself awake, but threw the rest of his toast into the bin. He knew he would regret it later; seeing a dead body on an empty stomach was never a good idea, but that didn't make him any hungrier. He knew the routine afterwards. Bacon sandwiches from a roadside van just down from the station. It was life-affirming, that on seeing an end to a life the team had urges to celebrate their own and suspend the diets and good intentions.

'Rushing off?' Alice said.

'Yes. There's a body.'

'There's always a body,' she said, turning away. 'You'll be late, I suppose.'

Sam sighed. It was too early for this. 'You know how it is.'

'Yes, I know,' she snapped. 'You remind me every time and it's up to me to take care of everything.'

'Alice, don't be like this.'

'What, feeling like I live on my own sometimes? Just go, Sam.'

Sam thought how to respond, but he decided to leave it. He wasn't ready for another argument.

By the time Charlotte's car, a neat grey Golf, appeared on the street outside his house his fatigue had disappeared, replaced by a keenness to get to the scene. Alice didn't say anything as he kissed Erin and Amy on their heads, before heading outside. When he climbed into Charlotte's car, he was met with a blast of her perfume, strong flowers that he felt seep into his clothes.

'Sorry about the early start,' she said. 'Hunter called and told me to get everyone together.'

Sam frowned. This was a murder, nothing unusual in Hunter being involved, but he remembered the discussion from the night before.

'Why Hunter?' Sam said.

'Why not? It must be something newsworthy. He'll be deciding on his press conference suit as we speak.'

'They ought to let you do it,' Sam said. 'You look like you've been getting ready for hours.' And he meant it. Not yet thirty, the energy of youth gave a shine to her soft brown skin.

'You must have sleep in your eyes,' she said, smiling.

As Sam watched the familiar sights of his neighbourhood rush past, open-plan lawns and bright new bricks, he said, 'So, what do we know about it?'

'Nothing yet,' Charlotte said. 'Hunter just told me where to go.'

'Why didn't he call me too?'

'Because he's sleazy. I think he likes the idea of talking to me when I'm still in bed.'

'Really?' Sam said, laughing.

'Hey, it's not funny. You know he made a play for me, when we went for that drink at Christmas.'

'No, I didn't know that. And he's married.'

'That's what I told him. It gave me a reason to say no, which sounded better than I didn't like the way he dyed his hair, or his tan, or his cigarette breath, or the fact that he's just too bloody old.'

The journey settled into small talk as they rounded southern Manchester and then started to head upwards, the land rising to the flat plain of the Pennine moors, a landscape of heather and rough grass, brown and barren of trees, except for where it fell away to deep ravines and glinting reservoirs. The sprawl of council estates and new developments built on the sites of torn-down cotton mills gave way to grey stone, some of it in the form of small cottages, but others were grand detached houses with imposing bay windows. Even that was lost eventually, as they started the long rise to the moors, where the road twisted and climbed and the city sprawl of Manchester was lost to the stillness and mist higher up.

Sam pointed at a cluster of cars and vans ahead, where a uniformed officer was stationed to wave on those who wanted to slow down and look. Sam pulled out his identification as they drew close and they were directed to a semi-circular patch of gravel that served as a car park. The view one way was spectacular, over a deep valley that ran to a reservoir in the distance, the morning sun glinting starburst flashes. It was where people went who wanted the moors but without the walk, so that they could take in the splendour from their car bonnets whilst eating an ice cream from the van that parked there on summer weekends. Straight ahead, though, it was just a long expanse of moorland, the white paper suits of the forensic teams the only bright spots.

As they stepped out, Sam wished he had brought a coat. The wind was sharp and damp, so he buttoned his jacket and thrust his hands into his pockets.

The main crowd was well away from the car park, although Hunter had stayed back from it, in deep conversation with DS Weaver, his sidekick, recruited into every investigation Hunter conducted. He was like a cheaper version of Hunter himself, his hair grey and scruffy, his cheap polyester shirt straining against the paunch of his stomach.

Sam and Charlotte set off walking. It wasn't

easy. The ground was spongy and rutted and with long moorland grasses that were made slippery by the morning dew. As they got closer to Hunter, Sam said, 'Morning, sir.'

Hunter turned round. He looked pale.

'Are you all right?' Sam said.

Hunter didn't answer at first, just exchanged glances with Weaver. 'It's a bad one,' he said eventually.

'Are you the SIO?'

Hunter nodded, although being the Senior Investigating Officer didn't look like it was a good start to his week. 'It's just on our side of the boundary so the Yorkshire boys were happy to hand it over,' he said. 'Looks like we're the lucky ones.'

Charlotte had walked over to a box containing the forensic suits and was slipping one on over her clothes to prevent contamination of the scene. Sam followed her lead, leaving Hunter and Weaver by the road, and once they were both ready, with white paper bonnets and masks over their nose and mouth, they walked towards the crime scene tape that had been stretched over the moors.

Their suits rustled as they walked. Even that early, and at a murder scene, the view was breathtaking. The moors stretched for miles ahead, no trees on the top, so that it looked ominous, secretive, the browns and greens broken only by the occasional black scar, where the peat soil shifted and exposed itself. The ground was never still.

The place was timeless, unchanged, blighted only by the occasional electricity pylon and the rumble of traffic. It was the high barrier between the two warring factions of Yorkshire and Lancashire, sometimes impassable in winter, so that they grew up as rivals, not neighbours.

Ahead the movement of more white paper suits breached the serenity. They were clustered around a white tent, bright and incongruous against the dark heather. Sam and Charlotte walked together but they didn't say anything. When they got to the tent, Sam looked in and then blew out noisily.

There was a woman's torso, pale, with the red and white of muscle and bone showing where the legs had been hacked away, and the same with the arms. The limbs weren't missing, though. They had been placed alongside the torso, so that the legs spread out from where they had been positioned just above the hips, the arms the same, so that her body made a grotesque X shape.

He backed out of the tent and lowered his mask to suck in some clean air. Charlotte did the same.

'What the hell does that mean?' Charlotte said eventually, her voice quiet.

Sam shook his head. 'I don't know, but it clearly means something. A lot of care has gone into the placement of the body.'

'But why up here? So desolate.'

'That might be the whole point. Who's going to see you putting her here?' Sam glanced back at the woman's face, illuminated by the occasional flash from the crime scene photographer. 'We'll be able to get fingerprints from her, and DNA, and look at her ankle.' He pointed. 'There's a tattoo, a small butterfly. If she isn't on any database, that might help to identify her because a missing person report will mention it.'

'I don't get the point of the deliberate display, though,' Charlotte said. 'Why go to all the trouble of cutting a body apart to make a statement and then display it somewhere so remote?'

Sam looked around and saw what she meant. There were walking trails across the moors, just small snaking gaps in the tangle of heather, but none near the body. You wouldn't come across it unless you ventured from the trails.

'So how was it discovered?' Sam said. 'Her body looks freshly dead, no real decomposition, and whatever slim chance there was of her body being discovered, it happened straight away.'

One of the crime scene officers looked up and pointed further along, back towards the road. 'There's a trail just over there, not far from where you parked. Someone came up here this morning looking for some birds or something, was scouting the hills with binoculars when his lenses picked up a flash of white. He walked over for a look, and this little display spoilt his morning.'

'What's Hunter been like?' Sam said. 'He seems quiet.'

'He's been bloody useless. The body was probably brought along the path that you walked along, but he's just let everyone trample all over it. It was buggered as a crime scene a long time before you trampled it a bit further.'

'So what now?'

'We get her to the lab. Once we move her, we might find something left behind, but we've heard nothing about search teams coming up here.'

'She won't have been killed here though, will she?' Sam said. 'This is just a dumping ground.'

'So what's the most crucial thing?' the CSI said. 'The route the killer took, of course, from wherever he parked to where he placed her, but people have wandered all over here in their boots and even parked their vehicles in the layby. We don't know what is new and what is old.'

'That doesn't seem like Hunter,' Sam said.

'He's losing his touch. He retires next year. Perhaps he's thinking of the beaches too much.'

Sam looked back to where Hunter was standing. He was apart from everyone else, his hands thrust into his pockets, looking towards the scene as if he didn't want to get any closer, Weaver pacing behind him.

Something wasn't right.

Fifteen

The morning had started slowly for Joe, his waking head filled with thoughts of Carl Jex and Aidan Molloy. It was the Aidan Molloy case that intrigued him. Carl Jex was really just another small piece of strangeness in a world that was often filled with oddities.

It had been a long time since Joe had looked forward to getting to work.

The decline had set in slowly for him. A year earlier, Joe's profession had defined him. It wasn't just what he did but it was what he was. A lawyer. And not just a lawyer, but a criminal defence lawyer. He helped people. They didn't always deserve the help, Joe knew that. Not everyone could blame their past for how their lives had turned out. Sometimes it was about greed, or impulsive stupidity, and occasionally it was pure wickedness, where people with a skewed moral compass expected Joe to help them stay free so that they could do it all again. Joe understood that and had learned to rationalise it. A fair society needed someone like Joe to maintain its balance. Everyone deserved fairness, and the state shouldn't pick and choose who deserved it and who didn't.

He never forgot the victims, though. He had felt the raging fire of being one himself, the memories of how his eighteenth birthday had ended with his mother screaming his sister's name. The unhappiness of the victims was just something he had learned to live with; he couldn't ease their pain by letting his clients down. No one wins then.

Then Monica happened.

She had been a trainee solicitor at the firm, young and vibrant, with her whole life and career ahead of her, but working with Joe had exposed her to danger and he hadn't spotted it. A dangerous client saw something in her that he wanted, and he took it. There was no reason why Joe should have realised – lawyers rarely fall victim to their clients – but that didn't make it any easier. All that was left to show for her time at the firm was a plaque on a wooden bench.

It hadn't affected Joe too much at first, or so he thought. He had to keep going to show that he couldn't be beaten, so he went into work every morning with a fake smile on his face and wondered when his spark would return. It took him a while to realise that it never would. He found it hard to find the same outrage or momentum; nothing seemed as important any more. He lost interest in his moaning clients and the gripes of his bosses at the declining fees. It seemed like he was watching everything he had strived for just slip away and he didn't have the energy to stop it.

But this morning seemed different. He wanted to get into work, to see if there was an update. He thought about Aidan Molloy's mother, Mary, getting her stall ready for another day of empty campaigning.

He recalled Lorna Jex's certainty that something was wrong. Her paranoia about the police took on a different hue when it became apparent that she and Carl were related to a missing detective. It didn't seem straightforward any more, and that intrigued him.

He clambered out of bed and wandered into his living room, the next room along the short corridor in his apartment – the joys of cramped city living. White walls, black sofa, no clutter apart from the shelf of vinyl records and compact discs, most of them old blues and country music, the new digital tracks losing too much of the crackle and hiss. It was a cliché, he knew, the room screamed bachelor at anyone who happened to pass through, but it had been a long time since anyone had added any flourish or warmth to his home.

The morning light put a smile on his face as he headed for his balcony, squinting into the sun that rose over the red brick of the railway viaduct that took the trains and trams northwards. The view ahead was idyllic, a small area of tranquility. It was almost ironic because it was the site of the start of the industrial revolution, where railways and canals converged, yet now it was the most serene part of the city. It was part of a ripple effect: as the ripples had spread outwards it was the first area to become still.

He let the light bathe him for a while and then he went back inside, still smiling. The day felt good. The first one in a long time.

Sixteen

The day came back into view slowly for Carl.

It started as faint sounds in the background. Tiny intakes of breath, a soft shuffle of feet. At first he didn't know where he was. His mind seemed to take a long time to focus, the noises coming in waves, fading in and then out again until he became aware of the cold hardness of the floor against his body.

He wanted to sit up, but when he tried to move his arms he couldn't. They were fastened behind him, something tight around his wrists, the ovals of harsh chain links digging into his skin. He groaned, confused, and opened his eyes, but had to close them again quickly. The view ahead seemed to lurch at him, tilting from side to side like a rocking boat. He took some deep breaths but had to grit his teeth as sharp jabs of pain rushed at him.

'What's going on?' he said, although it came out muffled.

And then it came back to him. The images crept in, like the steady reveal of a slow stage curtain. He remembered coming to on the floor, confused, hurt, and the man coming towards him, and then something being forced into his mouth. After that, it was darkness once more.

He opened his eyes quickly. The woman. He remembered the woman. Her body cold and stiff on the floor. He swallowed back the pain. But she was no longer there. The cellar was in darkness and where she had been lying before there was a sheen along the floor like black ice.

'If you move too quickly, you'll die.'

Carl jumped at the voice. It was low and quiet, but with menace in every syllable. He winced and gasped as a jolt of pain shot to his forehead and then something tightened around his neck. The acidic taste of bile rose quickly. He tried to swallow it down but his throat was too constricted, stopping his breaths.

'What did I say? You need to be careful where you move,' the voice said, and then there were hands at the back of Carl's neck. It was a rope, like a tow-rope. It was loosened slightly.

Carl took some deep breaths and then said, 'Where are you?'

There was a click and a light shone in his face; the bright glare of a desk lamp, whoever was behind it just a dark outline. He grimaced against the brightness.

'How long have I been here?' Carl said.

'A while. I gave you some water, but I put in some sleeping pills to help you drift off. You were in awful pain. I had to do something.'

Carl let his head hang down, the rope digging in again but not as tightly. Sweat stuck his fringe to his forehead, despite the cool of the cellar. 'If you care so much, let me go.'

'I can't do that.'

'Why not?'

'You'll tell.'

Carl looked back to the floor, where the woman had been. 'Where has she gone?'

'Who?'

'The woman on the floor. She was dead.'

'Was she?'

'I saw her.'

Silence.

'Who was she?' Carl said.

'Does it matter?'

'She was dead. There will be someone wondering where she is, worried for her.'

'Like there is for you?'

That made tears jump into his eyes. He thought of his mother. She would be worried. He blinked them away, and the thought of her replaced some of the fear with anger.

'So what are you going to do?' Carl said.

Another pause. Longer this time.

'I don't know,' the man said eventually. 'I really don't know, but you need to be careful with that rope around your neck.'

Carl swallowed hard. He tried to stop the tremble in his legs but it was impossible.

'So now I want you to do something for me,'

the man said.

'But I don't want to.'

'I'll kill you if you don't. So think again.'

Fresh tears sprang into his eyes and a small whimper escaped.

'Stand up,' the man said.

Carl shuffled around so he could kneel up, which was hard with his wrists tied together behind his back. He grunted with effort as he rose to a standing position.

'What now?' he said.

The man laughed and then pulled on the rope, tightening it again, and then fastened it around a ceiling joist. Carl gasped.

When the man finished, he said, 'Have you ever been in control of your own destiny?'

Carl gulped and swallowed. 'I don't understand.'

The man stepped closer, his face in shadow against the brightness of the desk lamp. 'It's a slip-knot. If you pull against it, the rope will tighten and you'll die. You're at the very limit of the rope's slack.' He stepped forward and loosened the noose slightly. His breath was hot on Carl's cheek. 'Your wrists are tied up like that so that you can't pull it away from your neck.'

Carl licked his lips. 'But how can I sit down or anything?'

'You can't. That's why everything is in your control. You fall asleep and slump down, the rope will tighten and you'll die. You move away or try to sit down, the rope will tighten and you'll die. Think about that when I come in and ask you questions about why you were in my house. I'll give you time to reflect.'

Before Carl could say anything, the lamp was switched off. 'Where are you going?' Carl said, his voice betraying his panic.

'You don't need to know.'

Carl put his head back against the wall as the man's footsteps went across the cellar floor and then up the stairs. A brief sliver of light shone down from above and then it was darkness once more.

Joe skipped up the few small steps to his office building. The receptionist looked up as he walked in.

'Good morning, Mr Parker.'

'Hello, Marion,' he said, chirpier than normal. He didn't quite manage a whistle, but he was definitely a little quicker than usual on his way up the stairs.

He had almost made it to his room when he heard someone shout. 'Joe!' He turned to look back along the corridor and saw it was Tom Newman again, the senior partner.

'Hello, Tom. How are you?' Joe's voice was cautious. Twice in two days told him that this wasn't a social visit.

Joe let him walk past and into his office before he followed him in. He knew this was round two of the fees debate, so he closed the door behind him as he went in.

'I've just been into the secretaries' room,' Tom said. He was grinning again, his head cocked to one side nervously. 'I've told them that you're deciding what to do, and how things might be changing.'

Joe felt his energy evaporate. 'You mean you've told them that it's up to me whether I sack some of them or give up my own job to save them?'

'They're entitled to know. You'd like to make me out to be the villain here, but this is a business.'

Joe didn't respond. He stared at the Aidan Molloy papers, still on his desk from the night before.

'Just let me remind you that we need your proposals by the weekend,' Tom said.

And with that, he left the room.

Joe sat back and rubbed his face with his hands, deflated. He stared at the ceiling until the sound of footsteps disturbed him. When he looked, it was Gina.

'Late night?' she said.

'No, just a good morning turning bad.'

'I saw Tom,' she said. 'What did he want?'

Joe thought about whether to answer, but he respected Gina too much to keep anything from her. 'You know what it's about. The department's in trouble. We've got to make money or make savings, starting with the wage bill. But we can't invent criminals and we can't invent a need for what we do.'

'So what do we do? Some of the secretaries have got families, they need the money.'

'Tom says that he can employ the secretaries elsewhere,' Joe said, and he shook his head. 'He's given me the choice: sack people or sack myself.'

Gina didn't say anything for a few seconds, just toyed with her hands. Joe knew what she was thinking, that if the criminal department closed, she would lose her job along with Joe. Her career had always been about crime. Thirty years in the police and then her job with Joe as his case-worker, his clerk, his investigator, his just about everything. She couldn't do anything else.

When she looked up, she said, 'What are you going to do?'

Joe looked at the box of papers. Aidan Molloy's mother came back into his mind, and Lorna Jex. 'Fight,' he said.

'How?'

'Make it embarrassing for them to close us,' he said. 'I'm going to make a splash, give us a profile. It probably won't make any money, but it might just make it awkward for Tom to shut us down.' Joe pointed at the papers. 'I'm going to see Lorna Jex. I want to know what it is about Aidan's case that obsessed her son, and once I know, I'm going to stand side by side with Aidan's mother with this firm's logo held high. Speak to the papers, the television. Let's see Honeywells close us down then, with the local media watching.'

Gina frowned. 'Would that work?'

'I don't know, but have you got any better ideas?'

When Gina stayed silent, Joe knew that she didn't.

Seventeen

Sam sat at the back of the room, a notepad open in front of him.

They were in one of the empty rooms next to the Incident Room, everyone around a long table with a flipchart at one end. Briefings were best somewhere quiet, with all phones switched off.

The previous hour had been all about setting up the procedures and allocating roles. Hunter had, as usual, appointed Weaver as his deputy. That had been anticipated as soon as the nature of the murder was revealed. Hunter had the experience and the clout, but above all else it gave him the chance to practise for yet another heartfelt television appearance, Glory Hunter in full flow.

DI Evans had been given the role of Office Manager, to keep control of the Incident Room. The other roles were dished out: the Outside Inquiry Manager, Crime Scene Manager, Forensic Manager, Media Manager, House-to-House Manager. But it all came down to common sense in the end: what was suspicious and what wasn't.

At least the investigation had started.

Hunter paced at the front of the room, acting with more composure and assertiveness than he had at the crime scene.

The atmosphere around the room had the expectant air that always comes with the start of an investigation. Everyone attentive and silent, not the chair-twirling, joking and pen-tapping that comes later, when the initial shock has died down. It doesn't matter how long you have been doing the job, the sight of a dead body, someone's loved one snuffed out, still provokes anger and a desire for capture. When it stops doing that, it's time to stop doing the job, because you'll begin to miss things and killers will go unpunished.

Hunter stopped and looked around the room.

Sam knew all about Hunter's reputation.

Ruthless and flamboyant, he dominated Incident Rooms and inspired loyalty amongst those who worked under him.

This was Sam's first time as one of Hunter's team, as the DCI switched from unit to unit, following the big stories, but still Sam thought there was something missing. Hunter seemed nervous and was mopping his brow, as if the heating in the room was turned up too high.

He started by asking for ideas or motives. He got back the usual collection of ex-boyfriends, angry husbands and random stalkers, so he listed them on the first sheet of the flipchart.

Someone asked about the post mortem, and Hunter replied that he expected it later that day. They needed to know how the body was cut up; it might help in linking it to any tools found with a suspect. It would give a better time of death and provide a better clue of what she had been doing. Had she just eaten and, if so, what? Had there been any sexual activity, and was there any sign that it was non-consensual? Were there any minute traces of the killer left on her that were not obvious from the scene?

The suggestions were limited in the absence of the victim's identity, although Hunter preferred a domestic angle. More than half of all murders fall into that category and it was all about playing the odds.

Sam looked around the room to see if anyone was going to ask any questions, but most people were content to just look straight ahead and seem interested. He glanced at Charlotte and raised his eyebrows. She gave him a small shrug. No one had asked the question they had asked each other at the scene.

Sam coughed and raised his hand slowly. Everyone looked round to him, and when Hunter pointed, Sam said, 'Why did he choose that spot to dump the body?'

Hunter's eyes narrowed. 'What do you mean?'

Weaver sat down in a chair at the front, facing the room. He folded his arms and crossed one leg over the other.

'It looked like a display, the way the body was laid out, as if it meant something,' Sam said. 'We were supposed to see it, and he had the whole of Saddleworth Moor to choose from, but he picked somewhere away from a path. It's as if he didn't want anyone to see the display straight away.' He swallowed as he became aware of the awkward silence in the room, because he had raised something important before Hunter had. He continued regardless. 'She was found by a fluke, by that birdwatcher, and the moors don't get busy with the walkers until the weekend. So why make a display if it isn't going to be found straight away? Perhaps the location of the body is important.'

Hunter stared at him for a few seconds before he answered. 'But it was found straight away, so your theory doesn't stand up. White flesh on that dark ground and you're saying it wouldn't be found?' He shook his head. 'As for choosing the moors? You know what it's like up there. At night, it's complete darkness. The simplest answer is usually the likeliest one, that the body could be dumped without being seen.'

'But why all the way up there?' Sam went on.

'Why not some woods somewhere nearer the city? It seemed symbolic somehow.'

Hunter folded his arms. 'How long have you been on the Murder Squad?' When Sam didn't answer straight away, Hunter continued, 'I've been investigating murders for two decades. So go on, tell me: what am I missing? What experience do you bring to the team?'

Sam felt his cheeks burn up. He knew how it would sound when he voiced it, that it was just a year, that his previous cases had been paper-shuffling, investigating financial crimes.

Hunter must have spotted Sam's embarrassment and guessed at the answer. He wasn't going to let it go. 'I want to know. How long?'

Sam took a deep breath. 'A year.'

Hunter didn't smile or laugh, which was worse. He just shook his head as the rest of the room squirmed for him. Weaver snorted a laugh. Sam thought he had slowly worked his way into the squad. They knew he wasn't the sort to snipe and gossip behind people's backs, or one of those muscle-junkies who enjoyed barfly banter too much. Sam just got on with his job and applied the attention to detail he had picked up in the financial investigation unit. Yet no one was prepared to stand up for him in the face of Hunter's scorn.

'No one here has to be a profiler,' Hunter said, no longer looking at Sam. He was playing to the gallery again. 'Chase the forensics, the crime scene people, the house-to-house. You all know what you're doing. Hard work solves murders, not looking for hidden patterns.'

Sam tapped his pen on his paper in frustration, until everyone looked round as a young detective burst into the room, his eagerness obvious from the sharp crease in his trousers and the way he ducked his head slightly as he advanced towards Hunter. 'We've got her name,' he said, and handed over a piece of paper.

Hunter read it and then folded it into his pocket. 'Sarah Carvell,' he said. 'She appeared in court when she was younger for shoplifting and her fingerprints have just matched.'

Charlotte looked up. 'She was reported missing yesterday,' she said. 'I've got the paperwork on my desk.'

Hunter held her gaze a second too long. 'I'm heading to her house,' he said, and pointed at Sam. 'And you're coming with me.'

Sam was surprised as he looked up from his doodles, jagged boxes, showing his frustration. 'Me?'

'Yes, you,' Hunter said, and headed for the door.

Sam glanced at Charlotte, who shrugged and whispered, 'He must want to keep you close. A loose cannon already. You should be proud.'

'Yeah, right,' Sam said. 'I'll let you know how it goes.'

He stood still in the living room, looking down at the floor with his fists clenched, at where she had been before he had dragged her to the cellar.

Things had changed. He had changed. He had never cut up before. This was something new. Visceral and dark. What had gone before had been about disposal, nothing more.

114

No, that was wrong. It had never been about disposal. It had been about burial, somewhere symbolic, part of why he did what he did. Chopping her up seemed more brutal somehow.

He closed his eyes. It was there again, that growing noise in his head, like a vibration, getting louder. It was growing harder to ignore. Things were changing. He searched for an emotion, some kind of panic, but he couldn't find it. Instead, it was a need to strike out, to hurt; the thing that he kept restrained wanted to burst out. He didn't think he could stop it, and neither did he want to.

It wasn't his choice. It was the chain of events, the face at the window, the police involvement. The boy in the cellar. The intruder. Everything was changing. He had to do something about it, so he had left her as part-taunt, part-insurance. If it was the end for him, he wasn't going to go down alone.

It had been the noises that had been the hardest. He'd clenched his jaw as the saw dug into the flesh, the firm squelch of a butcher's shop followed by the tougher grind as the blade met the gleaming white of the bone.

He looked up to the photographs on the wall. His mother stared down at him, her face stern, her arm around him protectively. He turned away. Now wasn't a good time to think of those days.

The air in the room seemed suddenly stale. He opened a window and let the cool breeze take away the sweat from his forehead.

He thought about that. Sweat. What he'd done was too risky. It left traces. A spot of blood could bring everything crashing around him, or if they swabbed her and his DNA came back. He knew his guilt would be inescapable if their trail some-how led to him.

He closed his eyes and grimaced. The vibration got stronger, like a steady hum. It made him think of the others. Those who had tried to walk away.

He gritted his teeth as he pulled his phone out of his pocket. He searched for a number and heard it ring until a quiet voice said, 'You can't ring me at home, you know that. I'm not alone.'

He swallowed and tried to will away the tension in his head. 'Emma, I need to see you.'

Silence at first, and then, 'I can't. I've told you why.'

'I'm not accepting that. One last time. At least give me that.'

A pause. 'When?'

'Tonight. Come to my house. I'll collect you. Usual place. Eight o'clock.'

'Okay. I'll see you then.' She clicked off.

He put the phone against his forehead and took some deep breaths. One last time. Yes, that was right.

Eighteen

Joe drove to Carl's house, through stone villages where blackened millstone buildings crowded the main streets. Some had been turned into shops that sold second-hand books and locally made food to cater for the walkers who thronged

116

the streets in summer, fronted onto narrow pavements and old stone bridges that strangled the main road into tight passing places.

The villages didn't suit the sunlight – the sun brightened the hills and took away some of the menace of the nearby moors. They looked best in the rain when the stone cottages acquired a shine and everything turned from gloomy to brooding.

The view changed as he turned into the lane that led to Carl's house. Leaves trailed along the side of his car as the lane narrowed, but it didn't open out into a line of stone cottages, as he'd expected. It had an idyllic country setting, with thick green hedgerows bordering fields where sheep grazed, the rise of the Pennines just visible further ahead. The small spread of houses was a blight, with grimy pebbledash and windows and doors that looked faded and old.

Joe parked on the drive, then reached across to the passenger seat, to where he'd put Carl's papers from his visit to the police station. He skimmed through his scrawling handwriting, in case he had been wrong about not making a note of where Carl had been arrested. If there was any link between the arrest and his disappearance, it might be important. Joe sighed when he saw he hadn't noted it down. The arrest had been too late and too routine.

Lorna Jex appeared in the doorway. Even through the windscreen, he could make out the dark rings under her eyes and the paleness of her skin. He climbed out of his car.

'I haven't slept,' she said. 'Come in.'

As Joe followed her in, he asked, 'No sign? No news?'

Lorna shook her head. 'It's been two nights,' she said, and led him along a dark hallway that smelled of old cigarettes and into a kitchen of dated brown tiles and mock-oak cupboards, a relic of the eighties. Photograph frames cluttered the walls, displaying family pictures that had faded into light browns to match the surroundings. As Lorna clicked on the kettle and spooned instant coffee into two cups, Joe said, 'Has Carl ever done anything like this before?'

Lorna shook her head. There were no tears. She looked as though she had used up all of her reservoir.

She waited until the kettle boiled, poured the water and then passed a cup to Joe. 'He would have called; he knows I'd be worried.'

Joe took a sip out of politeness and said, 'I want to help.'

Lorna looked at Joe through the steam, her hands around her cup. 'I thought you couldn't, that everything was confidential.'

'I've thought about that,' Joe said. 'You're not going to complain about that, are you?'

Lorna shook her head.

'So neither will Carl,' Joe said.

'Not if it helps him.'

Lorna shuffled into a living room that was a similar shade to the kitchen, with wallpaper yellowed by cigarette smoke and a carpet whose pattern was hidden by the hairs left by the scruffy terrier that curled up in a chair by the window. The dog opened an eye to look at Joe, but closed it again with a large sigh that made his body blow up and down like bellows.

Lorna sat silently in her chair so Joe started the conversation.

'He was walking along the lane when I left him,' he said. 'It was very early in the morning and he said I would have to turn around if I drove him down, and that I would wake people up.'

'He's very thoughtful. Did you watch him go?'

'There wasn't much to watch. The trees and the bend soon swallowed him up, so I set off.'

'So you definitely didn't drive down the lane?'

'No. I let him out and went.'

'The lady next door said she heard a car right outside in the early hours. It set off quickly. So that wasn't you?'

Joe shook his head. 'Definitely not.'

Lorna stared at the floor for a few minutes and Joe let her take her time. Her cup trembled in her hand. 'So what did Carl tell you?' she said eventually.

'That's just it,' Joe said. 'Carl didn't tell me anything.'

'I don't understand.'

'He'd been locked up because he was creeping around a house, looking in. A neighbour called the police. I asked him for an account and he wouldn't tell me, was worried about someone listening in. Why would he think that?'

Lorna looked down and she clasped her fingers together. 'Because of his father.'

'I don't understand.'

'Do you know about my husband, David?'

Joe nodded. 'Carl didn't tell me, though. Nor

you. Why not?'

'He was scared. Carl was trying to find out what happened to his father. He'd become obsessed by it.'

'Carl mentioned the Aidan Molloy case.'

Lorna looked up sharply at that and her chin quivered as tears rolled down her cheeks. 'That name,' she said, and her jaw clenched. 'So Carl did tell you something.'

'Just that it was connected somehow. He didn't go into any detail. Why did Carl have a special interest in it?'

Lorna paused and looked at Joe, her gaze sterner now, more focused. 'That's not the question you should be asking.'

'What do you mean?'

'You should be asking why my husband had a special interest in it. Carl was just following on from where David left off, trying to get some answers about what happened to him, except Carl doesn't know all that David knew.'

Joe leaned forward and said quietly, 'So tell me about David.'

'What is there to know? He went missing six months ago. No one knows where he has gone.'

'Including you?'

'Yes, of course including me.'

'So how did it happen?'

Lorna took a deep breath and wiped the back of her hand over her eyes, making them red. 'Like most missing people, I suppose. One night he went out and never came home. There were no warnings, no letters. All I knew was that he had become obsessed by the Aidan Molloy case.'

'And now Carl.'

Lorna nodded. 'And now my son,' she said, and began to sob loudly. 'Don't let Carl disappear like his father did. Please.'

'You need to talk to me,' Joe said, taking her hand and clasping it in his. 'If I can help, I will.'

'That must be why he chose you,' she said, through her tears.

Joe gripped her hand a little tighter. Lorna's words had just dragged him deeper into the case. He felt the need to know more, and an enthusiasm he hadn't felt in a long time.

Nineteen

Hunter and Weaver walked quickly to the doors that would take them outside, as they headed to the home of the dead woman, Sarah Carvell. It was time to break some bad news.

They were talking to each other quietly and earnestly, excluding Sam. At first Sam thought it was just about making him jog to keep up, to belittle him, but then he started to wonder whether it was deliberate, so that he couldn't hear their conversation. Hunter opened the door by slapping the green release button and then slamming the palm of his hand against the glass.

As Sam caught them up outside, he said, 'Can I ask you something, sir?'

'Fire away,' Hunter said, staring straight ahead.

'Why do you want me with you?'

Hunter exchanged glances with Weaver. He stopped and turned to face Sam, his hands on his hips, pulling his jacket back. 'Don't you want to be with us? Prefer swooning over that pretty thing next to you? What's her name?'

'DC Gray.'

Hunter's mouth twitched a smile, although it contained little warmth. 'But you don't call her that, do you?'

'Her name is Charlotte.'

'Well, I'm sorry to tear you away from her.'

'No, it's not that, sir. It's just that you didn't seem that keen on my input.'

Hunter stepped closer to Sam and said, 'The investigation needs to be focused, to have a direction. I don't want you there as a distraction.'

'A distraction?' Sam said. 'I thought you wanted ideas, that's all. I haven't been on the team that long, I know, but I've been a detective for a few years and I don't need treating like some errant child, or a cadet who needs showing the ropes.'

Hunter moved even closer. He was breathing heavily through his nose. 'This is your role, to stay close to me, so that you can report back to the rest of the team. That good enough for you?' When Sam didn't respond, Hunter pointed to a silver BMW, Weaver holding open the door. 'You'll do whatever I tell you to do, and for whatever reason I have. So stop whining and get in.'

Sam gritted his teeth. Weaver glared at him as he climbed in.

Sam pulled out his phone as they set off, both men silent in the front, Hunter driving. He texted Charlotte.

I've annoyed H&W. Still think I'm right about location. Can you check on reports of unusual activity there? Go back five years. Dumping bodies not a daily thing.

He looked out of the window as they drove on, conscious of the silence and with no desire to break it, only the steady drone of the engine filling the car. His phone was in his hand, set to vibrate. After a few minutes, his fingers felt a buzz. He checked the screen. It was a text from Charlotte.

I'm not ur gimp, but ok. I'm blaming you if Hunter starts bitching.

Sam smiled to himself and put his phone away.

Sarah Carvell lived in a small town in a valley to the north of Manchester. It was an old cotton town of terraced houses and small mills, rejuvenated as a commuter town for those who wanted the city offices but the country living. They drove onto a modern estate of cul-de-sacs that branched off from one circular road, checking each road sign as they went, Sam dreading what lay ahead. He knew too well how the arrival of the police to deliver bad news devastated families. His sister's murder drove his father into a grave and his mother into the bottle, the only blessing being the birth of his little sister Ruby two years later.

Hunter came to a stop. They were in front of a boxy detached house, with a small porch that jutted out at the front and a driveway shared with the house next door, the two houses connected by adjoining garages.

'Come on,' Hunter said, although it was directed at Weaver, not Sam.

Sam followed them both up the driveway.

Hunter straightened his tie. Weaver hoisted his trousers onto his paunch and tucked in his shirt. Sam looked around as Hunter rang the doorbell. There was a view along the valley towards the grey shadow of Manchester in the distance, obscured slightly by the pink petals of cherry blossom on a tree at the edge of the garden, the gentle breeze scattering them across the neat square lawn.

The door was opened quickly, angrily almost, by a tall man with dark hair swept back, only his temples showing tinges of grey.

He stopped and then paled, as if he knew straight away what it was about. 'Sorry, I thought you were someone else,' he said, licking his lips, tears already in his eyes. 'What do you want?'

Hunter pulled out his identification and introduced himself. Nothing else needed to be said. It was the pause that did it, the respectful smile and slight nod of the head.

'Sarah?'

'Can we come in, sir?'

The man turned and went into the house, walking slowly along the short hallway, his shoulders slumped, until he was able to reach the sofa in the living room. He sat down and perched forward. Hunter indicated with his head that Sam should get him a drink.

Sam went into the kitchen and listened as Hunter broke the news and closed his eyes when he heard the man wail. When he opened them again, it was the ordinariness that struck him. The kitchen looked out over a rectangular lawn, visible through a wooden pergola trailing honeysuckle and clematis just coming into flower. There were little touches that showed the woman who had lived there. Small magnets stuck to the fridge, souvenirs from holidays that she used to secure notes and drawings and the scribbles of young children, at school for the day, about to come home and find that their mother never would. Things would be different now. Grief changes everything.

Sam filled the kettle, and once it had boiled he took a mug of tea through.

The husband's name was Billy. He wiped his eyes with the heel of his hand. He was staring forward, his expression a mixture of disbelief and misery.

'She told me she was going to Wendy's house, one of her friends,' Billy said.

'Wendy?' Hunter said.

'Wendy Sykes. Sarah used to go out with her a lot, and she stayed out late sometimes. I have to be up early for work, so I didn't think anything of it when she hadn't come home before I went to bed. Then when I woke up and she wasn't there, I called Wendy. Sarah was never there. Wendy wouldn't say anything more, so I guessed that, you know...'

'Sarah had been with someone else? Another man?'

Billy nodded, tears running down his face. 'How did she die?'

'She was found on Saddleworth Moor.' Hunter didn't elaborate on that, but he delivered it in the smooth tones of someone used to dealing with bereaved relatives. 'I'm sorry to have to ask you

125

these things, but we need to know, and the sooner we know, the faster we can act. How was your marriage?'

After a few moments of silence, Billy said, 'What are most marriages like? We argued, we didn't talk to each other much sometimes, but it was just something we had to work through.'

'And were you working through it?'

Billy just shrugged.

'What does that mean?'

Billy exhaled. 'I don't know. Something was different. She was buying smarter clothes, making herself look nice, but only for when she went out. When she was here, she was distant, as if she wanted to be somewhere else and all we had was too much drudgery.'

'And she went missing the night before last?'

Billy nodded slowly.

'And where were you that night?'

He looked up, anger in his eyes now. 'I was here, looking after my children. It's what I do when she goes out. Sarah went out with her friend, so she said, and now this.'

'Do you mind if my colleague looks through her things, just to see if there is anything that might give us a clue where she went?' Hunter gestured towards Sam.

Billy looked at Sam and shrugged. He didn't have the will to fight anything.

Sam went upstairs and into Billy and Sarah's bedroom. It was so ordinary. Silk cushions on a purple duvet. Clothes on the floor, waiting for the wash. Photographs of Sarah and Billy in happier times, their heads together, grinning at the

126

camera. Sam's mind went back to the grotesque display on the moors. How had Sarah gone from the happy woman in the photograph to how he had seen her not long before?

He went to the drawers at the side of the bed and went through those that contained Sarah's underwear. He rummaged at the bottom. Billy wouldn't go through her underwear drawer, so any secrets might be kept there, but there was nothing unusual. Some headache tablets, small bottles of perfume, like free samples thrown in after a shopping trip.

The wardrobe was all about Sarah. There were some shirts to one side, and a suit that had dust on the shoulders, but they were squashed by the blouses and jumpers and dresses. Shoes and boots were thrown in untidily. Sam was looking for boxes, anything that might contain souvenirs of what she was doing away from the home, but nothing struck him as unusual. He couldn't find any diaries or letters.

When he went back downstairs, he said, 'Do you have her bank statements?' When Billy looked confused, Sam added, 'If she's been doing something out of the ordinary, it might show in her spending.'

'We do online banking, but I think Sarah kept her passwords in a pocket in that case.' And he pointed to a laptop at the side of a bookcase. 'Sarah looked after that kind of thing.'

Sam was disappointed. He wouldn't be able to touch the laptop until a copy had been made of the hard drive, so that they could look for traces of long-deleted emails and online chats without spoiling the evidence. Paper copies would have given him something instant.

He rummaged in the pocket of the laptop case and found a piece of paper. There were lists of on-line accounts and hints and clues to passwords, things that she would know. It showed some degree of caution, just in case the laptop case was lost.

Sam recognised the name of a bank and underneath the words 'dob 79' and then 'cat 999'. Hints and clues.

He got the answers from Billy to all of the clues on the piece of paper, her date of birth and the name of her cat, and gave the nod to Hunter that he had what he needed, the sheet of paper with passwords in a sealed plastic bag.

There was a knock at the door. Sam went to answer. It was a female detective Sam knew from his early days in the Force, Nicola Sharp.

When Sam showed her through, she said, 'DI Evans sent me. I'm your FLO.' Then she looked at Billy. 'I'm the Family Liaison Officer. I'm here to help you during the investigation.'

Billy looked and nodded, but didn't say anything. He was retreating into himself.

Hunter looked irritated. Sam couldn't understand why. Nicola was a woman who exuded sympathy but she could also read people well. The FLOs were experienced detectives, not hand-holders. If Billy was hiding something, Nicola would spot it.

Hunter forced out a smile and got to his feet. He headed for the door, Weaver with him, leaving Billy with Nicola. Sam thanked Billy for his help and followed. When he thought of what devastation awaited the children, he was relieved to be leaving.

Twenty

Lorna Jex looked down before she spoke, as if she was trying to work out what to say. Eventually, she looked up and said, 'I don't really know when it started, David's obsession with the Aidan Molloy case. It just crept up on us. Why should he have been obsessed with the case? He'd been on the investigation, knew all about it. But he was, and I couldn't understand it.'

'When did you first notice?' Joe said.

She shrugged. 'A year ago. Perhaps a bit less. It was as if he suddenly started to feel bad about something, but why should he? He put a bad man away. David had put a lot of really bad men away, but this seemed different, as if it really affected him. He started to collect things, newspaper reports, things like that, and would go to see people, spend all night sometimes, driving around. I don't know where he went, didn't want to know really.'

'What was his thing about the case, though? Did he ever say?'

'No, but I would catch him sometimes, just staring into space, like something was bothering him. And I remember that he became obsessed about our debts. He said we would have to clear everything, so we didn't book a holiday last year and stopped buying treats. We just put everything towards the credit cards and mortgage.'

'Do you think he was planning on running away? Perhaps he was making sure you could cope after he left.'

'What, because we were clearing debts? I don't think so. He could have just told me he was going and left. That would have been better than what we have now, this uncertainty.'

Joe frowned. 'Did David think that they'd got the wrong man in Aidan Molloy?' When Lorna looked at him, he added, 'Why else would he become obsessed with the case? Like you said, Aidan was locked up, David's job done. What else was there to do?'

Lorna shook her head. 'He never said.' A pause, then, 'Do you want to see David's notes?'

Joe raised an eyebrow. 'Yes, I do.'

She got to her feet wearily and walked towards the living-room door. Joe took it as a sign to follow her, and he creaked his way up the stairs behind her until they got to the small bedroom at the front of the house.

'This was my daughter's bedroom, before she got married,' Lorna said, and she pushed open the door.

The room wasn't very big. Just enough room for a bed that ran to the window sill, space saved by storage underneath, raising the bed so that anyone tall would sleep with their feet on the windowsill. There were old white cupboards and shelves opposite that had been taken over by black filing folders, with a computer and monitor

130

resting on a small desk at one side. There were newspaper clippings pinned to a cork board and maps taped to the wall.

Joe stepped forward, expecting them to be all about Aidan Molloy, but as he got closer he saw that they were missing person reports from newspapers. As far as he could tell, there were six women mentioned, the clippings pinned alongside each other with string going to a point on a large map of Manchester. Four of them were just small pieces, as if they were hardly worth of a mention, whereas two were bigger spreads, with appeals from their families. Joe remembered one of them from the media buzz. A law clerk called Mandy, blonde and pretty with cute children. There were a few tearful appeals and the public mood had turned on her husband because he hadn't cried at the press conference.

'He was spending more and more time in here,' Lorna said, her voice flat and emotionless. 'And drinking. He'd always drunk at weekends or while we were watching a film, but then it turned into something he did on his own, up here.'

Joe turned away from the clippings. 'Tell me about the night he disappeared.'

Lorna leaned against the wall. 'He'd been getting worse. He was drinking more and not turning up for work. They were going to discipline him, but he put in a sick note and went off with stress. Then one evening he was different. He seemed happier, excited almost. He said he was going out but wouldn't tell me where, but he hugged me, and he hadn't hugged me in a long time. He said he loved me but he had to go out, and that was it. He never came home.'

'Where do you think he went?'

'I just don't know, but something was different that night.'

'What did you do?' Joe said.

'I reported him missing.'

'What did the police say?'

'That's just it. They didn't say much. They put out an alert, some pictures in the paper, stating that they were worried about him, but they seemed to think he'd just run away.' She wiped her eye. 'I don't think they liked it being public. He was on sick leave for stress, so it hinted that whatever happened was somehow their fault.'

'Did he take any money out of his bank? If he was still getting his wages when he was off sick, he would have money to take out and he would need it.'

Lorna shook her head and tears appeared in her eyes again. There was the truth, and she knew it. He was dead.

'So what about Carl?' Joe said softly. 'Where does he fit into all this?'

'Carl loves his dad. Worships him. David's a policeman, strong and protective. What teenage boy wouldn't love a father like that?' A smile through the tears. 'That's how we met, through the police. My car was broken into and David was the person who came to see me. He didn't solve the break-in, but he was so sweet. Tall and strong, just started out in the job. I asked him out. He was a good man. Carl couldn't cope with David walking out, and he suspected it was something to do with all of this.' She pointed towards the clippings.

'So he started going through it all, to try to find the answer.' She wiped her eyes again. 'I told him to stop, that he had schoolwork to do, but he wouldn't listen. He became as obsessed as David, up here all the time, going through things. He started to stay out a lot, always late, and the school told me he was skipping lessons.'

'Did Carl say where he was going the other night?'

'He said he was going to see a friend. When he didn't come home yesterday morning, I called the police. They told me he'd been arrested, so I came to you.'

Joe looked back towards the newspaper clippings, and to the black file covers. Two missing persons, father and son, both connected somehow to Aidan Molloy, and none of this would earn any money for the firm.

But as he looked at the shelves, he knew that the answers to whatever had happened were in those papers.

'I want to help,' he said.

Lorna reached out for him and put her hand on his arm. 'Thank you,' she said softly.

His phone beeped. He held up his hand in apology and looked at the screen. It was a message from Gina. *Where are you? Client downstairs.*

Joe sighed. He knew he should go back to the office, but he was more interested in Carl Jex. 'Excuse me,' he said, and called Gina. When she answered, he said, 'I won't be back in time.'

'Where are you? You're not booked in the diary anywhere.'

'I'm just checking something out.'

'Aidan Molloy?'

He glanced at Lorna to see if she was listening, but she was gazing at the clippings on the wall, her husband's obsession. 'Yes. I'm with Lorna, Carl's mother.'

There was a pause, until Gina said, 'I know you want to make a splash, but I don't think Tom will care. Make some money. That's what talks with Tom.'

'If he wants us out, there's nothing we can do. You suck up to Tom if you want, and he might keep you on. Me? I'm gone, I know it.'

'And what about your client?'

'You see him and tell him to find another lawyer.'

With that, he hung up and went back to looking at the news clippings and the map on the wall. Did the locations mean something? They had meant something to David Jex, as he had drawn attention to them. Or perhaps he was just trying to find a pattern somewhere, shapes in the mist, although Joe didn't really know why.

The files on the shelf had titles on the binders. *Statements* was prominent on seven of them, and the name of Aidan Molloy and the six remaining people listed on the missing persons reports. Each had a date written on the spine and all six people had gone missing after Aidan Molloy had been arrested. Joe shook his head. It all meant one obvious thing: David Jex didn't think Aidan Molloy was guilty. Neither did Carl. And now both had disappeared.

Twenty-one

Hunter drove quickly, heading to the home of Sarah Carvell's friend, Wendy Sykes, where Sarah was supposed to have been on the night she went missing. He glanced in his mirror at Sam. 'You're Joe Parker's brother, right? The defence lawyer.'

Sam was unsure whether Hunter was just making conversation; he didn't seem the type for idle chat. 'Yes. He's doing well for himself.'

'That's a matter of opinion. He's at Honeywells, isn't he?'

'Has been for a couple of years now.'

Hunter didn't comment any further, just concentrated on his driving. Sam didn't know if Joe's job made things better or worse for him, in Hunter's eyes. Did Sam get some credit for choosing the right career or was he tainted by association?

Whispers in the canteen gave defence lawyers mixed reviews. Most of the police accepted them as a necessary evil, but they thought they also derailed investigations and left victims without justice. Some played fair, but too many didn't.

But Sam knew something else too: no one fights dirtier than a copper in trouble.

The journey wasn't far, a couple of miles. Wendy lived in a similar house to Sarah, built on the gaps made by the bulldozing of industry, modern and clean and on a street of sweeping curves and short driveways and garages that never housed a car.

135

The routine was just the same. The slow walk along the path. The quiet knock on the door, as if it came with an unspoken hope that it wouldn't be answered. But Wendy Sykes opened the door as they all did, with her face a mix of fear and shock and then tears. Another life changed for ever.

Wendy let the door swing open as she walked back into the house. She was small with short dark hair, dressed in jogging trousers and a T-shirt. She went straight to the kitchen and asked everyone to sit down at a long rectangular table. There was a slow-cooker on the side, filling the room with the aroma of warming stew.

Wendy turned to look out of the window, wiping her eyes. 'I thought you were here about my husband, or maybe, you know...' And Sam noticed that she glanced at a picture of two smiling young boys in a small wooden frame on the wall close to her.

She was still looking out of the window when she said, 'How did she die?'

'We can't tell you, I'm sorry,' Hunter said.

'But she was killed, right? It wasn't an accident, or suicide?'

'I can't tell you very much,' Hunter said. 'But yes, it looks like she was murdered.'

Wendy closed her eyes at that and took a deep breath. 'Billy?' she asked.

'Why do you say that?' Hunter said, leaning forward.

She opened her eyes and turned round. 'I don't mean anything. I thought you always looked at the husband, that's all.'

'Had Sarah ever said that Billy was violent?'

Wendy shook her head. 'No. Just the opposite. Too placid, like she wanted to shake him up a bit, that everything was a bit steady. But everyone has a snapping point.'

'Why would Billy snap?' Hunter said.

Wendy paused before she said, 'No reason.'

'Billy said Sarah was with you two nights ago. Is that correct?'

Wendy looked to the floor for a few seconds. She let a tear roll down her cheek and then said in a low voice, 'No, she wasn't. I stayed in.'

Hunter exchanged small nods with Weaver. Billy's story was checking out. 'Did you know that Sarah said she was with you?'

'So Billy said.'

'But why would Sarah say she was with you if she wasn't?'

'I don't know. I just know I was here, so I don't think I can help you.' The tears had gone now, replaced by tension.

'Did she text you or call you?' Hunter pressed.

Wendy reached for a mobile phone that was plugged into a wall socket, charging. 'Have a look,' she said, and skimmed it across the table to Hunter.

Sam watched over Hunter's shoulder as he went to the messages folder. It was blank. Too blank, as if there'd been a clear-out.

Sam held out his hand. 'Can I have a look?'

Hunter passed him the phone. A Samsung. Sam clicked on the phone icon and went to the logs, a list of all the texts and calls received and made. All the logged calls had a contact name next to it. Wendy was right. There were none from Sarah.

Sam passed it back to Wendy. 'Thank you.'

When she took it from him, she said, 'Can you go now?'

'Not yet,' Hunter said. 'A woman has died. I want answers.' Wendy folded her arms defiantly but Hunter went on regardless. 'Do you know if Sarah was seeing someone else?'

'What makes you say that?'

'If she told Billy she was with you and she wasn't, you're an alibi. I don't know how close you are to Billy, whether he would call to check, but an alibi like this only works if the other person knows about it. So did you?'

Wendy pursed her lips and shook her head. 'You saw my phone. I don't know anything.'

Hunter softened his tone. 'Your friend was murdered. It's time to leave behind whatever you're protecting. It will come out.'

Wendy didn't say anything for a while and Hunter let the silence grow. Eventually she said, 'I don't know anything.'

'And you don't know where she was the other night?'

'No.'

'And you don't know if she was seeing someone else?'

A tear ran down her cheek and her lip trembled. She wiped it away and shook her head. 'Like I said, I don't know anything.'

Hunter stood up and took a business card from his jacket pocket. 'If you think of anything important, call me.'

Wendy took the card without looking and held it in her hand as she watched them leave.

138

When they were back in their car, Hunter looked back at the house and said, 'That puts the husband in the frame.'

'How come?' Sam said, surprised.

'She's hiding something. She must be protecting Sarah, which means that whatever she knows would hurt Billy.' He turned to look at Sam. 'What do you think?'

Sam knew he was being tested. 'It's not a simple domestic,' he said. 'Billy seemed too plausible. Everything about him seemed genuine. And why display Sarah's body like that if it was anything to do with him?'

'To make people like you think of a different suspect,' Hunter said. 'Simple distraction.'

'But why not just bury her and pretend that she'd run off?' Sam said. 'He risks forensic discovery in the hope that we interpret it differently? That doesn't seem right.'

'You've got to play the odds,' Hunter said, his tone sharper as he started the engine. 'That's why you always start at the most obvious place.'

As Hunter set off, Sam wondered why they hadn't searched Billy's house more thoroughly. There could be blood or some forensic traces. Instead, they'd left with nothing but suspicions. If Billy was a serious suspect, Hunter didn't seem to be doing a great job at investigating, and that worried him.

Twenty-two

Joe walked back towards his office through Crown Square, his car back in the underground garage beneath his apartment. He had gone the long way round, taking streets that avoided his office to bring him back round to the purpose of his route: Aidan's mother.

Mary Molloy was in her usual place, where Joe had seen her so many times that she had begun to fade into the background. Her placard was against the small wall in front of the sloping grass verge that rose up to the Crown Court windows, just part of the daily noise and bustle. She was handing out leaflets to whoever was prepared to take them outside the place where it had all happened, putting in the hours in front of the building in which her son received his life sentence.

Joe watched her for a while. Her smile was engaging, lit her up, gave her some bounce and persuaded people to take leaflets, but whenever there was a gap in the flow of people it was re-vealed as a mask. She would return to her placard, her face filled with grim determination, her jaw set, eyes looking around, waiting for the next person who might come along, hoping always that the leaflet might end up in the hand of someone who could do something to change things. Behind the brightness of her smile, given up for whoever was passing, there was sadness. Joe hoped that her

140

moment had come the day before, when he had taken one from her.

She sat on the low wall and rested for a few moments. Joe watched her. Her hair hung forward as she looked down, her feet tapping on the floor absent-mindedly, her arms resting on her knees. On some, it might have looked carefree. For Mary, it highlighted her sadness, showed that her thoughts were elsewhere.

Reaching into his pocket, Joe produced the leaflet he had been given the day before and held it up as he approached her.

As he got closer, she looked up and regarded him with suspicion, as if not used to someone approaching her, but then she regained her composure. 'Can I help you?' Her soft Irish accent took him by surprise again, having none of the sharp Manchester edges.

Joe smiled, trying to put her at ease. He looked at the leaflet and then back to Mary. 'I just wondered if I could have a talk with you about your son's case.'

'Sure. Tell me first, who are you?'

'My name is Joe Parker and I'm a lawyer at Honeywells.'

Her warmth disappeared and an angry look flashed into her eyes, her temper quick. 'What's wrong? You worried that I'm soiling your reputation?'

'I don't understand.'

'My son trusted you to prove the truth, but you didn't, and now he's in prison for something he didn't do and you're getting all prissy about me letting the world know.'

Joe realised that she blamed Honeywells for their part in the fiasco of her son's imprisonment.

'This is nothing to do with Honeywells,' he said, his hands out, palms down. 'I wasn't at the firm when Aidan went to prison and no one knows I'm here.' He held up the leaflet again. 'I'm here to find out answers of my own.'

'About Aidan's case?'

'Yes.'

Her brow furrowed and her lip jutted out, the look in her eyes a mix of confusion and suspicion. 'Why the sudden interest?'

'Some strange things have happened recently, and I wonder whether they are somehow connected to Aidan's case. Until I talk to you, I don't know.'

She stood up and folded her arms. 'What kind of things?'

'Come with me and we'll talk.'

She paused for a few moments, and then nodded. 'Let me call someone first.'

'Who?'

'Just a friend who's helping me out. A reporter. We decide on strategy together, that's all.' When Joe shrugged, she stepped away and whispered into her mobile phone. A few seconds went by as she listened. When she looked back to Joe, her head cocked, her hand over the mouthpiece, she said, 'Tell me where to meet you and I'll come along as soon he gets here.'

'The Acropolis. A café, just along there.' And he pointed towards Bridge Street.

'I know it,' she said. She spoke into her phone and then to Joe, 'Give me thirty minutes.'

Joe agreed and set off walking, ready for his wait. He didn't have an urge to do much else with his afternoon.

The Acropolis was a greasy spoon in a narrow street not far from the court, run by an ageing Greek man who served milky coffees and large breakfast platters. The door tinkled as Joe went in and Andreas waved from behind the counter. Joe ordered an omelette and coffee and then sat and waited, his view out of the large windows obscured by the steam.

When Andreas brought over his food, he said, 'I don't see you in here so much, Joe.'

Joe smiled. 'It's no reflection on your food. It's just, well, you know.'

'We all have bad patches in our job,' Andreas said, and he put his hand on Joe's shoulder. 'That girl who worked with you. I heard about it, and it wasn't your fault.'

For a moment, Joe felt grateful for the contact, wanted to sit Andreas down and tell him all about how he felt about it, a friendly face who wouldn't judge him, but as quickly as the emotion arrived, he pushed it away.

'Thank you, Andreas,' he said.

'Ten years ago, I wanted to just close this place and go, but now?' Andreas shrugged. 'It's my place in the city.'

Joe raised his cup. 'I'm glad you stayed.'

Andreas trudged back behind his counter and to the back door, from where small trails of cigarette smoke drifted into the café.

For an hour, Joe watched the occasional passerby and tried not to listen to the conversations of the other customers. Some were workmen who were renovating a derelict government building and knew that a greasy dinner from Andreas would get them through the afternoon, whereas others were just single old men with nothing to do but walk the streets, and staring into a coffee worked off an extra couple of hours. He wondered whether he had been stood up by Mary when he saw her.

He wiped the steam from the window, just to make sure it was her. There was a man walking with her. Tall, and slim, in a blue corduroy jacket and grey trousers.

Mary nodded at Joe as she walked in, the man with her looking back into the street, scanning it, before closing the door.

Mary slid into the table opposite Joe, the man alongside her, squeaking on the long green vinyl seat before leaning against the large tiled mosaic of the Acropolis.

Joe waved for three coffees and said, 'I'm Joe Parker, from Honeywells.'

The man with Mary reached across with his hand to shake.

'Sorry, I'm being rude,' he said. 'Tyrone McCarthy.' And he gripped Joe's hand hard as he shook it. It was meant to be noticed but Joe didn't grimace. 'I'm a reporter. I've been helping Mary with her campaign. I hope you don't mind, but she asked me to be here when you spoke with her.'

'Irish too?' Joe said, thinking about his name.

Tyrone smiled. 'It's what drew me to her story at first. We've a lot in common. I was born here, but my parents are Irish. I felt some affinity.'

'But why do you have to be here?'

Tyrone put a voice recorder on the table and switched it on. 'Come on, Mr Parker, you're a smart man, you know how it is. You work for the firm who acted for Aidan, who let him get convicted, and now you want to speak with her. If I'm helping Mary with her campaign, then I should know what you're going to say.'

Mary peered into the mug as Andreas put the drinks on the table. 'Think of it as latte,' Joe said, which made her smile, the first real softening of her exterior, but it disappeared again as quickly as it had arrived.

Joe considered Tyrone and said, 'Why were you looking around when you came in?'

Tyrone frowned. 'Someone has been following me. Probably Mary too. I don't know if it's the police, worried about what we might uncover, or someone else.'

'Someone else?'

'We're making a lot of noise, and people start to take notice. And it's not just the police. Aidan did not kill Rebecca Scarfield, which means someone else did and that person will not want us looking at the case too deeply. Think about it: whoever killed her is still free because everyone thinks Aidan did it. If we prove otherwise, someone is going to get worried.'

Joe looked towards the window. 'So who did you see?'

'I don't know, that's just it. It was just that sensation of being followed.'

'So who do you work for?' Joe said.

'The *Evening Press*,' Tyrone said. 'I keep on at my editor to do a spread, but he won't let me yet. He's worried about a backlash from the police, because of who Rebecca's father is, the assistant chief constable.'

'So why do you carry on?'

'If I can find that one thing to persuade my editor to run with the story, to back a campaign, then it will be worth it.'

Joe saw it then. Mary was Tyrone's ticket, nothing more. Tyrone hoped that he might make a name for himself on the back of her story. Joe felt a small tug of guilt – he saw something of himself in that equation. For him, Mary was also a means to an end.

Mary put down her mug and leaned forward. 'So what has happened that involves Aidan?' she said. 'If it doesn't help him, I'm not interested.'

'Does the name David Jex mean anything to you?' Joe said.

Her eyelids flickered and her lips tightened. 'Yes, it does, and you know why, if you know anything about Aidan's case.'

'One of the detectives on his case,' Joe said, nodding.

'What about him?'

'He's gone missing.'

Mary looked confused. 'I know. That was months back. I've read about it.' She ran her finger round the edge of her mug, her nails short and bitten. 'Do the police think he's dead?'

'I haven't asked them.'

Mary looked into her drink for a while. 'Does he have a family?' she said eventually.

146

'A wife and two children. A son and daughter. They don't know where he is, but this is the thing: he was obsessing over Aidan's case before he disappeared.'

Mary looked up, and Joe saw that the shadows had appeared around her again. 'Perhaps it's guilt for framing Aidan.'

'Framing?'

'Yes, exactly that. They lied. The police. The witnesses.'

'How do you know that?'

'Because I know my son,' she said, her voice raised, her hand pressed against her chest. 'If he was a murderer, don't you think I would know? I know what happened on that night. I know what time he got in. I told the police something different, I realise that, but I was confused, scared. I see now, and I can look myself in the mirror and be sure that I'm right, but I don't think the witnesses can. That couple who saw Aidan's car? Liars. Those girls who reckoned Aidan had threatened that woman? Liars. The detectives who worked on the case? Liars.'

Tyrone reached across and put his hand on hers, squeezing tightly, supportive.

Mary's anger was strident, insistent, almost accusatory, but there was a touch of desperation about her that touched Joe. She was a lone voice, with only some reporter on the make to help her.

Mary took a drink before putting her mug down with a loud clink. 'So what is it?' she said.

'What do you mean?'

'What is special about what you know that can help me?'

'I just feel that something isn't right, but I don't know what it is,' Joe said.

Tyrone tutted. 'So you've come to get information from us? You're going to have to do better than that.'

Mary looked at Tyrone and then back at Joe before she said, 'There's something else too, I can tell. You wouldn't just come to me because a detective went missing a few months ago. So what is it?'

Joe wondered how far he could go. He had a duty of confidentiality, but Joe had always been prepared to overlook his professional duties if the case demanded it. Being a lawyer is about helping people, and sometimes that meant doing the wrong thing for the right result. It isn't about what you do, but about what will catch you out, and right then, there was a reporter with a notebook and a voice recorder. He didn't see anything in Mary Molloy that was a threat, but he wasn't sure about Tyrone.

'This has to be off the record,' Joe said, pointing at the voice recorder. 'I'll tell you when you can go on the record.'

Tyrone looked at Mary, who nodded, so he clicked off the voice recorder.

'David Jex's son has gone missing too,' Joe said.

Mary looked surprised for a moment, but then she recovered her composure. She looked out of the window and took another sip of her coffee, before she said, 'But how does this help Aidan?'

'Because he had become interested in Aidan's case too, and he knows it's linked somehow to his father's disappearance. Has he ever got in touch with you? Carl Jex? Just a teenager.'

'No, he hasn't,' Mary said, and Tyrone shrugged and shook his head when she looked at him. 'I would have recognised the name. It's unusual.'

'How do you know that he isn't trying to prove that his father was right?' Tyrone said. 'Perhaps he's worried that we're starting to change people's minds about Aidan?'

'That would make you a suspect in their disappearances,' Joe said.

Mary's cheeks flushed purple. 'Apple doesn't fall far from the tree, eh?' she said. 'Is that what you mean?'

Joe leaned forward and softened his tone. 'We shouldn't be enemies,' he said. 'Just tell me where to start looking.'

'And what's in it for you? More money for your firm? Didn't you make enough last time, when you failed?'

Joe sighed. Mary was a difficult person to get on with, but Joe tried not to judge her too harshly. He knew what it was like to lose a loved one. Mary still had her son, but every day she believed he was being treated cruelly for something he didn't do. Joe had felt the hard smack of injustice through his career, where a case had gone the wrong way, but the feeling had never lasted long. There was always a new case to move on to.

'I just want to do the right thing,' he said, looking at both Tyrone and Mary. 'My time at Honeywells is nearly done. If you don't use me now, I won't have access to Aidan's file any more.' Mary didn't respond, so Joe continued, 'If I find anything out, will Aidan talk to me, if I go to see him in prison? I can't do anything without his permission.'

Mary looked at Tyrone, who shrugged, before she turned back to Joe. 'If you can help him, Aidan will see you,' she said, her voice quiet.

'So where do I start?'

'With those lying witnesses,' she said, the snap coming back into her voice. 'They couldn't look at me at court. They knew they were lying to get Aidan locked up, and if you can untangle their lies, the case falls away.'

Joe dug into his pocket for a business card. He slid it across the table. Mary picked it up to look at it, turning it in her hand.

'I can't promise anything,' Joe said. 'Perhaps I'm being selfish, but if I can make a difference it will help me, and it will help you, and Aidan.'

Mary nodded and then she took Joe by surprise by reaching across and grasping his hand. She held it tightly and stared hard at him, leaning forward so that he had no chance of avoiding her stare. 'Don't fill me with false hope, Mr Parker, that's all I ask of you.'

'I won't, I promise,' he said, and in the fast blinks that followed his reply, he got a glimpse of the sadness behind her campaign, her yearning to have her son back home with her.

Mary reached into her pocket for her phone and sent a short text, reading the number from Joe's business card. A few seconds later, Joe's phone buzzed to let him know that he had a message.

'You have my number now,' she said. 'I want to know if there is any news. Anything at all.'

Joe nodded his agreement and went to slide out

of the seat. As he went, he looked at Tyrone and promised himself that he would try to make more of a difference than Tyrone had. Once he'd returned to the warm glow of daylight outside, Joe felt the rush of a new cause, the feeling that he could make something happen. He just had to prove it now.

Twenty-three

As they arrived back at the station, Hunter and Weaver walking ahead again, excluding him, Sam said, 'What now?'

They both stopped and turned round. Hunter said, 'You dig the dirt on the husband. Don't rush it though; he might have covered his tracks well. We don't want him to know he's a suspect. Look at her social media stuff and for any bitching about him. You've got access to her bank accounts. Get his. Take our time and we'll find something.'

'And you're sure it's him?'

'We can never be sure, but he's the main focus until something else comes up. Remember, this is how policing works. It's not about theories. It's about putting in the hard work.'

Sam bit back his retort that he wasn't a complete novice. Hunter had an opinion of him and nothing he could say would change that. He would have to come up with what Hunter needed to gain his approval. The problem was that Sam was convinced Hunter was getting it wrong.

Once they were back in the Incident Room, Hunter and Weaver retreated into a huddle in one corner. Sam wasn't invited, so he took a seat next to Charlotte and logged onto the computer.

'How did it go?' she said, speaking with a mouthful of some chewy health bar, her hand over her mouth so that she didn't spit oats over him.

'Not great at the victim's house. It's the part I hate the most, seeing the news given over.'

'Brings back bad memories?'

'Something like that. You see a life changed for ever by just a few words, where everything crumbles in front of you.'

She screwed up the wrapper and put it in the bin under her desk before asking, 'What did you make of the husband? Is he a suspect?'

'Hunter thinks he's the number one.'

'And you?'

'He seemed genuine to me. Hunter thought differently. Said it's all about playing the odds, how it's always the husband or boyfriend until something tells you otherwise.'

'And Weaver?'

Sam shook his head slowly. 'He let Hunter do the talking, as if he's just his bagman.'

Charlotte shrugged. 'Isn't he right though? Unless there is something else, it is always the man in their life.'

Sam exhaled. 'You saw the body this morning. That was a display, a taunt. Why would the husband do that? Or even a boyfriend. She was sawn up, for Christ's sake. Who could do that?'

'To deflect us, if he was planning it?'

Sam gave a small laugh. 'You sound like Hunter.

Okay, I get it, maybe I'm the one getting it wrong. I'll do the background checks, speak to her friends and family. Not straight away though.'

'Why, what are you doing?'

'I just want to do more on the victim. She was up to something. She told her husband she was at a friend's house, but it turns out that she wasn't. And what are people usually doing if they are using a friend as an alibi?'

'Having an affair,' Charlotte said.

'So there should be a change in her spending habits.'

'Why?'

'She was married, early thirties, with two children, both at school. My guess is that she wanted to put some sparkle back in her life.' His mind flashed to Alice and he felt a stab of guilt over the hours he put in at the station, followed by a rush of panic as he wondered whether he was describing his own marriage. He resolved to take Alice out for a nice evening soon. 'That can involve money,' he went on. 'I'll look for an increase in buying clothes, or perhaps even the odd hotel in her accounts? If we can find the man who was getting the benefit, we can find out where she was before she was killed.'

'And it gives the husband a motive,' Charlotte said. 'He follows her, knows she's being unfaithful, and he kills her to make it look like some sick attack, maybe even to humiliate her. Perhaps her lover even left his semen inside her, meaning we will go straight to him. Billy portrays himself as the victim, not her, and sobs away at the press conferences so that no one suspects him.'

'Except that everyone suspects whoever does the press conference now,' Sam said. 'The killer has to do it so that he doesn't raise suspicion, but all people do is point at the television and accuse the person crying into the microphone. I've done it, and I bet you have. Sometimes I'm right. Sometimes I'm not.'

'But you don't see it as the husband?'

Sam shook his head. 'No, I don't, but I'll do my job first.'

He started to search for previous reports of domestic violence, under both Sarah and Billy's name, and then the address. A lot of violence in the home goes unreported, but anything that makes it as far as a phone call to the police gives a good snapshot of a relationship, a desperate and dark glimpse into a couple's private life. Too often the police were unable to make a difference, where the pattern of reports and retractions is played out, just empty promises to change that only last until the next six-pack of lager.

When he searched under Billy's name, Sam found two reports. One from a neighbour who was concerned that she could hear a woman's screams coming from the house, and another one from Sarah herself, complaining that she had been hit. When the police got there, she didn't want to tell them anything.

Sam thought about the area. Quiet, suburban, aspirational, the first stop for those trying to get away from the rougher estates. Enough for Sarah to not want to give it up? Did that make her put up with a bully who took it too far?

He put the exhibit bag that contained the list of

password hints onto his desk, and next to it the list of answers he had got from Billy.

Sam logged onto the bank account first, and once online, got the screen to display a list of all transactions from Sarah's current account for the preceding two years. He printed it off and spent a few minutes taping the sheets together, so that it was a long scrolling bank statement. He rummaged in a drawer for highlighter pens, sorting out five colours in total, so that a quick glance would show whether there had been an increase in types of spending. He separated them into categories of what were obviously perfumes and clothes, identified from the online names, and then hotels, and high street chemists and department stores. As he worked through, he could see from the frequency of the strikes that there was an increase in department stores and online perfume shops. She was making herself look nice for someone, and Sam guessed that it wasn't for Billy.

He logged onto the credit card account next, and was struck by how her spending had changed. It was increasing, becoming more extravagant. The credit card was in her own name, according to the account details, whereas there was a joint account listed alongside the current account. The credit card account was harder for Billy to see.

As Sam went through the months, he saw some hotel bills, along with department stores. He could also see that she had been paying back less than she had been spending. Whatever extravagances she had been enjoying, she hadn't been able to afford them.

Before he could look any further, Evans came

155

into the room. She looked pale. She headed to the centre and clapped her hands, making everyone look round.

Evans waited for the murmurs to die down before she said, 'I've just been to the post mortem.'

'That was quick,' Hunter said, sitting on the edge of a desk in the corner of the room.

Evans turned to him and said, 'The ritualistic way in which the body was displayed helped it to jump the queue. They're still slicing and dicing in there, but I thought I needed to give everyone an update.'

Sam noticed that it was the group she wanted to update, not Hunter. Evans was setting out where her loyalties lay.

Evans made sure she had everyone's attention before she continued. 'The key questions were whether she was sexually assaulted in some way, whether she died on the moors, and whether she was alive or dead when the amputations started.'

'Why is it important whether she died on the moors?' Hunter said, stepping forward, his hands on his hips.

'For the same reason that the location of the body is important. I agreed with Sam Parker earlier – if the choice of that location was deliberate, it means something.'

Hunter glowered at Sam and clenched his jaw. He didn't stop Evans, though.

'The doc says that there is no evidence of a sexual assault,' Evans said. 'That doesn't mean that there wasn't one, but there was no tearing, no semen deposits, no bruising at the top of the thighs.'

156

'Perhaps a condom was used,' someone said from the other side of the room.

Evans agreed. 'They'll swab for lubricants, but there were no signs of force around there. There are some bruises around her wrists, the back of her head and on her shoulder blades, so it looks like she was held down with her hands held over her head.'

'So how did she die?' Hunter said.

'Strangulation or suffocation,' Evans said. 'The little red marks in the eyes are there.'

'That sounds like an angry killing,' Hunter said.

'The husband offed her before she met up with lover boy,' Weaver said, stepping forward. 'Killed and dumped her to make it look like a sick killing.'

'Perhaps,' Evans said. 'The doc would agree that she didn't die on the moors. It was a dumping ground, nothing more.'

'How does she know?' Hunter said.

'The wounds are clean cuts, done after she died. If she had been alive, there would have been a struggle of some description, making the wounds more jagged. There were also some small pieces of green plastic stuck in the flesh, like she had been rested on strong garden bags and the saw had caught and snagged them.'

'Do we know it's a saw?' Hunter said.

'That's the best guess. The limbs have been sawn off like a lamb's leg for the butcher's window – there are small lines in the flesh that criss-cross each other.'

'The forwards and backwards of the saw-blade?' Hunter said.

'That's the one,' Evans said. 'It's looking like she was strangled and then dismembered so that she could be dumped. The body parts would fit into a car boot a lot easier. Which means that the location was selected. So why there?'

Hunter looked over at Weaver before he said, 'So we would find it. It's remote enough to let him dump her without being seen at night but near enough for the ramblers to find her in the morning. He's distracting you. You're buying the bluff.'

'He?'

'Husband. It looks like she was playing away. She told him she was at a friend's house but she wasn't, and her friend won't give up her secrets. So he plans it so that he kills her and dumps the body in a way that an angry husband wouldn't. Is there a history of violence?'

Sam raised his hand. 'A couple of reports.'

Hunter smiled, although there was no warmth to it. 'There you are.'

'So what now?' Evans said.

'I'm going back to the victim's house,' Hunter said. 'Except this time I'm taking a CSI with a search team with me. We're looking for green garden bags and traces of blood where she was cut up.'

'And don't forget the car,' Evans said.

Hunter took a deep breath through his nose. 'Thank you, Inspector, I've done this before.' And then he left the room, Weaver going with him.

Charlotte leaned into Sam. 'It looks like you're no longer teacher's pet.'

That brought a smile from him. 'I don't think we gelled,' he said. 'First dates are like that.'

Evans turned to Sam and raised her eyebrows, as if to query whether Hunter could be right.

Sam shrugged, avoiding a proper conclusion, and then he shook his head. No, he didn't believe it. Hunter was getting it wrong, and Sam wanted to know why.

Twenty-four

Carl tried to keep track of time but it was impossible. The cellar was in complete darkness. He didn't know if it made time go more quickly or whether it dragged out every minute so that he had only really been there for a few hours. He was waiting for hunger to hit him, but the fear was keeping that at bay.

The pain in his head was easing now but his back and shoulders were still shooting sharp twinges through his body, the bruises from the fall down the stairs. He had learned to manage it by moving slowly, just tiny stretches, but his fear of moving made him stiffen up more, the tightness of the rope around his neck a constant reminder.

He put his head back against the cold wall as he fought against the tears. He should have told his mother where he was going. Or his lawyer. No one knew where he was and he had to find a way to stay strong. It was hard, though. His legs were aching from standing, and he was scared of the man coming back.

He couldn't believe it had come to this, being tied up in a cellar, all because of his father's obsession.

Carl had once been so proud of him. He was a detective, and Carl had wanted to grow up to be just like him, even wanted to follow him in his career, but he wasn't sure any more. The job had changed his father. It had taken him away. All he had wanted to do was find out why.

It had started more than a year earlier. Just another routine day.

Carl had been in his room when his father came home. He was upset, angry, throwing things around. That wasn't like him. Carl had been upstairs, just browsing the internet, but he had stopped and listened. His parents didn't argue often, and his father never ranted like he did that day – he wasn't making any sense. He had mentioned a woman's name, so Carl had closed his door and put his hands over his ears. He didn't want to hear that.

His father went into the smallest bedroom, his sister's old room, and slammed the door. When he emerged a few hours later, it was if the argument had never happened, but from then on his father was different. There were moments of distraction, his thoughts elsewhere, where his father would suddenly stop eating or be caught looking out of the window when he was watching television. When he was in his room, he spent a lot of time on the telephone.

A few months later, his father went out and never returned.

So Carl had been searching for him, and his

search had ended up here. He took a deep breath. Is this where his father had been, too? In this cellar, tied up? If he had, he hadn't left alive, and Carl knew with growing certainty that he had to find a way to get out. He couldn't trust whoever the man was to let him go and, if he didn't escape, his mother would be left alone to wonder where both the men in her life had gone. He couldn't bear the thought of that.

There was a noise outside, the faint rumble of a car. Carl tensed. He waited for the anticipated sound of the door through the ceiling, which was followed by footsteps on the wooden floor, slow and deliberate. Carl held his breath as it fell silent above him. There were flutters in his chest as the quiet was broken by the sound of the cellar door being unlocked. He listened to the slow clomp of footsteps down the stairs until the lamp was clicked on. Carl winced in the glare, turning away.

The man stood in front of the light, so that he was just an outline. Carl got the upward flick of his hair and the scent of aftershave.

'I've got something for you,' the man said.

His tone was soft, which surprised Carl. There was the rustle of a plastic bag and then a drip of liquid onto the floor. Carl yelped when something cold was placed on the back of his head. It was a bag of ice.

Carl grimaced at first, but then the pain started to recede and he was able to put his head back against the wall, jamming the ice pack in place.

'So what do you know about me?' the man said.

'I don't know anything,' Carl said.

161

A hand shot forward and pushed Carl's head back. He cried out as the ice cubes dug into his scalp.

'Don't play games, that is my advice to you,' the man said, his face close, so that Carl felt the warmth of his breath and the spray of his spittle.

'I'm not playing games,' Carl said, grimacing.

'So answer my questions. I'll get the answers one way or another, so make it easier on yourself. Tell me what you know about me.'

Carl closed his eyes, his mind racing, filled with panic and fear, yet understanding that the man in front of him wanted desperately to know how much he knew. It was the only bargaining position he had. 'I don't know anything about you,' Carl said. 'I was just watching the house, to burgle it.'

Another push to Carl's head, so that it banged against the wall. He shouted out and grimaced as he tried to put his hands to where it hurt, remembering belatedly that they were held back by the chain.

'I want your name,' the man said.

'It's Carl,' he said, the words coming out as a gasp. 'Carl Jex.'

The man reached forward and pulled the ice away. 'All right, Carl,' he said. 'So tell me again what you were doing outside my house.'

'I told you. I was going to burgle you.'

The man put his face close to Carl's, making him recoil, although there was nowhere to go. All he got was the smell of his breath. Stale whisky, some coffee. 'And I've got so many nice things that you thought you'd have another go?'

Carl didn't respond. Instead beads of sweat ran

down his forehead, despite the coldness of the cellar.

'Why should I keep you alive?' the man said. 'You've seen things in here, so you know I can't let you go. If you're just Carl the burglar, I could end this now.'

Carl swallowed and looked away for a moment.

The man's fist slammed into his cheekbone, knocking Carl to the side, his fall prevented by the taut yank of the rope making him gasp as it pulled tight around his neck. Blood flew from his mouth and onto the floor and half a tooth went with it.

He bucked and gasped as he tried to draw in air, his legs unsteady, swinging around as the rope went tight. He panicked and his bladder gave way, soaking his trousers. After a few seconds he felt arms around him, pulling him back to his feet and pushing him against the wall. There were fingers behind the rope, digging in and scratching Carl's neck, loosening it again, allowing him to breathe.

Carl sucked in air but the intake of coldness caught the nerve endings in his broken tooth, making him screech in pain.

'Don't lie to me again,' the man whispered into his ear, with a menacing hiss. 'I can leave you down here to die. Just remember that.'

Carl nodded that he understood. A tear ran down his cheek. 'How long am I staying here for?'

The man moved away. 'Until the end,' he said, and he turned and walked out, throwing the cellar into darkness as he clicked off the light. The cellar door slammed.

Carl put his head back against the wall and sobbed. Despite the new pain in his teeth, he let

163

the cold air rush in as he wailed in despair. He'd seen so little of his life, and he knew then that it was going to end in darkness, the faint shadows ahead of him the last things he would ever see.

Twenty-five

Sam put the phone down after another call revealed not very much.

Charlotte looked up. 'You seem frustrated.'

'I am. I'm finding nothing out about Sarah's husband that makes him a suspect. There are those calls to the police, but her friends say he's a quiet man. Perhaps too quiet for her, but that's all.'

'Quiet to the outside world doesn't mean he's the same behind closed doors.'

'I know that, but no one has suggested Billy might be responsible apart from Hunter. And why would he leave his children at night to do what he did? He seems pretty devoted to me.'

'So what are you going to do?'

Sam thought about that, and about how DI Evans had supported his suspicions about the location. 'I'm going to speak to Evans.'

'Why?'

'Because I don't like the way this is going.'

Charlotte glanced to the front of the room, where Hunter and Weaver were talking still, just whispers in the corner. 'Don't make Hunter your enemy,' she said.

'Sometimes it's about doing the right thing,' Sam said, and walked out of the Incident Room to Evans's small office next door. She was staring into a coffee cup when Sam knocked lightly on the door and walked in.

She looked up. 'Sam?'

He closed the door behind him. Now that he was standing there, his notion to speak to her didn't seem like the greatest of ideas. Although he sensed the tension between Evans and Hunter, he didn't know how far they went back or where her loyalties lay. His gaze flitted between her raised eyebrows and the framed photographs on the edge of her desk. Family pictures. A young girl, Evans smiling with her.

'Come on, get on with it,' she said, impatience showing in her voice.

He took a deep breath and said, 'It's about the investigation. I'm concerned.'

'Why?' Evans said, frowning now.

'It's DCI Hunter, ma'am.'

She pointed to the chair in front of her desk. 'Sit down.' When he followed her direction, she said, 'Talk to me, Sam.'

He looked at his hands, unsure how to start, not knowing if he was about to begin a dialogue he would later regret. But he realised that he was too far in to stop now. There was only one way to say it: as it was.

'I don't want to appear out of tune here,' he said, 'and if you think I'm saying things I shouldn't be saying, tell me and I'll carry on doing what I'm supposed to be doing.'

'Just say it.'

He took a deep breath. 'Hunter has fixated on the husband, and I don't know why,' he said. 'I saw him, the husband, and the shock was genuine. Hunter has already allowed the crime scene to be messed up, and now he seems set on making it about the husband.'

Evans sighed. 'Hunter has been around a long time and thinks that whatever answer is obvious to him can be the only answer; and with his history, who could tell him he's wrong? He's put away a lot of really bad people.'

'So I just get on with it, assume he's right?'

'He's the senior investigating officer. For as long as he's in charge, that's just the way it is. If you take on the mantle of maverick cop, you won't last long on the team, or maybe even on the Force. Your job is about obeying orders. You catch crooks, yes, but by doing as you're told. Like it or not, that's what you signed up for.'

Sam gripped the wooden arms of the chair as if to stand up, but Evans held out her hand to stop him. A smile twitched at the corner of her mouth. 'What do you think might have happened?'

Sam settled back down again and scratched his temple before he spoke. 'I don't know, but that's my point. I'm keeping an open mind. What troubles me is that it is a lot of fuss to wrap up the body limbs just to leave them there. He could have just buried her and reported her as a missing person. Her body was meant to be discovered, but why, and why that spot? And why like that?'

'But you agree that it has to be somewhere, so why not just there? There's not necessarily some hidden meaning.'

'I understand that, but it's not like that area is just some local woodland. There's nothing around it for miles. Yes, there's less chance of being caught with the body, but why go onto the moors as far as he did? The body was found around a hundred yards from the closest place to park a car, which is a long way to carry a torso. Why not just dump and arrange the body closer to the car and get out of there? The longer he's carrying limbs to and fro, covering himself with her DNA all the time, the other body parts still in the car and awaiting transportation, the greater the chance of discovery.' Sam stopped and took a deep breath.

'And?'

'And why would the husband go to all that trouble of driving to the moors to avoid discovery, with the risk of being stopped by the police, and then spend longer up there than he needed to? It doesn't make any sense.'

Evans stayed quiet as she thought, her fingers steepled and tapping against her pursed lips. 'If it doesn't make sense, it usually means there's something else,' she said, almost to herself.

'That's what I was thinking. By concentrating too much on the husband, I think we might miss something.'

'I can't tell you to go against Hunter,' she said.

'So what are you saying, ma'am?'

She sat back and put her hands on the desk. 'That I won't tell Hunter what you're doing if you follow your own inquiries. Speak to her friends to see if she complained about being followed. Look for anything similar, if there could be such a thing. Chase old reports of men being caught

167

hanging around the moors.'

'And if Hunter finds out?' Sam said.

'You're on your own. Unless...'

'Unless?'

'If it isn't the husband and whoever did this strikes again, wouldn't you rather be the person who looked at everything, the one in the squad who got it right?'

'And then?'

'Then I'll take the credit.'

Sam smiled. 'So I'm on my own if I have it wrong, but if I'm right, I'm operating with your guidance?'

Evans returned the smile. 'Power is just a bitch, isn't it?'

Sam nodded and got to his feet. 'Thank you, ma'am.' He turned towards the door but then stopped as his hand reached the door handle. He turned back to Evans. 'Does Hunter get it wrong much?'

'No,' Evans said. 'He gets his man. Every time.'

He clenched his jaw and closed his eyes as the first tremors of anger shook him. They were back, the vibrations in his head, stopping him from thinking clearly. It had been like that ever since the boy had told him his name: Carl Jex.

The house seemed silent, more so than usual. No ticking clocks. No computer hum or the clicks of cooling radiators. There were just the fast taps of his foot on the carpeted floor as he stared towards his wardrobe. Soon, he would lose everything.

He took deep breaths to let his anger subside.

His emotions bubbled up sometimes. He knew he should have more control, but it was hard to stay rational.

He got to his feet and went to the wardrobe. The door opened slowly, revealing the neat row of suit carriers. He reached for one from a couple of years earlier, the package rustling as he took it gently from the rail. He sat down on the bed and put the carrier over his knees. It calmed him as he moved the zip slowly, and once it was halfway down he lifted it to his face, inhaling deeply. He closed his eyes and let out a deep sigh. There were still soft traces of her perfume, the heavy flowers that reminded him of her, those nights spent with her, when he had given her a new life. The life she deserved.

It was always the smells that brought them back. They were evocative, sensual, overpowering, much stronger than any other of the senses. They could catch you unawares and carry you back to a different time. Hot tarmac. Cut grass. The smell of someone baking. It's not just the memories. The scents take you back to the actual time, transport you back there, to that place.

He surrounded himself with her scent. Her faded perfume, along with that musky smell all of her own, heady and warm, so his mind was flooded with memories. Her laugh, joy-filled, exuberant, different from how she was when he first met her, when she seemed quiet, almost flat, as if she had forgotten how to enjoy herself. He thought back to their first time, when she had seemed timid, stopping him, stopping herself really, knowing that she was getting carried away,

169

not wanting to expose her true self to him.

He had changed that. He had released her, helped her find the real woman within, the person she always knew was underneath. He had been damn good for her. Why hadn't she realised that?

Why would she want to walk away, to go back to what was waiting for her at home? He had saved her.

He buried his face into her clothes and took another deep breath. Her scent lingered in the air as he zipped up the suit carrier.

He hung his head as he thought about how it was all over. He stayed like that for a moment, then he put the suit carrier back into the wardrobe, making sure it was in the right place, before walking slowly towards the room next door. His parents' bedroom.

He didn't go in there much. It was the place where he weakened. He leaned against the doorframe as he pushed at the door, opening slowly to reveal the bed. He could still smell the mustiness of a Sunday morning, the room heady with warm bodies and stale booze.

His mother's clothes were in an old wardrobe along the wall next to his room. He looked down at the floor before he stepped over the threshold, his tongue running over his lip as his foot pressed into the carpet. It was thicker than anywhere else in the house, dark brown swirls that spoke of a different time.

The wardrobe door clicked as he opened it and he gasped as the odour rushed at him, swamping him in memories of being clasped against her, his face buried in her clothes as she held him close, her arms around him, protecting him, the rage from his father muffled.

He held one of her dresses against his face and she was still there. Stale cigarettes and cheap perfume. Nights in front of the fire rushed back to him. Music and booze, laughter and dancing. Two people swaying in the flickering light. Until things changed. It always went wrong.

His eyes dampened and his throat felt thick. By moving on, he'd be leaving this behind too. Could he do that?

But with the identity of his captive in the cellar confirmed, he knew he had no choice.

The boy had ruined everything. All of his memories would be snatched from him.

The vibrations came back. He would make him pay.

Twenty-six

Joe had wanted to avoid the office after his meeting with Mary Molloy, so he decided to go back further into the story, to a person who was one of the subjects of Mary's anger: Hugh Bramwell, Aidan's solicitor at Honeywells.

Joe had joined Honeywells after falling out with the people at the firm where he trained, when his fiancée decided she preferred the attentions of one of the married partners to Joe's. Hugh had given him a way out, allowing him to take over as the criminal lawyer at Honeywells when the older man retired.

Hugh Bramwell had been one of the last old-school defence lawyers in Manchester, full of country-set charm, well-spoken and impeccably dressed, in tweed three-piece suits and a pocket watch, as if setting himself apart as the city's eccentric would get him more clients. And it did.

The law didn't attract characters like Hugh any more. Joe had been drawn to it because of what had happened to his sister. It was a way of keeping alive his hope of meeting her killer. For most young lawyers the returns in crime were too low, so criminal law had become a magnet for chancers, failures, and those who lived lives not too far from the clients they represented.

Joe contacted Hugh and arranged a meeting, and as it could be his last week at Honeywells, he decided to have the meeting in a pub.

He paid the taxi driver and stared up at the Horse and Jockey. It looked like an old country pub, with Tudor beams and a low roof, except that it was in leafy suburbia, with its view over what people called 'the Green' lending a village feel, although in reality it was just a triangle of tired grass with an old Victorian lamp in the centre.

He texted Gina.

Out for the rest of the day. It's relevant to Aidan's case. Will fill you in tomorrow.

A reply shot back.

You've got a client at 4.

Send him away.

Joe set his phone to silent. He didn't want to be distracted.

It had been a few years since he had been in the

Horse and Jockey. It was in the Chorlton area of the city, an area settled by the urban professionals, those who wanted the buzz of the city and to enjoy the thought that they were just a short drive from some of Manchester's roughest edges. They were only ever places to drive past, though, not stop in – danger experienced through a windscreen. He knew Kim Reader didn't live far away, in a first-floor apartment in one of the high Victorian buildings, with large windows and peaked roofs. Kim had opted for original features over the bland newbuilds. It had been a few years since Joe had been there, too.

Joe spotted Hugh sitting outside, as he said he would be, drinking from a foamy pint that sat on one of the long dark tables.

As Joe got closer, Hugh lifted his glass as a welcome before he drained what was left.

'It looks like it's my round,' Joe said.

'I knew you'd get the message,' Hugh said, chuckling to himself.

Joe dipped his head to get in through the doorway, returning shortly afterwards with two pints of bitter, the head running down the side of the glass like spilled cream.

Hugh didn't say anything until he had made the top three inches disappear.

'I thought they'd ruin this place by letting the children in,' Hugh said, 'but they make up for it with the beer.'

'The barman knew what you wanted.'

'I'm here whenever the sun comes out.'

Joe was about to ask him what his wife thought of that, a throwaway comment, but then he remembered with a jolt why Hugh had retired: his wife was dying of cancer and he had wanted to be with her. Joe had heard the news that she had died a year earlier. As that came back to him, he looked more closely at Hugh. His clothes looked worn and in need of a wash, and he had stubble on his cheeks, whereas in work he had always been immaculate. His eyes were red and his veins were showing as tiny red scratches across his nose and cheeks. Joe guessed that sitting in the Horse and Jockey was better than sitting in a silent house, with only his memories to keep him warm.

'How's retirement, Hugh?' he asked, knowing the answer.

Hugh looked over. 'Slow,' he said, smiling softly, realising why Joe had asked. 'But I'd rather be here, where the beer is good, than where you are, wasting your years.'

'Not for much longer,' Joe said. When Hugh raised his eyebrows, grey and bushy, strands pointing skyward, he added, 'Honeywells are ditching crime. There just isn't the mark-up any more so they're packing it in.'

'When?'

'They won't see out the year, is my guess. They want me to trim the department or give it up altogether.'

'But they'll miss the post-Christmas bonanza. The burglaries, the pub fights, the family arguments that end up as brawls. It's a time of great joy.'

Joe smiled. 'They don't share it.' He paused. 'Don't you miss it? Truthfully?'

Hugh took another swig before he answered. 'I

174

do, but not the way it is today. I miss the theatre of the courtroom, and seeing the other lawyers, and the police. I miss the clients sometimes, although not quite as much. But it's not the same these days. It's bureaucracy and form filling and box ticking, everything regimented and scripted. There's no room for someone with a little panache any more.' And he emphasised the word *panache* with a flourish of his hand. 'The Law Society had me doing so much in the name of quality control that I never had the time to do anything that needed controlling.' He shook his head. 'No, I'm well out of it.'

'There aren't many who think the law is a good place to be any more,' Joe said, his voice heavy with weariness. 'There's a long line of students ready to step in, but only because they are weighed down by debt. Once they get in, most with any sense want to get out again.'

'And do you, Joe?'

Joe sighed. 'I just want to enjoy it again. Is that too much to ask?'

'So you've come to me, an elderly sage, so that I can scatter wisdom down onto you and make you love the law again?'

Joe laughed, despite himself. 'Not quite,' he said. 'Perhaps I like your company?'

Hugh leaned forward and put his hand on Joe's forearm. 'What is it, Joe?' he said, his voice low. 'You can talk to me.'

Joe moved his arm away and took another drink of his beer. 'I'm here about a case, an old one of yours. Aidan Molloy.'

Hugh's eyes widened. He took a long pull at his

beer until he emptied it. He held up his glass. 'I'll need another one for this. And fill yours too. I don't like to watch people playing catch-up.'

Joe shook his head, smiling, as he went back into the pub. As he glanced back, he saw Hugh looking down, as if the solitude weighed heavily on him the moment it arrived. It wouldn't harm anyone if Joe kept him company for a while.

When Joe returned with two more creamy beers, Hugh looked up, and Joe saw that some of the joy had faded from his eyes.

'Aidan Molloy,' Hugh said solemnly. 'The one that got away.'

'What do you mean?'

'They don't come along very often, but now and again you get a client accused of something serious when you think they're innocent. And I don't mean *not guilty;* that's a whole different thing. No, I mean innocent, as in he didn't do it.'

Joe settled back into his seat. 'What makes you think that?'

'It was just the way he was. All the way through the case, he was different from the rest. You know how most are, that they feign some outrage and anger, but only because they want to make someone else believe them. With Aidan, it was different.'

'How so?'

'It was disbelief, not anger. I remember the way he looked at his mother when he was convicted. She couldn't watch the trial until after she had given her evidence, but she was there for the verdict, and when it all came crashing down around him Aidan looked across at her and just

176

shook his head and cried, as if he couldn't believe what was happening. That's when I believed him.'

'And before?'

'He was a client. It didn't matter whether I believed him or not.'

'So did you try to do anything about it?'

Hugh took a drink of his beer and, once he had wiped away the foam from his mouth, said, 'There was nothing to do. I took advice from counsel as to whether there were any appeal points, but there weren't. The judge summed it up just right, so it was all down to how the jury saw the evidence, and Aidan. The verdict was a reasonable one.'

'But a wrong one?'

'I think so, but you can't appeal it just because you don't like it, not without any other evidence. Once we gave Aidan the news, he sacked us. His mother took up the campaign on Aidan's behalf. She started out by slandering the firm, but we threatened her with legal proceedings, so all of her attention was directed towards persuading people by the strength of her will. The one thing she couldn't see, however, was that she was one of the problems.'

'I met her today. She's suspicious of everyone and angry at everything.'

'That's what I mean,' Hugh said. 'She was the same back then, and it was easy to take a dislike to her. The jury did.' Before Joe could say anything, Hugh raised his hand. 'I know, I know, it's not a talent contest, but sometimes all the witness has is the hope that the twelve people on the jury like and believe them. If they don't like someone, it makes it easier for them to think they're lying.'

'Lying? Is that what you think?'

'No, I don't, for what it's worth, but it didn't take much for the jury to think she was.' Hugh sighed. 'We tried to talk her out of giving evidence, told her she would only make it worse for Aidan, but she was insistent, which made Aidan insistent. In their eyes, we were part of the conspiracy, lawyers who all pal around together, so her opinion always won over mine.'

'Why was she such a problem?'

'Two reasons: the alibi and her character, and both reasons were intertwined.' Hugh jabbed his finger at the table. 'If she'd have listened to us, perhaps Aidan would have just swung enough reasonable doubt his way, but I was there when she was in the witness box, and you could see the faces of the jury harden. It was where the doubt slipped away and became a certainty of Aidan's guilt.'

'What was wrong with the alibi?'

'She changed it,' Hugh said. 'When they first pulled Aidan in, he told the police that he had got home at twelve thirty. That could still have made him the killer but would have ruled him out as the person dumping the body. Once Aidan had given them a time, the police spoke to her, before Aidan could get her to change her mind. She told the police two thirty, which meant that he could have been the person dumping the body. But she was insistent that she had got it wrong, that she had been tired when she heard him come in through the front door and had quickly glanced at the clock, not spotted the one before the two.'

'And when did she discover her mistake?'

'Once she had spoken to Aidan, who convinced her that she must be wrong. She wanted to tell the jury that.'

Joe shook his head. 'I can guess what happened,' he said.

'The prosecution waved her statement at her, the one she had given to the police, with the declaration of truth at the top, where she said it was two thirty, the first time she had been asked to recall it, and accused her of changing the truth just to help out her son. It was an easy point to make.'

'A very easy one.'

'And it wasn't the first time,' Hugh said.

'I don't understand.'

'Three or four years before the trial, Mary Molloy went to prison for perverting the course of justice. Six months. Her boyfriend was caught on a speed camera and he persuaded her to say that she was driving, except that they didn't think to ask to see the photograph before they embarked on their lie. Her beau had a lush dark beard and the camera captured it just beautifully. It split them up, because she resented him so much for it. When the police asked him about it, he said he had no idea about it, that Mary must have done it as an act of love. She went to prison. He didn't even get as far as a courtroom.'

'So she had told a lie before to try to get someone off,' Joe said, nodding to himself. 'If she would do that for a speed camera offence, how far would she go for a murder case?'

'Exactly,' Hugh said. 'The jury thought she was

covering up for her son, and if they thought that, they thought he was guilty.'

'Why couldn't you stop her? You didn't have to call her.'

'The client was insistent, and you know how it is. We might be the lawyers, but sometimes we have to look after ourselves.'

Joe sat back and took a drink. Hugh didn't need to spell it out. Joe had had many cases like it, where the last thing the case needs is for the client to get into the witness box, as all the hard work of creating doubt in the prosecution case can be wiped out by a defendant's lame excuses. But most defendants want to explain themselves, to have their say. Some will listen to good advice to quit while they are ahead, but others are so insistent that all you can do is give them their hour or more in the spotlight; if you don't let them and the verdict comes down as guilty, the lawyer gets the blame. It must have been the same in Aidan's case, where eventually Hugh had let Aidan dictate his defence, where the desire for Hugh to avoid a complaint was stronger than the need to do the right thing by Aidan, even if Aidan couldn't see it.

'What did you think of the witnesses?' Joe said.

'The couple who saw the car seemed decent enough, although they wouldn't budge on the type of car, or the partial plate. And the three young women who reckoned Aidan had threatened the victim?' Hugh shrugged. 'Why would they lie? Aidan's mother had a reason to lie. They didn't.'

'To say you believed him, you're putting up a good case for the prosecution.'

'No, I'm just saying why the conviction wasn't

a surprise. It doesn't mean it wasn't wrong.'

They sat there in silence for a few minutes, enjoying the beer. Joe began to feel his muscles relaxing, his worries about his future slipping away.

It was Hugh who broke the silence. 'So what are you going to do?'

Joe looked at him. 'I'm going to look into it.'

'Why?'

Joe thought about that, and said, 'I want to love my job again, to do something good, to right a wrong.'

'Your idealism is always the first victim to the job.'

'It doesn't mean it has to be gone for ever.'

'Promise me one thing,' Hugh said.

'What's that?'

'If I got something wrong, if I overlooked something that I should have spotted, know that I'm sorry. Truly sorry. If you can get him out of prison without ruining my reputation, I would be grateful, but if you can't...' And Hugh just sighed. 'Just get that man out of jail.'

Joe raised his glass in agreement. He planned to do that.

Twenty-seven

The cellar door opened and the sound of footsteps on the stairs filled the dark space. Carl stood away from the wall, fear pushing back the threat of sleep. If he slumped, the noose would tighten

181

around his throat. He grimaced and closed his eyes as he waited for the lamp to switch on, opening them slowly when his eyelids turned bright red. He turned his face away until he got used to the glare.

The man moved in front of the lamp and stepped close to him again, so that his silhouette blocked out the light. He was breathing heavily through his nose, as if his jaw was clenched in anger.

'What's going to happen?' Carl said, blinking.

There was a pause before the man said, 'You could attack me. Bite me or headbutt me. Don't. No one knows you're here. No one will hear you outside. You'll die from lack of water within three days if you annoy me. I will leave you down here for a week if you even try, so be very careful. That's if you can stay awake. You could weaken and then it would all be over. One slip, one sag of your knees, and you'll end your days spinning on the spot in here.'

'Why are you doing this?' Carl said, a sob choking his voice.

'Because you lied to me.'

'Don't hit me again,' Carl said. 'Please. I'm scared.'

'Why? You can leave whenever you want.'

Carl was confused. 'I don't understand.'

He laughed, his breath warm on Carl's cheeks. 'But you'll be dead when you do. It's a simple choice: either you stay here or you die. There is no middle way. All you've got to do is relax those knees and feel that noose go tight. It will feel like a release.'

Carl put his head back against the wall and closed his eyes. 'Why?' he said, his voice breaking.

'I'm a collector,' the man said. 'I choose, usually, but it looks like something has just washed up for me this time. So let's talk some more. We could try the truth for a change. I want to know why you've chosen me. Why did you come into my house?'

Carl didn't respond.

'You know you're going to die here, don't you?' the man said.

Carl nodded slowly.

'So talk, and make it easy on yourself.'

Carl felt a small burst of hope. The man wanted to find out what he knew, and whether anyone else knew. He put his head back and wondered what he could say. He guessed that his survival was still only as good for as long as he held onto his secrets.

'Like I said, I'm just a kid who wanted a look round your house.'

There was the swish of movement before Carl gasped at the sharp prick of metal under his chin. He tried to move his head away but he couldn't.

'Don't tell me lies,' the man said. 'One more and this blade will go so deep you'll be grateful for the noose, just to stop the pain.'

'Okay, okay, I'm sorry,' Carl said, a stammer in his voice. 'I'm looking for my dad, and I think he came looking for you, and now he's gone missing.'

'Why would he come looking for me?'

'I don't know. He's a policeman and he was looking into one of his old cases. He had a list of addresses, and your house was on it. So I was

183

looking at you when the police caught me.'

'So what do you know about me?'

'Nothing, I swear. Nothing at all.'

'What about my name?'

'I don't know anything about you. It's just an address. Let me go and I won't say anything.'

There was no response for a few minutes. Carl waited for another blow or a deeper push with the knife, but the man said, 'Tell me everything.'

'I've told you. It was just a list my father was looking at. I've looked at other houses too.'

'But you came back for me.'

'You seemed different from the people in the other houses I looked at, that's all.'

The knife left Carl's neck and the man stepped away. His hand went to his forehead, and he seemed to be grimacing.

The man turned back. 'Do you want to know about me?'

Carl swallowed and then shook his head. 'Not any more. I just want to go home.'

'Why? You might learn something.'

'Why would it matter, if I'm going to die?'

A pause. 'I can see your point.' A few more minutes passed before the man said, 'Like I said, I'm a collector.'

'Of what?'

'Beautiful things. You're too young to understand.'

Carl looked towards the floor. 'So what about the woman who was in here, the dead one? Did you collect her too?'

The man pushed the knife into Carl's neck, the tip just breaking the skin, making Carl cry out.

'Don't make it sound so cheap,' the man said, anger in his voice.

'I'm sorry, I'm sorry,' Carl said desperately. 'I don't understand, that's all. When you say collect, you mean that the woman on the floor was someone you just wanted to have?'

'I'd already had her,' the man said, and then he laughed, moving the blade from Carl's neck. 'Her problem was that she wanted to leave, to get away.' He shook his head. 'No one ever gets away.' He paused before he said quietly, 'I've got someone coming round later. Whatever happens now is your fault. You've accelerated this. I need to act quickly. I want you to know that everything that happens is down to you.'

'What do you mean, that it's my fault?'

'The end is getting closer. So I've just got some loose ends to tie up.'

The man reached into his pocket and pulled out some rags. Carl knew what was going to come and tried to pull away, but it was no good. One of the rags was jammed into his mouth and, before he had chance to spit it out, the other was wrapped around his head, keeping it in place, the knot tight behind him.

And with that, his captor turned and left the cellar, the key louder in the lock this time.

Carl put his head back against the wall, taking deep breaths through the gag. He needed to decide which put him in most danger: going along with the man, or against him. Hunger and fatigue weakened him though. His legs didn't feel strong and his body swayed.

He didn't know how much longer he could last.

Twenty-eight

'So what are you expecting when we get there?' Charlotte asked, keeping her gaze fixed on the road ahead.

Sam had co-opted Charlotte after leaving Evans's office under the pretence of speaking to some of Sarah's friends, to build up a picture of her husband, but he had disclosed his true purpose on the drive away from the station. They were heading for the spot where Sarah's body had been discovered to try to work out if there was anything special about it, anything that might indicate why the killer had chosen that place to leave her.

'You can back out, you know,' Sam said. 'Hunter will be unhappy if he finds out, and Evans won't back us up.'

'But Evans knows what you're doing?'

'She'll take the credit if I've got it right. Sell me out if I haven't.'

'That's okay then,' Charlotte said, smiling. 'Hunter has only got a couple of years left in him. It's people like Evans we should worry about. She's got another decade in her, and even if she sells us out on this case, she'll remember that we tried and be all right with us.'

When Sam focused again on the road ahead, she repeated her question. 'So, don't keep me in suspense, what are you expecting when we get there?'

'I just thought we would look at the scene with

fresh eyes,' Sam said.

They were driving uphill in Charlotte's car, leaving behind the late-afternoon Manchester rush hour.

As they got closer, the moors flattening out and creating a barren plateau of browns and purples, Charlotte sat forward, her arms on the wheel. 'It looks quiet,' she said, confusion in her voice.

Sam didn't say anything but a sense of dread crept into him. He had expected to see some poor uniformed officer stationed behind fluttering crime scene tape, hunched up in a coat and questioning his career choice. Instead it was all back to normal, as if the discovery earlier hadn't happened at all. There was only a small bunch of sunflowers attached to a post as a memorial.

Charlotte parked her car where she believed the killer must have parked his, in a small bay closest to the obvious route to the body, and stepped out. The wind was cold, despite the season. It seemed to whistle across the surface, fluttering the heather and making the soft white heads of the hare's tail grasses wave. The sharpness made Sam's eyes water as he reached in for his coat before heading to where the soft soil and heather began.

He looked at the spread of the moors, disbelief on his face.

'Hunter has released the scene already,' he said.

Charlotte walked beside him, putting on her own coat. 'They did a sweep this morning, the usual lines, dog and stick thing. What else is there to do?'

'It just seems too early. We'll have all the ghouls up here later, once the details come out.'

'It's a public space. We can't preserve it for ever.'

She was right, he knew that, but it seemed that the horror from earlier in the day had been forgotten as the landscape returned to normal. There was a small group of walkers in dark fleeces and heavy boots. Cyclists in Lycra rode past. A couple held each other as they looked at the view, her long dark hair streaming back in the wind and over the shoulders of her denim jacket.

'How far along was she?' Sam asked. 'It all looks the same once you get away from the road.'

'There.' Charlotte pointed to a cluster of grass a long way ahead. Sam could see where it had been flattened by the attentions of the crime scene investigators.

They both walked in silence before Sam stopped. He turned around, his hands on his hips, and shook his head.

'What's wrong?' Charlotte said.

'Look around.'

Charlotte turned. The moors spread as far as they could see. There was the barely audible hum of the motorway a couple of miles away. There was nothing to block the sound, no trees or buildings, just the long roll and tumble of grass and heather, so the noise hovered over the landscape like a loud whisper. In the distance there was the glimmer of a reservoir, trees clustered along its banks, the view down the valley giving a hint of the urban sprawl at the foot of the hills, the tower blocks of a satellite town just visible.

'What am I looking at?' she said.

'The view of the road is just the same here as it is where she was left. So why dump her there,' and he pointed, 'fifty yards further ahead? How long would it take him to get there? Legs, arms, a torso and a head. That's three trips at least. A hundred yards extra with each run. It could add on a minute each time, meaning he opted to hang around for three minutes extra, arousing suspicion the whole time. It makes no sense.'

'What if he used something to carry the body?' Charlotte said. 'A wheelbarrow or a sheet.'

'There'd be marks – a line of flattened heather or a wheel track. There's nothing.'

'So you're saying that the specific spot is important?'

'It's the only thing that makes sense,' Sam said. He set off again, the clumps of grass making his trousers wet, the ground soft underfoot.

When they got to the spot where Sarah had been found, Sam looked down and shook his head. 'It's all gone. No trace left. Everything back to normal as if it meant nothing.'

'They've done the sweep, the body has gone,' Charlotte reiterated. 'They can't close off the moors.'

Sam's mind flashed back to when his own sister was killed. The path through the woods was closed overnight, but by the next morning it had been back to normal, apart from the few ghouls it attracted, who like to gawp at murder scenes under the pretence of laying flowers. By the following day, it was as if her death had meant nothing. The path became quieter, some parents warning their children away, but over time Ellie was just forgotten.

When Sam looked at Charlotte, her brow was

creased with concern.

'What's wrong?' Sam said.

'You're taking this too personally,' she said. 'Follow the orders, submit your paperwork, don't make a hash of anything.'

'Murder is important. It can't be relegated to paper-turning.'

'Do you think I don't know this?' Charlotte said. 'That you're the only one who really knows what murder means because your sister was killed?' When Sam flinched, she softened. 'I don't want to fall out with you about this, Sam, but you need to be careful. If you get it right, bravo, and you'll get a reputation and some respect, but what if you don't? What if Hunter's hunch is right and the husband did it? You'll just be the man who almost derailed things by thinking he knows best. Your career will be finished.'

'And if I'm right and I don't do anything, I should just be happy that I followed Hunter's direction?'

'They'll blame Hunter, not you.'

'*I'll* blame me,' Sam said, exasperated. He looked down and shook his head. 'It shouldn't be about me. It's about the victim, making it right for her; I've got to go with how I feel.'

'And you're ready for the consequences if you've got it wrong?'

Sam nodded. 'I joined the police for emotional reasons. I'm not going to forget those.'

'Your sister.'

'Yes, my sister, and how the Force tried to look after us and make it right. When I approach a case, I think of how those detectives tried to do the right thing. I don't blame them for not catching whoever murdered Ellie, but I want to do the same, follow my instincts.'

'Not orders?'

'We'll do what Hunter says. I just think we should do a little extra too.'

Charlotte rolled her eyes and put her hands on her hips. 'All right, I can see you're not going to change your mind.' She smiled, despite herself. 'Go on then, Sherlock, look around. What do you think?'

Sam looked at the grass, flattened and muddied. The dumping ground.

'Why didn't he bury her?' he said. 'Think of those poor children murdered by Brady and Hindley. Keith Bennett is still under here somewhere. It's as if the soil just swallowed him up.'

'It moves,' Charlotte said.

'What do you mean?'

'Just that. It's peat, and it's soft, so sometimes it shifts around. It means a body can move from its original location. Even if Brady was willing to point to the exact spot where he buried Keith Bennett, his body might have gone walkabout through the decades, shifted around by the moving peat.'

'So all the more reason to bury her,' Sam said. 'She would never be found and go down as just another runaway. These moors could be a graveyard for a lot of people and no one would know. So, yes, the isolation makes sense, but why not bury her?'

'X marks the spot,' Charlotte said, a half-smile on her lips.

'What do you mean?'

'Think of how the body was set out,' she said. 'The arms and legs were splayed out like an X-marking. If the location is important, what better sign is there than a big cross spelled out by a dead body?'

Sam's smile spread as he thought about that. 'You might have something there.'

'So what now?'

Sam checked his watch. 'Now, we go home.'

'And tonight?'

'I do some research, see if I can discover anything about this location.'

'And if you find something?'

'I speak to Hunter. Hopefully he'll listen if I do.'

Twenty-nine

His hand clenched the steering wheel tightly. Carl Jex was still in the cellar. It had been a couple of hours since he had been down there. It made everything riskier but he couldn't stop now. Emma was next to him, sitting quietly.

She leaned forward and looked through the windscreen. They were outside his house. 'You've never brought me here before.'

'It feels like the right time,' he said.

He climbed out of the car and held out his arm for Emma to hold onto as they walked to his door. As they went inside, he reached for her coat to slip it from her shoulders. He hung it on a tall wooden coat stand as the light in the hallway flickered, as if the bulb was about to go. He glanced upwards and grimaced. The mood had to be right. He didn't want to spoil it by searching for spare bulbs.

'What's wrong?' she said.

He turned round. 'A bulb, that's all.' He pointed ahead. 'Go in. First door on the right.'

'You should have brought me here before,' Emma said. 'Hotels are nice and all that, but I'd rather see where you live.'

Her footsteps made loud clunks on the polished oak floorboards as she walked slowly, her hand trailing along the deep red wallpaper, the light bulbs shielded by purple shades with small tassels, so that the way in looked dark but warm.

He slipped off his silk scarf and wool jacket and hung them over the end of the banister.

The fire was smouldering as he entered the living room, so he went over to the brass bucket to put on more coal. As they clattered into the grate, the oily smell of the coal dust made his mouth water. It took him back more than twenty years, when it had been his job to do this, to keep the fire stoked on those nights in.

For a moment, he smelled his father's cigarettes, the atmosphere heavy with them, the smoke swirling around the room like a faint blue cloud, the aroma warm as it made his throat tickle.

He thought he heard a laugh. The sound of his mother. He whirled around. There was only Emma there, turning on the spot, her heels making small marks in the rug as she looked around the room. She wasn't laughing.

He swallowed. His parents came back to him more each time. As he watched Emma he saw his mother dancing, just turning on the spot, swaying, singing.

This was the time he loved the most, the anticipation. It was more than lust. It was excitement, felt by the fast hammer of his heart, the tightening in his throat, the room fading as he thought of what lay ahead.

He tried not to betray his nerves. 'I'll get us a drink,' he said, and walked over to the cabinet on the furthest wall.

Emma sat down but she didn't relax. She was sitting forward, her knees close together. She was wearing what she thought was glamorous, a short dress, silky and blue, off the shoulder and set off by black stockings. Her hair was tied back.

Facing away, he poured whisky into two tumblers, and topped hers up with cola. She knew how to ruin a good drink. Then he reached into the cabinet and pulled out a small bottle. He poured a generous quantity of the ground powder into the drink, swirling it quickly. He paused to let the powder dissolve and then went to her.

She smiled as he handed her the glass.

He sat in silence for a few minutes as she drank. She looked around the room, her finger wiping at the condensation on her glass. She asked him about the things she could see, whether they were antiques or just long held by his family.

He answered but said little. He let her fill the gaps by taking long sips from her glass.

After around twenty minutes, he walked over to the record player, the old Dansette. He'd had to have it repaired a few times, but he refused to give it up. It had provided the soundtrack to his weekends as his parents put on records of what he used to call 'golden oldies', which made his mother laugh. They had worn out more than one rug as they held each other and twirled and laughed.

At least that's how it started.

The Dansette buzzed as he turned it on and then there was a fizz through the speakers. It made him look over to the high-backed chair near the fire, and for a second he thought he could see his father's fingers gripping the arm, his legs jutted out in front of him. He looked again. It was just a moving shadow made by the fire.

He lifted the stylus arm gently and blew some fluff from the needle. He reached for the small record collection next to it and took the record from the front, as always.

He took the vinyl out of its sleeve, holding it by the edges, wiping it gently with a cloth before placing it onto the spindle. His tongue flicked onto his lips as the plastic arm clunked onto the record and, as he pulled on the start lever, it slapped onto the turntable.

He closed his eyes and listened to the sweep of the stylus arm, the tick of the mechanism, and gasped as the needle lowered and emitted a loud crackle as it hit the groove.

The first bars of the song filled the room, loud and distorted. The room seemed to contract. His mother's giggles, getting tipsy, stumbling into the furniture. His father's irritation, growing through the evening, fuelled by the whisky. The singer's opening line, deep and mournful.

'Dance with me,' he said, as he opened his eyes.

Emma took another long sip from her glass. He went to her and held out his hand, and she rose to her feet.

She was about to put her drink down when he shook his head. 'No. Drink up.' He raised his glass to his lips and downed his, breathing through his nose at the fire in his chest. 'We're here to have fun.'

Emma smiled and said, 'Okay,' before draining her glass.

She swayed as she walked over to him. He was much taller than her, so he was able to pull her close and put her face into his neck, inhaling deeply, taking in her perfume. It was the one she always wore and all their previous times together rushed at him. The passion, the fun, those promises she had made to him, her pleasure at being free.

Broken promises.

He held her like that as the song played out. The needle creaked back to the beginning of the song, and she giggled as it started again. As the song wore on, she started to sway and slump in his arms, and then the needle clicked its way back and all there was left was the light fizz from the speakers and the crackle of the fire.

He laid her on the floor carefully, making sure she was on the floorboards and not on the rug, so that no fibres would be transferred. He lay next to her and put his face into her hair so that he was enveloped by the smell of it, warmth and shampoo and perfume and her own scent, the one that assaulted him on those few times they had spent the full night together, her own aroma filling the hotel room.

Her head was hard against the floor as his hand went around her neck. Her bones were brittle under his grip, her skin warm. He squeezed, and he thought he could hear her heels beating a fast rhythm on the floor, gasps and shrieks slowly rendered mute. When he looked, she was still, the flunitrazepam taking effect.

He squeezed again. It would soon be over.

Sam leaned against the kitchen worktop and looked down. It was quiet, his children were in bed and the house had distilled down to the hum of the fridge and the slow rumbles of the central heating.

He had gone into the kitchen to load the dishwasher, but he had become thoughtful and distracted as he mulled over the day's events. DI Evans's words came back to him. If his theory about the body was wrong then he would have to deal with Hunter's wrath on his own. The uncomfortable creep of self-doubt came over him, the sudden certainty that he should do his job and nothing more. Follow orders, work the leads, avoid going up against anyone.

He thought back on what he had found out about Sarah Carvell. She had everything, it seemed: a husband who loved her, children, a nice house. Sam remembered how the credit card bills showed Sarah's other life; the one she thought about when her husband was out at work.

He reached across the worktop to where the

post was piled up. Junk mainly, waiting to be dumped in the recycling bin, but there was that other pile. The bills, reminders, bank statements.

Alice was in the other room, watching television. Sam reached across and flicked through the statements until he saw one with Alice's name on. A credit card bill. It had been opened but the statement was still in the envelope. He looked back to the living room, visible through the glass in the door, to where he could see Alice staring at the television.

He pulled out the bill slowly and opened it out. Just over four hundred pounds owed on it. He skimmed the entries and shook his head, angry with himself. It was just petrol and things for the house, some children's clothes, obvious from the shop names.

He jumped and looked up when he felt a hand on his arm, just a gentle touch. It was Alice, her hair swept back, her skin pale and shiny from whatever late-night skin routine she had followed. Her eyes looked pink from the lack of mascara.

'Checking my post?' she said, her eyebrows raised.

He put the bill down, feeling guilty. 'I know, I'm sorry. I was curious, that's all.'

He took her face in his hands and kissed her softly on the lips. Her warmth, those unexpected hugs, the occasional stroke of his back as she went past him, those were things that kept everything together. She had been his school sweetheart, his first serious girlfriend, and from the things they had shared, first times, great times, close times, he knew she would be his last.

Alice pulled away.

'What's wrong?' he said.

'Nothing,' she said, although her tone told him otherwise.

'Talk to me, Alice.'

She folded her arms and looked down, her lips set. His unease grew until she said, 'I feel lonely sometimes.'

'What do you mean?'

'Just that. I'm alone at the moment. You're out all day and come home late, and when you do come home, you don't really, because in here,' and she tapped the side of her head, 'you're still absorbed in whatever case you're wrapped up in.' She paused as she blinked away tears. 'You're never here. Not in your head.'

He sighed. He didn't know how to respond. At work he saw things that were too dark to bring into his family home. He tried to leave them behind, so that his home stayed untainted by the evil that seemed to roam the city streets, but they stayed with him, he knew that.

'You used to think about all the fraud cases, too,' Alice said. 'But it seems different with the murder cases. They consume you. Sam, you don't have to feel personally responsible for catching every murderer. It's a job. You're part of a team.'

'If someone has been killed, it's important,' he said.

'And so are we. Your family. Your children. Don't forget about us in the process. You don't have to attack each case as if you're trying to make it up to your sister.'

Sam exhaled sharply. 'That's not fair,' he said.

He could feel his anger starting to bubble. He took a deep breath. He didn't want the argument. 'I will never bring Ellie back and I can't control too much of what happens at the station, but if I can just help to bring a killer to the prison gates then I feel like I've got a little closer to making it right for not protecting her.'

'You're not to blame for Ellie's murder. We've been through this so many times!'

'I know that – you're right – but it doesn't stop me from feeling it.'

'So what about us? When do we get a piece of you?'

'I can't help how I am,' he said.

Alice stormed away at that and slammed the kitchen door. He raised his eyes to the ceiling in exasperation. He knew he would have to make it up to her, and to his two girls, but for the moment he couldn't shake off his thoughts about the case.

So his mind went back to it. To the way he felt about Hunter, and the investigation; the release of the scene and those secrets that might still be up there, left to get blown away by the rolling breezes that rippled across the heather. Suddenly, he remembered what Charlotte had said: X marks the spot.

He went into the living room, where Alice was sitting with her knees drawn up underneath her on the chair, her arms folded tightly.

'I'm going back up there, tonight,' he said.

'Where?'

'The moors. That crime scene isn't finished yet.'

Thirty

He grunted at the ache in his shoulder as he moved. Perspiration speckled his forehead. He wiped the sweat away with his forearm before reaching down to smooth Emma's hair. He moved it away from her face and kissed the top of her head, pausing for a moment for one deep inhale of her scent. It would be impossible to recall it. That's the way with smells, but once he smelled it again everything would come flooding back.

No one leaves. He had offered her escape and she had rejected it. He had to save her.

He closed his eyes as he remembered the screams. The bad nights always ended with screams, even though they always started the same way. A warm fire. Some music. His parents dancing. But he would see the transformation as the whisky flowed. Sometimes it would stay as laughter, and he would sit in the corner of the room and watch his parents dance and hold each other, two people drawn together.

But there were always the other nights, when things would take a different turn.

They started with the tight grip of his father's fingers on the chair arm, that little sign that the whisky was feeding his darker side, where his resentment lived, that spine of hatred that propped up his feelings. Then came the grabbing and pulling, with hisses of contempt in her ear.

All she had to do was leave.

His mother would see the signs, and a nod of the head towards the door, a flick of her eyelids, told him that he should go to bed. He knew what it meant. There were things he shouldn't see.

But he did. He heard it and his imagination did the rest. The loud slaps, the screams, the gasps of pain. Sometimes she would fight back and he would get angrier. The slaps became punches, or the loud crack of his father's belt, and he would creep downstairs and watch through the banister.

All she had to do was leave. But she never did.

Joe watched the afternoon turn to evening, as the large houses around the Green became silhouettes. The hours were passed in good company, though, the conversation with Hugh moving away from Aidan Molloy's case and to updates on legal gossip. Who was getting divorced, which firms were in trouble, who was merging with whom. Joe enjoyed Hugh's company and he could see Hugh's pleasure at talking about his old life, however much he pretended he didn't miss it.

As the clock wound round towards ten, Hugh rose to his feet and stumbled against the table. He laughed to himself. 'It's my own personal alarm,' he said. 'It used to be a telephone call. I would call home every hour, and when Patricia couldn't understand me, she would come and collect me. Now?' He laughed again. 'My first wobble sends me home.'

Joe stretched. He could feel the night air beginning to spin and he knew he should stop, but he didn't feel like ending so early and going back to an empty apartment.

'How far have you got to go?' he said.

Hugh pointed, his finger swaying in time with his body. 'Just down there. You watch from here, just to make sure I don't fall over.'

Joe laughed and shook his hand. 'Look after yourself, Hugh. We should do this again.'

Hugh waved and then set off, his feet not always following the straight line he aimed for. Joe watched him until he swayed into a front garden fifty yards along and disappeared into his house. When the front-room light clicked on, Joe drained his drink. Standing up, he felt the pavement shift under his feet. He was drunk, but he still wanted another drink.

He pulled his phone from his pocket.

It was the familiar pull he felt when he was drunk, although it was usually the bare walls of his apartment that prompted him to seek out company. It was usually internet chatrooms, strangers meeting on darkened screens, except that it had become harder to avoid the seedy stuff. It was the companionship Joe was after, just brief and fleeting, a distraction, but it had become a compulsion for him. The nights seemed too quiet to be drunk alone, so he had tried to break the habit.

His thoughts had gone to Kim Reader. She lived a couple of streets away, and being so close made him want to seek her out, to check whether she wanted a drink. He didn't feel ready to stop.

He thumbed through his contact list. The crowd outside the bar had grown, groups of men mainly, their chatter loud but sober, just enjoying a midweek drink. As Joe looked around, he realised that he was the drunk one, the images coming in like buffering video.

When he found her, he texted her.

Just been for a drink with Hugh Bramwell. He seems well. He said to say hi.

Joe set off walking, his eyes glancing downwards to his phone, waiting for it to buzz in his hand. When it did, he read:

Hugh? Were you at the Jockey? Should have told me.

He sent back:

Didn't want to disturb.

His phone stayed quiet for a few minutes, until it buzzed and he read:

Never a disturbance.

He had walked two streets and turned towards where she lived. The light was on in her apartment. Desire was driving his actions, steered by alcohol. There had been moments when they were both young law students, when drunken nights had ended in drunken sex, although it had always meant more to Joe than he had let on. Since then, when their careers re-converged in Manchester, they had skirted around each other, their contact limited to professional jousting and occasional pub sessions, but the pull had always been there. The problem was that they had never been single at the same time.

His phone buzzed again.

How many have you had? Hugh is a bad influence.

I was keeping up with him.

LOL. A lot then.

Enough to make me wobble. I just wanted to text.

I'm glad you did.

He was outside her apartment, looking up at the shadows of the television against her white blinds, flowers on the window sill.

Are you still there? she texted. *I could come and meet you.*

Where's Simon?

There was a pause of a few minutes, as Joe swayed on his feet. *It's complicated,* came the response eventually.

That text made Joe close his eyes. All he had to do was ring her bell and she might let him in, and a memory of one of their nights together came back to him. Kim's soft murmurs, the warmth of her skin, her hands pressing into his back.

But there was Simon. Joe didn't mess around with attached women. He had felt the sting of infidelity himself. He wasn't going to inflict it on someone else. *Complicated* wasn't the same as being single.

He typed, *Shame. I'm in the taxi, heading home.* He paused before tapping the send button, and he looked up at the sky as it went, his words bouncing between the phone masts and ending right above him, where Kim was waiting.

Okay. Another time, came the response.

He walked away, and although with every step it felt like he was making the wrong move, he kept on walking.

Thirty-one

For Carl, the evening had been one of waves of images and sounds, fading in and out, tiredness and hunger making it hard to stay on his feet. He was able to press his hands against the wall to give himself some support, but he was weakening.

He thought of his mother. He had to stay strong for her.

The darkness enveloped him, magnifying the noises, something for his mind to lock onto as it swirled around, lost in some half-sleep, unsure if he was dreaming. He could hear steady breaths sometimes, as if someone was watching him closely, bathing him in their warm breath. Perhaps it was just a draught finding its way in from somewhere and mixing in with his own semi-consciousness.

Other times, he heard sounds above him. The knocks of sharp heels on a wooden floor, the creak of a chair, the distorted wail of a song. Laughter. Then it had fallen silent. Carl had tried to listen out, to keep himself awake and focused, but it had got harder as the hours passed. His head was bathed in perspiration, his clothes sticking to his chest.

Then the cellar door opened.

Carl flinched. He stood up straight, set his feet apart. The rope dug into his neck but didn't tighten. There were loud swishing noises, the sound of something heavy being dragged, and then grunts of exertion.

Carl knew what it was before he saw it. He closed his eyes, not wanting the truth to be confirmed, but the sounds that filled his head were somehow worse. The sickening slap of bare flesh against stone steps echoed round the cellar, making him open his eyes.

The man was pulling someone, although he was visible only as a slow shadow in the light that streamed down from the open doorway. He had his hands under the person's arms and the body jolted as he made his way down the steps. When he got to the bottom, Carl saw that it was a woman, naked. The man dragged her across a few feet more and then laid her gently on the floor. The faint light caught beads of sweat and made them glisten. It was Carl's first proper look at his face. He saw a glare in his eyes that made him shrink back.

The man looked down at the woman's body and said, 'Just meat now.'

He started to pace, a moving shadow against the light. His hands went to his head, running over his hair, fast and edgy, his pacing getting faster.

Carl stamped his foot, angry for her, screeching through his gag.

The man looked up, surprised, almost as if he had forgotten Carl was there. He stepped over to him and pulled at the knot on the gag at the back of his head. He reached into Carl's mouth to take out the rag that had muffled his screeches of horror.

Carl put his head back, swallowing, his mouth

dry. 'What have you done?'

The man gripped Carl around the jaw, forcing his head upwards. He didn't say anything at first. He took deep breaths through his nose and pushed Carl's head back.

'You're hurting me,' Carl said, gasping.

'You started this,' he snarled. 'You came looking for me. Well, you've found me now. Do you like what you see?'

'You killed her,' Carl said.

'No, you killed her,' the man said, gripping harder. 'Don't you see that? You interfered, brought it forward. Look at her.'

'I don't want to.'

The man gripped Carl's jaw harder and moved to one side. 'Look!'

Carl blinked away a tear. He couldn't see much. Just a dark outline on the floor.

'She's just a piece of meat now,' the man said. 'All stiff and pink like pork. There's no soul, nothing special. We all come down to this in the end. Slabs of meat.'

Carl looked again as his eyes got used to the faint glow of light. He could make out her pale skin, her limbs flaccid, and fought against the rise of bile in his throat.

The man pushed Carl's head back again, knocking him into the wall. Carl rocked backwards. The rope dug into his neck. 'So what do I do with you?' the man said. 'I can't let you go.'

'You can. I won't tell anyone. I promise.'

'Why would you do that? You've nothing to lose by talking. Not like her.'

'What do you mean?'

'You want a lesson in life? How's this: we all pretend. Take Emma here. If all she wanted was fun, why choose me? Fun is transient, meaningless. We were more than that. No, *I'm* more than that, and she said she was too, that she wanted more than just a fling. We connected. I was the man for her. I made her laugh, was the witty and intelligent guy for her. I could be whoever she wanted me to be. That's how I am. Emma wanted to feel the strong arms of someone round her, just a trace of the passion she used to feel for her husband. I gave her that, but still it wasn't enough. How could she say that?'

'But if she was married, she was never going to be yours.'

'You're so naïve,' the man said. 'Marriage kills passion. It burns out the fires until there is nothing left except resentment and loneliness and bitterness. People who pretend otherwise are lying to themselves.'

'My parents were happy,' Carl said.

The man shook his head slowly. 'No, they weren't. They just pretended they were for your benefit, to keep you feeling safe and secure, so you didn't have to worry about all the shit that heads your way in life. I mean, how often did you hear them laugh, and I mean really laugh?' Carl didn't respond. 'Never is my guess. Emma was the same, and I was going to rescue her. I wanted to show her a different way, to explore all her dark corners. We all have them, you know, those hidden desires we won't tell anyone. All she had to do was expose herself to me, show that it wasn't just some romp, that it was no cheap thing. She had to give herself to me, surrender everything. Let me know her every thought, every fear, so that I had her completely and she was unable to go back.'

'And once you had that?'

'I'd let her go.'

'Dump her, you mean.'

The man laughed, although it came out as a sneer. 'What else would there be for me to see? I brought her out of herself, found the real Emma. It was my gift to her.'

Carl's mind was racing. The man seemed less hostile in this frenzied state. If he could keep him talking, perhaps there was a way out. 'It sounds like a game,' he said. 'You make her love you just so you can mistreat her. But she would have given up everything she had for you, ruined her own life.'

'But she wouldn't give herself up, so I had to rescue her twice over.'

'I don't understand.'

'I rescued her once, when I showed her the real Emma, but do you think I could let her go back to her life, the one she had? Empty, soulless. It would kill her from the inside, except she wouldn't even know she was dying, because it would be slow and lingering. But still she clung onto it, always scared, because one wrong telephone call from me, a careless word in someone's ear and all she had would have been gone. Her home. Family.' He smiled, as if he was proud of himself. 'So I've rescued her again. She's free now.'

Carl looked over at Emma's prone form and anger crept in. 'You don't collect,' he said. 'You destroy, like those people who say they love butterflies when really they just want them dead and pinned inside a frame. If you can't destroy a person by breaking them, you kill them.'

The man's eyes narrowed. 'If you collect, you don't give away.' He cocked his head. 'Maybe I'm not a collector? Perhaps I'm just a thief? I like to collect other people's things.'

'But it won't last for ever,' Carl said. 'They might trace her to you and they'll come down here and find me.'

The man clenched his jaw before yanking on the rope and drawing it tight. 'You're not making a convincing case for being kept alive.'

Carl gasped. 'I'm sorry,' he said, panic clear in his voice. 'I won't say anything like that again. But it's a good question. How do you know they can't trace me to you?'

The man's eyes flickered at that. 'Can they?'

'I found you, didn't I?'

'Ha! That's what you're holding out for? The rescue. The white knight on his charger. So let's speed things up a bit.'

The man reached for his waistband and Carl heard the same swish as he had earlier in the night, the sound of a knife being drawn from a leather sheath.

He waited for the blade to appear under his chin again. It didn't. It came at him lower down, just above his knee.

The man leaned in so that he could whisper into Carl's ear. 'Can you feel the knife? Just one thrust. How long would you last on one leg?'

'Don't hurt me, please,' Carl said, tears running down his face.

'These walls are filled with memories. I'm going to lose them all now, because of you. Shouldn't I let you share my pain?'

'No, no, it doesn't have to be like this.'

Carl shrieked as the blade pierced the skin on his leg and moved down towards his kneecap. Blood soaked his trousers. It felt like flames as the knife was dragged through his skin, until the man pulled it out eventually and wiped the blade on Carl's clothes.

Carl gritted his teeth in pain.

'There, I'm helping you,' the man said. 'Your legs might give up a bit sooner now. If this is hell for you, that cut might end it more quickly by getting you swinging. Until then, think of the pain you've caused. If you're still around the next time I come down, I'll help you a little more.'

'No, please, don't,' Carl said, sobbing, desperate to bend down but prevented by the rope.

'Don't you see?' the man said. 'I'm giving you the power, making it your choice when you go. A lot to take in at your age, but you have no idea how much pain you have caused me. I'm just spreading it around.'

With that, the man pushed the gag back into Carl's mouth and turned and walked out of the cellar, slamming the door shut at the top of the stairs. Carl tried to stay balanced on one leg, sobbing, swaying, feeling the rope grip a little tighter.

As the darkness settled around him, the silence broken only by his own sobs, Carl could think of nothing else but the agony radiating from his leg that prevented him from putting his foot down.

It would all be over soon.

Thirty-two

The low rumble of tyres almost numbed Sam to sleep as he completed the last part of the journey onto the moors.

The argument with Alice was still in his head, but it had been pushed away by the compulsion he felt to find out why the crime scene troubled him. For Sam, the location was important, even if Hunter disregarded it and was interested in no one else but Sarah Carvell's husband. Charlotte's words stayed with him: X marks the spot.

The drive was becoming all too familiar now. This was his third visit in twenty-four hours. It was his first time at night but the climb and swerve were just the same. His high beam swept the sky as he got higher but once the road levelled out it spread over the moorland, catching the eyes of the sheep that dotted the fields. Rabbits darted across the road before disappearing back into the heather. Despite the wildlife, it felt like he was completely alone, far from everywhere.

His car lights caught the sign ahead that heralded the arrival into Yorkshire, the pull-in just behind it. The steady hum of his wheels on tarmac turned into the crunch of dirt and gravel as he came to a stop.

Stepping out of the car, the first thing he noticed was the cold. The wind felt like it had gathered pace as it rolled across the open countryside with

213

no trees to break its path. He shivered and pulled up the collar on his coat. He knew he was going to be there for some time and suddenly wished he had brought something warmer with him.

Then there was the silence.

His footsteps crackled like small fireworks. A sheep bleated. There was a car in the distance, but Sam knew it was a few miles away. He looked upwards. He was away from the orange glow of the city and all he could see were the glorious silver pinpricks of stars against the dark blanket of night sky.

He opened the car boot and took out a sack of logs that he had stored in his garage, for the garden heater he had bought the year before. He had wanted something torso-sized and it was all he could find. He decided not to use a torch at the start, as he guessed that whoever had carried the body would not have wanted to be seen. He hoisted the sack into his arms and started walking.

The ground was soft, with large puddles of water where the spring rain was too much for the peat soil. It was slippery underfoot and the heather grew in such clumps that Sam almost went to the floor a few times in the first fifty yards. He worried about breaking an ankle and spending the night there in agony. But it told him what he needed to know: whatever had made the killer take this path must have been important.

Sam struggled for a bit longer before he stopped and put the sack down. He was out of breath and his back was straining from holding the sack and struggling to stay on his feet. His feet had slithered on the soft ground and the logs that weren't heavy soon felt that way. He looked back. His car was just a dark block, an outline, and as he looked at his feet they were just shadows. It was truly dark. There would be no need to go any further to dump a body and yet there was still a way to go to where the body was found.

Then there was a car. The headlights were long streaks as the engine noise grew steadily louder. Sam stopped to watch. It wasn't travelling fast but the beams were on full. The road got brighter as the car got closer and as it passed his own car he saw that the beam didn't reach him; the slight rise of the land at the roadside soaking up the light.

A passing car would not have seen whoever dumped the body even this short way onto the moors. There was no need for the killer to go as far as he had, which meant that he did it for a different reason. Sam was more certain now that the location was significant.

He went back to his car, dragging the logs this time, and sat in the passenger seat. He checked his watch. Three a.m. It wouldn't be light for another couple of hours. His shoes were wet, his trousers too, and it would be a few hours before it would get warm again.

There was a flask of coffee behind his seat, just to keep him awake so that he could drive. He poured a cup and the moorland faded from view as steam misted his windscreen.

The time passed slowly. He thought about sleeping, but it was too cold for that. He huddled in his seat, his arms folded tightly, watching the slight hint of daylight to the east turn into the slow spread of dawn. The hills opposite turned blue before they faded slowly into a light mist as the first creeping rays of sunshine played with the dew that glistened on the slopes. Now was the time.

He stretched when he got out of the car, his joints popping some life back into his body. He was getting to the difficult part.

He went to his car boot again and took out a spade, before setting off across the moors once more. His trousers were still wet and his soles squeaked as he walked, mud clinging to them from his earlier effort. He had expected birdsong, the usual early-morning clamour, but there was silence, as if it was a landscape where nothing moved. He concentrated hard as he went, keeping a look-out for where he was. There were few distinguishing landmarks but if there was any point to what he was doing, he had to get the right spot.

He followed a path between the clusters of heather, made by the rivulets of water that ran down from the top of the rise, and ahead there was the flattened area where boots had gathered just hours before. In the centre of the muddy patch was a less spoiled area, where her body had been, left untouched as the forensic people did their work around it and combed for minor clues once she had been taken away. It made finding the exact spot easier than he had imagined.

If Charlotte was right, there had to be something underneath because there certainly wasn't anything on top.

The spade felt heavy as he paused, wondering if he was doing the right thing, but he hadn't spent the night freezing in his car to have doubts

216

now. He thrust the spade into the ground.

It was soft and he was able to get a good spade-full with his first dig. The peace of the early morning was broken by the sound of his exertion: his grunts of effort, the squelch of the soft soil. It wasn't long before he had made a square hole around four feet wide. It wasn't deep, although it seemed enough to work out whether there was anything to be found. He checked his watch. Nearly six o'clock. There was more traffic noise now, just hums in the distance, and the occasional engine roared along the road by his car, but it was still pretty quiet. He would have to go home and get ready for his day at work soon so he couldn't stay too much longer. If something was buried here it wouldn't be in the first layer, as it would be exposed too quickly as the peat soil moved, creating new cracks in the surface. One more spade depth and he would leave. No one would know he had been there.

The sound of the sheep seemed to get louder as he raised his spade in the air, their bleats carried over the moors. A large bird of prey circled over him, its wings wide, swirling against the bright blue.

It was after the second thrust of his spade that everything changed.

The spade didn't go in as far, as if it had met some extra resistance. He threw it down and dropped to his knees, the tension in his throat telling him that this was something different. The moisture soaked his trousers and dirt started to coat his cuffs as he moved the soil with his hands, but he wasn't going to stop. He brushed it away and felt something under his fingers. It was cloth. His hands moved faster and as he cleared the soil, he saw a blue-checked shirt, dirty now, but there was a button. One more sweep with his hands and then Sam felt himself turn cold. His fingers had brushed against something hard, and as he moved them along and realised what it was, he sat back on his haunches and looked up at the sky, not wanting to see any more. It was the bony ridges of a ribcage.

Thirty-three

Joe raised his head from the pillow, bleary-eyed, his mouth dry, his tongue sticking to its roof. There was a noise, familiar but distant, the real world taking its time to come into view. As the mist in his head cleared, he recognised it as the buzz of his phone, dancing on the bedside table as someone waited for him to answer. He glanced across at the clock. Not even eight o'clock.

When he grabbed for it, he moved too quickly, so that his head felt like it had gone in a different direction. He wasn't going to answer, but he saw that it was Kim Reader. He groaned when he remembered the texts he had sent when he had been drunk the night before, when he had almost gone to her place.

He pressed the answer button and drawled, 'Hi.'

'Come on, sleepy bones. Get up and let me in.'

Kim's jauntiness was like a jab at his conscious-
ness.

'Uh huh?'

'I'm outside, and I've got coffee and bacon
sandwiches.'

'I could have been out at a police station.'

'Not if you'd been with Hugh all evening, and
your blinds are still closed.'

'Okay, okay,' Joe said, swinging his legs out of
bed. 'Hang on.'

His steps were uncertain as he walked out of his
bedroom, picking up clothes on the way, before he
buzzed to unlock the external door and left his
apartment door open. Kim would find her way.
He went into the bathroom, so that by the time
she came in, shouting his name, he had splashed
and cleaned himself into some semblance of
normality.

When he emerged back into the living room, he
saw that Kim had moved onto his balcony, the
coffees and two bags of sandwiches on the small
table outside. Joe joined her. 'Morning,' he said.
It came out slow and deep.

He looked down at himself and ran his hands
across his stubble. His grab for clothes hadn't got
further than a pair of grey jogging trousers and
an old blue T-shirt. Kim looked, as always, a
picture of elegance. Her blouse was crisp white,
open-necked, under a navy trouser suit, tight
around the long stretch of her legs, but not so
tight that it was inappropriate for a court appearance. Her dark hair was tied back in a silver clasp.

She handed him one of the coffees. 'I guessed
you would be in no mood for making me one, and

that there'd be even less chance of breakfast.' She pushed over one of the bags, the outside made grey by grease. The aroma assaulted him and reminded him that he hadn't eaten the night before.

He sat down and started to eat. It tasted good, the bacon sloppy and brown sauce leaking from the bread.

Kim peeled off the plastic top from her coffee and said, 'I like your view.' She was squinting into the brightness outside, the balcony facing towards the slowly rising sun.

'It's what sold it to me.'

And that was the truth. The water shimmered as the first shards of sunlight lightened the rooftops on the other side, turning red tiles into bright pink. Even the screeches of the trams and the occasional rumble of a train were like soft murmurs to Joe, his morning soundtrack.

'A bachelor pad with a view,' he said between mouthfuls. 'All television and gadgets. It needs some warmth.'

'A woman's touch?' Kim said, her eyes dancing with mischief.

'I wouldn't insult you by saying that.'

'So that's a yes?'

Joe grinned and raised his coffee in salute.

He took a drink and his brain slowly came into focus. 'How come you're so early?'

Kim eyed him for a few seconds over her drink, taking her own sandwich out of the bag and placing it on top. 'I've got some files to look at before I go into court, and I was wondering why you texted me last night.'

Joe took another bite as he tried to recall

whether he had said anything inappropriate, but it was a fog. 'I was just being friendly.'

'No you weren't.'

'What do you mean?' He winced. 'Did I say something wrong?'

'You wanted to come round. Why else would you text?' Kim blushed. 'And you should have done. I was glad you called.'

'Simon would have minded.'

'Simon wasn't there.'

'Okay, I would have minded.'

Kim reached across and placed her hand on Joe's. 'I was hoping you would come, and when you wouldn't I was angry with you, because you made me think that you could have done.'

'I'm sorry,' he said. 'I thought of you and it seemed right to contact you, but then, well, you know how it is.'

'No, I don't know. You tell me.'

'You've got Simon,' he said. 'Haven't you?'

'Like I said, it's complicated. I broke off the engagement, but we still see each other.'

'That changes things,' Joe said. 'It changes us.'

Kim scowled and took her hand away. 'There isn't an *us*. Do you want there to be?'

Joe took a deep breath. 'I don't make plans like that. I can't expect you to leave Simon just so you can have something with me. What if we don't work out? You'll have given up everything, and for what? Some fling with an old flame?'

Kim leaned in and looked deeply into his eyes. She had gone beyond the boundary of friendliness and was in his space, her eyes boring into his. His fog lifted enough for him to see the fire in there. And he felt it too. A yearning. A need to have her arms around him. Her perfume filled his nostrils, delicate and flowery, and he breathed it in, wanting to drag her closer, to feel the soft kiss of her lips.

He sat back and shook his head. 'I can't do this,' he said, frustration in his voice, pushing the sandwich to one side. 'It's not fair on Simon.'

'And not fair on me for you not to,' Kim said, hurt in her voice. 'I want you, Joe Parker. I've always wanted you.' She looked down and concentrated hard on her coffee. 'You've made me feel cheap.'

Joe took her hand this time. When she looked up, he thought there were tears in her eyes. 'I don't think you're cheap,' he said, squeezing her hand. 'I wish I could think differently, but I can't. I'm sorry.'

Kim wiped her eyes with the back of her hand. She gave a small embarrassed laugh. 'Okay.' She exhaled. 'I'm sorry. I'm being stupid. Eat your sandwich. Let's talk about something different. Work. Why were you with Hugh? Old times?'

'It's a case I'm working on. Hugh used to be involved with it.'

That made her frown. 'Which one?'

'Aidan Molloy.'

'Still thinking about that?' Kim exhaled loudly. 'You don't mind making yourself unpopular.'

'It goes with the job, unpopularity.'

'But why are you involved with that case? It's long dead.'

'Not to Aidan's mother. And it just piqued my interest.'

Kim's eyes narrowed. 'Is there some development?'

'Come on, I can't spill stuff like that.'

'So there is.'

'I didn't say that,' Joe said, and sighed. 'Okay, maybe I am thinking there is something. Do you know David Jex? A detective?'

Kim frowned as she thought about that. 'Is he the one who's gone missing?'

'That's the one.'

'I remember people talking about it. He'd been acting a bit strange so people think he's just gone wandering, maybe even dead somewhere.'

'His son was arrested the other night, creeping around someone's house, and he wanted someone from Honeywells. I turned out but he wouldn't tell me anything about it. Now he's gone missing too, so his mother came to see me. She said they were both obsessed with the Aidan Molloy case, that it started with David and then Carl started looking when David went missing. When I saw Mary Molloy campaigning I spoke to her. I'm not getting paid for this but I'm trying to do the right thing, except I don't even know what the right thing is.'

'You're drifting, Joe,' Kim said, her tone softening.

'What do you mean?'

'I can see it in your eyes when I see you in court. Your heart isn't in your job any more. Don't use Aidan Molloy's case to rescue yourself.'

Joe frowned. He wanted to tell her that she had read it wrong, that it was justice for Mary, because something wasn't right about the case. But

223

he knew Kim was right.

'What do the people in your office think about the Aidan Molloy case?' he said, drinking his coffee. 'Am I wasting my time?'

'If we weren't sure about the conviction, we would say so. I don't know that much about the case, I wasn't involved in it, but I have heard people talk about it, and no one seems concerned about it. Just that Mary Molloy is like the annoying wasp that won't go away.'

'She's fighting for her son.'

'She's wasting her own life.'

'What about DCI Hunter?'

'I don't understand.'

'There are many officers I trust,' Joe said. 'They brief me truthfully about the evidence before the interview, even though they know it means showing their hand. But there are those I'm never sure about, where it's like a slow game of reveal. They only tell me what they think I should know, keeping back the surprises, so you never know if what you're being told is the whole truth.'

Kim smiled. 'I know that feeling.'

'What, they play games with you too?'

'Not in the same way. Sometimes it's a battle about whether to charge someone, and the stuff that will make a charge less likely has to be teased out rather than volunteered. But like you say, that's the game.'

'And DCI Hunter?'

Kim took another drink of coffee. 'He's a powerful figure. Involved in a lot of big cases.'

'That doesn't tell me much.'

Kim put her cup down, empty now, and stared

at it for a few seconds. 'Is this just between us?' she said, when she looked up again.

'Yes.'

'I don't like him. He's from a different era. He was popular a few years ago but most of the old guard have gone, retired or taken redundancy. Most of the lawyers are a lot younger than Hunter and trained in a different time. Hunter acts like a sheriff, you know, riding in to clean up the town, his little team of deputies with him. He creeps me out a bit. Stares that linger a second longer than they need to, and treats prosecutors like an inconvenience. It's like he wishes he could run the cases through the courts himself.'

'He was there the other night, when Carl Jex was arrested. It wasn't his case, but he seemed interested, was loitering.' Joe grimaced. 'I should have paid more attention to him. I didn't make a note of the address where Carl was arrested. It was late, and it was a routine case.'

'I can't help you there,' Kim said. 'If Carl is charged, you'll find out, but I'm not ringing round for you.'

'I wouldn't expect you to.' A pause. 'Do you trust Hunter?'

Kim raised an eyebrow at that. 'I don't trust anyone with that much power.'

Joe smiled. 'Thank you. That's what I wanted to know.'

Thirty-four

Carl put his head back against the wall. He was finding it hard to focus. His eyes were heavy, his body aching. Sounds seemed to come to him on a slow loop, as if everything was dragged out, his head moving too slowly. His knees trembled, his shoes wet from his piss. His legs were cramped up but there was no safe way to ease the pain. His cut leg made him shriek through his gag, but he had to use it to support himself.

He was going to fight it, though. His mother would be out there looking for him. She had the files; she'd speak to the right people.

His mind was twisting things. The sounds from upstairs came as loud echoes and his memories of the rest of the house seemed like something from another lifetime.

He knew it was daylight because the cellar had got warmer. Was this to be the last morning he saw?

The cellar door opened and the man came down the stairs. His shirt collar was up, and a tie hung loosely around his neck. He was carrying a glass. He didn't seem as concerned about being seen.

'You still here?' the man said, and laughed to himself.

Carl nodded. 'Let me go,' he said, the words muffled through the gag. 'Please.'

The man stepped over Emma's body. He didn't

226

even look down. 'I'm going to work. I'll be gone for hours. That's how long it will continue at least. Do you think you'll last?'

Carl didn't answer.

The man raised the glass to Carl's lips and let a small amount of water dribble over the gag. Carl sucked at the cloth in desperation, but just as quickly the glass was pulled away.

The man grinned and placed the glass on the floor close to his feet. 'There it is,' he said. 'Precious water. You just need to bend down for it,' and he laughed again.

He started to knot his tie. 'Goodbye, Carl. If you don't make it through the day, it's been a pleasure. No, it really has.' And with that, he turned and left the cellar.

Carl closed his eyes as tears came once more. It was hopeless. He wouldn't last the day. All the fight he had started to store up inside just leaked out of him.

He kicked out in frustration, sending the glass across the floor. It shattered against the wall and the cellar fell back into silence.

Sam was sitting in his car with the door open. He had been there for a few hours now, watching the pitch of the forensic tent and the arrival of the crime scene investigators, and fatigue was setting in. His legs were restless and it took just a few moments of quiet for a blink to turn into a rest and then into a short doze, jerking awake each time.

He was drinking the last of his coffee when his phone rang. It was Joe.

'Hi, Joe,' he said, his weariness showing in his voice.

'I need to ask you a favour,' Joe said.

Sam sighed. He didn't need this.

'Not now,' he said. 'Things are getting a bit crazy.'

'But this might be important.'

'No, Joe, not now,' Sam snapped, and clicked off his phone. Irritation swept through him, fuelled by tiredness. He wasn't going to let Joe use him as a shortcut. Sam hadn't joined the force to be a defence lawyer's man on the inside.

DI Evans arrived on the scene. She'd parked much further down the hill, the verges already clogged with forensic vehicles and squad cars. Sam noticed more press interest too, with a helicopter in the air and television vans parked in the distance. Evans looked tired as she walked towards him, her short hair bedraggled, as if she'd foregone a shower to get to the scene quickly.

He raised his cup to her but didn't smile.

'So you were proved right,' she said, as she got closer.

'I don't feel much pride in it,' he said. 'I've had no sleep and when everyone else was eating their breakfast, I was running my hands over a buried corpse.'

'Well, put that way, I can see why you're not celebrating.' She looked over to the forensic tent in the distance, pitched in the same place as the day before, a white block surrounded by small white figures. 'So what did you see?'

'Not much,' he said. 'I saw the shirt and felt the ribcage, and I knew I shouldn't dig any further. I

228

called it in.'

'So if you could feel the ribs, it had been there for some time.'

'It certainly didn't feel fleshy, thank goodness.'

'Could you tell anything about the body? Was it male or female, adult or child?'

Sam thought back to his sight of the body, the feel of it under his hand, and said, 'I'm guessing a man, from the style of the shirt and the size. It certainly wasn't a child, which is perhaps the thought that is interesting them so much.' And he pointed down the road, to the press cameras.

Evans followed his gesture. The evil deeds of Ian Brady and Myra Hindley still haunted the moors and it only took a police forensic tent on the barren slopes to get the media twitching. 'Yeah, I see what you mean,' she said, and reached down to the box of paper suits wrapped in cellophane. 'Come on, get suited up. Let's take a look.'

Sam groaned as he eased himself out of his car, his knees cracking as he straightened. As he ripped open the plastic to unwrap the plain white coveralls, he said, 'Have you heard from Hunter?'

'He's with the superintendent now. You got lucky. Hunter is angry about your insubordination, but the discovery of a body should save you.'

Sam smiled at that, before putting the paper mask over his nose and mouth. 'You'll take some of the credit, I suppose,' he said, his voice muffled.

'The joys of command,' she said, and Sam saw the twinkle of her eyes above her own mask. 'Come on, let's walk. You're the hero of the hour.'

Sam followed her along the same track he had taken before, past where he had stopped with the sack of logs. 'He could have stopped here,' he said, making Evans turn round. 'The headlights missed me when a car went past and it's still a long way to go before you get to the body. That's what made me dig. It just didn't make any sense.'

'Logic always works best,' Evans said. 'People like Hunter think it's all about instinct and hunches, but instinct is just ego. A proper case theory is about logic.'

Their suits rustled as they walked, the heather scraping against their legs. They stepped to one side to let two crime scene investigators walk past carrying plastic crates filled with soil. From the redness of exertion showing above the masks, Sam guessed that they were feeling heavier with every step. Someone would have the job of going through that later, just to see whether anything had been dropped into the hole as the body was buried.

When they got to the forensic tent Evans held the flap open for him. It was warm inside, even though it was still early and the day hadn't acquired any heat on the outside. There were four people squashed in there. A forensic scientist he recognised from the bushiness of his grey eyebrows and the way his stomach pushed out at the paper suit, and three crime scene investigators, one with a camera and two more with small brushes, treating the body like an archaeological dig.

The hole Sam had dug earlier was still there, but it was deeper, the soil being removed from around the body. There seemed less doubt now about gender. The face looked well-preserved, although the features had grown tight to the skull and looked leathery, as if the dead person was very old and had spent too long in the sun. It was undoubtedly a man's face. The clothes were dirty, with empty-looking jeans and a hollow blue checked shirt, except for where the ribcage stuck up.

'How long do you think it's been there?' Evans said.

The forensic scientist looked up and tilted his head as if he was thinking about it, although Sam guessed that he had been trying to work it out ever since he arrived.

'Hard to say,' he said. 'In peat soil like this, the bodies can stay preserved for years. What rots a body is oxygen and it lets the insect world in to munch away at it. Peat soil doesn't let in much oxygen and it's very acidic, so it makes the body go waxy like this. It's more than a couple of months though, because there has been some decomposition. The coldness in winter will have slowed it down, but I reckon it's months rather than years.'

'It gives us some kind of starting point,' Evans said, looking back into the hole, her forehead creased.

One of the crime scene investigators was brushing away the soil behind the body's neck when she knelt up. 'We've got something here,' she said.

That made everyone pay attention. Sam moved closer, Evans with him.

The investigator brushed at some more soil before she reached in with her gloved hand and pulled at something. It was a blue ribbon, wet and soiled, but still bright enough to see. As she pulled, there was something white and plastic attached to it. Once it came free, the crime scene investigator looked at it and drew a sharp intake of breath.

'What is it?' Evans said, and reached out for it.

Sam looked over her shoulder as she took hold of it. 'Shit,' he muttered.

It was an identification badge, the logo on the front familiar to everyone in the tent. Greater Manchester Police. Evans wiped away the dirt, and Sam swore again as the photograph and a name were unveiled.

David Jex.

Thirty-five

Joe paused in front of the Magistrates' Court.

It rose high in front of him, red sandstone and dark glass, but for all of its modern glamour Joe knew what was waiting for him. The excuses of defendants, handed over to him so that he could repackage them as something heartfelt and earnest.

Joe was carrying two files. Neither were guilty pleas, so he knew he wouldn't see out either. Honeywells would close the department and his clients would be left to find alternative represent-ation. One of the young lawyers from Mahones, Damien, approached the court entrance, all ill-fitting cheap suit and nerves. Joe stuck out his arm.

'Damien, can you look after these for me?'

Damien looked down at the files and then at Joe. It was common for lawyers to ask others to mind a client, a quid pro quo in exchange for a small agency fee, so it was something else that made Damien frown. 'Are you all right, Joe?'

Joe closed his eyes for a moment, feeling the fast beat of his heart as the thought of going into court overwhelmed him. 'I'm just fine,' he said, and started to walk away, sweat prickling his forehead.

'Joe, what am I doing with them?'

'Keeping them, if you want,' Joe said, and he kept on walking. He knew where he was going, but he had to go into the office first.

Gina was walking along the first-floor corridor when Joe walked to his room. He didn't say anything to her as he passed her. Instead, he closed his door firmly, giving out the message that he wasn't to be interrupted. Gina ignored that, she had known him too long, and barged straight in.

'What's going on?' she said, her brow furrowed by concern.

Joe was in his chair, looking at his computer screen. He logged straight onto the prison website, to get the phone number. Emergency legal visits were unusual, but Joe was relieved to see that Honeywells was still the firm on the prison's records. He explained that something had come up unexpectedly, and was told that if he could get there in a couple of hours, they could accommodate a visit.

'Joe?' Gina said, her hands on her hips now.

He fished around for some notes Carl had made, given to him by Lorna the day before, and headed for the door. He paused to kiss Gina on the cheek. 'We're done here, with this firm. I'm going to do this before I go.'

'Joe, you can't do this,' she shouted after him, but he wasn't listening. He had a prison slot and he had the address of the young couple who had found Rebecca Scarfield, Aidan's supposed victim, the details jotted across the top of their witness statements.

They lived in a town in Yorkshire, on the other side of the Pennines but only a few miles from where the body was found. It was a different county, a whole different place, but it was on the way to where Aidan was imprisoned at the high security prison in Wakefield.

Carl gritted his teeth as the pain in his legs grew. He fought the urge to sit down, the back of his legs cramping, his calves tight and desperate for rest. He was thirsty and his stomach groaned. He felt light-headed and it was hard to keep his mouth hydrated; the gag soaked up any saliva he could muster.

Fatigue scared him the most. One quick drift into sleep, even standing, would make that slip-knot tighten and he would die, the last view of his world being the starkness of the cellar and the dead woman on the floor in front of him. He tried to concentrate on something else instead, just to keep his mind alert. He needed some anger or adrenalin, so he thought about how he had ended up here.

The man's house had been just one more on a list of addresses he'd found at the back of one of his father's files. Carl had been working his way through the list, trying to work out what his father might have seen. Night after night of hanging around houses, looking for something about the occupant that struck him as off-key, to notice the thing his father had noticed. Then there had been this house, the next on the list.

Something about the man had struck him as being unusual. He had seemed secretive, looking around whenever he got into his car. He was friendly with his neighbours, but it seemed too much, as if he was more interested in getting them to like him than in becoming friends. He was the man who rushed from his car to help the elderly lady with her shopping bags, or laughed overly loudly as he exchanged banter with the postman. A good neighbour, everyone loved him, but Carl had seen him change whenever he thought he was alone. His smile slipped as soon as the postman moved on, and he checked around him whenever he went into the house, as if he didn't want anyone to see inside.

So Carl had gone back for another look and he had been arrested. That had made him want to go back again, certain that there was something else to see, and he had ended up in the cellar instead, clammy, cold and hungry. It was dark, the light off, and even though his eyes had adjusted to the gloom, it was still impossible to make much out. There were the lines of shelving and, ahead in the darkness, the grey outline of the woman's body.

He thought he could hear her, like soft breaths, but he knew it was his mind playing tricks. What would happen to her now? How had he disposed of the others? How many were there? Would he have to witness it, some carve-up with a saw or perhaps wrapped in plastic and taken away?

Carl looked down and blinked away some tears. He readjusted his feet, just to keep the circulation going in his legs. A sob choked up his throat. As much as he resolved to be strong, misery crept up on him and assaulted him in waves. Helplessness, anger, despair, confusion and disbelief swirled around him. What must his mother be thinking? Another one of the men in her life leaving the house and failing to return. She would spend the rest of her life wondering where they had gone and whether they were ever going to come back.

The sob escaped this time. It came out as a pitiful low moan, muffled through the gag, and then short bursts as he broke, tears running down his cheeks, his body quivering in the dark, making the rope scrape against his neck. He closed his eyes, seeking sanctuary in the darkness, for a moment taken away from the gloom of the cellar.

He stopped.

There had been a noise. Just soft but it had seemed loud in the dark. He opened his eyes and looked around. He was no longer alone.

It was there again. Something moving against the floor – a soft shuffle, barely audible but still there. Goosebumps broke out on his skin as fear rippled through him, making him cold.

There was a groan, low and steady. Carl jumped and yelped. It was coming from the floor, from the woman. He stared hard at her grey outline. Then he saw it: her leg moved.

His chest pumped hard as he took in fast

breaths through his nostrils. He'd heard about this, bodies moving as they contract, rigor mortis setting in, expelling air that comes out as moans. He couldn't bear the thought of that in the dark. He closed his eyes again. The hours ahead were filled with added dread now, wondering what changes she would go through as her body began its long transition to dust.

The noise changed and he yelped again. It was louder this time, the groan more audible. He opened his eyes, needing to see, and then he sobbed as she raised herself on one elbow and said in a muffled voice, 'Where the fuck am I?'

Thirty-six

Sam rubbed his face with his hands when he walked along the corridor. It was quiet, with many people still up at the scene, but there was still the chatter of the Incident Room ahead. He wasn't ready for that yet. He was tired, having had virtually no sleep.

As he got closer, Evans was in the doorway of her room, talking to someone inside. She turned to him and gestured with a tilt of her head that he should go in. She was unsmiling. Sam did as he was told, and then paused when he got in there.

There was a superintendent sitting behind her desk. He was in uniform, with a silver crown on his epaulettes and his hair full and grey. He bore that relaxed air of a man who has done well in his career, but his eyes were cold. He wasn't there to congratulate anyone.

'DC Parker,' he said, the tone of his voice rich and deep. 'Sit down,' and he gestured to the chair in front of the desk. 'I'm Superintendent Metcalfe.'

Evans leaned against her door as Sam took his seat. He crossed his legs nervously. He brushed non-existent lint from his trousers.

'Sir?'

Metcalfe smiled, but it was quick. 'You've caused us a problem, Sam. Can I call you Sam?'

Sam nodded. 'A problem? Why?'

'Because we had that scene finished off yesterday, but it turns out that one of our officers was buried on the same spot, uncovered only when an off-duty detective went for a midnight dig. It makes us like look amateurs, saved by some maverick.'

Sam uncrossed his leg and then back again. 'That wasn't my intention, sir.'

'So why the hell did you do it?'

Sam turned to look back at Evans. She was staying quiet, her arms folded. Seeing where the blame was going to rest, he reckoned.

'I raised it yesterday, in the squad meeting,' Sam said. 'It just seemed that the location of the dead woman was significant.'

'And what was said when you raised it?'

'DCI Hunter dismissed it.'

'So you went against a direct order?'

'I got it right, sir. That's why I did it. I knew I was right.'

The superintendent looked up at Evans before

he sighed. 'Between us three, Hunter is a dinosaur, but a damn good copper. However,' and he frowned, 'his ego gets in the way sometimes. That didn't mean you had to go on a frolic of your own.'

Sam coughed nervously. 'Isn't it more important that we found the body, not how we found it?'

'It isn't just about one case,' the superintendent said, his tone acquiring an edge. 'We have to think of how the Force will look. We can't be seen as some kind of Keystone Kops outfit.'

Evans stepped away from the door. 'I told Sam he could follow that angle,' she said.

The superintendent looked up, surprised.

'He came to me yesterday and said he thought the investigation was too narrow, focusing too much on the husband and not on other possibilities.'

'So you told him to go get a spade and dig up the moors at sunrise?' Metcalfe said, leaning back, his eyes wide.

'No, I didn't,' she said. 'But I did say that I would back him up provided he did everything Hunter asked him as well. I thought that if it came to nothing, then nothing was lost.'

'Ordered,' the superintendent said. 'Hunter doesn't ask. He orders.'

Evans stayed quiet. She had made her point, and Sam was grateful.

The superintendent twirled in his chair. He looked out of the window for a few seconds before he turned back to face Sam. 'We need to manage it then,' he said. 'You gave him authority and he was acting under direction, pursuing many lines of inquiry. The fact that Sam was alone won't come out until the trial.'

'If there is one,' Evans said. 'We need to catch the bastard first and, thanks to Sam, we've got more chance than we did this time yesterday.'

'That's the line, then,' the superintendent said. 'Sam was no Lone Ranger. He was acting under orders, waiting until the end of the night, to see if the killer returned to the scene. If it was meant as a display, some kind of marker, the killer would think we'd missed it and might have come back with a spade of his own. It was a bluff, a piece of misdirection. When he didn't show, we dug ourselves.'

'It sounds good,' Evans said.

'Sam?'

He nodded. 'I didn't do it for the glory. I did it because it wasn't being done right.'

The superintendent nodded, satisfied. 'It's hard to be happy, because it's one of our own on the moors, but well done.'

Sam smiled. 'Thank you, sir.'

The superintendent got to his feet. He held out his hand to shake. Sam took it. 'Thank you, Sam. Just remember the line. Bluff and misdirection. It makes us look cunning. I like it.'

The superintendent left the room. Evans closed the door and let out a sigh of relief. 'That could have gone badly,' she said. 'He's all about image, not results.'

Sam stared at the closed door for a few seconds before he said, 'How does someone lose their way like that?'

'Simple. They never had a proper way. It was only ever about the slippery pole. Some people are born to climb, kissing every arse they pass on the way up. Promise me one thing, Sam.'

'Yes?'

'Don't be like him. Or like them.' And she pointed to the room next door, to the Incident Room. 'All puffed chests and back slaps.'

Sam smiled. 'Thank you.'

Before he left the room, Evans said, 'If this bluff is going to work, you had to be on duty last night, so right now, from this minute, you're off-duty. We're not paying you overtime for a lone crusade.'

'So I have to go home?'

'I didn't say that, but you should. You look tired.'

He left the room, grateful for avoiding censure, and leaned against the wall in the corridor. He closed his eyes and exhaled loudly. More important than avoiding disciplinary action, he had been right.

He opened his eyes and looked towards the Incident Room door. The chatter seemed louder now, the detectives on the phone or discussing the case. He thought about what Evans had said.

In that moment, he felt more apart from the others in the Incident Room than he ever had.

'Emma?' Carl said, but it came out muffled through the gag.

She yelped and then groaned, holding her forehead. 'Where am I?' she said, her voice croaky. She coughed. 'My throat hurts. There was something in that drink.'

Carl grunted through the gag, to attract her attention. He stamped his foot.

241

She cried out and shouted, 'Who's there?' Her voice echoed.

'Over here,' he tried to say, but again it was muffled.

She started to cry. 'I'm cold. Where am I?' A pause. 'I've got no clothes.'

He stamped his foot again.

There was silence, and Carl knew she was trying to work out her situation. The night before, she had expected some kind of romantic evening and now she was waking up cold and naked in a cellar, with someone grunting at her from the darkness.

'Please, over here, help me,' Carl said, his voice lowered, trying to speak more slowly, the words coming through clearer this time.

There was a pause, and then Emma shuffled across the floor towards him. She was reaching out with her hands, sweeping the floor in wide arcs, until her fingers hit his feet.

She yelped and jumped back. There were a few moments of silence, and then she said, 'Who are you?' There was fear in her voice. 'You're watching me. I can't see you.'

'No, no, no,' Carl said. 'Please.'

There was another pause, and then she started towards him again, her hands on his feet. She started to work her hands up his legs, then his body, towards his arms. She was silent as she searched him, until they finished their slow journey and she felt the cold metal of the chain around his wrists.

She stopped. 'What's this?' she said, stepping back.

Carl shook his head urgently and said, 'Help me,' the words still muffled.

Her cold hands went back along Carl's arms and towards his neck. There was a gasp when she felt the rope, and when her fingers hit the gag, she reached round to the back and pulled at the knot, fumbling in the darkness, weak and tired, until the cloth went slack. She pulled it away and yanked out the rag that had been rammed into his mouth.

'Thank you,' Carl said, swallowing hard, trying to work his mouth back into some kind of normality.

'Where am I?' she said, stepping away from him.

'You came here last night, to see a man.'

There was a pause and then she said, 'I've got no clothes on. I'm cold. And what happened to me? My throat hurts.'

'You're supposed to be dead.'

'What? I don't understand.'

'It's what he does, the man who lives here. No one leaves.'

Thirty-seven

The journey across the Pennines was busier than normal, with extra traffic streaming onto the motorway from the direction of the moors. The radio had said that there was a police operation there and Joe guessed that the road had been blocked off. He had called Mary Molloy. She was surprised but she wasn't going to let Joe blunder into the case unsupervised. She wanted to meet him in Wakefield. Joe couldn't say no.

He dropped down into one of the small towns on the Yorkshire edge of the Pennine hills, where the couple lived, his satnav leading him to a small stone terrace on a cobbled road that ended in a high wall. The rise was steep, the houses leaning against each other for support. Joe had to park on a different street, the cars hogging their own piece of precious parking space so that there was no space left for visitors.

He hesitated before he knocked on their door, his hand poised, knuckles clenched. There was someone inside, given away by the murmur of the television, and he knew he was about to make them relive an awful memory. They had discovered a dead body. It would have been traumatic, not helped by the ordeal of a court appearance, and he was about to make them dredge it all back up again. He hadn't even spoken to Aidan Molloy yet, and there he was, traversing the north, chasing a case he didn't really have. Except that Joe wasn't doing it for Aidan. He was doing it for himself, he knew that. Did he have the right to be so selfish?

He knocked on the door, a short rap, before he talked himself out of it.

When the door opened, a young woman was there, wiping her hands on a cloth, a little boy hiding behind her legs, perhaps only three. He stared up at Joe, confused, suddenly shy. Cooking smells drifted from inside, spicy and hot.

'Nicole Grant? My name is Joe Parker,' he said,

and he handed over a business card. She looked at it, confused. 'I've come from Manchester to talk to you about the Aidan Molloy case.'

Nicola paled. 'Why didn't you call first?' she said, brushing away a loose strand of blonde hair, the rest of it tied up at the back.

The truthful answer was that Joe knew she would refuse or call the police. He had no instructions to talk about Aidan's case, but Carl Jex gave him justification.

'It's urgent, and important.'

Nicole hesitated, looking back into the house, suddenly flustered, until she moved away from the door and said, 'You better come in then.'

When Joe went inside, she asked him if he wanted a drink, her politeness kicking in. He asked for coffee. A hot drink would give him twenty minutes at least. He walked into the living room, where there were toys strewn across the floor and crayons on a table. He sat down and waited, the young boy now watching him warily from the corner of the room.

As Joe looked around, he could tell that they weren't used to dealing with lawyers. Many people dragged into court cases were those who lived in the same world inhabited by the defendants, made victims by their lives on the wrong side of everything. But sometimes, and only sometimes, people who preferred an ordinary life found themselves pulled into the whirl of criminal proceedings, usually just the wrong people in the wrong place at the wrong time.

When Nicole came back in, holding a cup, she said, 'Sorry about the mess.' She handed Joe his

245

drink and began to pick up toys, throwing them into a hamper in the corner of the room.

'There's no need, honestly,' Joe said, smiling, trying to put her at ease. 'You've got a nice house. Children bring something to it.'

'Chaos?' she said.

'Happy chaos,' he said, smiling, and he meant it. His job had taken him to some of the worst homes you could imagine, seeing clients in their houses with empty booze bottles lying around and dog faeces spread over the floor. Nicole's house was nothing more than a family home, with all the noise that it brings, a welcome change from the clinical emptiness of Joe's own apartment.

Nicole went to shout up the stairs for her husband, and a rumble of feet through the ceiling told Joe that her husband Dan was on his way. The little boy sat in a chair opposite and stared.

'What's your name?' Joe said to him.

'Matthew.'

'That's a nice name,' Joe said, and was then rescued by Nicole's reappearance, his repertoire of child-talk exhausted.

Nicole told Matthew to play upstairs as Dan came into the room, pulling on a jumper, his hair wet.

'I've just finished work, sorry. An early shift.' He held out his hand and Joe stood to shake it. Dan's hands were hard and calloused, his grip hard, as if to say that Joe shouldn't forget who was the man of the house. His face was ruddy, from outside work was Joe's guess, his hair shaved to stubble.

As Nicole sat in a chair at the side of the room, Dan stayed on his feet and leaned against a stone fireplace. 'So what's this about?'

'Aidan Molloy. I'm from the law firm that represented him.'

Dan looked across at Nicole and said, 'We've nothing else to say about it. We said it in court back then. It's years ago.'

Joe spotted the family dynamic, that Dan would speak for both of them.

'I've been getting some good information that suggests that the police got it wrong, that Aidan Molloy is innocent,' Joe said. It was a lie, but he wanted them to talk.

'That's nothing to do with us,' Dan said. 'All we did was tell the police what we saw.'

'Which was what?'

'A car, and then our headlights flashed against some skin. It was her, Rebecca. What else can we say? We called the police and that was it.'

'Did you get a good look at the driver?'

'I've been through this before and if you're genuine you'll know what I said.'

'I've been doing this job for long enough to know that not everything goes in the statement.'

Dan stayed silent for a while, which told Joe that there was more, although when he spoke he said, 'No, we didn't see the driver. He was pulling away. We saw just the back of the car.'

'What sort of car was it?'

Dan exchanged glances with Nicole before he said, 'A blue hatchback. An Astra, I thought.'

'Is that what you thought, Nicole?' Joe said, turning to her. He had noticed that she wasn't looking up as Dan spoke, and he was still talking for both of them.

'Hey!' Dan said angrily. 'We're not in the witness box. This is our home.'

'I'm sorry,' Joe said, raising his hand. 'It's just that I know different people often see the same thing differently.'

'That's what you do, you lawyers,' Dan said. 'That's what the police said back then. Lawyers like you would try and trip us up and make us look like we were unsure so that he got away with it.'

'Perhaps *he* didn't do it.'

'We saw what we saw and the murderer is in prison. Why is it that all these murders are always miscarriages? Why can't there just be one guilty one?'

Joe looked across at Nicole. She was looking back at him, but she wasn't showing the same level of anger as her husband. Instead, she seemed uncomfortable, looking down at her hands.

'Are you sure the right man is in prison?' Joe said to her. 'Could you be wrong? It was dark, you got a quick glimpse, the car was driving away quickly.'

'It wasn't just on us,' Dan said, his anger rising. 'Leave. I want you to go. We've had all this before.'

'Who from?'

'Some young lad. He didn't say how he knew about us. Just came over on the bus.'

'Can you remember what he was called?' Joe said, even though he guessed who he would be.

'No. Why should I? Now go, please, or I'll throw you out.'

Nicole looked up. 'He was called Carl,' she said.

'And what did you do when he came round?' Joe said.

'We told DCI Hunter.'

'Carl has gone missing,' Joe said. 'He's one of my clients and he's only fifteen. He was looking into the case and thought he was getting close to the truth.'

'Missing?'

'He didn't go home, no one knows where he's been, so I'm trying to find out how close to the truth he got.'

Dan went towards the front door. 'The jury saw the truth. So it's time for you to go and let us get on with our lives.' He opened it. 'Goodbye.'

Nicole didn't look up as Joe went towards the door. As it closed behind him and Joe was back on the street, he knew that the trip had been useful. They had been defensive, which told him that they were hiding something.

All Joe had to do was find out what.

The Incident Room fell quiet when Sam walked in. He didn't know what to expect. He felt like he had done something good, but it was hard to feel like the hero when a colleague's body had been discovered.

Everyone looked up. There was a pause, before someone started to clap at the back of the room. Within a few seconds, everyone had joined in. Someone stepped forward and slapped him on the back. No one was smiling, but he could see their appreciation, that a mystery about one of their friends had been resolved, and they were grateful.

It felt like the first time they had really noticed him.

He went over to where Charlotte was sitting. She

sat back and folded her arms. 'So that's what you were up to yesterday,' she said, pretending to be hurt.

'I didn't think you'd enjoy midnight digging. You got it right though: X marked the spot.'

'And if we solve one murder, we will probably solve the other.'

'That's the hope.' He looked around. 'So what now?'

'We're having to go through all his old investigations, just to see if anyone had made a threat against him.'

'It goes with the job sometimes, but I've never known a threat be carried out.'

'No, me neither,' Charlotte said. She looked over Sam's shoulder and said, 'Uh-oh, trouble.'

Sam turned round. It was Hunter, Weaver following. They both made straight over to him.

Hunter was grinding his teeth as he got closer. 'We need to talk,' he said, and jerked his thumb back towards the door.

Sam sighed. It looked like whatever was going to be said, Hunter wanted to keep it private.

They walked out together, Hunter moving quickly. Weaver walked behind, but he didn't have the same urgency. They rounded the corner at one end, where most of the rooms were vacant, ready for the sale of the building.

Hunter pointed towards an office, banged on the frosted glass and went inside. The room was empty, apart from four desks that were gathering dust, the walls scarred by sticky tape, discarded pieces of paper gathered against one wall. Hunter went to the window, his hands on his hips so that his jacket splayed outwards.

Sam leaned against the wall as Weaver came in, avoiding Sam's gaze. This was no official meeting. It was Hunter letting off steam, angry with Sam but knowing he could do nothing about it, because Sam had been proved right.

When Hunter turned back around, he shook his head, his lips set, sweat prickling his nose and forehead. 'You stupid little prick,' he said in a hiss. 'Who the fuck do you think you are? Going up there, with no official backing, digging around a murder scene.' He turned and started to pace, winding himself up.

Sam stood straight and folded his arms. 'I did have official backing,' he said, trying to hide the tremble in his voice.

'Not from me,' Hunter said, and jabbed his own chest with his finger. 'You tried to make a fool of me.'

'No, I didn't. I just did the right thing.'

Hunter went quickly towards him, and for a moment Sam thought he was going to hit him. Instead, he flushed and pointed in Sam's face, before turning away, both of his fists clenching and unclenching.

'You're going to come out of it all right anyway,' Sam said.

Hunter whirled back around. 'What do you mean?'

'Superintendent Metcalfe is going to spin it that we reopened the moors to trick the killer into coming back, to make him think that we hadn't spotted the reason for her being left there. Bluff and misdirection, he said.'

'That's not the fucking point.'

Before Sam could say anything else, the door burst open and one of the detectives from the Incident Room was there, out of breath.

'Yes?' Hunter snapped.

'I've been looking for you,' he said. 'The press have been on, trying to speak to you. They've got wind of something big. Is there going to be a conference?'

'Yes, at some point. Superintendent Metcalfe fancies the limelight, so I've heard.'

The detective looked surprised. 'And Lorna Jex is downstairs, David's wife. We've kept her in the lobby.'

Hunter looked at the ceiling and muttered something under his breath, before pointing at Sam. 'You dug him up. You talk to her.'

The detective put his head back out of the room and let the door close.

'Don't think I've forgotten this,' Hunter said, pointing at Sam before storming out of the room. Weaver followed, as always.

When the door slammed, Sam shook his head and let out a long sigh. It was turning into quite a day.

Thirty-eight

Joe checked his watch. Mary Molloy was late.

He was in front of some advertising hoardings at the bottom of a hill that ran away from the centre of Wakefield, the toughness of the former mining city an apt setting for one of the country's highest security prisons. He was waiting for Mary, amongst the din of city traffic and the occasional rumble of a train that passed over a nearby bridge.

His phone rang in his pocket. He thought it might be Mary, calling to say she had changed her mind, but when he looked at the screen, he saw that it was Kim.

He put a finger in one ear so that he could hear her over the noise. 'Are you stalking me?' he said, jokingly.

'You wish,' she said. 'Where the hell are you? It's noisy.'

'About to visit Aidan Molloy in prison.'

'Do you know what we prosecutors call a co-incidence?'

'Proof of guilt,' Joe said. 'Coincidence is too easy an explanation.'

'That's right,' she said. 'They make me sus-picious.'

Joe frowned. 'So what's coincidental?'

'David Jex.'

'Carl's father? Why? What's happened?'

Joe heard her take a deep breath. 'He's turned

253

up dead on the moors.'

Joe's mouth dropped open. He looked around, to check no one could hear him. 'Dead? How come?'

'This is the bizarre thing,' she said. 'Your brother dug him up.'

'Sam? I don't understand. Is this public yet?'

'Not yet, but it won't take long. Someone mentioned it back at the office. They were on the phone to the police and it was the news at the station. Keep it quiet for now, it's not officially confirmed yet, but I just thought you ought to know after what you were saying this morning.'

Joe was struck silent by the enormity of what he had just been told. He recalled Lorna Jex and her worry for her husband. What was she going through right now? Of course, Joe knew exactly what she was going through; he had seen it first hand when his own sister died. And what did that mean for Carl? He had been looking at the same thing as his father. Had he met the same end? Lorna didn't deserve to lose them both.

'If it's got any connection with Aidan Molloy and I find anything out, will you help me?' Joe said.

'Me?'

'I thought prosecutors were all about truth and justice, all those clichés that help you sleep every night.'

'I'm a lawyer, like you. I just chose a different side.'

'So do the right thing, if I find anything out.'

Kim was silent for a few seconds, and then said, 'I've got to go back into court.'

'Kim?'

'I told you about David Jex because I thought you should know,' she said. 'Everything else, I've got to remember which side I'm on. Goodbye, Joe.' His phone went silent.

As Joe put his phone back into his pocket, he felt the divide between them grow once more – Kim always on one side, him on the other. He thought about David Jex, and Sam's involvement. He still needed to speak to Sam, even though he had hung up on him when he had tried to talk to him earlier in the day. They had talked about Carl Jex at his mother's house the other evening, but that seemed like an awfully long time ago.

He looked up at the sound of someone walking towards him. It was Mary. He waved. She didn't wave back.

When she reached him, she hoisted her bag back onto her shoulder, folded her arms and said, 'The train was late.'

'I told you, I could have done this on my own.'

'If you're going to take on Aidan's case, I want to know what he says, how he is, not wait for you to write to me or call me.'

'I understand,' Joe said, and they walked towards the prison entrance together. He felt a pull on his sleeve. He turned round to see Mary looking up at him, and for a second there was a crack in her tough exterior.

'I've never got close to freeing Aidan,' she said, her voice soft, fear in her eyes. 'If you let me believe that I can and it's all a fake, then it'll be like going back to the beginning and I can't cope with that.'

255

'I can't promise anything, Mary, but I will be honest with you, and I'm no fake,' Joe said, trying to smile reassuringly.

'I wanted Tyrone to be here, to make sure you're not trying to make a fool out of me, but he's busy.'

'I'm not doing that. Trust me. Call him later.'

Mary thought about that for a moment and then set off ahead of him, to the concrete façade of one of the country's most notorious prisons. The facilities were modern and comfortable, behind high sandstone walls but within earshot of the city centre. The sounds of the nearby West-gate nightlife drifted over the walls on still nights, taunting the prisoners with the life they had left behind. From terrorists and psychopaths, serial killers to child murderers, Wakefield's inmates made the prison reverberate in the press. Dennis Nilsen, Ian Huntley, Mick Philpott, Levi Bellfield and countless others. Aidan Molloy had joined them in Wakefield due to his notoriety, the press whipping up his story, his supposed victim white and pretty and the daughter of the assistant chief constable. She was a decent married woman, cast aside and left on the moors like fly-tipped waste.

The prison entrance was through a glass-fronted office that acted like a small lookout in a seventies exterior that broke up the long sweep of the prison walls.

Joe turned to Mary. 'I'm booked in as a legal visit,' he said. 'I can't take you in with me.'

'I know that,' Mary said. 'I'll wait here. I just want to know everything straight away.'

'I can meet you in the pub back there, if you

want, or a café in the centre.'

She shook her head. 'No, I'll wait. Thank you.'

Joe left Mary loitering outside as he pushed his way in. The passage through reception was the usual thing, even though he was a lawyer. Bag scan and a body scanner and then a wave with a wand when something on him set off the beeper. No phones or metal objects, everything left in a locker, his identity proved with his passport, before a final slow walk past a drug-dog.

A guard led the way, although there was no idle conversation. Joe was placed in a small room as he waited for Aidan, the walls painted gunmetal grey, the table and chairs bolted to the floor, so that there was no chance of anything being used as a weapon or to create a hostage situation. A red light flashed on the camera in the corner. He waited for around ten minutes before there was movement at the door and, as he looked up, he saw a guard and then a figure behind. Aidan Molloy.

Aidan wasn't how Joe had expected. The image from his mother's leaflets was of someone smiling, big and gentle, his arm around Mary's shoulders, the loving son big enough to protect his mother. The Aidan Molloy in front of him was much thinner, his complexion grey and pale and he had dark rings under his eyes. He seemed sombre, and an air of defeat hung around him.

Joe stood to meet him, holding out his hand to shake. The grip he got from Aidan was limp and wet.

'So you're from Honeywells,' Aidan said as he sat down, his arms out in front of him, his palms flat on the table. His tone was flat, neither hostile nor friendly.

'Yes, Joe Parker. I've been looking at your case.'

'Why? What's the sudden interest?'

'How much has your mother told you?'

Aidan shook his head and scowled. 'She knows better than that. The calls from here are recorded.'

Joe pondered on how to begin. He was still shocked by the news about Carl's father. 'Thank you for seeing me,' he said at last. 'I've got a client whose case seems linked to yours.'

Aidan's mouth twitched as his expression softened. 'Okay, I'll listen. Who's your client?'

'Someone called Jex.'

Aidan's eyes widened and he sat forward. He opened his mouth as if to say something but then sat back again, shaking his head. Joe let the silence spin out until Aidan said eventually, 'David Jex?'

'No, his son, Carl.'

'I don't understand,' Aidan said, looking confused.

'Neither do I, at the moment, which is why I'm here speaking to you. I'm trying to work out the connection and I get the feeling that the answer is going to help you.'

Aidan thought about that for a few moments. 'When you said Jex, I thought you meant the detective, that perhaps he'd been arrested for perjury or something.'

'Why him?' Joe said. 'It was the witnesses who implicated you: the teenage girls, the young couple. It wasn't David Jex.'

'They were told what to say by the police, David Jex included.'

'You might think that, but we'll never prove it.'

'I don't think it. I know it.' When Joe raised an eyebrow, Aidan added, 'David Jex came to see me. He told me, more or less.'

Joe was surprised. 'When?'

'Eight months ago. Although I didn't know what he wanted. It was almost as if he'd come to say sorry but couldn't. He sat where you are and told me that he believed me now, that I hadn't killed that girl. What use was that to me? The camera doesn't record sound, because it's only there to watch out for an attack. What is said in here is supposed to be private. So I told him to go out there and do something about it. An apology from him won't get me out of here. And neither will you being here, just satisfying your curiosity.'

'I didn't come for that, Aidan. I came because it seemed like the next logical step.'

'So tell me.'

Joe sighed. 'David Jex went missing.'

'I heard,' Aidan said.

'It sounds like it wasn't long after his visit here.'

Aidan looked more thoughtful, sitting back again.

'David Jex became obsessed with your case,' Joe said. 'His son doesn't know why, but David was looking into it again, and then he went missing. His son was trying to find him, by working out what his father had found out. That brought him into contact with me and now he's gone missing as well. So how was David when he came here?'

Aidan pursed his lips as he cast his mind back. 'Remorseful,' he said eventually.

'Did he tell you anything about what he might have found out?'

'Do you think I'd be sitting here if he had,' Aidan scoffed. 'He can be as remorseful as he likes, but for as long as I wake up in here every morning, it's just self-pity. If he has done something foolish, like topped himself, that's just too bad, but at least it was a quick way out. For me, here, it's just a slow death, waiting for someone to see the truth.'

'The witnesses weren't the only ones telling lies though,' Joe said. 'You lied too.'

'I was scared,' Aidan said. 'Rebecca was seeing someone else, so I'd been driving around, trying to find her. I panicked and tried to cover up our affair. Lying doesn't make me a killer.' He folded his arms and they both sat in silence for a few minutes.

Joe exhaled loudly. 'This isn't official yet, but David Jex is dead. I've only just found out. I didn't know whether to tell you, but I think you deserve to know.'

Aidan paled. 'I didn't mean anything when I said about suicide,' he said. 'If he had a family, well, that's awful. I'm sorry.'

'It wasn't suicide,' Joe said. 'He was found on the moors, buried.'

Aidan's eyes opened wide. 'I don't understand.'

'Neither do I, yet.'

Aidan stared at the table for a while, taking in the news, so Joe asked, 'How are you finding it?'

'Prison?' Aidan said, looking up again. 'How do you think?' He sat forward, intensity in his eyes for the first time. 'Do you know what it's like to wake up every morning knowing that you're the victim, that you're in the wrong place? I feel like screaming every day at how wrong this is. Sometimes I cry, and sometimes I just sit and seethe in disbelief, but what can I do? I have a cell to myself, isolated, but that's how I like it. I don't want to be with the rest of them, because then I'll end up like them, guilty, waiting to be allowed out. I'm not guilty. I'm just angry. So I sit in my cell and go over my papers, reading them over and over, looking for a chink of something, a sign that other people have missed. And I write letters. To the judge, to the newspapers, but none of them are published. My mother helps. She feels as useless as I do, but we don't know what else to do. Give up? I even wrote to your firm once, but I got a letter saying that there were no avenues of appeal left. Do you know how that felt, to be dumped by your own legal team?'

'I didn't know that.'

'Why should you? I'm just a file number to people like you, a tale to bring up at the dinner parties.'

'I wasn't at the firm then. I don't know if this makes you feel better, but last night I was talking to Hugh Bramwell about your case. He said that he believed you, that yours was the case where he always believed there had been a miscarriage but could never prove it.'

'So why isn't he here, or campaigning with my mother?'

'We're criminal lawyers, Aidan. Clients tell us they're innocent all the time. There are some we believe, but we can't keep on fighting the battles after they've been lost, not without something new, or else we'd have no time left for the other battles we've got to fight. It doesn't mean that we won't come back for you when there is something new.'

'And is there something new?'

Joe thought about that. 'I want to know what David Jex found out.'

'He didn't tell me,' Aidan said.

'But it must have been important for him to come and see you.'

'That's no comfort if his discovery disappeared with him.' He paused. His voice softened when he said, 'Do you know I made myself a stab vest once?'

'A stab vest?'

'It's the blades you've got to watch in here, because people see me as a trophy. The prison let me have magazines, so I kept them, just for something to read, or so the guards thought. I got hold of some parcel tape and taped a few together so that I could put it over my head and hide it under my T-shirt. The guards stopped me wearing it, told me that it made me more of a target, made it look like I was frightened. Which I was. So instead, I spend my time hoping for a new child killer or serial rapist, just so that he would take some of the hatred away from me. How is that a way to live?'

Joe nodded that he understood. 'I'll do what I can, I promise you that much.'

And as he stood to go, Joe knew that he meant it.

Thirty-nine

Lorna Jex was sitting on one of the fold-down chairs that lined the wall of the waiting area when Sam walked in.

He knew how he appeared. Tired-looking, stubble on his cheeks, a weary drawl to his voice. Lorna Jex was owed more than that by the police force that had employed her husband. But he could still show her kindness.

The station was no longer open to the public. There was no front desk, no access unless you were allowed in by someone, so Lorna was alone, her fingers wrapped up in a handkerchief, tears staining her cheeks.

'Mrs Jex,' he said, his voice gentle, reassuring. 'I'm Sam Parker. Come through, please.'

She got slowly to her feet, following Sam into the gloom of the station, away from the eyes of the press that were gathering outside.

He led her along the corridor and into what was once an interview room, the table and chairs still bolted to the floor, the alarm sensor that ran round the wall no longer in use. No windows, no comfort, but it stopped Sam from walking her through the whole station, or being gawped at through open doorways.

As he sat her down, he went to a chair on the other side of the table. He reached across and took hold of her hands. 'I'm so sorry, Mrs Jex. We found David's body this morning.'

She hung her head and started to cry, her sobs making her tremble, tears running from her cheeks and making spots of moisture on her blouse.

'Hasn't anyone been to see you?'

She shook her head. 'I've been out, speaking to Carl's friends, trying to find him. It was only when I got back and there was a reporter on my drive that I thought something must have happened. So I came here. I thought it might have been...' And she let out a long breath and looked up to the ceiling, blinking fast, so that more tears hung from her eyelashes. 'I thought it might have been Carl.'

Sam squeezed her hand and she gave him a watery smile. 'How did he die?' she said, pulling her hands away to wipe her eyes.

'We don't know yet. He was found buried on the moors.'

She took a deep breath. 'So he didn't kill himself?' she said.

'No.'

There were more tears and Sam let her cry herself out.

'I've always known this day was coming,' she said eventually, her voice more even. 'I feel bad, because I feel relieved somehow, that at least it's all over, and that it isn't Carl. I thought DCI Hunter might have been here though. He and David were close, as far as I could tell.'

'He's very busy with the investigation, that's all,' Sam said, his instinct to protect Lorna's feelings taking over from his anger at Hunter. 'I'm sure he'll come and see you.'

Lorna smiled her gratitude.

'Just one thing,' Sam said. 'I'm Joe Parker's brother, Carl's solicitor. I know about how Carl went missing. Have you heard anything?'

'What, you think it might be connected?'

'I don't know,' Sam said. 'We have to take it seriously, though.'

Lorna started crying again. 'And Carl might end up the same way?'

'I don't know,' Sam said. 'But knowing everything might help us get to him in time.'

Lorna shook her head. 'No, I don't know anything. He was secretive, like his father. I didn't really look in his files. Just the odd glimpse.'

'Files?'

'Yes. My husband made files of whatever it was he was looking into. I didn't pry. He told me it was police work. When he disappeared, Carl did the same.'

'And still you didn't look?'

'Not properly. It was just old statements, that's all. To do with that Aidan man, Aidan Molloy, the one who killed that woman on the moors.'

'Where are the files now?'

'Your brother has them all.'

Sam gave her hands another squeeze. He hadn't wanted to involve Joe, not after Hunter's dig about him, but Sam knew there was no choice now. Joe's case and his case were linked.

It was time to speak to his brother.

Forty

As soon as Joe turned his phone back on, he saw that there was a message from his office. He rang as he approached the prison doors, Mary still outside, pacing, waiting for him.

'Hi, Marion; it's Joe.'

'Mr Parker, the woman you spoke to earlier has called. Nicole. She wants to speak to you again.'

Joe smiled to himself. It was the young mother who had found Rebecca Scarfield, along with her husband, Dan. Joe had known she would call, although it had come quicker than he expected. Despite the fact she had stayed silent earlier, her body language had told him that she disagreed with her husband, even though he had been speaking for her. He made a note of her number and called her before he got outside, not wanting Mary to hear it.

She told Joe that he had to meet her away from the house, so that Dan would never guess she had spoken to him. He told her he would be there in half an hour.

When Joe got outside, Mary turned, her face expectant.

'How is he?' she said.

'Like I expected. Angry, bitter, but you know all of that.'

'So what now?'

'I've got to see someone.'

266

'Connected with the case?'

'Yes.'

'Can I come with you?'

Joe thought about that. He needed to keep Mary onside but he didn't want her to frighten Nicole away.

'If you keep your distance,' he said.

'Why should I?'

'Because I've spoken to her once already, and her husband took over. There's something she wants to tell me. Let's not scare her off.'

'Who is it?'

'Nicole Grant.'

Mary nodded to herself, she recognised the name, and agreed.

Mary was quiet on the walk back to his car, and during the journey to Nicole's, although Joe could feel the sense of expectation that she was trying to hold back now that the glimmer of hope was shining a little brighter. He told her about David Jex, how it seemed that his brother had found him, and that brought more life into her conversation. But as they got closer to Nicole's, her shutters went up again and her public face returned: the survivor.

When they arrived in Nicole's village, he pulled over where Nicole had told him. He turned to Mary.

'Wait in the car. I'll tell you everything she tells me, but if you come over, she might clam up. Be patient.'

Mary stayed silent as Joe got out of his car and went to sit on a park bench.

He waited for thirty minutes, and had started

to wonder whether he had got her directions wrong, when he saw her walking towards him, her head down, her hands thrust into the pockets of her jacket.

She didn't say anything when she sat down next to him, so Joe stayed staring ahead, watching the sway of the branches of the trees that towered over the bench. She would talk eventually, he knew that. She had called him.

'Thank you for seeing me,' Nicole said after a few minutes. She was chewing gum, her jaw fast and nervous. 'I can't stay too long. I've left Matthew with a friend.'

'Where's Dan?'

'Playing snooker. He'll back for his tea, so I can't hang about.'

They were in a park just up the hill from Nicole's house, a wide patch of green with some wooden climbing frames set in bark chippings, the stone houses surrounding it set against the green hills behind it, looking away from the dark brood of the Pennines and towards the more gentle roll of industrial West Yorkshire.

She looked around. 'I bring Matthew here sometimes, when I need some fresh air.'

'I don't blame you, it's a nice spot,' Joe said, not rushing her.

She turned to Joe. 'Do you really think Aidan Molloy might be innocent?'

Joe looked at her. Her hands were in her lap, her fingers clasped together. Her eyes looked heavy, a flush to her cheeks giving away that she had shed some tears since his visit earlier.

'I don't know, truly,' Joe said. 'All I know is that

I've spoken to people I trust and they think he is.'

'Which means that he's in prison for something he didn't do, because of something we said.'

'And more than that,' Joe said. 'It means that the real killer is still out there, still posing a threat.'

Nicole sighed and put her head back. 'This is never going to end, is it?'

'Cases like this never do. He won't be released if he won't admit his guilt, and there is no chance of that, so he'll carry on waking up behind bars. I've met his mother.' He tried not to give away that she was watching from his car parked just further along the road. 'She's a fighter who won't give in.'

Nicole stayed silent.

Joe turned round to her, his knee on the bench. 'You said something strange just then.'

'What do you mean?' Nicole said, her voice suspicious.

'You said Aidan was in prison because of something you said.'

'Yes. That's right, isn't it?'

'But why didn't you say that it was because of something you saw? Not said. Unless, of course, what you saw was different to what you said.'

Nicole slumped forward and lifted her hand to her eye to wipe away a tear. 'I won't get in trouble, will I?'

Joe was keener now. There was something here. 'I don't know. I can't promise anything, but isn't this about doing the right thing?'

She exhaled loudly and her lip trembled. 'I don't want to go to prison. I've got a young child and I didn't mean to do anything wrong.'

'Talk to me, Nicole.'

'Dan will be angry.'

'Sometimes you've got to tell the truth.'

Nicole took a deep breath and said, 'We got the car wrong.'

Joe's eyes widened. He knew the importance of the car, and the partial registration. It was a key part of the case.

'Tell me about that night,' he said softly, trying to hide his excitement that something new was coming out. 'I'm not writing anything down. It's just you and me.'

Nicole let the silence drag on, broken only by the loud giggle of a small girl on a swing.

'Dan and I didn't live together then,' she said eventually. 'We had to find places if we wanted some privacy.' She blushed. 'You know how it is.'

'So you were looking for somewhere quiet?'

'I'm not ashamed. We were younger, just having fun, and there's a track you can drive down with some old derelict cottage at the bottom. It says private but the gate was never locked, and you only had to go a short distance to be hidden from the road. We used to go up there a lot, but we stopped after we found her, Rebecca. It didn't feel right after that.'

'So what did you see?'

'It was just like Dan said. We were pulling in but there was a car already there. We stopped, but then someone ran to the car and drove away really quickly. He almost scraped our car as he went past and headed towards Manchester, not the way we'd come. When we drove further in, our head-lights caught Rebecca.' She shook her head. 'It was awful. It was just as if she'd been dumped

270

there like an old mattress. I'll never forget it.'

'So what did you get wrong?'

'The car. We got the car wrong.'

'But Dan seemed so certain.'

'I know. He is, but he wasn't at the time, and now he's convinced himself.'

'So tell me.'

'It wasn't a blue Astra, like we said. It was a red Ford Focus.'

'That's quite a difference.'

'It wasn't bright red. A dark red, and with a quick look in the dark you might say it was dark blue. And they are similar-looking hatchbacks.'

'So it could have been a blue Astra?'

Nicole shook her head. 'I might be a woman but I know about cars. I like them, always have, but why would I know? I'm just the woman who gets ignored in car showrooms; the salesmen talk to Dan, even if I'm the one who's buying. So why listen to me when I said it wasn't a blue Astra?'

'But if you were so certain?'

'I got scared and doubted myself. That detective explained it that way; it was dark and a quick glimpse and perhaps I was wrong. The killer has a blue Astra, so I backed down. He told me that he would get away with it if I created doubt, and that he was the killer and we had to stick to the story or else he would be freed to do it again.'

'But your car was wrong.'

'I know, but Dan was less sure than I was. He didn't get as good a view because he was driving and then he was distracted by the body. I watched the car for longer and I know what I saw.' She wiped her eyes. 'So I lied, and Dan said that I was doing the right thing. The police said I was doing the right thing. How could I live with letting Rebecca's murderer go free just because I said it was a different car? He might have swapped cars or borrowed one.'

'What about the partial registration?'

Nicole shook her head. 'We didn't get a partial registration. Not really anyway. The police told us what the letters might have been and we just went along with it.'

'The car was part of the jigsaw,' Joe said. 'You were a witness. All you had to do was tell the truth and let the facts determine the outcome.'

She looked at Joe, suspicion in her eyes. 'It's different for people like you,' she said. 'It's all a game. The police said we were making sure a murderer stayed locked up and that we would stop him from doing it again. How could we fight against that?'

'Who was the officer?'

Nicole thought for a moment. 'Hunter,' she said.

He should have guessed.

'Will I get into trouble?' she said.

He thought about that. He could lie and say no, that justice would prevail, but he couldn't do that. Five years earlier she was certain it was a blue Astra. Now she was certain it was a red Focus. All that was certain was that she had lied.

But it wasn't enough to get Aidan out of prison. No, he had to find out more – perhaps even find the real killer – and for that he needed something more than a person who changed her mind a few years later.

Forty-one

Emma had stayed silent for a long time. Whether she was groggy, or was just trying to work out what had happened, Carl wasn't sure, but she had stayed curled up against the wall. He had tried pleading with her to speak, to remove the noose, but she had remained silent.

He jumped when she said, 'Is there a light in here?'

'There's a lamp on a table just over there,' he said.

Emma made her way carefully to it, the table moving with a scrape as she found it. She felt around the base before finding the switch. Carl squinted into the glare. He could only guess at how he looked, standing with a noose around his neck.

'Help me, please,' he said.

She went as if to rush over to him, but she gasped and put her hand to head. 'My head hurts,' she said. 'And I'm so cold.'

She put her arms around herself, as if to warm herself, and then went to him. She pulled at the rope, loosening the knot and slipping it over his head. He sank to his knees in relief, gasping and falling to one side, enjoying the feel of the cold floor against his cheek. His legs felt like they were on fire as they got used to not taking his weight, blood flowing through his cramped muscles again.

'Thank you,' he said.

He moved his head to get a better view of her. She was on her knees, huddled, rocking backwards and forwards, her teeth chattering.

'I think he threw my coat in the corner over there,' Carl said. 'It will keep you warm, and, well, you know, cover you up.'

Emma nodded and walked quickly over to the opposite corner of the cellar. She found Carl's coat and put it on. She was slim and the coat was too big for her, so she was able to cover herself up properly. She wrapped it tightly around her body, her mousey hair trailing over the collar.

'Thank you,' she said, and ran to the stairs. When she got to the top, she pulled on the door handle, but it was no good. The door was locked. She banged against it with her shoulder, but the door didn't move. She sat down on the top step with her head in her hands and started to cry. 'What's going on?' she shouted through the tears, and stamped her foot twice, before whimpering with pain.

Carl let her cry for a while before he said, 'He thinks you're dead.' She stopped crying for a moment and looked down at him. 'That's why you're here. He was going to get rid of you later.'

'Dead? But why?'

'Because you were going to leave him.'

She shook her head in disbelief. 'What a fucking mess,' she said, more to herself than to Carl. Then she looked across the cellar. 'And why are you here, like that? Is this some kind of sick game?'

'I got too close, so he locked me up. He hasn't decided what to do with me yet. I think he's going to kill me but I'm different to you.'

'How?'

'I'm not a woman.'

'It's as simple as that?'

'It seems that way.'

Emma paused as she thought about that. Then she walked over to him and knelt down opposite. She stayed silent for a few minutes and Carl didn't try to interrupt her thoughts. Eventually she said, 'So tell me what you know?'

And Carl did. He explained to her about his father and why he had ended up at the man's house and then in the cellar, with a dead woman to start off with and how he had watched the man drag Emma down the stairs.

'He must think he killed you, but for some reason he got it wrong.'

'There was something in my drink. One minute we're dancing, the next I'm down here.' Her hand went to her throat. 'It hurts,' and then, 'What now?'

Carl thought about what the man would do when he came back into the cellar, and he knew that there was only one thing he would do: kill her. 'We need to sit and wait for him to come back, then hopefully surprise him. Can you find anything to break these chains with?'

Emma went looking through the shelves, lifting up tins of paint and boxes of weedkiller. 'It's just household stuff.' She carried on searching before shouting out in pain, lifting her foot. She winced and bent down. 'There's broken glass down here.'

Carl closed his eyes in apology. The glass he had smashed earlier.

Emma carried on looking around the shelves until she said, 'No, nothing.'

She knelt down next to Carl and pulled the coat closer to herself. 'So what do we do?'

'We wait, I suppose.'

They both stayed in silence for a few minutes, until Carl said, 'Who is he?'

Emma thought about that for a few moments. 'I don't know really,' she said. 'He told me he was called Declan, but I don't know if I believe that any more. Most of what he told me wasn't true. Why should I believe his name?'

'So how did it start?'

Emma looked at him and said, 'What do you mean?'

'My dad went missing because of whatever this Declan does. If I'm going to understand this, I need to know how it works.'

'How old are you?'

'Fifteen.'

'So you won't understand.'

'My father is missing and I want to know everything about this man, so I can try to understand that at least.'

When Emma didn't respond, Carl said, 'He told me that he's a collector, whatever that means, and that once he collects, he doesn't give up.'

'That's about right,' Emma said, almost to herself, her lips curled into a snarl. 'It's not too difficult to imagine, is it, even for someone of your age. Good old-fashioned flattery, and I fell for it. I feel so stupid.'

'Tell me more.'

Emma was quiet again for a few minutes, until

she said, 'I work in a pub in the city centre. Nothing special. It's a cliché, isn't it, a barmaid going out with a customer? But Declan wasn't like the usual drunken crowd.'

'How?'

'He was intelligent, thoughtful, well-dressed. He's big but there's something soft about him. No, not soft. Feminine. He always wore nice jumpers and shirts, and it was his shoes I noticed. Always brown brogues, with leather soles. I could tell they were expensive, but nothing flashy. Declan was always expensive but understated. It just marked him out as different.'

'So what made him choose your pub?'

'I don't know. He just came in one lunchtime and started drinking and talking. I thought at first he was trying to be cool by hanging around with people who he thought were beneath him, but he made an effort. He seemed interested in people, didn't seem to look down on anyone, and he knew stuff. It's hard to explain, but he would just seem to know about whatever people were interested in. He seemed to latch onto me straight away. I don't know what it was. My shifts changed and he started coming in the evenings. Never getting drunk. Just sitting at the end of the bar, drinking quietly, and I would end up talking to him. He was interesting, but it was more than that. He was interested in me. Wanted to know about me.' She shrugged and looked down, embarrassed. 'I was flattered. How stupid is that?'

'So you became his girlfriend?'

She thrust her hands into the coat pockets. 'Not straight away. I'm married. Two children. I love my husband, I really do, but it was too safe. You'll understand this when you're older. He does his thing, I do mine, and we both make sure the children are all right, but I felt taken for granted, ignored, and there was Declan. Always telling me how nice I looked, always interested in me, and I liked it. It's vain and it's silly, I know, but when you get complimented all the time you don't want it to stop. It wasn't long before he started asking me out.'

'What about your children? I'd be hurt if my mum did that.'

'Don't judge me, Carl. That's not fair. You don't know anything about life. I said no for a long time, months really, but he seemed determined. He got my number from somewhere and would text me constantly. Late at night and in the morning. I fought it for a while but then he told me he wouldn't accept my refusal, and soon it got to the point where I didn't want him to stop. You might understand this more when you're older, but sometimes it's just nice to hear good things said about you when your life is all about working and making meals and watching television. So eventually, well, I'm sure you can guess.'

'So how did it come to this, where he tried to kill you?' Carl asked. 'He said it was because you were going to leave him.'

Emma wiped away a tear that snaked down her cheek. 'I had to end it, and he didn't understand. When I first started seeing him, he was a real gentleman, and it got pretty intense. He told me he could take me away from everything, that all I had to do was give myself up to him. I just couldn't get enough of him. I thought of him all the time, but then he started to change.'

'How?'

'He knew my situation, right, I told him that. I didn't want to leave my husband, but he wanted me to, and you have no idea how exhilarating it is to have a man want you so much. But then he got more demanding. Too demanding. He wanted me to do things that I didn't like. Sexual stuff. You wouldn't understand, you're too young, and I wouldn't leave my husband. It sounds hollow, but my family comes first every time. I just wanted to be cherished. Is that so wrong?'

'So what happened?'

Emma raised a hand to her face and wiped away more tears. 'I caught him out, just by chance. I had a night off when I was supposed to be at work, about a month ago, and I went for a drink with some friends. We went into a pub and I saw him at the bar, and he was talking to the barmaid just like he did with me. Attentive, smiling, and I could tell from her face that she was lapping it up, just like I had. I felt such a fool. He had wanted me to give up everything for him, but I was just another woman, part of a game. I almost lost everything because of him.'

'So what did you do?'

'I told him that I didn't want anything more to do with him. I was staying with my husband.' Her toes traced circles on the concrete floor as she thought about it. 'I'd seen him for what he is, the devil sitting on a married woman's shoulder, whispering, nudging, persuading her to join him in his soulless life. That's what he is, an empty shell. He just wants to destroy what other people have and that he knows he never can. He is just dead inside; he knows it and it kills him.' She shook her head. 'I told him he had sold his soul. He got angry because he knew it was true.'

'But why were you here last night if you had ended it?'

'Do you think he was going to let me just walk away?' she said, her voice raised. 'Everything had to be on his terms. I wasn't allowed to be in charge. I've met him a couple of times since, to end it, but it always come back to the same thing, that he won't let me leave.'

'Last night?'

She looked down, embarrassed. 'I was going to have one last night with him and show him that I could use him, let him know what he was going to miss out on, and then walk away.'

'But you didn't.'

'No,' she said. 'I woke up here.' She looked at Carl and wiped her eyes. 'So what now?'

'We try to get out. Use that broken glass. Attack him with it.'

'How can I do that? He's big and strong and I feel awful. I don't know what he put in my drink.'

'We do have one big advantage though.'

'Which is what?'

'He thinks you're dead. So he's going to get a surprise when he realises you're not.'

Forty-two

Mary Molloy was quiet as they headed back to Manchester. Joe had told her what Nicole had confessed – that the police had talked them into putting Aidan's number plate into the statement – and Mary's anger increased. She sat with her knees pressed closely together in the passenger seat, her tan leather handbag perched on top with her fingers gripping the handles.

Joe tried to make small talk but Mary barely responded, just yes and no. It was only when they left some of the clutter of West Yorkshire behind and started up the long motorway rise towards the Pennine tops that she prompted a conversation.

'Can you see how hard it is for Aidan now?' she said, staring forward, her jaw clenched. 'You've had proof from her that his case was based on lies. Aidan has to live with that every day.'

'I saw,' Joe said. 'Angry, resentful, but resigned in some way to his fate, that not much is going to get him out of there.' He glanced across. 'A bit like you.'

Mary looked back, some flare in her eyes, but as she turned away to look out of the passenger window, Joe knew that she was fighting with herself to keep it together. Out of the corner of his eye, he saw her brush the long sweep of her hair to one side and wipe at her eye.

The motorway droned on, all the towns gone

and replaced by rolling green hills and meandering lines of drystone walls. The sunlight twinkled on a reservoir surface. Mary turned to look forward.

'It's hard for Aidan,' she said quietly. 'Every day is wrong for him. He is scared and angry. How can anyone live their life like that?'

Joe noticed how her Irish lilt became more pronounced when she spoke softly. When she was talking tough, her accent became blunted by the years she had spent in England, but when she softened, and became more of the woman she had been before her son's injustice had toughened her up, a bit more of Ireland returned.

'I don't know,' Joe said.

She fell silent again, lost in the worries she had for her son, Joe's involvement being one more fight in a life of fighting, and it stayed that way for the rest of the journey.

The motorway came off the high points and the drive turned into a long descent into grey sprawl, the fast sweep becoming the stop-start of city traffic as Joe turned off. The journey ended with grids of terraced streets whose names were familiar to Joe from filling out criminal legal aid forms. The area was just layers of immigration, first settled by the Irish and slowly fleshed out by families from Asia and then Africa. Joe stopped outside a small terraced house whose bricks had been painted with anti-graffiti paint.

'It's to stop people daubing things on,' Mary said, following Joe's gaze.

'Why don't you move?'

'Why should I? I've nothing to be ashamed of.

And neither has Aidan.' She turned to Joe. Her face looked stern but there was pleading in her eyes. 'So what now?'

'I just keep digging and see what I can find.'

'I've been looking for longer than you,' Mary said. 'Why do you think you can do better?'

'I don't know if I can, but this case has come to me for a reason.'

Mary looked back at her house. 'I didn't want my life to be this hard,' she said. 'I've done some things I shouldn't have done, and I've taken knocks, but this?' She shook her head and let out a long sigh. 'I used to think that it made me more interesting, like who would you want dinner with: Johnny Cash or Cliff Richard? But now? I think I've put up with enough.'

'Tell me your story,' Joe said. 'What brought you to England?'

She paused as she thought about that. 'Escape,' she said. 'And Aidan.'

'What do you mean?'

'It's an old, old story.'

'I'd like to hear it.'

'What is there to tell?'

'Where are you from and why are you here?'

'On the edge of Dublin, on the way out to a little place by the sea called Howth.' Her eyes misted over as she thought back. 'I was eighteen and got myself a job in a pub. The Green Dolphin. All the men used to pour in there after Mass, and there I was, all innocence and smiles, and in he walked. Fergus. He was tall and dark and his smile was just too easy. I fell for him.' She rolled her eyes. 'I had to fall for the married one, and you can work out

283

how that went down. Fergus is Aidan's father.'

'If it's too private, you don't have to tell me.'

'I know, but you'll understand then how I am like I am. I believed what Fergus told me. He made me promises, told me that we were meant to be together, that he didn't love his wife any more, and I believed him. It feels like it's always been that way, that those close to me let me down.' She allowed herself a little smile. 'There's a beach nearby, at Dollymount. Sand dunes and grass and a view towards Dublin. I loved it there. We'd all go there, me and my friends, and those dunes were our own little Lovers' Lane. And Fergus would take me there in his car, this orange Mazda. I can still see it in my head. The feel of its seat under my skin, the squeaky vinyl. That summer was just the best ever. I was besotted.'

Her eyes had become animated as she talked about it, but then they darkened when she said, 'It changed when I got pregnant. He became cold, wouldn't talk to me. He made his peace with his priest and his wife and that's all that seemed to matter to him. I was nineteen. A single woman carrying a married man's child.'

'So what did you do?'

'I did the one thing you aren't supposed to do if you're a good Catholic girl from Ireland: I decided to get an abortion. It was the best thing. For me. For Fergus. Even for his wife, so that she wouldn't see his child being pushed around in a pram.'

'I don't know much about Ireland,' Joe said, 'but that doesn't sound like an easy thing to do.'

'It wasn't. Still isn't. I had to come to England

284

for it, except my mother found out why I was going and, well, things got a little crazy. She screamed at me. My father hit me, the first time he had ever done that. The things they said to me were awful. Truly awful. Child killer, evil little woman, marriage-wrecker, and I expected it, but it hurt the same. My older brother attacked Fergus in the pub. The priest was round all the time, trying to talk me out of it and telling me that the sin of carrying a married man's child was nowhere near the sin of killing it. I was nineteen, for Christ's sake, with enough to worry about, and all this on top. I had to leave, get away, just to get some breathing space. They told me that if I had the abortion, I was gone from the family for ever and that they could never forgive me.' She looked down and swallowed. When she looked up again, she had choked back the tears. 'So that was it.'

'What, they turned away from you completely?'

'I was preparing to kill the unborn child of a married man. You have no idea how that sort of thing went down in Ireland back then. Even now. So that was it for me too. I turned my back on them; I was going to make it alone. I stepped off the ferry at Holyhead with all my savings in my purse, just a few hundred pounds, some daft young woman in a floppy hat not knowing where the hell to go or what to do.'

'Why did you come to Manchester?'

'I had friends in London and my parents would look for me there first, if they ever got the urge, but I knew someone who'd moved here and that there was an Irish community of sorts. I reckoned I could just lose myself here.' She gave a little laugh. 'It was only meant to be short term. I had this dream that I would get the abortion and then see the world. Maybe an apartment in New York overlooking Central Park, because once I was no longer pregnant I could go wherever I wanted. The world was at my feet.'

'But you didn't have an abortion. You had Aidan.'

Mary nodded. 'I backed out. I'd travelled to England, with my family hating me for it, but I couldn't do it. I thought at first it was because I'd had the evil of it knocked into me by the nuns all of my life, but it was something different to that. It was about the life I had growing inside me, the one part of Fergus I could still hold onto. So I had the baby. Aidan.' She took a deep breath. 'I never told my parents. I didn't want them to know. They were prepared to turn their backs on me, and as far as they knew, I'd had the abortion and I wasn't welcome any more.'

'But if you'd told them what you'd done, that you'd given birth, it would have been all right, wouldn't it?'

'Probably, but it became about how they had treated me, not how they had been right all along.'

'Did Aidan ever ask about them?'

'Of course he did, but I couldn't go back, even though I had done what they wanted, had the baby. I was stubborn, and a couple of years just became a couple of decades.'

Joe sighed. Criminal law usually had some family dysfunction as a background, but for some reason Mary's story got to him. 'Do you miss them?' he said. 'Do you want to see them again?'

Mary nodded, tearful again. 'But the things they said. My brother, Stephen, he did a piece in one of the papers after Aidan was sent to prison, saying how he should have been aborted, how Rebecca would still be alive if I had stuck to my reason for leaving. He made it all my fault.'

'The papers might have twisted that.'

'Perhaps, but it hurt.'

Joe reached across and put his hand over hers. 'So we'll prove them wrong. We'll get Aidan out and look at rebuilding whatever you've left behind.'

Her lip trembled. 'You'd do that for me?'

'I'm trying to do the right thing, for me. So yes, I would.'

'I'd like that,' she said, wiping tears away from her eyes with her fingertips. 'My parents are getting old now. I just want to sit on Dollymount Beach and listen to the slow ripple of the sea, feel the salt thicken my hair. I want to see my daddy smiling at me, and not with the disappointment and anger he had when I left. But too much has been said, too much time gone past.'

'Let's finish this first,' Joe said. 'I promise I won't let you down. No one should have to make it alone, Mary.'

She looked him in the eyes. 'Some of us have to,' she said. 'And that's the hard thing. Aidan going to prison is bigger than anything I've gone through before. If I begin to trust you and you then let me down, I'm not sure I'll recover.'

Joe knew then that he carried a heavy responsibility. 'I'll do what I can,' he said.

Mary nodded her approval and patted him on

the hand as she climbed out of his car. As he drove away, Joe saw in his rear-view mirror that she didn't loiter on the street. She walked quickly across the pavement and into her house. It gave Joe a sense of her isolation in her own community and for the first time he started to admire her.

Her whole adult life had been a struggle, but she wasn't giving in.

Forty-three

Sam had found himself a quiet room in the station, trying to avoid Evans. He was supposed to be off-duty. He couldn't clock off yet though, despite what had been said. The case was still his, the body he discovered, and he wanted to see it through as much as he could.

It was the room used by the old tape librarian, where old interview tapes were stored on shelves that ran around the room. The shelves were empty now: the tapes stored off-site since the use of digital interviews. The room was bare, apart from a small brown chair and a desk that bore the scratches of cufflinks and watches and rings from where defence lawyers and prosecutors had rested their hands as they counter-signed the self-seal strips that wrapped around the boxes, when the opening of a master tape had to be witnessed to prove that there had been no tampering with evidence.

It rankled with Sam sometimes, how protection

for criminals meant mistrust of the police, but the pages of history told how power could be abused whenever people were left to do the job however they felt like it.

He closed his eyes for a moment, just to rest them, but sleep swamped him, his head drooping to his chest, until the images rushed back at him, but distorted by dreams. The dig was different. The chop of his spade was louder, more frantic, and then David Jex was still alive, his hands reaching upwards, his mouth open, soil filling it slowly.

Sam jerked awake. He groaned. His legs were twitchy from fatigue.

His phone buzzed in his pocket. When he answered, it was Alice.

'Hi,' he said, his voice husky.

'What are you doing?' she said.

'Just keeping an eye on things down here,' he said. 'Has there been anything on the news yet?'

'It's on the radio but only a brief report on the television.' A pause. 'You need to come home, Sam.'

'I can't yet. Not until I've seen it through.'

'You need to stop doing this.'

'Doing what?'

'Pushing yourself so hard. I can hear it in your voice. Let other people take over. Please, Sam. You'll just wear yourself out one day. And the girls want to see you.' She must have heard the reluctance in the long pause, as she said, 'Meet me later. Just have a break.'

He rubbed his face to take some of the sleep away. 'Okay. But I've got to speak to Joe as well. He's got some information on the case.'

Alice went quiet for a moment. 'Don't just fit us in,' she said. 'That's not fair. We'll still be here, needing you when this case is done and finished. Just remember that. It's just another case.'

Sam closed his eyes and pinched his nose with his fingers. He wanted to say that it wasn't just another case, that every victim deserved his efforts, and the memory of seeing David Jex's laminated badge wouldn't leave him. Someone just like him, taken away and perhaps never meant to be found again. Until now. But why?

But she was right. He needed to see Erin and Amy too. Every day that he couldn't kiss them goodnight was one he knew he would regret.

But until he found out the reason behind it all and was able to tell Lorna Jex the truth, Sam knew he wouldn't rest.

Joe took his car home and walked to his office, enjoying the few extra moments where he wasn't cooped inside, dodging the attention of the senior partner. It was always good to feel the warmth of the sun, a pleasant break from the indoor office routine, although the memory of Mary Molloy hung heavily. Aidan had become more than just an old case.

His phone rang in his pocket as he strolled through the small park near his office, glancing across at Monica's bench, as always.

It was Sam.

'So you're speaking to me now?' Joe said, remembering how he had been cut off earlier.

'I've just had your client's mother here,' Sam said, his tone sombre.

Joe closed his eyes. He'd hardly thought of the impact on her. It had become all about the case.

'Lorna, how is she?' Joe said, although he didn't need to be told that she was distraught.

'As you might expect,' Sam said, and added, 'We need to talk.'

'What about?'

'Your case. About Carl. Everything seems linked somehow.'

'All right,' Joe said. 'I'll give you a call to let you know when I'm free. I'd rather do it informally.'

'So you can deny the confidentiality breach later?'

'Something like that,' he said, and clicked off the phone.

He clinked through the small gate and walked quickly for the last few yards to his office, trudging up the pale stone steps. As he got inside, the reception desk was unmanned, Marion elsewhere. There was laughter along one of the corridors, and as Joe got closer he couldn't stop his smile. He recognised Hugh Bramwell's low boom.

As Joe went through the door towards the sounds of conversation, Hugh was talking to Marion and some of the secretaries and for a moment Joe saw some of the old flirt, the friendly old man whose spark had been extinguished by his wife's death.

Hugh turned as Joe got closer. He beamed. 'Hello again, Joe. How's your head?'

'Was foggy this morning,' Joe said. 'Just passing?'

'No. I've come to see you.'

'Me? So soon? People will talk.'

'It's about what we discussed last night.'

Joe caught the interested glances of Marion and the secretaries, so gestured for Hugh to follow. As he set off walking, their laughs faded as Hugh parted with one last flirt before he caught up with Joe.

'Thank you for last night,' Hugh said.

'What do you mean?'

'Just talking about the old days again. Or at least a case. I've missed it.'

'You said you didn't.'

'I was a lawyer for nearly forty years. It was a big part of me.'

'And you got home and thought just about the good parts and fancied some more of the action?'

They turned into Joe's office. Gina was at the end of the corridor watching as Joe closed the door.

'Some of that,' Hugh said. 'But the house is lonely and empty. I know that's partly my fault.'

'For your wife dying? Hardly.'

'No, for the fact that it fell so silent when she went. I've got two grown-up children, but they don't stay in touch that much. I feel like I'm the man they don't really know, because I spent too much time here. I dressed it up as putting food on the table or getting them nice things, but it wasn't. It was all about being here. Fighting cases. This was where the planning was done, the strategies, the groundwork. The courtroom was all about the battle, the punch and counter, the misdirection, the fake punch to disguise the body blow. I gave up my family for it. And I miss it.'

'That makes me sad,' Joe said.

'Me too, but it's all I have left. The family battle is already lost.' Hugh looked over to the desk. 'Can I?'

'Of course,' Joe said, and gestured with his hand that Hugh could take another look around.

Hugh ran his fingers over the wood and the green leather inlay and smiled nostalgically. He sat down and turned the chair so he could see out of the window, his enjoyment of the familiar creak obvious on his face.

'It hasn't changed,' he said, his voice distant.

'I used to like it for the same reasons you do,' Joe said. 'Not for much longer though.'

'I know. The world changes. People of my generation milked the system for too long, and you're getting the rebound.'

'Milked?'

'It wasn't hard to make a good living from legal aid, but some got too good at it. Calling lawyers greedy is easy, so we were always going to be the first to suffer when the money got tighter.' He leaned forward, Joe sitting in the client's chair, a wide wooden seat with leather pads to match the desk.

'So is this just about nostalgia?' Joe said.

Hugh looked up. 'Not really. I want in.'

'In?'

'Yes, I want to help, in Aidan Molloy's case. Be involved again. Think about it, Joe. I know more about the case than you do. You've read a file, spoken to a few people, but you know that a case is more than what is written down. It's also about impressions and people and rumours and sometimes what you think is the real truth, that middle

293

ground between what the statements say and what the client tells you, and none of that comes from those dusty pages.'

'We can't pay you.'

'I'm doing it for me, and for Aidan. I don't need the money.'

Joe grinned. 'Welcome back.'

Hugh sat back and clapped with delight. 'Right. What have we got so far?'

Joe told him about the change in the vehicle seen up on the moors, pulling away.

'So what's next?'

'The three young girls who said they'd overheard Aidan threatening to kill Rebecca. I'm going to see them.'

Hugh grimaced. 'You need to be careful with those three.'

'What do you mean?'

'They were stroppy little madams. They enjoyed the limelight, and they won't take kindly to you saying they got it wrong. And anyway, does it matter? So what if Aidan threatened to kill her? It doesn't mean he did. What will you gain if you speak to them? A complaint to the police and for no real advantage, that's what.'

'But they might admit being pressurised into saying what they did by Hunter. One more strand of evidence gone.'

'They won't. I saw how they were.'

Joe frowned. 'Only one thing for it then. The most difficult visit of all. Rebecca Scarfield's home.'

Hugh was surprised, his eyes wide. 'His victim?'

Joe nodded. 'We need to speak to her husband.'

'You have her address?'

'No, but I know a woman who will.'

Hugh jumped to his feet, dangling his car keys. 'I'll drive.'

Forty-four

He clutched his head and looked down. He threw his phone across the desk. He was getting updates on what was happening, but they just made the vibrations stronger. People were looking at him, he could tell. Every time he looked up, he caught the quick movement of people glancing away.

'Are you all right?' a voice said.

He looked up. 'Just a migraine,' he said, and tried to focus once more. But he couldn't escape the pounding sound, like a steady thump, thump.

He tried to focus on something else. Something ordinary that would calm the noise in his head, but his mind went back to Emma. He tried to think of happier times, when they had been close, but every thought took him back to the night before. The feel of her throat under his hands, the sound of her feet on the floor, kicking and struggling.

But she hadn't struggled. No, that was someone else. He grimaced as the memories came back.

His parents. That's who it always came back to. The arguments, the drinking, but that night had been more than that.

It had started as an argument, his mother drunk, his father shouting. He had stayed in his room and put his hands over his ears. But it didn't end the usual way, with the sound of his mother's cries as his father beat her, his fists raining down in some blind-drunk fury. There had been a scream, as always, but it was cut short. Then the sound of furniture being knocked around. He thought he heard a table knocked over, a vase smashed, but there were no more screams.

He had tried to stay away, not because he was scared of his father's rage turning on him, but because he couldn't bear the shame in his mother's eyes whenever it happened. Why should she feel like that? But the silence had gone on for too long.

He had crept down the stairs and slowly pushed open the living-room door.

He flinched as the memories came back to him. His mother's feet sticking out from behind the sofa and kicking against the floor. His father over her, saliva hanging down from his mouth, his teeth bared, sweat glistening from the glow of the fire.

Then her feet had stopped moving and the room fell silent.

He had listened for a sound that told him everything was all right, that it was just another fight. He had been desperate to hear her scream, to strike back, to cry out at the weight of his fist, just anything. There was nothing.

His father came towards him and he had braced himself to be hit, but his father just walked past and went upstairs.

When he was alone in the room, he went to his mother. As he looked down, he saw how she had died. Her blouse was torn in the struggle, but already there were bruises on her neck.

He lay next to her, his head on her breast and his arm across her, not long enough to reach all the way.

All she'd had to do was leave.

He opened his eyes quickly. His heart was beating fast and there was sweat around his collar. His life became a lie from then on. His mother had gone missing, or so the story had gone. His father had provided the narrative – she was an alcoholic, had been depressed, and one day she left the house and never came back. That was what he was told to say, and he couldn't afford to lose both his parents.

The young man in his cellar had made everything different. He had to plan the rest of his day. He had made some preparations, knowing it would come eventually, but still it was hard to think that he'd be leaving the house. So much had happened there.

There were still things he had to do first. He reached for his phone and went to his contact list. He dialled. When he heard the familiar voice, he said, 'I need an address.'

When he said whose address he wanted, there was silence for a few seconds, and then agreement, quiet and sullen.

He tapped his cheek with his phone when he hung up.

Those who hurt him got hurt back. That was how it worked.

Forty-five

Hugh and Joe headed out of the city, on their way to see Rebecca Scarfield's husband. Joe had spoken to Mary, and she'd told him that he worked for a car dealership. Joe had called ahead, to make sure he was there.

As Hugh drove, Joe turned to him and said, 'Hunter is a dominant figure in all of this.'

They were in Hugh's old champagne-coloured Mercedes coupé, a relic from the eighties that he had clung onto for no other reason than it had never let him down, with cream leather seats and a polished walnut steering wheel. No iPod docks or Bluetooth.

Hugh didn't respond at first. He just gripped the steering wheel and stared through the windscreen.

Eventually, he said, 'Hunter was a big part of the case. They used him in all the press conferences and reconstructions. He liked the cameras, and the attention. I think he fancied himself as someone the television people would use when he retired, like some kind of consultant.' He frowned. 'I remember one television reconstruction where he strode across some wasteland towards the camera, in a black shirt and long black trenchcoat, as if it was an audition, not an appeal for information.'

'Vain?'

'And some. But it wasn't just vanity. It was

298

about power, and I don't mean the power you get from promotions. It was the power over people, like he enjoyed their thrall. Now he's just like me, a figure from a different time.'

'I caught the back end of those times when I was training, but that was just Friday drinking,' Joe said.

'I remember those well,' Hugh said, rolling his eyes. 'That's what has changed. For all their bluster, and ours, we were all playing the same game. It was the Friday tradition back then, everyone to the pub for the afternoon, even though they were supposed to be on duty. A little cellar bar near St Ann's Square, and that would be the start of the weekend. We'd trade blows and spin tall tales and Hunter would sit in the middle on a high stool as the other detectives, his gang, boasted and bragged and drank.'

'I've heard some of the tales,' Joe said. 'I never knew if they were just urban myths.'

Hugh raised his eyebrows. 'No, they're not. And you'll have just heard the pub stories, the ones they boast about. The worst cases were the ones you never hear about. It was a different world, and Hunter was part of it.'

'Like what?'

'What do you think?' Hugh said. 'Beatings, sleep deprivation, threats against family. I heard of one instance where someone was hung out of a second-floor window.'

'They can't be true.'

'I heard too many things from too many clients to think otherwise. Spend some time with old retired detectives and you work out that you'll

299

only hear the stories they're prepared to share. Even I could work out the little bribes and deals, information exchanged for lesser charges, especially with the Drugs Squad. I'd be waiting for my client to have his flash and dabs, photographs and fingerprints, and he would emerge from some small room with a detective behind him, holding a pad full of notes.'

Joe gave a small laugh. 'Junkies just lose themselves, don't they? They help the police to keep them off their backs for all the thefts and burglaries and then they end up in court, happy to go to jail just to get away from their dealer for a while.'

'But legal empires are built on the back of them.'

'So is it better now, or then?'

Hugh pondered on that for a few seconds. 'There are some winners, some losers. The police are more professional now, but sometimes it pays to deal with criminals on their own terms. Crack some heads, kick down some doors. Everyone knew where they stood. Now, the criminals have the power.'

'Problem was that the lines got too blurred, so I heard. People were convicted of crimes they hadn't done. Aidan Molloy was only five years ago. Perhaps the times haven't changed as much as you think.'

'Times have. I'm just not sure Hunter has.'

Joe looked back out of the window. 'That is what I'll miss about the job. For every bit of crap and bureaucracy, there is some human drama that is interesting, an anecdote you can tell.'

Hugh glanced over quickly. 'Are you really

thinking of walking away?'

'I don't know what I'm going to do. I could learn to do some civil law, work in one of those accident factories by the motorway.'

'You'd suffocate.'

'I know that, but I've still got bills to pay.'

They carried on in silence for a while until Hugh said, 'If you stop practising, just make sure you give it up for something worthwhile. Don't leave it too late. Like I did.'

'You? You had it all.'

'Just a shell, Joe, just a shell. A nice house, two lovely children, a wife who kept everything together, financial security, but none of it means anything if you're not there to see it. Your children just want you there, to show you things, to tell you about their day. And Patricia too.'

'So why are you here? Go see your kids.'

'That battle has been lost. This is a battle I can still win.'

'Aidan Molloy? This is what it's all about for you, making up in some way for whatever went on before, proving your worth?'

'Isn't it for you, Joe? You're using him to get back your spark. So what are you going to do?'

'We look into Hunter.'

'But what difference will that make?'

'It might persuade some of these witnesses to break cover, if it gives them the chance to show how it was Hunter who manipulated things, changed them, told them what to say. We need someone who can give us more dirt on him. If we can find more cases where he has done it, then it might give the witnesses more confidence.'

301

'Someone on the inside?' Hugh said.

'Why not? It makes most sense.'

They drove in silence the rest of the way, until Hugh came to a stop. 'Here we are.'

Joe took a deep breath. They were outside a glass cube, with used cars lined up outside and new ones parked up inside. He wasn't looking forward to this. He turned to Hugh. 'Are you coming in?'

Hugh looked towards the showroom, his arms on his steering wheel, and shook his head. 'No, thank you. I'll sit this one out. I'll wait in the car.'

Joe followed his gaze. 'It's times like this when you realise the hurt the job creates. We're dealing with people's lives – not just a game, some theatre show.'

'It's Aidan's life too, don't forget that.'

'Good point,' Joe said, and stepped out of the car.

There were no other customers there as Joe walked inside. A smart young woman in a blue suit was sitting at a desk. She smiled and asked if she could help. Joe asked to speak to Roy Scarfield. When he came down from an office on the floor above, Joe handed him his card and suggested they spoke in private. Roy tapped the card against his knuckles and told Joe to follow him.

Roy was tall and slim, his hair cropped short and greying in patches. He had that car salesman swagger, clearly he thought that he could persuade anyone of anything.

'Thank you for seeing me,' Joe said, as they went into his office. It was a small room with a view over the showroom. Missives from head office fluttered on a corkboard. 'I want to talk about Rebecca, if you're okay with that, and Aidan Molloy.'

Roy sat down and his jaw tightened. He looked at the business card and then at Joe again. He gestured for Joe to sit down, and said, 'Why? Are you his lawyer now?'

'Yes. I'm looking into whether I can help Aidan with an appeal,' he said. He owed it to Roy not to feed him a line. Before Roy could ask him to leave, he added quickly, 'I'm not going to spend my time with someone who I think is guilty.'

'The jury said he was guilty.'

'I know, and if I thought they'd got it right, I'd walk away and let Aidan Molloy rot in his cell.'

He scowled. 'Lawyers don't do that.'

'This one does.'

Roy picked up a pen and started to tap it on the desk. Eventually, he said, 'So why do you think I'd be interested in helping you?'

'You'll want Rebecca's killer locked up.'

'He is. In Wakefield Prison.'

'I hope you're right, but my worry is that if he isn't, Aidan Molloy has wasted five years of his life.'

Roy pursed his lips at that. 'But why is anything I have to say important?' he said. 'It wasn't back then. I was just the poor sap they put in front of the cameras. That made me a suspect in many eyes and for as long as Aidan's mother campaigns, people wonder whether it was in fact me. Who am I but the jealous husband? For every bit of Aidan's case they start to unravel, it comes back to me. But just so you know – it wasn't me. I can look you in the eye and say that and I can look my children in the eyes and say that I had no part in her death.'

Joe knew there was some truth in what he said. If there was even a chance he could direct some blame towards Roy, he ought to do it. The law isn't about truth. It's about proof, and that can be undone by doubt, whether there was any truth in the doubt or not.

But this time Joe wasn't working an ordinary case. If this was going to be his farewell at Honeywells, he wanted to remove the shadow of Aidan's case before he left.

'I'm not thinking of pushing any blame towards you,' Joe said.

'So why do I matter all of a sudden?'

'What do you mean?'

'This. Your visit. Why are you interested in anything I have to say? No one was back then.' Roy shook his head, his anger increasing. 'Three weeks that trial lasted, and do you know how many times the prosecuting QC spoke to me, the victim's husband? None. That's how many. He spoke to Rebecca's parents, because that was sucking up to the assistant chief constable, but I didn't seem to matter.'

Joe sighed. Some senior barristers were like that. For them it was all about maintaining independence and not being swayed by emotive voices. Or so they said. Joe was sure that it was just one more case for them. Why get into the emotional stuff when you can get someone else to do it?

'It isn't right,' Joe said. 'But who knows more about Rebecca than you? This case is very much about Rebecca.'

'Yeah, right, like I knew her at all,' Roy said. He

leaned forward, his arms on the desk. He spoke quietly but there was menace in his tone. 'Rebecca was sleeping around. Okay, I get that. I've met someone else, moved on from that hurt, but knowing that the little bastard who was fucking her also took her away from me – and not just me but my two children – well, let's just say that I don't have much desire to set him free.'

'What if the only thing he did wrong was to get involved with Rebecca? He doesn't deserve a life sentence for that.'

Roy didn't answer that. Instead, he just breathed heavily through his nose and sat back again.

Joe spotted a framed picture on a shelf behind. There was a woman in it but she was nothing like the pictures he had seen of Rebecca in the file. Rebecca had been a redhead, her hair long and bright, her skin pale. The woman in the picture was darker, Mediterranean-looking. Roy was wearing a ring. He had remarried.

'So what is there that makes you think that he might not have done it?' Roy said eventually.

'I spoke to Aidan today,' Joe said. 'I believed in him. I've read what he said back then, that he was driving around on the night Rebecca died because he thought she was seeing someone else.'

'Yeah, so he said in the trial. Then again, he said a lot of things, and changed his story whenever something else came up.'

'He was scared and he panicked. He didn't want anyone to know he had been seeing Rebecca. She was married and he knew it was wrong.'

'So he's a liar.'

'Yes, he lied about being involved with her, but

305

that shouldn't get him a life sentence. And there are other things, too.' Joe hadn't wanted to disclose too much, but he wanted Roy to open up. 'Like the couple who saw the car pulling away. They might have got it wrong.'

Roy looked down. When he looked up again, some of the anger had gone from his eyes. 'Have you any idea what it's like to lose someone like that, where you can't help but think you're somehow to blame and that if you had behaved differently, she might still be alive?'

There it was. The slap that came back to him when he least expected it. Ellie flooded into his mind. He saw her walking home from school on his eighteenth birthday, turning into the wooded path, wearing headphones, oblivious to the man loitering further along. Just a man in a hooded top. Except Joe had seen him. He had watched him as he followed Ellie and he had done nothing. She was going to be all right. Everyone used that path.

Ellie never made it home and Joe had learned to cope with the guilt by blocking out the pain and replacing it with a desire to find her killer. Every morning he called the custody desks around Manchester, the pretence of trying to pick up clients hiding the need to know about any rapists who had been locked up. He became a lawyer because it gave him access to people like Ellie's killer. He dreamed that one day he would meet him.

But he wasn't going to say any of that to Roy Scarfield.

'I can only begin to imagine, Roy, and I'm sorry for your loss,' he said, focusing hard on keeping his tone even.

Roy shrugged and blew out a long sigh. 'I think there might have been someone else,' he said.

Joe raised his eyebrows. 'Why do you think that?'

'It had been going on too long for it to have just been Aidan Molloy.' He sat back in a slump. 'Sometimes you can only see it when your mind works backwards and you look again at things. Her sister told me she was lonely. How could that be? I'd given her two beautiful children. All of my family adored her and we had friends too.'

'Her friends or your friends?'

'Just other couples we knew. Like my old football friends and their wives. It was our social circle. And does it matter?'

'Sometimes people want their own world, and not just to be a part of someone else's.'

'That's not fair.'

'But you were telling me that her sister knew she was lonely. I'm just guessing at why she might have been. And why Aidan might not have been the first.'

'She started going out more,' Roy said, sadness creeping into his voice. 'She said she was seeing friends, but she wasn't. There always seemed to be someone leaving her workplace, so there was another leaving do, another excuse to stay out. She started isolating herself more from me, as if she no longer wanted to hear what I had to say, and she wouldn't say anything to me either. We co-existed, that's the best way I can describe it. A co-existence.'

'So who was he? This other man?'

'I don't know,' Roy said. 'I'm not even sure

307

there was one, but Aidan said he had been seeing her for around four months. Rebecca had been distant from me for much longer than that. A couple of years, maybe.' Then he frowned.

'What is it?' Joe said.

'Just memories. Suspicions. Things that didn't seem right at the time. She was marked sometimes.'

'Marked?'

'Yes, like deep scratches, as if they had been inflicted deliberately. I don't think I was supposed to know, because they were always somewhere private, like the inside of her thigh, but I would catch her looking sometimes. I asked her once but she always had an excuse. Aidan Molloy couldn't have done something like that. He wasn't man enough. He was a wimp, a coward, and that's why he did what he did. He couldn't deal with Rebecca trying to dump him, and that was what she was trying to do. She wanted to come back here, to her family. He was an escape, that's all, and he just couldn't see it.'

'Before Aidan, where did she work?'

'Just in the library. Nice and quiet, except when the kids wanted to hog the computers.'

'And it was no one there?'

'They were all women who worked there, so no.'

Joe nodded slowly. 'I'm sorry for bringing all this up again. I'm sure it must be painful. And I hope you're right, because it means that the right person is in prison.'

Roy clenched his jaw. 'And if he isn't the right person?'

'I aim to find out who it is and get Aidan out of that cell. Then perhaps I'll have done something useful with my career.'

Forty-six

Carl closed his eyes as he thought about what would happen next. He felt hope for the first time since the man had locked him up. There was someone else to help him. An adult.

The cellar had been returned to darkness, the lamp turned off so that the man didn't spot it as he returned home. Emma was still wrapped up in Carl's coat, leaning against him for some extra warmth, but she would have to give it up when he returned. Her skin felt cold against his, goose bumps on her legs, and she was shivering. All they were doing was waiting. Carl couldn't do much, his arms still chained behind his back. They had tried to find a way to undo it but there were no tools in there. It was a high-quality bike lock threaded through some chain and needed more than the pieces of broken glass strewn across the floor. There wasn't even anything they could have used as a screwdriver, so that she could have taken the lock from the door and raise the alarm. It was just an empty cell. So it was all down to Emma.

'I'm not sure I can do this,' she said, her arms round her knees.

'You've got to,' Carl said, suddenly desperate.

'He thinks you're dead. If he finds out that you're not, he'll just kill you all over again.'

She was quiet, and then, 'I know, I know.'

'Can you use it?'

There was the soft tinkle as Emma tapped the broken glass on the floor. 'I'm going to have to.'

She had torn some of the lining from Carl's coat to wrap around one end, so that she would have some protection as she fought with it.

'Just grip the base of the glass and shove it hard into his neck,' Carl said. 'You'll have the element of surprise. Get right under the ear, cut off the blood supply to the brain. He'll die straight away.'

'How do you know that?'

'My biology teacher told us. You've got to make it good. He's got to die or we'll never get out.'

Emma put her head to her knees. 'I've never hurt anyone. Not physically, not on purpose. This is so extreme.'

'So is dying. And that's what waits for you if you don't do it.' Carl was trying to stay calm, he needed to keep Emma with him, but he knew he was making her take all the risks. He spoke quietly when he said, 'You can't die. You've got children. They need you. That's your choice. Do it for your children, if no one else.'

A pause, and then, 'All right. For them.'

They sat in silence for a few more minutes until there was the sound of a car outside. Emma tensed.

'Quick, we need to be back where we were before,' Carl said. 'Throw my coat into the corner.'

Emma helped Carl to his feet and placed the noose loosely around his neck, so that he'd be able to pull his head out if there was a way of helping her. She put the gag back in place and scuttled across to where she thought she had been lying before. She gasped as she took off the coat, the cold air hitting her naked body. She tried her best to adopt the same position, one arm pointing along the floor, the other down her leg.

Then there was silence.

The engine was turned off. Carl listened to the slow crunch of the man's footsteps outside as he made his way to the front door. Carl tried to slow down his breathing, but his chest was pumping hard, nervous, scared. The front door clicked and then slammed, followed by the steady thumps of his feet on the wooden hallway.

The man didn't come down the stairs straight away. Carl willed him to, so that they could try to end this, but there were just everyday sounds upstairs. The hiss of the kettle. The ping of the microwave. The radio was turned on, a local channel filled with chat and the occasional song. Nothing modern. Emma stayed in her place and more than an hour passed before the cellar door opened, the time measured by the sound of the news bulletins floating down to them. Carl tensed and closed his eyes. He wanted to cry out for his mother, but he couldn't give anything anyway. The man began his slow journey into the darkness of the cellar, the light from the hallway framing his body.

The light stayed off. Carl was pleased. The man wouldn't see the light rise and fall of Emma's body as she breathed, or the tenseness in her limbs as she waited to pounce. Carl knew the broken glass was curled into her palm, so that it wouldn't catch a glint from the light that filtered down from the hallway.

Carl groaned, but it was deliberate, to let the man know that he was feeling low, to keep his concentration on him and away from Emma on the floor.

The man stepped over her, the rise and fall of his leg caught in silhouette. That made Carl angry. He had treated her like discarded rubbish, like Emma was just something he had to clear up.

When the man reached him, he pulled down Carl's gag with one hand. Carl made a show of stretching his mouth and swallowing, as if he had been desperate for hours for the release.

'Let me go, please,' Carl said, his voice low.

'I can't do that,' the man said. 'I thought you'd be dead by now.'

Carl shook his head. 'I want to survive this.'

The man stepped closer, his face right in front of Carl's. 'No one leaves. Haven't you got that yet?'

'Why not?' Carl said. He had to keep him talking, so that his attention was on him.

Emma moved. She was pushing herself up from the floor, slowly, quietly, her body framed in the faint light.

'You could still leave,' Carl said, as Emma stood up and turned towards him, her movement exaggerated and careful. The broken glass was held out like a dagger. 'They'll track you down to here anyway. You could just let me go and run.'

Emma crept forward, hunched over, just a few feet behind him now. Her arm was raised.

Carl swallowed. 'What difference does it make if you kill me?' he said, his voice getting faster. 'I

312

could tell them what you told me, why you did it.'

The man cocked his head, looked almost amused.

Emma screamed as she lunged at him.

He turned, surprised.

Emma's arm came down hard, twice. She screeched with effort. He cried out and fell towards Carl but Emma kept on coming, slashing at him, the broken glass like flashes of brightness in the dark. There was a splash of something on Carl's face, sticky and warm.

'Keep going!' Carl shouted, and pulled his head out of the noose and kicked out. The man shouted out in pain. He was stumbling backwards. Carl ran forward, kicking out some more, screaming obscenities. The man fell to the floor. Carl was stamping, his foot finding the man's stomach.

Emma pushed past Carl and raised her arm high for one more strike down when the man kicked out towards her. His shoe smashed into her left knee and she cried out in pain. Her leg crumpled, her hand on her knee, shouting, desperate and scared now. There was a tinkle as the broken glass skittered across the floor.

The man moved quickly, scrambling up and pushing his shoulder into Carl's midriff and charging him. Carl was propelled across the floor until the wall stopped him, the scene ahead blurring as his head banged against the bricks. He slumped down, groaning.

Emma was on the floor, crying out. The man rushed towards her, snarling. He straddled her. His hands went round her neck.

'Emma!' Carl screamed, trying to get onto his

knees to help her, but his head was still dazed, so that he stumbled back onto his side, every movement made harder by the chains around his wrists.

Emma was on her back as the man pushed down on her.

Carl was crying out, scared. He tried to shuffle towards them, but he was too dazed. Emma was lashing out with her fists, trying to knock him off, her head thrashing, her good leg kicking out, but it was no use. The man was using all of his strength to pin her down, his hands tight around her throat. A stream of saliva hung down from his mouth as he bared his teeth in a grimace. He was winning the fight. Emma's struggle became less frantic, more laboured. Carl got to his knees again, his head forward, sucking in breaths, trying to clear his vision.

Carl ran towards them, kicking out, but the man ignored them.

'No, don't!' Carl screamed.

The man was screaming too, in effort, in anger. Emma's feet were kicking against the floor but he just carried on, until after a few more seconds her body went still.

Carl sank to his knees, his forehead on the cold floor, and sobbed.

The man sat back on his heels, his hands on his thighs, his face upwards, breathing hard, gulping in air. There was blood on his face, glistening in the light that shone from the hallway.

After a few minutes, his head dropped forward, his chest not rising and falling as much, and then he pushed himself upright slowly, as if he was exhausted.

He went to Carl and grabbed him by the hair. 'You're next,' he hissed into Carl's ear, and threw him to the floor.

The man staggered towards the stairs, his footsteps unsteady, using his hand for support against the wall as he went upwards. Before he closed the door and thrust Carl back into darkness, there were wide red streaks visible along the wall.

Silence didn't fall on the cellar this time. It rang with the sound of Carl's cries, lying on his side, deep sobs wracking his body. Emma was dead. And the man was right. He was next.

Forty-seven

Joe threw down his keys as he walked into his apartment, Hugh behind him. Sam had called again, wanting to see him privately. Joe had chosen the apartment, where he wouldn't be disturbed.

He pointed towards the balcony doors and said to Hugh, 'Shall we go outside?'

Hugh looked around. 'Yes. I'd rather sit somewhere with a view.'

'Are you saying my apartment is austere?'

'Functional.'

'Cold?'

'Lacking a warm glow.'

There was a buzz on the intercom, and a quick check of the camera revealed it to be Sam. Joe buzzed for him to come up and opened the apartment door so that Sam could walk right in.

Hugh led the way, Joe following, and as they settled on the chairs on the balcony the door to the apartment clicked shut. Sam had arrived.

When he appeared, his work suit was looser than usual, with his tie pulled down and his top button undone. He looked at Hugh and said, 'I thought we'd be alone.'

'Hugh is helping me with Aidan's case,' Joe said. 'He was Aidan's lawyer first time round.' He pulled out a chair. 'Sit down.'

Sam followed the instruction, nodding politely at Hugh.

Joe gestured towards Hugh. 'Have you two met?'

Sam thought about that for a moment, and a flicker of his eyelashes betrayed the return of his memory. 'A few years ago, when I was a younger cop.'

'And you remembered?' Hugh said, beaming.

'Yes, but not for the reasons you might like. You weren't courteous to me at all. A bit pompous, in fact, beaming in your suit like I was just someone to trick.'

'And were you? Tricked, I mean?'

'Some mugger walked away from what he had done, knocked an old lady over for her purse and left her frightened for the rest of her life.'

Hugh's smile faded slightly. 'I was doing my job,' he said. 'By the sounds of it, a bit better than you.'

'I know we all have jobs to do,' Sam said. 'It just seems like mine is the one that ought to go the smoothest, because right is on my side, isn't it?'

Joe sat back down again and said, 'That is probably a good place to start.'

'What do you mean?'

Joe rested his arm on the balcony rail. 'I know what drives you, Sam. Ellie, justice, doing the right thing. I wish I could be that noble sometimes. You do your job because you think you're on the right side. But what if you came across a case where the wrong thing had been done, where there had been a grave injustice, and all due to the actions of someone from your side? What would be the right thing then?'

'Are you talking about Aidan Molloy?' Sam said, his eyes narrowed.

'Humour me.'

Sam sighed. 'Okay, if you really want my opinion, that isn't going to happen. If a case goes anywhere, it has got to convince a lot of people. Us, the prosecution, and then a judge. If there is something wrong, it will be found out.'

'But if it is founded on lies, and the lies are believed, who would know?'

'That's always been the way, Joe, but don't get all precious,' Sam said, his tiredness making him react to the argument he'd had with Joe too many times. 'I don't know how often I've seen people get away with bad things just because people like you have presented some fake alternative that explains the evidence. It just isn't right that you get it the easy way.'

'You allege it, so you prove it. That's how it should be.'

'All I know is that we have to have some degree of certainty before we take anyone to court. All you need to do is spin a bit of doubt, so everything is weighted in your favour.'

'I'm talking about something different this time.'

'How so?'

'What if we could show with some certainty that a person was innocent, and that police lies had put that person in prison?'

'That's a pretty serious thing to say, Joe.'

'I know.'

'And this is about Aidan Molloy?'

Joe nodded. 'I'm still looking at it.'

Sam paused as he thought about that. 'I'm here for the same reason.'

'What do you mean?' Joe said, confused.

'You've heard about me finding David Jex on the moors?'

'Hell of a coincidence.'

'Yes, I suppose so, but that's just how things are sometimes.'

Sam rubbed his eyes. Joe knew he was just creating a space for his thoughts. Eventually, Sam said, 'If you're going to accuse a police officer of telling lies to get Aidan convicted, you need good proof, solid unassailable proof.'

'And if I had it?'

'I'd take it higher.'

'What if that was part of the problem?'

'You need to stop talking in riddles,' Sam said. 'We're sharing here. If you won't tell me, just let me go home and I can spend some time with my family.'

Joe exchanged glances with Hugh, who gave a small nod of his head.

'How much do you remember about the Aidan Molloy case?' Joe said.

'He was convicted of killing the assistant chief's

318

daughter,' Sam said. 'That raised his profile, and his mother is always in the paper, and campaigning and leafleting.'

'Mary Molloy,' Joe said, nodding. 'She's a powerful woman. Has never stopped fighting for her son.'

'But since when was justice about who had the loudest voice?'

'It's not. It's about getting the right person for the right crime. Aidan is the wrong person, and the reason for that is someone in your force.'

'Who?'

'DCI Hunter.'

Sam started to respond, but then stopped, surprised. 'Hunter?'

Joe nodded slowly, letting Sam's thoughts catch up.

'So tell me,' Sam said.

'He convinced witnesses to change their stories to fit his theory that Aidan had done it. I've spoken to two of them. A young couple. One admitted it, more or less, and I think I can get her to repeat it in court. There is no other evidence. No DNA. No saliva. No blood spatter. It is all based on eye-witness evidence and items that could be planted.'

'But why would Hunter do that?'

'Because he's a glory boy.'

'Where's the glory in getting the wrong person?'

'Plenty, provided no one realises. He was under pressure – it was his boss's daughter. He had to get a result. He convinced himself that Aidan was guilty, and made sure the evidence proved it.'

Sam shook his head. 'There must be something else. I can't investigate my own boss. It would be the end of my career. Even if it were true, there would be too many who would never trust me again. I'd be the grass, the snitch.'

'What about doing the right thing?'

'Come off it; don't lay that one on me. Why don't you just take the case back to court, if these witnesses will talk?'

'I thought you'd want more than just an unsafe verdict, Sam.'

'What do you mean?'

'What if there was another murderer still out there, because of Hunter's lies?' When Sam looked confused, Joe added, 'If it wasn't Aidan Molloy, the real killer is out there, and he might have killed again.'

Sam thought about that for a moment. 'Tell me what you've got.'

'The evidence in Aidan's case was strong but not so strong that it couldn't be false. Three young women said Aidan had threatened to kill Rebecca, overheard in a pub car park. They knew Aidan. His car was seen fleeing the scene. A spade was found in his boot, but he lived in a terraced house with a concrete yard, so he didn't need it for gardening. Not the strongest case, except his mother gave conflicting accounts of when he got in that night.' Joe shrugged and held out his hands. 'The stories are made up. The threats were just tall tales by silly teenagers who wanted some attention. Problem is, when these things start they are impossible to stop. That's what led the police to Aidan's door and I don't know what it was about him that made Hunter think he was guilty, but the whole case was then shaped around Aidan. Hunter put pressure on the witnesses to change the description of the car at the scene so that it matched Aidan's. The spade was planted in the boot. It can be the only explanation. Hunter believed that Aidan Molloy was a killer who was going to get away with it, so he padded the case. Except that Aidan Molloy isn't a killer, and I think there's been another murder since, by the real killer.'

Hugh sat forward. 'What are you talking about, Joe?'

'David Jex,' Joe said. 'He became obsessed with Aidan's case, and his son was scared of Hunter. And where is David Jex now?'

'Dead,' Sam said quietly. He chewed on his lip until he said, 'Just a detective who went missing, they said. Marital strife, they said. They kept expecting him to turn up hanging from a tree or something.'

'There's more to it than that,' Joe said. 'What sparked his obsession with Aidan's case? It was all done, neatly wrapped up, Aidan behind bars.'

Sam's eyes widened. He was starting to catch up. 'If he found something out that suggested that Aidan was innocent.'

'And what could do that?' When Sam didn't respond, Joe added, 'What about another murder?'

Sam pulled a face. 'Come on.'

'Why not? Rebecca was murdered, and if it wasn't Aidan, why not another murder? The whole case was built around the fact that Aidan was Rebecca's lover. What if she had another lover and Hunter went after the wrong one? Why would David Jex become obsessed with the case? I'll tell you: he's a murder detective, like you, and what

321

would upset you more than anything?'

'Missing something that allowed a killer to get away with it,' Sam said.

Joe shook his head. 'No, it wouldn't. What would eat away at you would be if you missed something that allowed a person to kill again. But what if you did something deliberate that led to that? What if you had caused one person to be a suspect and allowed the real killer to remain free? It's against all the reasons you became a murder detective. Aidan's case is solved, all done. So what changed? What made David become obsessive?'

Sam pondered on that. 'So you're saying David Jex was put there by Rebecca's real killer?'

'It's what makes sense.'

'Why would the killer highlight it, though?'

'What do you mean?' Joe said.

'I went digging on that spot because of a body found there the day before. It was set out as if it was a sign. I thought there might be something else at the scene, and there was: David Jex. Why would the killer want me to find him?'

'Sometimes people just want to be caught,' Joe said.

'There is one thing though,' Sam said.

'Go on.'

'Hunter has been acting strangely, ever since we discovered the body yesterday,' Sam said. 'He's even worse today.'

'He might know the same thing David found out, and now David's body points the spotlight at whatever David was doing before he went missing.'

'Which was looking into the Aidan Molloy

case,' Joe said.

'So you think there might be another murder connected with whoever really killed Rebecca Scarfield, and Hunter knows that?' Sam said.

'I'm guessing, surmising,' Joe said. 'This is where you come into it.'

'Me? How come?'

'You can have a look. See if there are similar murders. Has anyone else been caught or suspected? And get me the address where Carl was arrested. That's why I called this morning. It must have some relevance.'

Sam let out a long breath as he thought of that. Eventually, he said, 'You have to do something for me too.'

'Which is what?'

'Let me have copies of the files Carl had. Lorna told me about Carl's obsession. That's why I'm here. She told me that you had the files.'

Joe smiled. 'So you know what I'm saying is right?'

'I don't know. I would need some kind of clearance to go after Hunter. More likely it will go to a different force.'

'That will take a long time,' Joe said. 'All the time Aidan is locked up. So why not go off-plan? Do something yourself. Work with us.'

'I can't. I have to do it properly. You're going after Hunter because he broke the rules and you want me to help by breaking the rules too. Only a lawyer could think like that.'

'Is there any connection between Rebecca Scarfield and the woman found yesterday?'

Sam thought about that. 'Apart from the fact

that they were married women having affairs, nothing.'

'Isn't that enough, when you throw David Jex into the mix?' Joe said.

Sam sighed. 'All right, I'll speak to my boss.'

Joe smiled. 'I knew you'd see it my way eventually.'

Forty-eight

Joe and Hugh watched Sam drive away, back into the city-centre traffic.

'Do you think he'll come up with the right things?' Hugh said.

'Sam gets it done, don't worry about that.' He looked at Hugh. 'So what now? I'm going to head to the office, to see if I've still got one. What about you?'

'I'll join you shortly,' Hugh said, checking his watch. 'Just got an errand to do. Niece's birthday. Got to get a card in the post.'

Hugh set off walking towards Deansgate, his head down, and Joe headed off on his preferred route, along the canal and under the bridges, where the cars didn't disturb him.

As he threaded through restaurant tables on the other side of a long footbridge, his phone buzzed. A message. When he looked, it was from Kim Reader. *Come to the Crown Court. Alone. Need to talk about Molloy.*

He texted back. *On my way.*

Joe was curious. It was the *alone* part that troubled him.

He was soon at the Crown Court, through the now bored-looking security people, the wave of the radar wand perfunctory, and then up the stairs.

The Crown Court is a long corridor, with high windows on one side, and rows of seats for those awaiting a court appearance. Facing them are the heavy wooden doors into the courtrooms, controlled by ushers in long black gowns and clipboards, often retired police officers.

It was a different atmosphere to the Magistrates' Court, where Joe commonly plied his trade, which is chaos and noise, nuisance offenders making nuisances of themselves, a sea of strut and snarl. There are some flashes of dread, those who only fall foul of the law once or twice in a lifetime, the drink-drivers, the neighbour disputes, but the rest is drink and drugs and fights and theft and a never-ending stream of wasted lives.

The Crown Court is where the serious cases end up, so those who go carry more fear in their eyes, that the view they have through the huge windows could be the last one for a few years that isn't through thin metal bars. They edge around nervously, bite fingernails, receive words of comfort from girlfriends and mothers, have more open space to ponder their fate, the corridors quiet and pensive.

Kim was sitting on one of the chairs near the large windows. Her court wig was on her lap, her legs crossed, her demure look ruined by the fatigue in her eyes and her ruffled hair.

The court day was drawing to a close, and the only people left were those who had been made to wait all day, the end of the list. Barristers walked quickly along the corridor. Some of them still wore the horsehair wigs, but they were cock-eyed, tired-looking, whereas others were done for the day, their court dress tucked away in leather bags, their wigs in black oval tins. Theatre was over.

'Rough day?' Joe said.

Kim looked up and smiled. 'You know how it is. Six briefs in four different courts, with the judges bellyaching in each one. Let me tell you, Joe, that if you want to make sure your case in court four gets called on, just go and sit in court seven and start dealing with that case. You can guarantee that court four will suddenly need you.' She sighed. 'Then this evening is crossed out with the preparation for tomorrow, and I daren't think about having some of the weekend free.'

He sat next to her. 'I could take you away from all of this,' he said. 'I've always thought we should have gone into practice together. Parker Reader Solicitors.'

'I think Reader Parker sounds better,' she said, some mischief returning as a glint in her eye.

'We'll talk about it over coffee,' Joe said.

'I thought you wanted out?'

'Well, yeah maybe. But what else can I do? Push trolleys around a supermarket car park?'

'First things first. Aidan Molloy. I've got someone you might want to meet.'

'Have you got me down here to tell me to stop wasting my time?'

'Just follow me.'

She stood and went towards the nearest court-room.

The door was heavy, solid wood, and despite the concrete look of the building's exterior the courtrooms were styled on the courts of old, with wooden panelling and brass rails. There were three rows for the lawyers. The QCs' slot at the front, the everyday barristers behind and the clerks and caseworkers at the back. Behind the last row was the wooden dock, the brass rail along the top usually marked by the moisture of thousands of sweaty palms, gripped tightly as verdicts or sentences were announced.

Along the middle row was a barrister, sitting on the desk, his trouser leg riding up as he raised one foot onto the cushion of the chair, his socks held up by garters. Joe recognised him. Martin Barlow. He wasn't from the chambers he usually used, but sometimes the work gets swapped around as people become double-booked.

'Mr Barlow?' Joe said, curious. 'This is all a bit clandestine.'

'Martin, please,' he said, and smiled, small grey eyes under short grey hair. 'I haven't seen you in a while, Joe.'

Joe held out his hand and shook. 'I'm still around,' he said.

'Young Kim here said you're looking at resurrecting the Aidan Molloy case,' Martin said.

'Just thinking about it at the moment,' he said, although he knew he had already gone further than just thinking.

'I defended him,' Martin said. 'I was the junior on it.'

Joe was surprised. 'So this is about telling me that I'm wasting my time?'

'No,' Martin said, surprised. 'Just the opposite, in fact. Aidan was one of the few I believed.'

'I'm pleased to hear it.'

'Hear him out, Joe,' Kim said, irritation in her voice. 'I'm doing this for you. We can all go home and forget about Aidan if you prefer.'

Joe leaned against the desk. 'Okay, I'm sorry. Go on.'

'I've heard you're working with Hugh Bramwell again,' Martin said.

'Yes. Like you, he thinks Aidan is the innocent one and wants to try and get right what he didn't last time.'

'That might take some time.'

'What do you mean?'

'Well, Hugh did very little right last time. To the point where I wondered if he was trying to lose the case on purpose.'

'What do you mean?'

Martin started to undo his collar to remove his tabs, fastened with a brass stud at the back. 'This is going to be kept between you and me for now, but it might help you decide where to look. Hugh had a reputation for not fighting very hard. In the Molloy case, he was asked to look more into the witnesses, to find something we could use against them, like attention-seeking or false reports. We wanted them to be interviewed, and we asked Hugh to get the permission from the police, but he didn't do it. He said it wasn't ethical. It was Hugh who got Aidan to insist on his mother giving evidence, almost as if he was determined to

328

lose the case.'

'But you were in charge of the case in court, not Hugh.'

'No,' Martin said. 'Aidan was in charge. He's the client, you know how it works. We advise, we don't instruct, and the advice he listened to was that drummed into him by Hugh. The thing is, he should have looked into the witnesses more.'

'Why?'

'I came across one of them again. One of the three girls who said she'd heard him threaten to kill Rebecca outside a pub.'

'I was going to visit them before, but Hugh talked me out of it.'

'Lucky for you that I met one of them. She got in trouble for looking after drugs her boyfriend was selling, when she stored them in her loft. I defended her and she was angry because she said she'd been promised she would be protected.'

Joe frowned. 'Protected? I don't follow.'

'She told me that she would be tipped off if the police were ever going to visit her with a drugs warrant, as if it was her reward for giving evidence in Aidan's case. She was running around with some pretty dodgy people, but she was one of the ones you wouldn't think of. From a nice home, she looked the part, clean and wholesome, but she had a taste for the bad boys. She felt she had been betrayed, especially when she got three years.'

'So she told you she had lied and you didn't say anything?'

Martin shook his head. 'You can't lay that on me. What she told me was confidential and she didn't say she had lied. She just hinted at inducements, and wanted her reward for locking up the killer.'

'I read the file notes,' Joe said. 'Aidan had argued with Rebecca the night before, but said he was just being emotional because she was ending their relationship. No threats to kill were made. He made a fool of himself, that's all, crying and pleading.'

'And that is probably what happened,' Martin said.

Joe let out a long sigh. 'The woman who saw the car drive away is convinced it was a different car to how she described it in her statement. She said Hunter put them under pressure to remember it differently, and her boyfriend went along with it because he trusted Hunter's judgment more than her ability to recognise cars. Even the partial registration was down to Hunter.'

'And it will be the same with those three silly little teenagers,' Martin said. 'The truth is embellished to make it fit. They might even believe it themselves now, and this is the thing, that no one was doing it to lock up an innocent man. Even Hunter. They all thought they were patching up holes that would let a murderer walk free. If Hugh had done his job properly, perhaps those holes would have been seen.'

'So he's trying to make amends,' Joe said.

Kim shook her head. 'It's more than that,' she said. 'I asked around after we spoke earlier. We haven't got many of the old guard left, but the ones we have remember Hugh of old. His reputation wasn't good.'

Joe was surprised.

'Don't get me wrong,' she said, raising her hand. 'Everyone liked him. He didn't cause us problems and was always charming. Sometimes you just want to get through the day as smoothly as possible, without someone taking every useless point just to wear you down. But we talk about defence lawyers, ask ourselves the question of who we would go to if we were in trouble.'

'And?'

'If we were guilty, the same names cropped up, those who were good at the tear-jerking speeches, who could be the difference between Christmas at home or a prison breakfast. Hugh could do that. He had that old-school charm. If he said his client wouldn't do it again, the magistrates would go all doe-eyed and believe him.'

'But?'

'No one would go to him if they wanted a not guilty verdict. We know who fights well and clean. Hugh wasn't one of them. Not one of us would have used Hugh if we were in trouble.' Kim grimaced. 'And there were rumours.'

Joe was becoming uncomfortable. 'What kind of rumours?' Kim looked at Martin, who nodded.

'That he was too close to the police,' she said. 'He entertained them, bought them presents.'

'Everyone did back then.'

'No, it was more than that.' Kim sighed. 'Don't be angry, but I called Gina before. I asked her to look into Hugh, to use her old police contacts, and she didn't sound surprised.'

'So is Aidan innocent or not? What does it matter about Hugh?'

'Because Hugh might not be involved for the

reason you think,' Kim said. 'If Aidan Molloy is innocent, I hope you prove it. I've never wanted to lock up an innocent man just to say I could. Don't let Hugh derail that.'

Martin got to his feet and put his wig on top of some papers in an old leather holdall. He didn't want to keep his wig clean. A mark of experience was a tatty wig. He was keen on making it look more tatty. 'He was negligent, in my view, but that isn't how Aidan or his mother saw it. As far as they were concerned, Hugh made sure their voices were heard.' He gave a wry smile. 'You know how it is. Sometimes it's better to say nothing, but it's a tough call. Aidan had his case heard, but it was very weak because Hugh didn't do enough for him.'

Kim reached out and put her hand on Joe's. 'If Aidan is innocent, get him out. Just keep an eye on Hugh.'

Joe nodded and let go of her hand.

When he left the courtroom, he wasn't sure what anything meant any more.

Forty-nine

Sam rushed into the restaurant, looking for Alice. She waved when she saw him, although her smile seemed slow in coming.

It was one of those themed restaurants, American chrome, mock-diner style, with guitars and neon signs on the walls. It was all burgers, shakes and chicken wings, although the servers didn't quite provide the *have a good day* cheeriness that the style tried to project.

It was easy for Alice, though; she could let the girls play on the climbing frames and slides in the large room at the back so that they blew off some of their energy before she had to get them into bed.

Alice was at a table by the play area and she was eating chicken wings. Sam leaned in to kiss her and ended up with a blob of barbecue sauce on his cheek.

She tilted her head and smiled, and her eyes got that dreamy look that had first attracted him when they were still teenagers – soft and wistful, it had made him fall for her quickly. Too quickly, his father had said, but his mother liked Alice. She said she was good for him, that all that mattered was that she put a smile on his face.

'Sorry I'm late,' he said.

'You look tired, Sam.'

'I'll be fine,' he said, reaching across for a chip. 'How are the girls?'

'They've been manic today. When I told them we were coming here, they wouldn't calm down.'

'It'll tire them out,' he said.

Her smile wavered and was replaced by a look of concern. She put her food down and said, 'Come home earlier tonight. You can't keep doing these long shifts.'

'What do you mean?'

'You know what I mean,' she said. 'We had the conversation last night. It seems like every time someone is murdered you drop everything, even us, to try and sort it out. You get blinkers on and stop seeing what is around you, as if we no longer matter.'

'I'm on the Murder Squad,' he said. 'It's what I do. And this morning I dug up a corpse, so I feel a little invested in this one.'

'So how long are you working today?'

'Until I can't work any more,' he said. 'Joe thinks he has got something useful. I need to follow up on what he came up with.'

Alice frowned and glanced towards the play area. 'Go and say goodnight to your children, then.'

'Don't be like that,' he said, irritation in his voice. 'This is important.'

'So are they.'

Sam took a deep breath. He could feel his anger building, but he knew it was partly tiredness, and also because he knew Alice was right. She was always right, but that didn't stop him from going back to work.

'Okay, I won't be late, I promise,' he said.

Alice didn't respond.

'I've just got a couple of things to look at, then I'll come home.' He reached across and took hold of her hand. 'I promise.'

She looked at him, tried to maintain her frosty look, but then a smile flickered at the corners of her mouth. 'Okay, Sam Parker. If you promise.'

He grinned and kissed her hand, before standing and going into the play area. Erin and Amy ran towards him and wrapped themselves around his legs. He kissed them each on the heads, the scent of their hair mixed in with fast food and drinks, the grubby smells of happiness. They went back to their play and he watched them for a few minutes, showing off as they climbed and played and jumped into ball-pits, enjoying his attention.

The desire to stay with them was strong as he left the restaurant, but so was the urge to carry on with the case.

He kissed Alice goodbye and went back to his car, his mind returning to the case. Just a few hours more and he would let his life go back to normal for a while.

Joe was preoccupied as he walked quickly up the office steps and rushed through reception. Marion tried to pass him some telephone messages but he waved them away and carried on towards his office. He paused when he got to the top. Gina was standing there, her arms folded.

'What have you found out?' Joe asked, his tone accusatory.

'So you've spoken to Kim?' When Joe nodded, she said, 'So where is he, your little helper?'

'He's gone on an errand.'

'Did he say where?'

'A birthday card for his niece.' Joe frowned. 'What's going on, Gina?'

Gina put her hands on her hips and stared at the floor for a few seconds. When she looked up again, she spoke more softly. 'Let's go to your room. We need to talk.'

Joe followed her along the corridor. When he closed the door to his room, Gina sat down. She swivelled towards the window and stared at the view for a few seconds before saying, 'I'm surprised that you let Hugh back into the case.'

'I'm starting to think the same.'

Gina turned back towards him. 'How well do you know Hugh? And I mean really know him.'

'You know how I got the job. He did it before me and wanted to retire, and I had just left my old firm. I knew him from around the court and I used to enjoy his tales. War stories are fun sometimes.'

'We had a different view of him in the Force.'

Joe frowned. 'Tell me,' he said. 'I need to know everything. Kim gave me a taste, but I need more.'

'This case is all about DCI Hunter,' Gina said, leaning forward onto the desk, her hands clasped together. 'I know what Hunter is like. I was in the same Force as him. He won't have changed much, although the Force has, and is better for it. The legal system has probably gone the same way.'

'You're being too cryptic, Gina.'

'Did you know that Hugh was once arrested?'

Joe was surprised. 'No, I didn't.'

'It was about ten years ago. Before your time, I suppose. The top brass had become nervous about how close some of the defence lawyers were to the court clerks and judges. They thought it gave them an unfair advantage and looked into it.'

'The clerks and judges are lawyers, just like me,' Joe said. 'There are bound to be friendships. Look at Kim and me, and I've even had a drink with judges away from the courtroom.'

'But did you try to bribe them?'

'Bribery?'

'Yes, bribery, or so went the allegation. Undue influence and gifts. Football tickets for judges, court clerks being wined and dined at matches. It was corporate hospitality for those who were supposed to keep their distance.'

'So what happened?'

'Nothing, in the end. No one could prove that any case had been affected, but when they looked into Hugh, they found it went even further than court clerks. It went to the police too.'

'The police?'

'Yes,' Gina said, nodding. 'Does Hugh still have his apartment in Estepona?'

'Spain? I don't know.'

'Ask him, and then ask him about his guests, and when they stayed there.'

'No, why don't you tell me? You seem to know a lot.'

'Hunter has used it.'

'Hang on. Are you saying that Hunter and Hugh are old friends?' When Gina didn't respond, he said, 'How do you know?'

'I know Hunter. He goes for every favour he can, and there were rumours about Hugh.'

'Rumours? What are you talking about?'

Gina looked down and studied her hands for a while.

'Gina?'

'I'm breaching confidences here, and some of this is top secret, heavy stuff, secret squirrel information.'

'It won't go further than this room.'

'Hugh was an informant,' she said, and shrugged.

Joe was about to speak, but then he stopped himself, shocked, unsure as to what he could say.

'An informant?' he said eventually. 'He was a defence lawyer.'

'No, he was a businessman, and he found a way to keep the money coming in.'

Joe shook his head in disbelief. 'That can't be true.'

'Do you think he's a good lawyer?'

Joe hung his head. He remembered the conversation with Kim, and from what he remembered of Hugh's advocacy, it was mostly endearing bumble. Like Kim said though, the magistrates sometimes liked that, and when you've been around for long enough, people listen to you.

'He was never the sharpest,' Joe said, 'but I've known some very average lawyers get fierce loyalty from clients.'

'But you've got to get them through the door first, and most of all, you've got to get the police to arrest them. So Hugh used to tip off against some of his clients, so that they would be arrested and he'd get the work.'

Joe shook his head in disbelief. 'He would have been struck off if it had come out.'

Gina raised an eyebrow. 'Do you think that would have been his biggest problem if it had?'

Joe understood what she meant. Criminal lawyers act for dangerous people but for the most part are not threatened by them. If his clients had found out that Hugh had been briefing the police against them, then nothing would have saved him.

'That was where he went wrong,' Gina said. 'He couldn't think beyond the next pay cheque, but do you think Hunter would care about that? I don't know if it was just one bad year and he was under pressure to make more money, but once Hugh started selling out his clients, Hunter had him. Nothing explicit, but everyone knew about Hunter's regular free holidays, and he wasn't the only detective to enjoy them. And Hugh had to keep the tips coming, as well as more.'

'More?'

'Think about it,' Gina said. 'You've been involved in this case for a few days and you've started to pick it apart. Why couldn't Hugh?'

'I've been speaking to Martin Barlow, one of Aidan's legal team. He said Hugh did a bad job.'

'Hugh was smart. He did just enough to avoid an investigation from the Law Society, but I bet he could have done more. Hugh got his clients arrested, took the money, and the bargain with the police was that for their silence Hugh wouldn't fight the cases too hard.'

'He lost them on purpose?'

'I'm just saying he didn't fight very hard. Once it got round that Hugh was on a case, we used to think it was cut and dried. It didn't always work out that way, but it often did.'

Joe paced as he thought about that. There was logic to it. Law firms depend on the police locking up their clients, and it goes in quiet patches sometimes. Joe could understand the temptation to generate extra income if a quiet patch went on too long.

'So where do you think he is now?' he said.

Gina dug into her pocket for her phone and tossed it over. Joe caught it, confused.

339

'I haven't forgotten how to follow people,' she said.

Joe looked at the screen and his anger started to surge through him.

It was a picture of Hugh, and he was climbing into a car parked on one of the small cobbled streets near to Joe's apartment. Joe recognised the driver.

'Hunter,' he said, looking up.

'Straight after leaving your apartment,' Gina said. 'I waited for him after getting Kim's call.'

Joe was angry. 'So he offered to help just so he could keep Hunter up to date?'

'He might be worrying about himself more. His panic will have started as soon as you called him, because he'll know that if his world begins to unravel, so might Hunter's, and Hunter will take everyone else down with him. It will only take a few words in the right ears to put Hugh's life in danger, and he knows that.'

Joe leaned against the wall. 'Why didn't I spot what he was doing? I thought I could read people.'

'Because you trusted him. We can all be blinded.'

Joe stared at Gina's phone, finding it hard to believe the image. 'So what do I do?' he said eventually.

'You use him like Hunter is using him, except you feed Hugh the false stuff.'

'What like?'

'I don't know, but I'm sure you'll think of something.'

'So will you help me?'

'I was all along. It's just that you didn't realise.'

When Joe held up his hands in apology, she said, 'So what now?'

'We're looking for evidence of other murders or missing women. Something must have made David Jex act, and that can only be the realisation that they had got it wrong about Aidan. David had a bout of conscience and it cost him his life.'

'But now the police have found his body, won't they solve it all?'

'They didn't get it right with Rebecca Scarfield. I'd rather work this out for myself, just to make sure no one misses it.' He pointed to the box of files taken from Carl's house. 'Take one each and we'll go through them.'

He pulled out the first file. It was filled with the statements from Aidan's case. He had read his own version and, as he flicked through, he saw that the statements were the same. No amendments or deletions. He put the file to one side. Then he went to the list of addresses that he had seen previously, the one with lines through, as if Carl had been checking them off. As Joe went through them again, he frowned. The list seemed shorter. Joe was sure there had been five pages, but now there seemed to be one less. And as he looked at the names in the folder, he saw that there was a gap in the alphabet, where the street names went straight from K to R. The third page was missing.

'Have you been into these files for anything?' he said.

Gina frowned. 'Why would I?'

'I don't know. Curiosity?'

'I'm not paid to be curious.'

'There's a page missing.'

As Gina looked over, she smiled. 'That narrows it down, then. You might not have the address, but you know the range of the alphabet.'

Joe went through the other files but everything else seemed to be there. He was about to step away when he saw a blue cardboard wallet underneath the files. It was at the bottom of the box, half-folded into one of the flaps.

'What's this?' he said quietly. He reached in for it, and when he opened it he saw that it was filled with newspaper clippings, either photocopies of the page or printed articles from the internet.

'Have you seen these?' Joe said.

Gina leaned in. 'No. What are they?'

'They are all reports of missing women.' He flicked through them. 'Some of these go back ten years.'

'All local?'

'They're all from around Manchester, or just over the border, but not all are women. Some are missing teenagers, boys as well as girls.'

Joe looked through them quickly. Abductor and abusers go for similar types. It might just be age that selected them as victims, or even something more specific, like hair colour or dress sense, but not many mixed and matched. Someone who snatched children would not snatch an adult, and the reverse was true. It's all about the sick preferences that drive them, not just about opportunity.

'Sift them by geography,' Gina said. When Joe glanced up, she added, 'Familiarity is important, or else how could an abductor be sure that he wasn't going to be seen? If David Jex had seen something that made him think that Rebecca

342

Scarfield had been part of a series, then it had to be local.'

Joe went to his desk and made two piles of cuttings: one for the north of Manchester, where Rebecca lived, and the rest for elsewhere. Once he had sifted the pile by region, he discarded the ones of children. Rebecca had been a married woman. There was no point in looking for teenagers.

Joe was left with a pile of clippings involving seven women in total. Three were from Manchester. And there was one woman who made up most of the articles.

'Most of the clippings are about her?' he said, holding up the bundle.

'Melissa Clarke,' Gina said, reading the name. 'Went missing just over a year ago.'

'Thirty-two years old,' Joe said, skim-reading. 'No children. Had been married for three years. A pretty blonde. Just went out one evening and never returned. About the time David Jex starting obsessing about Aidan's case.'

Joe went looking through the other files to see if he could find any other reference to Melissa Clarke. There was nothing.

He read the articles again. Then he spotted something. It was a printout of a website dedicated to finding Melissa, and there was a telephone number to ring if anyone had any news.

He raised an eyebrow at Gina. 'Do we give it a call?'

'We won't find anything out if we don't.'

Joe smiled and reached for his phone. 'I knew you'd say that.'

Fifty

As Joe and Gina were heading out of the office, on their way to see Melissa Clarke's husband, Hugh was coming back in. He was out of breath, as if he had been rushing.

'You two going out?' he said, not quite meeting Joe's gaze.

Joe and Gina exchanged brief glances and both smiled. 'Errand all done, Hugh?' Joe said.

'Yes, thank you. Got to keep the family happy. Where are you two going?'

'Going to see another witness. Fancy a ride along?'

'Why not? That's why I'm here, to help,' Hugh said, relaxing slightly and falling in behind them.

The small group walked in silence to Gina's car, Joe unable to think of a way to start a conversation, still too shocked from what Gina had told him. Her car was parked by a meter outside the office, and as Hugh climbed into the back Joe and Gina exchanged stern glances. They were watching him.

The journey to where Melissa Clarke had lived hit all the rush hours. She was from the same area of Manchester as Rebecca Scarfield, one of the small towns on the climb towards the Pennine hills, and they were stuck in the stop-start through the shopping streets and then every small town on the way, until eventually they were driving uphill and away from the grey flatland of the city.

Melissa's address appeared to be a converted church, the high stone-gabled front boasting a metal plate with eight doorbells on it. It shouted young professionals, a couple who desired mill-stone living but without the means to buy the small cottage they really desired.

Joe reached the doorbells first and, once they were buzzed in, a short corridor at the top of a flight of new metal stairs led to an oak door that opened as they got closer.

There was a man there, tall and slim, stubble on his cheeks, although the shirt and tie he was wearing told Joe that life had returned to some degree of normality, that it was just the end of another working day.

'Thank you for seeing us, Mr Clarke,' Joe said.

'It's Chris,' he said, and walked back into the apartment, to allow everyone to follow.

The place was bright and airy, a small space made open plan to give it some light, with a kitchen at one end of the main room and a table in front of a window at the other, allowing meals overlooking the main road. A leather sofa and chair were grouped around a large television. There were some candles on the mantelpiece but they had never been lit, the wicks still clean. Photograph frames dotted the room, all showing a picture of the woman Joe had seen in the news-paper article not long before. The apartment hadn't become a shrine yet, but Chris was making sure he was tortured by her memory wherever he looked, his own way of ensuring that he didn't forget.

Chris must have spotted them looking. 'That's Melissa,' he said. 'Beautiful, isn't she?'

Joe had to agree, although it wasn't her gentle features or the kink of her blonde hair, but the brightness of her smile, the laughter in her eyes.

'Not knowing is the hardest,' Chris said, and sat down with a slump in the chair. Joe and Gina sat next to each other on the sofa, with Hugh sitting at the table in the window. There was a light hum of traffic from outside.

Chris looked at his hands before saying, 'You become all the clichés. All the things you've heard before and thought were just the things that people said for the sake of saying something, but they are all true. Every time I get a call or a visit, I wonder if it's the police to tell me that they've found her, or perhaps even Melissa to tell me that she was coming home, that she was sorry for whatever she had done and would I forgive her. And I would, if it was as simple as that. Knowing that she had been unfaithful and wanted to leave would at least give me something to get over, to try to rationalise, but this? Just a disappearance?' He blew out noisily and blinked away the moisture that had appeared in his eyes. 'How can you rationalise anything when you don't know what is true?'

He smiled, and this time the tears did come, until he wiped them away with the heel of his palm. 'I'm sorry,' he said. 'You didn't come here to listen to me feel sorry for myself. It's to do with Melissa, some news. So what have you got?'

'There are confidentiality issues relating to one of my clients,' Joe said, passing over a business

346

card. 'But Melissa's case seems relevant some-how, and if it is, it will help my client, and perhaps help resolve what happened to Melissa.'

'Resolve?' Chris said. 'That means whatever news there is won't be good. And it's all one-way? I tell you everything but you don't help me get any closer to what happened to Melissa?'

'It has to be that way,' Joe said. 'I'm sorry.'

Chris was silent for a minute or so, as if he was considering what to say. He wanted answers about Melissa, not just the chance to unburden himself, so they all listened to the hum of the fridge and the light chatter of a computer on a desk by the other wall. Eventually, he seemed to resolve his conflict as he nodded to himself. 'Melissa just went out one night and never came home.'

'As simple as that?' Joe said. When Chris nodded, Joe asked, 'Who did she go out with?'

'She said it was with her book group, but it wasn't; when I asked, no one else had gone out.'

Joe frowned. 'Where do you think she was really going?'

'I don't know. Why shouldn't I believe her? We'd only been married a few years. We have no children and we had social lives. We both worked hard but we saw each other enough.' He took a deep breath. 'We had been saving up for a house, not just this apartment, somewhere we could settle down, all the stuff you talk about, maybe even have children, so we put in the hours when we could.'

'What did Melissa do?'

'An accounts clerk at a local builders' merchant. I'm an accountant and we met through my job.' He shrugged. 'She knew my job was more pressurised than hers, that I didn't want to go out as much as she did. Sometimes you just want to get home and chill out, play some video games or stick some wine in the fridge. So I was used to Melissa going out without me.'

'But she lied to you,' Gina said.

'Yes, I know that now, and a few times before. When I spoke to her friends after she disappeared, it seemed like they hadn't gone out as much as she did.' He sighed. 'She was having an affair, I can guess that now.'

As had Rebecca Scarfield, Joe thought, although Aidan thought he hadn't been her only lover.

'Do you know who with?' Joe said.

'No, and I wish I did, because then I would have something to give to the police. All I get are polite smiles from them, as if they know I had something to do with it but can't prove it. She had no family really, her parents are dead and she was an only child, but none of her friends speak to me now. I have to deal with everything on my own. How am I supposed to work out how to do that?'

Joe looked over to Hugh, who was staring at the floor, frowning.

'No suspicions at all?' Joe said.

'None. But looking back, perhaps things weren't right. She became more distant, used to complain that I didn't show her enough affection or attention, and I thought she understood about my job. So I made an effort and it sort of worked back round again and I thought we were all right.' He shook his head. 'Obviously not.'

'So you had no idea who this other man might

be?' Joe said.

'None,' he said, and sighed. 'I can't keep going over this. The copper who first came to see me took all this down. Why don't you speak to him? I can't tell you anything else.'

'Can you remember his name?' Joe said, glancing at Gina.

Chris chewed his lip as he thought about it. 'Something unusual. Like Hicks or Heck or Jacks.'

'Jex?' Joe said.

'That's it,' Chris said. 'David Jex.'

Joe felt a tremble in his fingers. There it was. The connection.

'Does that name mean something?' Chris said. 'I can see it in your face.'

'No, it's nothing,' Joe said, stumbling over his words, unconvincing. 'But you're right, it's time for us to go. Thank you.'

He got to his feet and started walking towards the door, Gina behind him. Joe realised that Hugh wasn't following him and looked back around. Hugh was still looking at the floor, deep in thought.

'Hugh?'

He looked up and turned to Chris. 'Where was the book group?' he said.

'Darnside Library,' Chris said. 'They meet every two weeks.'

Hugh got up to follow Joe, grim-faced as he went past.

Joe looked at Gina, who shrugged. They needed to talk.

Fifty-one

He was behind her as she pulled into the car park of a small supermarket, the sort of place that you use to get the things you forgot and all the local kids hang around outside, their dogs and glares meant to intimidate. He parked two bays away and winced as he watched her. He'd wrapped a bandage around his neck, but the wound probably needed stitching. Emma had caught him well with that piece of glass.

Watching her took away some of the pain, though. He'd been following her since she left her house, first to the fast food place and now to here. Adrenalin coursed through him; he felt like he was on a timer, that he had so much to do before everything came to a stop. She was pretty, he thought, as she climbed out, although she had that weariness he had seen so many times, where the light has faded, and all that young glamour has been replaced by a tired look in her eyes and clothes that are just functional. Jeans and jumper, hair tied back but with loose strands.

She took her time unbuckling her two daughters, two sweet young things in blonde curls, who skipped and jumped their way into the shop. She laboured more slowly, stopping to pick up a basket as the two girls ran along the first aisle and then stooped to look at some comics.

He stepped out of his car and looked around,

just to see who was watching. He was going to walk into the shop, but then he remembered that there would be CCTV in there. He had to be careful. It would be what they play on the news when they talked about her, as she shopped innocently, not knowing what lay ahead. What would they call her? A stay-at-home mum? As if there was nothing else to her, her whole life defined by the way she dies a little inside the walls of what she calls home.

So he climbed back into his car and watched through the windscreen, his fingers tapping a fast rhythm on the steering wheel. This wasn't how he operated. Stepping away from the norm created risks. It was just something he had to do, knowing this was the end. No one leaves, but no one hurts him either. He had been hurt before.

The windows were large and he could see her as she queued at the till, her two girls pulling at her. She held a loaf of bread in one hand and a container of milk in the other, her purse hooked into her elbow. It was mundane, ordinary.

As she came back out and walked towards her car, her daughters running ahead, he stepped out of his car again. He fastened his scarf so she wouldn't see the bandage and made as if to walk past her, looking down, casual. He stopped. He turned to her as she was fastening the two girls into their seats. 'Alice? It is Alice, isn't it?'

She turned to him, wary, unsure.

'Sorry,' he said, laughing politely to put her at ease. 'I work with your husband, Sam. I'm on the same team. We met once before.'

'Oh,' she said, relaxing. 'Sorry. I didn't recognise you. How are you?'

Perfect response, he thought, not letting on that she had no idea who he was. They had never met before.

'I'm good, thanks.' He peered into the car. 'They're a pair of sweeties.'

She smiled. 'Tiring though.'

He returned the smile and detected a blush as she enjoyed his interest in her. Nothing he hadn't seen before, and for her it meant nothing, just the flattery of spotting something in a man's eye.

'I'll bet,' he said, showing that he understood her. She could trust him. 'Anyway, I'll let you get on. Good to see you again.'

Alice smiled. 'Thank you. And you.'

He went towards the shop but didn't go inside. Instead, he loitered in the shadows, and when she pulled out of the space, he walked quickly back to his car. He would catch her up and see where she went.

Her time was now.

'Melissa, she was the one,' Joe said, breathless as they emerged back onto the street.

'The one?' Gina said.

Joe looked towards the window of the apartment they had just visited, Melissa Clarke's husband watching them go, one last chance to find out what had happened to Melissa.

'The woman that made David Jex think again about Aidan Molloy,' Joe said. 'It was just another missing person, but then something clicked, and he started wondering about Aidan. Perhaps it brought a nagging doubt to the surface.'

'But what?'

'It was the library,' Hugh said, his voice quiet. 'It isn't far away.'

'The library?' Joe said, climbing into the car.

'Rebecca Scarfield was a librarian,' Hugh said.

'I know.'

'At the same library where Melissa had her book group.'

Joe looked at Gina, whose eyebrows were raised as she fumbled with her car keys. 'No, I didn't notice that,' he said.

'I suppose it didn't seem important enough back then, where she worked. The police had their man and everyone who worked there had alibis. It was just her job, nothing more.'

'How far did you look into those alibis, just to see whether the police had got it right, to see if there was another suspect?' Joe said.

'What, spread the blame? Make someone else suffer the pointed finger? I didn't work like that.'

Gina's hand reached across to touch Joe's, just to tell him to slow it down, but Joe gave her a quick shake of his head. The time was now.

Joe turned round in the car seat. 'It's not about blame.'

'We bear a heavy responsibility,' Hugh said. 'The courtroom is not just some theatre. It's about the lives of real people.'

'Sometimes those standing in the dock are people too.'

'I know that,' Hugh said, his brow furrowed, his voice more defensive.

'Do you?' Joe said.

Hugh put his head back, expanding his double

chin, and entwined his fingers over his stomach. 'Explain yourself.'

'Your job was to do all you could for them, but you saw it differently, so I've heard. Was that the deal – that you promised not to try too hard if Hunter kept on feeding you the work?'

Hugh paled and then frowned. He shook his head. 'What nonsense.'

'You were in Hunter's pocket, Hugh, only ever doing the minimum.'

Hugh exhaled loudly. 'In his pocket? You have no idea what you're talking about. And from you, Joe. I expected better.'

'How many holidays did Hunter have in your Spanish apartment?'

'What does that have to do with anything?'

'Come on, Hugh, getting cosy with the lead detective? Did you do anything else to make sure you got the work?'

'Joe!' Gina warned.

'What are you getting at?' Hugh said. 'Just spit it out if you've got something to say.'

Joe looked across to Gina, who was giving slight shakes of her head. He was getting close to something he shouldn't reveal. Not yet. He changed the line of attack.

'Why are you helping out here, Hugh?'

'I told you: I'm a bored widower trying to right a wrong. Now I'm wishing I hadn't bothered.'

'How very noble. So why are you feeding Hunter with updates?'

Hugh opened his mouth to say something but he stayed silent. Instead, he clenched his jaw hard.

'Have you seen Hunter today?' Joe said, his eyes

fixed on Hugh, trying to bore into him, letting him know that his secret was out.

Hugh's mouth twitched but said nothing.

'How about after you left my apartment? Your little meeting in his car.'

Hugh let out a deep breath and his head drooped. He inspected his hands for a few seconds, his right thumb stroking the palm of his left hand, before he said, 'It's not how it looks.'

Gina scoffed loudly. 'When men say that, it is usually exactly how it looks.' When Hugh stayed silent, she asked, 'So what is it then?'

Hugh looked out of the window, his jaw set, before he said, 'All right, I admit that I became involved in the case again because I was worried.'

'About what?'

'That I'd done the wrong thing back then.' He paused, as if working out how much to tell before he said, 'I meant it when I said that I thought Aidan was innocent, but I've thought that before and been wrong. So what, I pulled a few punches. Some guilty people avoided being acquitted and I made a good living. Would it have been less immoral if I had made a good living from helping guilty people get away with it?' He shook his head. 'I was a defence lawyer. Morals are murky, you know that.'

'And are all the ones you let down worth it for one Aidan Molloy, the one who didn't do it, the young man who spends every night in Wakefield Prison, waiting for a makeshift blade in his back just to fuel someone else's notoriety?'

Hugh rubbed his forehead. 'All right, I had a certain business model,' he said. 'I found a way of

355

getting the work, and it made me a good living.'

'You were paid to defend these people,' Joe said, exasperation evident in his higher pitch. 'They came to you for help.'

'No, they came to me to help them get away with something,' Hugh said, some snap creeping into his voice.

'That's how being a lawyer sometimes works.'

'So that trumps everything, does it? It doesn't matter about morality or right and wrong or punishing the guilty? It's just about giving everyone a free shot at getting away with it.'

Joe shook his head angrily. 'Don't try to justify what you did. You got greedy, plain and simple, and sold out your clients, so that people like Aidan Molloy stay in prison and women like Mary Molloy spend every day in torment, just wanting her child back.'

Hugh blew out a deep sigh and looked upwards. Tears moistened his eyes. 'Aidan was the one I worried about,' he said, a break in his voice. 'The others? I didn't care. They were guilty, so big deal, I sold my professional soul. What's the alternative? Just selling your own soul because of some professional promise? The reason is the same: to make money.'

'Let's visit Mary and see what she thinks about that.'

'And that's why I'm here, don't you understand?'

'Explain.'

'Aidan was the one who always troubled me, but Hunter, well, he convinced me at the time, and the evidence seemed good, so I let it ride.

But Aidan was the one who haunted me when I looked back, always the doubt, that maybe he was the one I got wrong.'

'And how did that make you feel?'

'Confused,' Hugh said. 'What I don't know is how I'd feel if someone I'd kept out of jail went and killed someone else. There are no easy answers. Aidan is suffering, but I was never sure of his innocence, and I thought that I had just read him wrong, that he was the most convincing liar out of all the liars who had ever passed through my office.'

'And now?'

Hugh sighed. 'I got it wrong all along.'

'It makes it one big fucking irony then, doesn't it?' Joe said. 'By letting Aidan go to jail, Rebecca's real killer stayed free, and killed again. Like Melissa.'

'You don't know that.'

'But you suspect it. I can see it in your face. And it's somehow connected to David Jex, because he found out and look what it cost him. So that's two deaths, and his son is still missing. How's your conscience now, Hugh?'

Hugh didn't respond. Joe gripped the back of the car seat. 'So why have you been feeding Hunter?'

'Like I said earlier, it's not how it seems.'

'Tell us, then. I'm just dying for this one.'

'I was trying to make him see what you were seeing, how he had got it wrong, that it was time to come clean if he had.'

'And his response?'

'That I was seeing things that weren't true, but if

357

I kept on reporting back to him, he might change his mind.' Hugh stared out of the windscreen for a few seconds before saying, 'So what now?'

Joe looked towards Gina, who gave him a small shrug. 'We're cutting you loose, Hugh,' Joe said. 'If we're going to prove Aidan's innocence, I don't want you around. You're too close to Hunter.'

Hugh nodded slowly. 'Just one thing though.'

'What?'

'Make it right. Don't worry about my reputation. Just make it right.'

And with that, Hugh climbed out of the car, shuffling off into the gloom of early evening.

Fifty-two

Sam walked more purposefully into the police station, trying to shake off some of his fatigue. Alice's words were still ringing in his ears and they had given him some renewed vigour, made him determined to finish the job.

He was looking for DI Evans, to speak to her about what Joe had said, when a tall bald man appeared in the corridor. The assistant chief constable, Desmond Archer. Rebecca's father.

Sam faltered, fought the urge to turn and go the other way, except the other way didn't lead to anywhere other than the way he had just come. It was no coincidence, though, and he knew he had to keep on walking. He took a deep breath to calm himself and smiled respectfully when he got close.

The assistant chief wasn't in the mood for pleasantries. He pointed and said, 'In here,' towards the room in which Evans was sitting.

As Sam went in, Evans looked up briefly, but then stared straight ahead. Sam looked at her to try to get a sign as to where this was heading, but from the way she stayed expressionless he knew it was serious.

The door slammed shut behind him.

Sam didn't sit down, even though there was a chair available. He stood with his feet apart, his head up, almost to attention, his hands clasped in front of him. The assistant chief's footsteps were quiet as he went round the desk, taking his place slowly in the chair.

The assistant chief was a career cop. No, more than that. He was one of the people for whom being a cop was his destination, his definition, as if he wouldn't have suited any other role. He was bald and humourless, his chest always out, taut and muscled from hours punishing himself on a bike. Sam knew too well how grief pushed people into distraction activities, as a moment alone can mean a moment to dwell. It was important not to forget, but sometimes remembering was too painful to handle.

'You know who I am,' he said to Sam.

'Yes, sir.'

'So tell me what you have been doing today.' He put his hands together on the desk but sat back, as if it was some way of stopping himself from springing at Sam.

'It's a follow-on from the discovery of David Jex this morning.'

'Go on.'

Sam swallowed. He knew he couldn't avoid it. 'Inquiries have led me to believe that it might be connected in some way to your daughter's case.' Sam tried to hide the tremble in his voice.

The assistant chief blinked quickly but otherwise he did not display any emotion.

'My daughter's case has been solved, Detective,' he said. 'Do you understand?'

Sam paused. 'I do, sir.'

'And do you think there is anything you can add to that?'

Sam thought back on what Joe had talked about, the inquiries he had made. He tried to ignore the fact that he was speaking to the assistant chief and tried to remember that he was speaking to a victim's father. This wasn't about procedures. It was about grief.

He softened his tone.

'I've received information that suggests, and only suggests, that Aidan Molloy might not have been your daughter's killer,' he said. 'I'm only looking into it as it seems somehow related to David Jex. If it isn't, I will stop looking.'

The assistant chief breathed in deeply through his nose before he said, 'You will not go off track on this case.' His voice was slow and even, but Sam heard the menace in it. 'Aidan Molloy is in prison, and he will stay in prison, and I will not have one of my own detectives looking around for any little specks of doubt to prop up an appeal just because his brother is involved.' Sam tried to protest but he was silenced. 'You know how it is, Parker. People like Aidan Molloy shout all the time, hoping that if they shout for long enough someone will believe them. Well, not with Rebecca's case. You'll drop this. Now.'

Sam glanced across to Evans, who didn't react.

'Do you understand, DC Parker?'

'I understand, sir.'

The assistant chief got to his feet and walked quickly out of the door. When it slammed, Evans let out a long breath and said, 'I'm sorry, Sam, but you're on your own on this one.'

'Who tipped him off?'

'Does it matter?'

'Of course it does. My brother reckons that Hunter got witnesses to change their versions to make sure that Aidan Molloy was convicted, and that David Jex realised they had got it wrong when someone else was murdered.'

Evans considered that, but then she shook her head. 'We can't go there.'

'Was it Hunter who tipped off the assistant chief? If it was, he's got what he wanted, which was for us to lay off the case.'

'There's no *us* in this, Sam. You got that?'

He sighed. 'Yes, I've got that, ma'am. Thank you.'

As he left her room, he felt deflated. It was either do the right thing or do as he was told. He knew which way he ought to go if he valued his career, but that wasn't the reason he joined the police.

He was going to do the right thing, whatever the cost.

Although it was getting late, the library lights were still on. It was an ageing prefab, with grubby yellow panels beneath flimsy-looking windows, but the glow from inside was bright, showing the rows of book-racks.

Darnside Library was the same as most, like a reminder of Joe's own childhood visits, with the library as a community centre and more than just about books. Posters on the walls advertised nursery groups and help centres for young mothers. Behind the desk there was a woman with glasses and short dark hair, who grinned warmly as they approached. Her badge said she was called Heather.

'We're closing soon,' Heather said, glancing at her watch.

'It's all right, we won't be long,' Joe said, and he slid a business card across the counter.

Heather read the card, her smile fading. 'Have we done something wrong?'

'I'm here about Rebecca Scarfield,' he said.

Heather looked confused for a moment before her eyes widened with recognition. 'She was here before me,' she said. 'She died about four months before I started. Everyone says she was really nice.'

'What were people saying then?'

'What do you mean?'

'I've been doing this job a long time,' Joe said, smiling. 'I know that there are the things that people will say to the police, and then there are things that they will keep to themselves, perhaps when they're not sure about something or don't want to make any trouble.'

'There was nothing really,' Heather said. 'Everyone said how sweet she was, and I know that people missed her, which made it hard for me at first. She was having an affair with the man who killed her, we all know that now, but that doesn't make her a bad person.'

'Aidan Molloy,' Joe said.

'That's him.'

'Were there rumours of any other affairs?'

Heather chewed her lip as she thought back. She shook her head. 'Not that I've heard, but people don't like to talk ill of the dead.'

'I understand,' Joe said, nodding. 'What about Melissa Clarke?'

'Oh Melissa. That's really sad. Melissa is lovely, and I feel for her husband. No one knows where she's gone at all.'

'How well did you know her?'

'Just from when she came here, for the reading group. Nice woman. Quiet, but there's something genuine about her.' She frowned. 'But you're not the first to ask this.'

'What do you mean?'

'There was a policeman, not long after Melissa went missing,' Heather said. 'I presumed that there was no connection with the group when he didn't come back.' She tugged on her lip and looked to the floor. 'I can't remember his name though. Jackson? No, too long. Jacks?'

'Jex,' Joe said.

'That's it. Jex,' she said, her face brightening. 'Yes, he came in asking about Rebecca and then Melissa, and we told him that there was no link, as Melissa only joined here a year earlier.'

'How long has the reading group been meeting here?'

'A long time. The members come and go, but

there's been a reading group here for years. Before I started.'

'How many are in it?'

Heather paused as she thought about that. 'About fifteen, although it does change. People leave and new ones join, you know how it is. We're trying to grow it because if we can keep the library busy, they might keep it open. We keep getting threatened with closure, but people need us. It's not just about reading books.' She pointed to the opposite wall. 'There's a poster there about it.'

Joe wandered over with Gina and stood in front of a large poster showing a group of people sitting in a circle, a book open on each of their laps. It was a mixed group, men and women of varying ages, all looking self-conscious and smiling, as if they knew they were having their picture taken.

Heather joined him at the poster. She tapped on the picture, at someone at one side. There wasn't much to see of him, just the top of his profile and a crossed leg jutting out in front of him, as if he was leaning back and putting himself deliberately out of the frame. Light brown cords and suede shoes.

'Melissa was friendly with him. Declan Farrell. He stopped coming not long after Melissa disappeared. I think he liked her, if you know what I mean.'

'Why did he stop coming?' Gina asked.

Heather leaned in so she could whisper conspiratorially. 'I heard he was warned off, that he was getting too fresh with Rachel, one of the other ladies. She stopped coming but her husband had words with him. Something about bombarding her with texts, talking about her marriage.'

Gina stepped forward and examined the picture. 'There's not much to see. Do you have any other pictures from this session?'

'No, I didn't take them.'

'So what do you know about him?'

Heather curled her lip. 'A supreme flatterer, in his mind, as if he makes an effort to get to know about everyone. Like there was one guy, he was into wine, and then Declan came in one week and started talking about wine as if he was really knowledgeable, and it seemed sort of creepy, as if he'd been researching it just to impress. One week he produced an article from a wine magazine and started to talk about wine, but the wine guy, well, he said that it was clear that he didn't know much beyond what he had read. He was the same with the women, as if he was always trying to find some angle to reach them, so that they'd be impressed by him. Some didn't like it and let him know, and he avoided those. Others thought he was nice. Entertaining, witty, knowledgeable.'

'And what did you think?'

'Honestly?'

'That's what we want.'

Heather pursed her lips. 'It was too false, as if he had no depth, no interests of his own other than getting people to like him.'

Gina stepped away, shaking her head. 'A narcissist,' she said quietly, almost to herself. 'Textbook.'

Joe looked at her. 'What do you mean?'

Gina shook her head. 'Nothing.'

Joe looked back to Heather. 'Do you have an address for Declan?'

'I can't give that out,' Heather said. 'I need this job. It's confidential customer information.'

'Can I ask you one thing then?' Joe said.

'Yes, go on,' Heather said, caution in her voice.

'Just go online and see if the address he gave was real.'

Heather's mouth twitched as she hesitated, before she relented and turned the screen back so that Joe couldn't see what was going on. A few clicks later and Heather paused, confusion in her eyes. She looked up. 'No, the street doesn't exist. It says 45 Whiteside Drive, but there is no Whiteside Drive in Manchester. There's a Whiteside Close in Salford, and a Whiteside Fold in Rochdale, but that's it.'

'A false detail,' Joe said.

'And a dead end,' Gina said. 'We don't know his address, or even if Declan is his real name.'

Joe turned to Heather. 'Will you contact the woman who complained about him – Rachel you said – ask her if she will meet me?'

Heather reached for her phone, and after a brief conversation, she said to Joe, 'High End Park in fifteen minutes.'

Joe thanked her and headed for the door. Before he got there, Heather shouted, 'So you think Declan might have had something to do with Melissa going missing?'

Joe exchanged glances with Gina before he said, 'As bizarre as it sounds, I hope so.'

Fifty-three

The Incident Room was busy. No one was going home, not with a dead copper pulled out of the ground. Some were ringing round the friends of David Jex, trying to get one piece of information they didn't collect when he went missing, whereas others were hunting down informants, trying to find out whether anyone had heard any rumours about some criminal kingpin offing a detective. It's something that would be a boast, so the whispers would soon start.

From the looks of exasperation, Sam knew that there was nothing positive coming through.

Hunter was in the corner, as always, but he didn't seem to be doing anything. He wasn't on the phones or directing any inquiries.

As Sam went over to Charlotte, Hunter looked up. Sam thought he looked wild-eyed. Sam held his gaze until Hunter got to his feet. For a moment, Sam thought he was going to march over to him, but instead Hunter stormed out of the Incident Room. There was a slam of an office door further along the corridor, followed by some shouting and the sound of chairs being knocked over.

Everyone exchanged glances and frowns.

'I'm keeping out of his way,' Charlotte said, as Sam reached her desk.

'How long has he been like that?' Sam said.

'Hours now,' she said. 'He just stares at the floor or paces around. He's not talking to anyone, not directing anyone.' She frowned. 'Why are you still here?'

'What, you mean still on duty, or still in a job?' he said.

'Ha ha.'

'I've had my wings clipped,' he said quietly. 'I've been told not to look at Aidan Molloy's case.'

Charlotte grimaced. 'And?'

'I'll think about it.' He pointed at Charlotte's computer monitor. 'So what are you doing?'

'Just cataloguing David's cases,' Charlotte said. 'His live ones and any closed within the previous three years, just in case it's revenge for something he'd done. I'm going through each one to assess the level of risk, whether he'd made any notes of anyone threatening him.'

'Found anything yet?'

Charlotte shook her head. 'Nothing. They're just cases, like we deal with every day. You know what it's like, people shouting threats when we arrest someone, their nearest and dearest losing it, but they always calm down, and some even become friendly, knowing we can update them. This is going to swamp us. We need something forensic.'

Sam sat down at the desk. 'Have they done the post mortem?'

'Yes,' Charlotte said, 'and it gets worse.'

'What, worse than being dead?'

She nodded. 'His body was pretty well-preserved. The peat does that. There was soil in his lungs, Sam.'

'Meaning?'

'That he wasn't dead when he was buried. He might not have been alive for long, but he took a few deep breaths of soil before he went.'

Sam closed his eyes. 'Jesus,' he muttered. Then his phone rang. He checked the screen. It was Joe.

He thought about answering, but the words of the assistant chief were still too clear. He would call back when he had time. It was time to play the dutiful soldier for a while.

Sam logged onto the computer and held out his hand. 'Pass me some case names. I'll help you out.'

'Shouldn't you go home? You look worn out.'

He shook his head. 'Not until I can't do any more.' Then his phone buzzed. It was a text.

He pulled out his phone. It was from Joe. *Look at Melissa Clarke* was all it said.

Melissa Clarke. Sam smiled to himself. It was a good place to start.

He tapped her name into the search bar. There were three in the system, but when he clicked on them, he saw that only one related to a missing person.

As he searched through the notes on the computer, the file information reports, the incident log, the statements taken not long after her disappearance, tremors of excitement started. There was a picture of her, one that was used in an appeal for information. Pretty, blonde, smiling. Joe was right. He had found something.

A married woman who went out one night and never returned. No explanation. Just like Rebecca Scarfield.

Charlotte looked up. 'What have you got?'

'Nothing,' he said, smiling, knowing the gleam in his eyes gave him away. 'I'm not supposed to be looking, remember.'

She grinned, but then it faded as she looked over Sam's shoulder. He turned round. Hunter was there, staring, not at Sam, but at the photograph showing on Sam's monitor of Melissa Clarke.

Hunter didn't move for a few seconds, just clenched and unclenched his fist, before he pointed at Weaver and then gestured towards the door.

As they left the room, Sam muttered, 'Shit.'

'You in trouble?' Charlotte said.

'Looks that way.'

'Then you might as well keep on going.'

He thought about that and smiled. 'Yes, I think you're right.'

Joe and Gina waited in a park by what would have been a country lane many decades earlier. The bright stream of the motorway had changed all that. A chain hotel and a faked country pub had been built opposite, and the lane was now a busy route to the small industrial estates that had sprung up, to take advantage of the quick access to the rest of the country.

The park still offered some respite though. Surrounded by trees, the grass in front of them was a taste of the countryside but with the cold northern breezes blocked out. Gina was sitting on a swing, rocking back and forth. Joe was leaning against one of the metal struts.

'What are you thinking?' Joe said.

Gina looked up. 'Is it that obvious?'

'You go quiet when you've something on your mind. Is it about the firm?'

Gina stayed quiet for a few moments, before she said, 'Hunter. If Aidan is innocent, why didn't he spot it? Whatever you think about him, Hunter is a murder detective, and he's old school, still about catching killers. Call it ego, or even call it little boys playing sheriff, but that's how Hunter is.'

'Would he let Aidan stay in prison if he knew he was innocent?'

'It isn't Aidan that would bother him but the killer being free. Aidan would be a casualty, nothing else. But letting a killer stay free? That's different.'

'Perhaps he doesn't know,' Joe said. 'Perhaps he's as convinced about Aidan's guilt as everyone else.'

'I'm not so sure about that. Why is he so interested in the case still?' Gina paused when there was a metallic squeak. When they looked to the gate into the park there was a woman there, in jeans and a long jumper, her arms folded, looking around. When Gina got to her feet, making the swing creak, she jumped, startled. Gina stepped forward, realising that she was in darkness. 'Rachel?'

A pause, and then, 'Yes, it's me.' Her voice was timid, reluctant.

Gina walked towards her, Joe just behind, but Rachel stayed where she was. When they got close, Gina handed over her business card. She looked at it and tapped it against her palm before saying, 'So what can I do for you?'

'Like Heather told you on the phone, it's about Declan from the reading group.'

'What about him?'

'Can't we sit over there, on a bench?'

Rachel looked and then nodded, walking over, her arms still folded.

She was pretty, her hair Scandinavian blonde, her skin pale and delicate, her figure slim underneath the baggy jumper.

As they all settled down, Rachel was quiet for a few seconds, before she said, 'Why do you want to know about Declan?'

'It's to do with a case we're working on and it could be important. We spoke with Heather at the library and she said that you and Declan got close.'

The clench of her folded arms got tighter when Gina said that.

'Heather shouldn't have said that.'

'She thought she was helping.'

Rachel stayed silent.

'Did you get close?' Gina said.

'Nothing happened,' Rachel said, glaring. 'I want you to know that. It's important.'

'So tell us what nearly happened.'

Rachel looked down, and Joe could tell she was working out what to say. Eventually, she said, 'I'm only talking to you because someone has to.'

'What do you mean?'

'Declan, he was, well, it's hard to explain. Dangerous, I suppose.'

'How so?'

'He was persistent. He got under my skin, made me doubt everything.'

'How do you mean?'

'Are either of you two married?' Rachel said.

'No,' Gina said, glancing at Joe, who was sitting back so that it was harder for Rachel to see him. 'I'm not interested in judging you. Neither of us are. We just need to know about Declan.'

'It might be hard for you to understand then, but things become routine,' Rachel said. 'It's not bad, that's life, everyday things, and sharing those things is part of everything, but it is hard to maintain the levels of excitement there once were. I understand that, at least I thought I did.'

'So what changed?'

'Declan.'

'Explain.'

Rachel shook her head as if angry at some forgotten memory. 'Declan is a handsome guy. Interesting, funny, engaging. It seemed like he knew me. I told him I liked flowers, doing arrangements and stuff, and he used to talk to me about them, as if he liked them too. He would come up to me before the meetings and tell me about some he had just bought, and it was flattering, as if he cared about the things I cared about. Then he got hold of my mobile number, and it changed.'

'What do you mean?'

'Before then, it had been a flirt at the book group, nothing more. I'd go home with the buzz of feeling that someone fancied me, but I didn't think anything beyond that, but then the texts started coming in. And they really started coming in. It was like scatter-bombing, constant, but it was personal stuff, saying that he was concerned about me, that I seemed unhappy. And I wasn't, or at least I thought I wasn't, but the things he was saying made me question everything. He didn't insult my husband, but talked about how nothing was exciting any more and how I had talked myself into a rut. I started to look at my husband and think maybe Declan was right. Did I still love him? Was it just a habit? Did I need some excitement?' She sighed. 'I asked him to stop texting me, because I knew he was sucking me in, but he just told me he wouldn't accept that answer. He would text me late at night and early in the morning, and Gary would ask who I was texting but what could I say? So Declan became my secret, and in between all the stuff that questioned everything was the fun stuff. The flattery, the jokes, the feeling that he was confiding in me about his own life and that I could confide in him.'

'It sounds like the start of an affair,' Gina said.

'It nearly was,' Rachel said, regret filling her voice. 'He invited me out. He said he would treat me, take me somewhere nice that my husband could never afford, but I was getting cold feet. I would have to get dressed up and I couldn't face lying to my husband.'

'So what happened?'

'He kept on and on, but I started getting suspicious about him, because it almost seemed too perfect. I'm just someone who works for the tax office to keep the bills paid and was doing a flower-arranging course at college. I've got this handsome guy who is interesting, and finds me interesting, and it was too good to be true. So I started to take notice of the things he was saying and it started to seem unreal. He said he was a writer, but it turned out he had never written anything. Or at least never had it published. And he would send me messages and make me feel like the most important person in his life, but then it would just stop. He would be quiet for weeks and I'd wonder if I'd done something wrong, just go crazy thinking about him and why he had stopped, and then the texts would start up again.'

'Why does that make him dangerous though?' Gina said. 'It just makes him sound like a player, nothing more.'

Rachel looked down and her chin started to quiver. 'I told him to leave me alone, and he got nasty, and I don't just mean angry. I'd followed him one night because I wanted to know who he was with, and I saw him with some woman, showing her into his house. I wasn't supposed to know where he lived, and when I followed him it wasn't where he said it was. I confronted him the next time I saw him, and there was something in his eyes I've never seen in a man before. A darkness, menace, like it transformed him, except his words didn't match. He was asking me to go to his house just once, to see how good it could be.'

'And did you?'

Rachel shook her head. 'He scared me. I refused, and when I wouldn't give in, he threatened to tell Gary all about us, how we had been exchanging late-night messages, the things I had said, the secrets I'd shared, about things I had done that Gary doesn't know about, can't know about, because it would hurt him. Just meaningless stuff, things that had happened on nights out but I'd felt bad about and ended up sharing with him.'

'How did it all end?'

'I changed my number. I stopped going to the reading group and that was it. Then I heard about Melissa going missing and I knew she had been getting close to Declan, so I wondered, well, whether he'd had anything to do with it.'

'Did you tell the police?'

She shook her head. 'Then all my stuff would come out. It's selfish, I know.'

'So why are you telling us now?'

'You're the first person to ask. The rest had just been my secret.' She looked at Gina. 'Do you think he might have harmed someone? Like Melissa.'

'I don't know,' Gina said. 'But something isn't adding up.'

'I wouldn't be surprised if he had.'

'What makes you so certain?'

'Just something in his eyes. I can't be more precise than that.'

Joe leaned forward. 'You said you followed him to his house.'

'Yes. He hadn't known I was there.'

'Where is it?'

'One of the streets off Greencroft Avenue, you know, the turning after the bowling alley. I can't remember which one.'

At the mention of the bowling alley, the memories of the police station visit with Carl rushed back at Joe. He hadn't written down the street name where Carl had been arrested, but on the drive home Carl had pointed it out. He'd forgotten about that. They had been driving past the bowling alley. *Down there,* Carl had said, and ges-

376

tured towards a street somewhere in the distance. Joe hadn't taken any notice at the time, it was late and it hadn't seemed important, but he remembered it now.

He turned to Gina, his nerves fluttering. 'That's the place.'

'What is?'

'Carl was arrested somewhere near there.' Joe looked at Rachel again. 'What kind of car does Declan drive?'

'A Focus. Dark red.'

Joe's eyes widened. Like Nicole had said, the one she saw on the moors. He grabbed Gina's hand. 'We've got to go.'

Fifty-four

Carl had hardly moved since the man left the cellar.

The man had ranted and kicked furniture, even thrown some around. Then there had been the slam of the door and the house had fallen silent.

Time had passed and all Carl could feel was emptiness. His head still throbbed from where he had been pushed against the wall, but that wasn't the reason. It all felt so hopeless. His one chance and Emma had died.

He'd let her down. He should have charged him, just to give Emma enough time to get to the door and make a run for it. She could have raised the alarm, and he could be waiting for the wail of sirens, instead of wondering what lay in store for him now. No, they had been too intent on striking out at him. Too angry, not thinking clearly enough. And now Emma was dead.

Carl couldn't look at her body, just a shadow in the murky darkness. Even if he was able to get out, seeing someone being killed was something he knew he'd never forget.

There was the sound of the car and then the slam of the front door. The man was back. Carl didn't move. Minutes passed, although Carl hadn't got any better at counting them, before the cellar door was flung open. There was a pause and then shadows flickered against the wall, lighting up the cellar with movement.

Carl struggled to a sitting position. The man was holding a large candle mounted on a white holder, the flame blowing slightly in the draught made by his movement. He walked slowly, carefully, his shadow cast as a moving giant, before he stopped to set the candle down on the floor. It lit up Emma, gave her skin some life. Carl turned away.

The man straightened and walked over to Carl. He was holding a newspaper in his other hand. His jaw was set in anger. There was a bandage around his neck.

He put the newspaper on the floor and then reached down for Carl, pulling him upwards by his hair. Carl cried out in pain as he was walked across to the noose. He struggled as the man placed it over his head again, but it was no use. Once it was back in place, the man yanked hard on the rope so that it went tight around him once more. Enough space still to breathe, but its tightness was an ever-present reminder.

Carl's legs ached straight away, even though he'd had some time resting.

The man bent down for the newspaper and thrust the front page in front of Carl. The *Evening Press*.

'Did you think I didn't know who you were?' the man said, snarling, spitting the words at him. 'Read it.'

Carl tried to focus, but the light was dim and the paper too close. 'I can't see,' but then the man moved the paper away and Carl saw his father's face.

Sweat jumped onto his forehead and his stomach rolled, the taste of acid sharp in his throat. He caught the headline. MISSING DETECTIVE FOUND BURIED ON THE MOORS. Carl didn't need to read the rest. He had found his answer.

The hot prickle of tears flashed across his eyes. His gut clenched and he let out a long moan. The cellar receded as he felt the hard slap of shock and memories of his father rushed back at him. His laughter, loud and happy; the strong man who held the family together. Splashing in the pool on holiday, falling asleep against his chest when watching films, the feel of his hand in his hair as he ruffled it. The images came in a flurry, so that he couldn't sift or sort them, and all he had now was the headline blurred through his tears.

He looked up at the man, and then back at the page, to the truth he had always known, but the hurt was still deep, the anguish of knowing that

379

the last faint hope of his father being alive was gone.

'You bastard,' Carl said, his voice thick with emotion. 'What did you do?'

'Me? Nothing, would you believe?' He smiled, although it was more like a cold sneer. 'But you'll never find out.' The man reached for the gag that had been thrown onto the floor. He fastened it tight, making Carl grunt with discomfort. 'I have to leave. I've got a few things to straighten out first. Remember, you started this, the end.' He paused to look down at Emma. 'I'm saving you this way, because you won't be able to live with it if I let you go. Choose your own way out, Carl. I'm leaving the gas on when I go. Whoever is first in will make the house go up with a bang, or maybe when the gas reaches that flame. That will be painful. Maybe go your own way first. Remember, all you need to do is sink to your knees.'

Then he was gone, moving quickly up the stairs, the door clicking shut.

Carl put his head back and let the tears flow. His father was dead. He'd always suspected it, but now his hope had truly been snuffed out. What about his mother? How would she cope?

He looked to the floor and felt the rope dig into his neck. His legs were weak, his energy sapped by the headline. He couldn't go on.

'I'm sorry,' he said, tears streaming down his cheeks. He'd let his mother down, by ending up like this. The man had gone. Carl knew he couldn't hold on.

Once more, his head filled with memories of his father. His smile, strong and funny, and the feel of his arms around his shoulders. His protector. His hero. Gone.

He couldn't last much longer. His legs ached, almost urged him to sit down. The man was right. It was the easiest way.

He wanted to say sorry to his mother. The flame was hypnotic, casting shadows over Emma. He thought of how it would be when the gas came down the stairs, curling around the bare space, sinking, finding the heat. Everything would end in a flash. He couldn't bear that.

It was time to go. He had no fight left.

Fifty-five

Gina was driving around the streets beyond the bowling alley. Sam still hadn't got back to Joe with the address, so they were looking for a dark red Ford Focus.

'So you think this is the man?' Gina said.

'Carl was here,' he said. 'Now he's missing. Whoever this person is, he is connected to a missing woman.'

Gina nodded at that, satisfied. 'I know this Declan.' When Joe looked surprised, she added, 'No, not the real Declan. I mean, I know people like him. How he thinks. I've come across people like him before.' Then she smiled ruefully. 'No, a person, not people.'

'Tell me,' Joe said.

'It was more than ten years ago now,' she said.

'I was living with a man but we'd become distant, although I still loved him. So along came Lloyd, another detective. Full of charm and wit, and he seemed to understand me, as if he knew what I was thinking, why I felt lonely. We had similar interests, or so I thought, but I felt bad about cheating. Lloyd wouldn't let it go though. He got hold of my number and texted constantly. It was just relentless, and eventually I gave in. So we went out. He made me feel special, fed me bull-shit, like we were star-crossed or something, and I just fell for him. I left my partner but as soon as I did, Lloyd dumped me. He'd got what he wanted, total devotion, capitulation almost. What further use was I to him?'

'Sometimes it's just the thrill of the chase.'

'No, it was more than that. And it's not just men; there are women like that too. He wanted to control me, as if it was just to prove that he could. But how can you walk away from someone you are so deeply in love with like that? So I made a fool of myself. I turned up at his house, sobbed and begged to be taken back, and he just abused it. He used me, like some plaything, knowing that I would do anything. He would leave it weeks without any contact, and I'd be calling and texting but nothing came back, until he decided he needed me, and I was desperate enough to jump at it. I realised what was going on eventually, that I was being stupid, but it took me a long time to get to that. And when I did, I walked away.'

'How did he take that?'

'Nastily. That was the thing with him, you see. I was supposed to be under his spell, and when I wasn't, he became spiteful. He threatened me with some photographs he had of me.' Gina blushed. 'Intimate ones. But I just kept on ignoring him and eventually he got the message. He ruined me though. I thought I was cracking up. I'd lost everything I had with my partner, so that was it for me. I decided I was staying single. No man was ever going to hurt me like that again.'

'You're too special to be alone, Gina,' Joe said. 'Any man would be lucky to have you.'

'Thank you.' She sighed in exasperation. 'I think I'm a decent person, but that was my flaw in the end. I thought he would treat me like I wanted to treat him, but I was naïve.'

'And you think it's similar to this?'

'I recognise the traits.'

'But being a bastard isn't the same as being a murderer.'

'It helps to be heartless though,' Gina said. 'And there are more connections you haven't spotted.'

Joe frowned. 'Go on.'

'What was the prosecution theory as to why Aidan killed Rebecca?'

'Rebecca was ending their relationship and Aidan became jealous and killed her in a rage. Her husband said they were trying to make another go of their marriage.'

'And think back now to Melissa's husband. What did he tell us just now?' When Joe didn't answer, Gina continued, 'That they had been going through a tough time but it seemed like they were pulling back together.'

'And?'

'Join the dots, Joe. Two married women having

affairs and both die or go missing just as they are trying to get their marriages back on track. Aidan says that Rebecca was seeing someone else too. Was Rebecca ending that relationship as well? It makes sense. She was cutting off all her extra-marital stuff and making another go of it, and it was the other person who killed her, not Aidan. Was that Declan?'

'So you think he killed Rebecca because she was ending the relationship, and then did the same with Melissa? Can you be so angry twice? Once is a loss of control. But twice?'

Gina shook her head. 'It's not about rage in the way you're thinking of it. If the killer is a narcissist, the loss of devotion will burn away at him. I've seen it and it's unpleasant.' As Joe took that in, Gina added, 'There's something else too.'

'Go on.'

'Everyone is married. Rebecca. Melissa. Then Rachel, even though she didn't succumb. It's not that he's a player, collecting beautiful women like trophies. What seems to attract him is women who belong to someone else. What they have is happiness, something special, togetherness, even if it has gone a bit stale. He has nothing and that eats away at him. So he wants to destroy the one thing he can't have, and that's happiness. That's just how Lloyd was. He liked to make out he was deep, but really there was nothing. He was a shell of a man, and he knew it.'

'It seems a stretch,' Joe said. 'Maybe he's just one of those men who have a lot of women on the go just so that he can boast to his friends. Deep down, there's nothing, yes, but it's all a game.'

'But all he has is the devotion of these women. When that disappears, how does he react? If it burned away at him, it might just have ended in murder.'

Joe thought about that as Gina drove, looking along the rows of identical-looking streets, long curves of high grey Victorian houses behind millstone walls and black metal gates. Then he saw it. A Ford Focus. Dark red. An 06 plate, so it would have been around when Rebecca was killed.

'There,' he said, banging his hand on the dashboard.

Gina stamped on her brake and scraped the wheels along the kerb as she came to a halt. She turned to Joe. 'You should have kept proper notes, so we knew for certain this was the actual address.'

'Lesson learned.'

'So what do we do?' Gina said.

'We could just knock on the door.'

'And how do you think that will go down? David Jex went missing. Carl Jex is missing. I know there are two of us, but I don't fancy turning it into a quartet.'

'I'll call Sam,' Joe said, and reached for his phone.

'And say what? Come and kick down a door because there is a car that is different to that mentioned in witness statements? It's not going to happen.'

'But it must relate to the body they dug up on the moors this morning.'

'Why? What real link is there?'

Joe turned, frustrated, knowing that Gina was

right. It was all surmising and guesswork in some hope that they could prove that Aidan was innocent.

Joe leaned forward and strained as he looked through the windscreen. 'Okay, let's watch for a while; see what we can work out.'

The houses on the street seemed pretty ordinary. They were spaced out, tall and imposing, with cars on the driveways, and just enough room to swing the gates closed behind. A laugh drifted through an open window and a car horn sounded from somewhere nearby. Midges danced in the faintest strains of daylight. The streetlights displayed faint glows as the sun disappeared behind houses at the end of the road, everywhere in evening shadow. There was no traffic noise – most people would be back from work – just the sounds of whooping children from a small playground visible through the gaps in the houses.

'So what do we think?' Gina said.

'That someone is playing around with married women, but he doesn't cope well with rejection,' Joe said. 'Like you said, what unites Melissa and Rebecca is not just that they were having affairs but that things were getting better – they both wanted to patch things up with their husbands.'

'And David Jex?'

'He spotted the link,' Joe said. 'He was the detective who spoke to Melissa's husband. He must have picked up on the same thing Hugh did – the library – and checked it out.'

'But why would he be so suspicious of the library?' Gina said.

'Because he was never convinced about Aidan

Molloy,' Joe said. 'He was swept along by his admiration of Hunter. But he was a good man and always felt uncomfortable about doing the wrong thing. Carl said he became obsessive about Aidan's case, looking into it again but in his own time. I think Melissa started that.'

'So what happened to him?'

'He got too close to real evil, is my guess,' Joe said.

'So we need to be careful.'

Joe nodded to himself as they sat in Gina's car, hoping for a glimpse of the occupant of the house.

'Someone's coming,' Gina said.

Joe looked through the windscreen. There was a car coming slowly down the road, and there was something about it that said that it wasn't just passing through. It was rolling slowly, as if the driver was looking around.

The car stopped outside the house where the Focus was parked, blocking the drive, so that whoever was in there couldn't get out.

'I recognise that car,' Gina whispered.

The driver door opened first, and Joe gasped when he saw who it was: Hunter, with Weaver climbing out of the passenger seat. 'We might have misjudged him,' Joe said, and his hand moved for the car door handle, until Gina grabbed his arm. 'No, not yet,' she said.

'Why, what's wrong?'

'Look around. How many other cars can you see? None. Just Hunter and Weaver. If this were an arrest, there'd be more. Hunter would want someone else to see it. And have you heard anything about him in the last couple of days that makes you trust him?'

Joe dropped his hand. He knew she was right. He watched as Hunter walked quickly to the front door, looking around as he went. He banged loudly, angrily. A couple of minutes passed before the door opened, and when it did, Hunter pushed it open and barged his way in.

'What's going on?' Joe whispered. 'That's not a social call.'

As he watched, Weaver blocked the door and the sound of raised voices drifted across in the dusk. A few minutes passed, then Weaver backed out, Hunter with him, pointing, snarling some threat about 'one hour', and then they were in the car and gone, driving quickly this time, the tyres squealing on the bald warm tarmac.

Joe watched them go and said, 'What was that all about?'

'I don't know,' Gina said.

'I could call Sam.'

'Why? He won't go against Hunter, and if Hunter has been and gone, there's nothing to do any more.'

'So let's just stay and watch. Just for a while. I want to see who's in there.'

Gina settled back into her car seat. Joe checked his watch. *One hour* had been the shout. So Joe might find out the answers he was looking for soon. It was just a matter of being patient.

They had to wait thirty minutes before the door opened. Something was happening. No one emerged for a few seconds, and Joe wondered if he had been seen, but then a man rushed out, a bag under his arm.

Joe's hand went to Gina's arm, his turn to grip her.

The man went to the car, to the Focus, and jumped in. He hadn't locked the door. He started the engine and reversed quickly.

'What is it, Joe?'

He looked at her, shaking his head in disbelief. 'It's all wrong.'

'What do you mean?'

'Him. The man, in that house, in that car.'

'You know him? Declan?'

'Yes,' he said, his mind racing. 'Except he wasn't called Declan then.'

'Who is he, Joe?'

'He said he was called Tyrone. Tyrone McCarthy. He's helping Mary Molloy with her campaign.'

Fifty-six

Joe stared along the road as the car disappeared. 'I don't understand.'

'Say that again,' Gina said. 'You're saying he's the reporter who's been helping Mary?'

Joe looked at her, and then back into the mist of exhaust fume that was just clearing. 'I must have it all wrong. Carl might have been here because he was trying to help Tyrone, perhaps just being overly curious.'

'What about Hunter?'

'He's making trouble for him. Tyrone is trying

389

to overturn one of his cases.'

'But we're not here because of Hunter,' Gina said. 'We're here because of his involvement with missing or murdered women, and because he gave a false address to the library. He's a predator, goes after married women. Of course he's going to use false names.'

Joe shook his head in frustration. 'So what do we have?'

'We have the one person who is somehow connected to all of it,' and Gina pointed down the road. 'He's connected to Melissa, whose disappearance was connected to David Jex going missing, because he was looking into Melissa's case when he started to become obsessed about Aidan Molloy. And he's connected to Rachel. He is the theme through all of this and now he's connected to Aidan through Mary Molloy. Joe, he's not helping Mary. He's monitoring, perhaps even manipulating.'

Joe looked across at the house, the lights turned off inside. 'I'm going in,' he said, and climbed out of the car.

As he strode across the road, Gina trotted to catch up. 'What do you mean, going in?'

'I'm not putting up with half-answers. I want to know what he's been doing, and I'll only find out by going inside.'

'But what if you're caught?'

'What, the firm will sack me?' he said. 'The Law Society will strike me off? I'll be out of a job any day soon, so let them. If I can do just one good thing before I walk away from it all, that will be freeing Aidan Molloy, and if Tyrone or Declan, or whoever the hell he is, turns out to be the key, then what is behind that door is crucial.'

Gina sighed. 'All right, I'm with you, but just be careful. I don't want to wake up in a police cell.'

Joe strode up the short path to the front door, their shoes loud in the street, and rattled at the front door handle. To his surprise, it was un-locked.

The door creaked as it opened, into a dark hall-way, the shadows of the stained glass around the door painting the way ahead. Joe walked slowly, not wanting to make a noise, even though he had seen the man drive away. There was a room to his right. He pushed at the door and it swung open into what looked like a living room.

Gina went to turn on the light, her hand on the switch. Joe held up his hand. He pulled out his phone to light up the room, wanting to keep his presence secret from whoever was outside. The light from the screen was faint but enough to make out what was there. A standard lamp in one corner and a sofa and two chairs clustered around a fire-place, the tiles around it old and flowered, the grate matt black.

Joe frowned. 'It's an old-fashioned place. Look at all this stuff.' And he pointed his phone to-wards the mantelpiece and a shelf by the fire. 'Just knick-knacks. Old photographs. Souvenirs from Ireland. I can't see anything new here. It's like an old person's house.'

There was a table in one corner with some envelopes. Gina walked over and noted the name. 'Not Tyrone McCarthy,' she said, lifting them up. 'Declan Farrell.'

'I'll make a call and see what we can find out,' Joe said.

He was about to dial Sam's number when Gina said, 'It smells fusty in here.'

Joe sniffed at the air. 'It's an old house.'

Gina left the room and went towards the stairs. Her feet made the wooden steps creak. Joe followed her out but then he stopped.

'Wait, what's that?'

Gina paused. 'I can't hear anything.'

'Listen,' Joe said, holding his finger to his lips.

There it was again. Some banging and muffled noises, like someone groaning.

'What is it?' Gina said, as she came back down the stairs. Some more bangs and thuds.

'It sounds like someone trapped,' Joe said. He tapped on the floor. There was an echo. The noises got louder, faster, more urgent. 'It's coming from below.'

Gina started to scour the hallway. 'Find a loose board. Maybe someone's under the floorboards.'

'No, it's not that. It's further away.' Joe moved along the hallway, looking for a doorway. He moved some coats. 'It's here!' There was a door, bolts along the top and bottom, and a lock in the middle. He slid back the bolts and pulled, but it was still locked. 'I'm going to break it open.'

'No, let the police do it. I'll call them.'

'The police have just been. Didn't you see?' Joe stepped back and aimed a kick at the door. It didn't budge, so he kicked it harder, his foot jarring as it hit the wood around the lock. It was damaged this time. One more kick, and the lock mechanism came loose as the wood splintered

392

around it. Joe yanked at the door until the lock moved out of its casing and it swung slowly open.

The way down the stairs was dark but the noises were louder. There was a flickering light ahead. A flame. The door slammed behind him, jolting him and creating a draught, blowing out the flame. The cellar was thrown into darkness and Joe stumbled on a step, losing his footing and letting go of his phone as he put out his hands to steady himself. It clattered noisily as it bounced down the stairs.

He felt his way slowly along. His hand brushed along dry paintwork and the occasional cobweb, which felt like light flutters on his skin as it was magnified by the darkness. His feet slapped the concrete floor as he got to the bottom. The noises were louder, like muffled screeches.

Joe moved slowly across the floor, his arms stretched outwards, fanning out, waiting to hit something. The air smelled of piss and sweat. Paper rustled under his feet, large sheets, like newspaper. The screeches were loud now, insistent, someone trying to say, 'Here, here,' desperation evident.

As he moved across, his foot hit something heavy and soft. He bent down to feel what he had struck and then recoiled as his hand touched something clammy, the unmistakable feel of cold flesh.

He swallowed, tried to control the fear that was rising in him, and felt again. It was a naked body. A woman, from the way her body curved. He pushed at her in case she was making the noises, in case she was injured, but she was heavy and immobile.

393

He got to his feet and moved around the woman on the floor. The noises didn't stop. They were further into the cellar. He kicked a foot, which kicked back at him. Joe dropped to his knees and followed the body upwards with his hands, along damp trousers and top, past the metal around two slim wrists.

Joe's hands found the gag. He wrestled with the knot, the cloth wet with saliva, until it sagged forward and he heard the person in front of him suck in deep breaths before sobbing loudly.

'Who are you?' Joe said.

'It's me, Carl,' he said, in between sobs. 'Gas. There's gas in the house. Booby-trapped.'

The smell. Joe realised what it was. He turned to shout, 'Gina! There's gas in the house.'

There were quick footsteps above, and the sound of Gina cursing. Joe listened out as she ran to the back door and flung it open. There was the scrape of windows being lifted upwards.

Gina opened the cellar door. 'He'd left the gas rings on. We need to get out.'

Joe closed his eyes and said a silent prayer of thanks. 'It's all right, Carl,' he said softly. 'It's over.'

He took the noose from his neck and Carl slumped to the floor. Relief flooded him as he thought how Lorna wouldn't have to go through her life not knowing about her son, but as the relief started to take him over, something else occurred to him: Mary Molloy. The man who had done this had left not long after Hunter had been. Where was he going? He wasn't coming back, that was for certain. Was it to the one person who might shelter him, the one person who had trusted him?

The weak light from the hallway reflected off his phone. The tumble down the stairs had made the cover come off and the battery skim across the floor. He felt around for them and reassembled it, pausing to look at the woman on the floor as he did so. She was dead, Joe could tell that. He didn't recognise her, though.

He helped Carl up the stairs and out into the street. Carl collapsed on the pavement, sobbing uncontrollably.

'Who's the woman in there?' Joe said.

Carl gulped in some air. 'She was called Emma,' he said.

'I've called the police,' Gina said.

'Gina, I've got to go,' Joe said, and got to his feet. 'Give me your car keys.'

'Where are you going?'

'You wait here for the police. I've got to go to Mary.'

Gina passed Joe her keys. His phone was working again, so he called Mary. When she answered, he said simply, 'Get out of your house. Go somewhere safe. It will all be over soon, but I'm coming to get you.'

And with that, he put his phone away and ran for the car.

Joe knew that this was a long way from over.

Fifty-seven

Sam had printed off what he could about Melissa Clarke's disappearance, so that he could read about the case away from prying eyes. He'd found another empty office. It felt like the rest of the station was crumbling around the Murder Squad. He spread the papers on the desk under the flickering glare of a faulty strip-light. He didn't know what Hunter had done about what he had seen on his screen, but he didn't want anyone looking over again.

Melissa Clarke. Like her husband had said, she went out one night and didn't come home again. There was a statement from someone at her book group saying that there was no meeting that night. Melissa's husband's statement read like a man who was suspicious about his wife's behaviour but didn't want to say the words, that she was having an affair. Just like Rebecca Scarfield.

Her friends couldn't explain it, although one did say that she thought she was unhappy at home. There was some focus on her husband, but with the rumours of an affair and unhappiness at home, she was listed as just another missing person. Her parents were dead and she had no brothers and sisters; there was no one to campaign for her. She was a woman involved with another man, and the only person who kept her in the area was the husband she didn't want to be with any more. Or at least that was how it seemed.

But it was more than that; it seemed like there wasn't enough being done, as if it was normal for young women to just disappear. There were so many other leads to chase. Benefit or tax checks, to see whether she was claiming or earning anywhere else. Driving licence checks. Had she been stopped anywhere by the police? Poster campaigns. No, it seemed as if the investigation was quietly shelved. David Jex was in charge of the investigation and then he went missing. No one else carried it on, and Jex became the next missing person. Until now.

Sam made some notes and knew where he was going next. There must be more victims. The book group was the starting point, Melissa's friends, and then treat it like a murder inquiry, not just about someone who has run off with her lover.

What he couldn't work out was why this hadn't been done earlier. Melissa had no history of erratic behaviour and hadn't taken her passport with her. An updated file information sheet said that her bank account hadn't been used for more than a month, signed off by David Jex. This wasn't a woman who didn't want to be found. She was a woman who couldn't be found.

He needed coffee. He knew the night was going to get longer, and if he could just find enough to persuade Evans to let him look further, or even back him up, then the lack of sleep was worthwhile.

He took his phone from his pocket. He was going to call Alice, just to see if he could make it right somehow, so that she understood why he was doing it, but then decided against it. If they argued, it would spoil his mood and distract him.

His phone started to ring in his hand. It was Joe. He pressed to answer.

'What's going on?'

Joe was out of breath. 'Look for Declan Farrell,' he said, almost shouting down the phone. 'We've found Carl Jex. He's alive, but we nearly didn't get here in time,' and Joe gave him an address.

'Carl's alive?' Sam said, surprised. He'd been too distracted to look for the address. He could have done it earlier.

'Are you looking into Melissa Clarke, like I said?' Joe continued. 'Well, we did, and it led us to this house. Carl Jex was trussed up in the cellar and there is a dead woman in there. Hunter and Weaver were here too.'

Sam's mouth dropped open. 'When?'

'Just before Farrell went. We looked inside and found Carl. He's your man, Sam. Declan Farrell. But I don't think he's coming back.'

Sam clicked off the phone and ran along the corridor, bursting into the Incident Room, making people look up. 'It's Declan Farrell, he's the one,' he said, out of his breath, holding up his phone. 'My brother has found Carl Jex.'

Evans looked up, startled, and pointed at two detectives. 'Go, now,' and then to Sam. 'You better be right on this.'

'I'm right,' he said, as the two detectives grabbed their coats and starting running for the doors. Sam followed. He was seeing this through.

He waited outside the house, suburban and safe,

away from the glare of the nearest streetlight. No one paid him any attention. He was filled with the tremors of anticipation. He thought of her scent, how she would be after a day with the children, imagined it filling his nostrils, a mixture of food and coffee and sweat and her own personal aroma. This wasn't how he did these things, but he was filled with an excitement of how different it was.

The lights went off and on in the house, tracking her movement. The bathroom and then the bedrooms. When the lights went off upstairs, it was time.

He reached for some gloves he had found in his house. Black leather driving gloves he had bought when he thought they added to his look. He waited until he saw movement downstairs, her outline against the window blinds.

His car door clunked softly as he closed it, the night air filled with the soft rustle of his clothes. He kept his footsteps light as he walked quickly to the door. Nothing suspicious or that would make anyone look out. He tapped lightly on the glass and waited.

She was a long time coming, but then her shadow grew bigger.

When the door opened, she seemed confused. 'Hello?'

He stepped forward quickly, pulling a knife from his pocket, an old fishing knife his father used for gutting whatever he had caught. He jammed it against her stomach and covered her mouth with his hand. 'One scream, one bad move, and I push it in and you die here.'

She whimpered, her eyes wide, her chin trembling.

He nodded slowly. 'Well done, Alice. Now listen very carefully. You're going to come with me. You're going to get in my car, in the boot, and not make any noise.'

Alice shook her head but he pressed his palm harder against her mouth. She glanced upwards, towards the stairs, and closed her eyes. The sound of singing came from one of the bedrooms, sweet innocence drifting down.

'No, you'll do as I say. The other choice you have is that I kill you now, and then I go upstairs and do the same to your daughters.'

Tears flashed across her eyes. She took some deep breaths through her nose and shook her head violently.

He pressed harder, sweat speckled his forehead. 'You're not listening, Alice. You'll do anything for your children, so do this for them. Come with me and they'll stay safe.' He raised his eyebrows and tilted his head. 'Yes?'

Alice stared at him, anger in her eyes now, but then she nodded.

'Good. Now turn around.'

Alice turned slowly, so that she was facing the wall in the hallway. He took his hand away from her mouth and pulled out some thin rope he'd found in one of his drawers, meant for a washing line. He put the knife between his teeth and tied her wrists quickly. He grabbed her coat from the hooks on the wall and put it over her shoulders, to hide the bindings.

She turned her head and bared her teeth. 'If you

go anywhere near my children, I will kill you.'

He pushed his body against hers, so that she slammed into the wall. His erection pressed against her. She felt it and closed her eyes.

'Don't get carried away, Alice. We're going now. Just remember, one bad move, one shout for help, and I run back inside and gut them in their beds. Do you understand?'

Alice took a deep breath and then nodded.

They walked along the driveway together, his right arm over her shoulder, his left hand pushing the knife against her ribs. He opened the boot quickly and pushed her in, folding her legs before closing it shut. She kicked against it once, but then she stayed quiet.

He closed his eyes. Now, Sam Parker, you're going to feel the hurt too. But your pain will never end, because you'll never know the truth.

Fifty-eight

Sam was first out of the car when they got to Declan Farrell's house, jumping from the back seat as the other two detectives were still undoing their seat belts. An ambulance was heading away, blue lights flashing, presumably with Carl Jex inside. A small huddle of neighbours watched it disappear. Gina was standing with them.

As Sam ran through the gate, she moved away from them and smiled wearily. 'Hi, Sam,' she said, and leaned in to whisper, 'it's not all happy

401

endings. There's a dead woman in there too.'

'I know,' said Sam. He turned round to the two detectives fastening their jackets. 'We need this sealing, and we need a crime scene team.' He was junior to the sergeants with him, but his tone got them on their phones. He turned back to Gina. 'What the hell has been going on?'

'He's had Carl Jex holed up in there since he went missing. The woman hasn't been dead long, but Carl said that she tried to attack Farrell to get out and he killed her.'

'Where is she?'

'In the cellar. Joe and I went all over the house, so we've ruined some of the forensic trails, but it's his house. I don't know how it will weaken anything.'

'And how's Carl?'

'Exhausted and frightened, but he'll be all right, although he knows about his father. Farrell told him. He's got that to deal with too.'

'Where's Joe?'

'Gone to find Aidan Molloy's mother. Declan Farrell was pretending to be a freelance journalist to stay close to her. He was deflecting and manipulating. I've spoken to the neighbours. He isn't a journalist. He works at the newspaper, selling advertising space. He went out and we don't think he's coming back. He booby-trapped the house, left the gas taps on and a burning candle in the cellar.'

'And he's gone after Mary?'

'It's one of the possibilities. If you can get on the ANPR cameras, I know his registration number,' and she reeled it off for him.

Sam made a note and called Evans, and once he had passed on the information he walked slowly past Gina, heading along the hallway. He could see towards the kitchen. Nothing modern. The units and appliances looked old. He pushed open the door into the living room. It creaked slowly. Just like the kitchen, dated, as if trapped in time. No modern equipment. No television. Just worn-out furniture and a rug with bare patches in the middle. There was an old record player, plastic and small.

'How old is this guy?' Sam said.

Gina appeared on his shoulder. 'Thirties. This looks like he's just moved into his grandparents' home.'

'What do we know about him?'

'Not much. Neighbours said he has lived on his own since his father died. His mother ran away, and then his father died a few years later. I think he's got a thing for married women and doesn't like it when they try to leave. But you need to check out his wardrobe.'

'What do you mean?'

'Have a look. Back bedroom. The front one is another museum piece.'

'What's your take on him?'

'Someone who can't let go of his past, from looking at the house.'

Sam left the room and went for the stairs. Everything smelled old and musty. Nothing had been replaced. Carpets or curtains or furniture.

When he went into the back bedroom, the wardrobe was still open, and he gasped when he saw what Gina meant. Women's clothes were sealed into suit carriers, different from the other clothes in there, all normal men's clothing. Jackets and shirts. The women's clothes were to one side, as if they had to be kept separate.

Souvenirs, he thought.

He closed the door. Although they were sealed, he wanted any DNA left on them to remain intact.

He was about to go downstairs when one of the detectives ran up the stairs. He was holding his phone, and there was a look in his eyes that made Sam stop, as if he was about to say something he didn't want to have to say.

The detective took a deep breath. 'It's your wife, Sam.'

Sam's stomach turned over, his mouth went dry, the sounds in the house retreated quickly.

When he said, 'What do you mean?' the words came out muffled, as if spoken by someone else from a distance.

He had to grab the doorframe for support when the detective replied, 'She's missing.'

Joe drove quickly on the motorway around Manchester, heading towards Mary, the lights along the carriageway painting shadows across his face as he went. What could he tell her? She had spent so much of her life feeling let down, building a new life away from her family in Ireland before being betrayed by the legal system when her son was accused. Hugh should have been there to do more, but he had been just another one of the men in her life who had failed her. Now Tyrone. Her supporter. Her campaigner.

As he turned off the motorway and into the tight complex of houses he saw her ahead, standing in the doorway of a small Irish club. It was a long one-storey building of dark windows, a Caffrey's sign above the door and a blackboard next to her advertising whatever act would be on stage later. She looked like she had just headed for a drink, in black leggings and a blue denim jacket, her arms folded as she leaned against the wall.

Mary looked up as he slowed down alongside. She crossed the pavement towards him and climbed in. 'What's the problem?' she said. 'Why the urgency?'

Joe set off before he answered. He didn't want her jumping out.

'It's about Tyrone,' he said.

Her gaze became fierce as he said it, her dark hair swishing with the sharp turn of her head, the glare from her hazel eyes making Joe realise how difficult this was going to be.

He told her, though. About how they had followed the trail, starting with Rebecca Scarfield and then to another missing woman, and how it had taken them to a house where Carl Jex was bound and gagged, a woman dead on the floor.

Mary closed her eyes. 'I don't understand,' she said eventually. 'He said he wanted to help me.'

'He was manipulating you, keeping an eye on what you had discovered. Was it Declan – sorry, Tyrone – who carried out a lot of the enquiries? Was he the one who promised to speak to witnesses?'

Mary nodded. 'They wouldn't speak to me, because of who I am. I put it down to guilt, that I reminded them of what harm they had done, and Tyrone...' She paused when she said the name. 'He said they might talk to him, because he's a journalist.'

'And did they?'

'He said they did but they weren't changing their stories.'

'He lied to you.'

She looked down, and for the first time Joe felt her resolve break. Mary was a tough woman, someone who had dealt with some of the harder things in life, and she stayed in one piece because she had learned to build up her defences. Don't get too close. Don't give away too much of yourself. Don't let others get too close. Joe guessed that Tyrone, or Declan, or whatever name he had used in the past, had got behind those defences, had told her enough untruths that she had decided to trust and rely on him. Finding out what he had been up to all along was the ultimate betrayal, as it prolonged the hurt for the person who meant most to her: Aidan.

The tears were slow in coming. She was trying to hold them back and her breaths came in gulps.

Joe stopped at the side of the road, in a bus stop just before an arcade of shops. He reached out for her hand. 'You don't always have to be strong,' he said.

She looked at him, tears running slowly down her cheeks and then she couldn't hold them back any longer. Her shoulders shook and her mouth curled in despair. Joe put his arm around her shoulders. She resisted at first, but when he pulled her closer, she relented. Her arms went around him and she wailed, sobbing into his shoulder, deep wracking convulsions. Joe's shirt became wet but he wasn't going to let her go. Her nails dug in into his back.

They stayed like that for a few minutes, until her grip relaxed and she pulled herself away. She stared into her lap for a few seconds before she said, 'Why are you doing this?'

'It's corny, but I just wanted to do the right thing. Aidan seemed to be it.'

'I should have trusted you, I know, but I've been let down in the past. It takes a lot. And I trusted Tyrone. It's because he was Irish, or so he said. That reminder of home made me lower my defences.'

'He's done worse to a lot of people.'

She wiped her eyes. 'Everyone lets me down in the end. It's always been the way, even back then, back in Ireland.'

'I haven't let you down yet,' Joe said. Mary smiled, her eyes shining wet. Joe was about to set off again when he felt his phone buzz in his pocket. It was Sam.

He answered. 'Hi, Sam. Have you found him yet?'

'Joe, Alice is gone.' Sam's voice was filled with panic.

Joe went cold. 'What do you mean, gone?'

'Just that. She left the girls alone. They're with me at the police station now.'

'Stay there. I'm on my way.'

Fifty-nine

Joe screeched to a halt outside the police station. His jaw ached from clenching and his fingers were white around the wheel.

'I should go,' Mary said. 'This is personal stuff.'

'No, stay with me, until I find out what it's about. Stay in the car.'

Gina was outside the station.

'What's going on?' Joe said to her, panting.

'I don't know,' Gina said. 'Sam got the call. He wanted me to stay with him, but they told me to wait here.'

Joe called Sam on his phone. 'I'm outside,' he said.

A pause. 'Someone will let you in,' Sam said.

Joe waited for a few minutes before the front door of the station opened. It was a detective Joe had met before. DI Evans. She glanced at Gina.

'She's with me,' he said. Evans looked like the argument about access was for a different day. She stepped aside and let them both walk past her.

As they went along the corridor, Joe said, 'Tell me what you know.'

'A neighbour called it in,' Evans said. 'She'd heard one of the girls crying. When she looked out of her window she saw that the front door was open and the crying wouldn't stop. She gave it five minutes and then went across. She found the girls there alone and no sign of Alice.'

'Alice is a good mother,' Joe said. 'She would never leave them alone.'

They turned into a room at the end of the corridor. Sam was in there, along with Erin and Amy. They were wrapped up in dressing gowns, their faces stained by tears, each holding a teddy bear.

There was a look in Sam's eyes that Joe had never seen before. Quiet panic, stark fear masked for the benefit of his daughters.

'Thanks for coming, Joe.'

'Has Alice texted or called or left any hint?'

Sam shook his head. 'She just wasn't there.' He looked up to the ceiling and blinked hard and fast, trying to control the tears.

'So what now?'

Sam shrugged, and in that brief gesture Joe saw all the helplessness of those whose loved ones go missing. The uncertainty, the complete lack of any answer, so that all they could do was keep looking until eventually they were either found, or they weren't.

'Can I have a quick word, in private?' Joe said to Sam, and looked at DI Evans, who thought for a moment before she nodded her agreement.

Joe stepped out into the corridor with Sam, leaving Gina and Evans in the room with the girls. Joe leaned in closely and said, 'Your colleagues will look into every part of your life. I've learned this past week that things behind closed doors aren't always as they seem. I'm speaking as your brother now. I think of Alice as my sister. She's the mother of my nieces, Sam, and I love them both. So you've got to be honest with me now. Is there anything in your life with her that makes you think you know where she might go? Or anyone she might go to?'

Sam looked down and gulped back tears. When he looked up again, he said, 'No, nothing. We made time for each other; it was just a normal marriage. And if what you're hinting at – that she might have run off with someone – was true, well, she wouldn't have left the girls on their own. I know that for an absolute certainty.'

Joe reached out for his brother. He put his arms around Sam and pulled him in closer. Sam resisted at first, as if he was awkward, but when he was close he sagged and put his arms around Joe. They stayed like that for a minute or so before Sam pulled away. He wiped his eyes.

'This won't find her,' Sam said. Then his phone beeped.

Sam reached into his pocket, and his eyes widened when he saw the screen. 'It's Alice.'

He pressed the button and read the message. He looked confused and then put his hand over his mouth. He handed the phone to Joe, who read, *Get Hunter and Weaver together. When you get their secret, Alice comes home.*

Joe was confused. 'What does that mean?'

'It means someone's got Alice,' Sam said, and rushed back into the room. He held up his phone for Evans to see. 'I've had a message.' His agitation was clear in his voice.

There was a brief moment of optimism on Evans's part, but it disappeared as soon as she saw the expression on Sam's face. She read the message and sucked in air. 'What the hell does that mean?'

'It means we speak to Hunter and Weaver,' Sam said.

'They're in the Incident Room,' Evans said.

Sam bolted out of the door. Joe followed.

They had almost got to the Incident Room when Evans caught up with them and put a hand on Sam's arm.

'What are you going to say?' she said, panting hard for breath.

'I want to know their secret,' he said.

'It will be to do with Declan Farrell and connected to Carl Jex,' Joe said.

'What do you mean?'

'Hunter and Weaver were at Declan Farrell's house not long before I went in and found Carl Jex tied up in a cellar,' Joe said. 'They gave Declan an ultimatum of an hour. It sounds like it was a warning to Declan that he had to leave, and we know he isn't coming back. He'd booby-trapped the house, set the gas taps going. If we hadn't been there, the whole house would have gone up.'

'What, and you think Hunter and Weaver are involved in all of this?' Evans said, her eyes wide.

'I know they are, but I don't know why. All I know is that they're trying to stop one of their prize scalps turning sour, because it all comes back to Aidan Molloy. The person in that house had ingratiated himself with Mary Molloy. He didn't use his real name, but I think he's the man who killed Rebecca Scarfield, not Aidan Molloy, and Hunter and Weaver don't want it coming out.'

'But why the hell would it matter?' Evans said.

'Because Hunter altered the evidence to make

it fit Aidan Molloy. The killer of the assistant chief's daughter getting away with it? He'd never live it down.'

'There was a lot of pressure to get someone for that,' Evans said.

'So Hunter got too keen, and now he can see all his hard work unravelling.'

Evans held up Sam's phone. 'But what about this? Who sent this text?'

'I'm guessing that it's Declan Farrell. Otherwise it's too coincidental. David Jex had been following the same trail we have, and I think at some point he realised they had got the wrong man in Aidan Molloy.'

'And then Jex went missing,' Evans said, her eyes narrowed, her voice quiet, as if her mind was trying to join up the dots, except that it kept on making a picture she couldn't accept as being correct. 'But why is it so important to whoever has got Alice that Hunter and Weaver spill some secret?'

'I don't know that part, but we should ask,' Joe said, and he jabbed his finger towards the phone in her hand. 'He has Alice.'

Evans's gaze hardened. 'There's no *we* here,' she said. 'This is police business.'

'Look, I've seen what this man can do. Carl tied up, his head in a noose, and a corpse lying at his feet. This is my family's business, and if you shut me out, I'll get in touch with a reporter – a real one this time – and I'll tell them what we saw. You'll all be tainted then, as if all you're interested in is looking after one of your own.'

'Don't threaten me,' Evans said, her voice rising a notch.

'It's no threat,' Joe said. 'It's a promise that I will do the right thing, one way or another. You have to decide which side you want to be on when it all goes public.'

'It's not about sides,' Sam said angrily. 'It's about getting Alice back.'

Joe turned to him. 'I know that, Sam, but over the last few days I've got the feeling that your colleagues don't quite see it that way.'

'All right,' Evans snapped, her hand in the air. 'We go in there, but remember that they are still senior police officers, and you're in a police station.'

Joe looked at Sam, who nodded. Joe was happy with that. If Sam trusted Evans, then so would he.

Sam pushed at the door to the Incident Room. Hunter turned round, Weaver too. Hunter paled and sat down.

Sixty

Declan Farrell looked around at the darkness.

It was a different kind. Not that eye-straining glow you get in the cities, where every street is picked out in murky orange, so that nothing is private but nowhere is clear. This darkness was complete; where even the bright dots of stars were only decoration, the speckled blanket untroubled by the light pollution a few miles away, the vivid dots of white only obscured when the rise and fall of the landscape made the horizon uneven, never enough to guide or illuminate.

It was reassuring. It gave him refuge from those who were pursuing him, and he knew they would be. This was the end, or at least a new beginning, the one he knew would come. He was going to do what he always did: spread some pain to those who had hurt him.

They were in the ruins of an old cottage, high on the moors, now just a frame of grey stone, with an open doorway and two empty windows, with wooden struts across the top. It meant they were hidden, his little secret, but it meant much more than that. He had been here before. Too often. The ground was easy to dig into, the peat soil soft and untroubled by tree roots. He had learned that from watching his father dig there, angry thrusts of the spade into the dirt, sweat sticking his shirt to his back, his gasps of breath filled with desperation, fear almost, but it hadn't stopped him.

He closed his eyes and she was with him again. His mother. She was always there when he visited, as if her body stained the walls but only he could see it. It was an outline of her body slumped against the wall, dragged there by his father. It had been done with his help, propped underneath the open square of what was once a window, a view towards dark spurs of moorland that followed the trail of a stream that headed to the reservoir in the valley below.

His father had dug a hole for her, but it was in the corner, because people don't dig in the corner when they search. They go for the centre each time, so he knew she wouldn't be found, forever their secret. That's what he'd said, that if people found out they would lose everything. He'd lost his mother. He couldn't lose his father too.

So he spent time up here, keeping the derelict cottage standing, like putting the stones back when they fell away and spreading branches and moss across the roof rafters to keep some of the rain out. He couldn't allow her resting place to become a swamp, the soil washed away to let the spindles of her fingers poke through the grass and nettles that were taking over. As much as he tried to stop it, the cottage was being reclaimed by the land, a little more crumbling each year.

The others weren't there, the ones he had brought. No one else had been buried there, not even his father. They were all out there some-where, under the peat soil and clumps of grass and the stars, the ones who thought they could say goodbye. No one leaves, he had told them that. So he had given them back to nature, bestowed on them the freedom of the open moorland.

It had been different when it came to his father's time. That had been so that he was never reunited with his mother. His mother had left his father for good, kept apart for eternity. Declan wasn't going to reunite them in death.

It had been one last taunt that had consigned him to an unmarked grave, dragged long into the night so that Declan wouldn't remember where he had dug. Forever abandoned.

His father had screamed in his face once too often, berating him, whisky spittle flying from his mouth. It brought back how he had been with her, one final reminder of why she should have left, got out of their poisonous union. But his father shouldn't have done it at the top of the stairs.

One push was all it took, his father's arms wheeling, suspended almost, his heels against the top step, and then he started tumbling, rolling, his head cracking against the steps. Something snapped as he landed, splayed on the floor like a puppet with cut strings.

Declan looked upwards towards the sky again, visible through the holes in the roof, most of it gone, except where he kept it covered over his mother. It looked like the stars had moved, as if they were being turned like a loose lid over the vast spread of the moors. It should have been idyllic, lost in the memories of his revenge, but he knew that everything had changed, that he had to either end it that night or move on and start again.

A sound disturbed his thoughts. Whimpers, pathetic and small. He turned round. Alice was against a wall, underneath where there was still some roof cover, most of it crumbled to rotting beams covered in moss, so that she couldn't be picked out by the infrared camera if they sent up the force helicopter.

This was different. It was pure revenge against someone who had never turned away from him. Alice wasn't the target of his revenge. She was the means, the tool, nothing more, but this was different, because it was goodbye too, to his life. Time to start over.

He trudged over and knelt in front of her. He cocked his head close to hers. He smiled, although he knew he was all in shadow.

'Poor little Alice,' he whispered. He reached out to move some stray hairs from her face, but she flinched and pulled away, the only protest she could muster. 'You know he will suffocate you, don't you? That good man of yours, Sam, the perfect husband, the one who catches bad people. You'll stay with him, and everything about you that is special will disappear. Your vibrancy, your fun. It will get sucked away by his needs. Ironing shirts, cooking meals, doing what you see as your duty. What about the other stuff? In bed? Is that duty now? Just enough to keep him from straying, but what about you?'

Alice shook her head. Tried to talk behind her gag, but it came out muffled.

'You'll never leave, will you? You promised to stand by him. Bravo.' And he put his finger under her chin and tilted her head upwards. He got closer and whispered, 'Will he get me?' He shook his head slowly and dramatically, his bottom lip out in a pout. 'I don't think so, do you?'

Her tears glistened despite the darkness, silvery salty tracks, her cheeks streaked with dirt. She shivered in her sweatpants and T-shirt.

'You know what will hurt him the most?' he said, as he straightened. 'Not knowing where you are, so that he can't give you a proper burial. He will spend every spare moment up here, walking over these moors, a spade in his hand, digging in places where he thinks you might be.'

Alice shook her head, her eyes clamped shut, her whimpers turning into muffled shrieks.

'He'll think he knows. He'll work out where the signal from your phone is, but that can only identify the nearest mast, and even then it will get bounced somewhere else if it's being overused, so it is only ever a guess. It still leaves the whole of the moors to cover. And he'll do that, because he loves you, walking the moors, looking, digging, but he'll never find your last resting spot. It's the start of your journey, as the earth pulls you around until eventually there is nothing left of you to find.'

He leaned forward to kiss the top of her head. She pulled away again, but he just laughed. 'I thought you needed it more than me.'

Alice didn't move as he stepped away out of the cottage, swinging his spade in his hand. He whistled, he knew it would upset her, and then stamped at the ground a few yards away, thinking about where the others were. Once he was satisfied that he had a good patch of virgin burial soil, he raised the spade high and thrust it hard into the ground.

Sixty-one

Sam marched straight up to Hunter.

'Tell us your secret,' he said.

Hunter's eyes flickered wide, just for a moment, but Sam noticed something else too: the process of information, a flick-book through all of his secrets and wondering where something was going to come back and hurt him.

'What do you mean?' Hunter said, but his voice was hoarse. His tongue darted onto his lip. Weaver sat in a chair and slumped against a desk.

Sam struggled to contain his panic, his concern

418

for Alice taking over everything. 'What do you think it means?' he said, an angry tremor audible. 'Someone has got my wife.'

'What has this got to do with me?' Hunter looked at Weaver. 'With us?'

'Where have you been this evening?' Sam said.

Hunter flushed. 'I don't like your tone.'

Evans rested her palm against Sam's chest. He looked at her, and she nodded at him slowly. *Calm down. Don't make it an attack.*

Hunter looked surprised when Evans said, 'It's a reasonable question, sir. Did you visit Declan Farrell earlier?'

Hunter's jaw dropped open. His nostrils flared as he weighed up whether to tell the truth or hide behind some bluster.

'Yes,' he said eventually. 'He said he had some information, but it turned out he didn't. We left. Why?'

'Half an hour after you left, so did he,' Evans said. 'When the house was searched, Carl Jex was found in the cellar, a noose around his neck, and a woman was naked and dead on the floor.'

Hunter put his head in his hands. Weaver groaned and put his head back.

Sam took a deep breath, making Hunter look at him.

'Do you know why I dug up the moor and found David Jex?' Sam said, stepping closer. 'Do you remember me telling you? X marked the spot was what I said, except you wouldn't listen to me, and let the scene get trampled to hell. Why would you do that?'

'We play the odds, you know that,' Hunter said,

419

but his voice was fainter, as if he was losing some of his fight.

'But the dead woman, carved up like that, laid out like that, was a sign to go looking for David Jex. Now it looks like whoever killed her and left her over the shallow grave of David Jex kept his son captive. And you were there. You were at the house, and you did nothing.' Sam took a deep breath as tears of anger began to flow. He jabbed Hunter in the chest. 'And now he has Alice.'

Hunter looked at the floor. 'How can you know that?'

'I got a text, telling us that Alice comes home if you tell us your secret!' Sam shouted, not caring about Hunter's rank. 'It was from Alice's phone.' He took it back from Evans. 'I'm going to call that number and find out why you're so important.' Sam pressed redial, but all he got was the unavailable tone. He looked at Evans, his eyes wide, panic rising.

Evans turned to Hunter. 'So is there anything we should know? At this moment, sir,' and the *sir* came with emphasis, 'things are not looking good for you. You missed the chance to dig up David Jex, one of our own. You missed the chance to rescue Carl Jex, the son of one of our own. And this somehow seems connected to the abduction of Alice Parker, the wife of one of our own. I might be speaking out of turn, but you're going to get pretty unpopular if you don't start talking.'

Before Hunter could say anything, Sam's phone pinged. A message.

Is Hunter there yet?

Sam looked up at Evans and then back at his

phone. He tapped in a quick *yes*.

There was a short delay, and then another ping. When he opened the message, the room swam in front of him. Hunter became blurred, and he might have been saying something but no sounds could make it through, as if his head had been plunged into water.

He didn't pass the phone over, it was taken from his hand, and the gasp Evans made was the sound that jolted him back into the room.

It was a picture message. Alice in dirty and wet sweatpants and a grey T-shirt, her outfit for a quiet evening in front of the television, the wind-down after a long day, except that she wasn't relaxing with a glass of wine. She was lying on the ground, a grubby gag across her mouth that pulled her cheeks back. No, that was wrong. She was *in* the ground, the muddied walls of a shallow grave visible.

It hadn't just been the sight of her in there that had made Sam nearly pass out. It had been the look in her eyes. Wide and frightened, terror in them that Sam had never seen before.

Another message came. Evans opened it this time and read out loud, 'I'm filling in the hole now, Alice inside. If Hunter tells you what happened to David Jex, and you tell me, I'll let you know where Alice is. You might get to her in time. I'll leave the phone on now, because I'm on the move, gone, disappearing, a new start. I'm just clearing out the deadwood before I leave.'

Evans pointed angrily at Hunter. 'You better start talking. If we find her dead and you said nothing, you're finished.'

It was Weaver who spoke up, his voice weak and defeated. 'He's finished anyway, if he talks. Me too.'

'This isn't about you any more!' Sam shouted, advancing towards him. 'It's about my fucking wife.'

Evans stood in front of him. 'Sam, not now.' She turned to Weaver. 'So if you're finished, at least do the right thing.'

Hunter's head turned between the two of them and then to Weaver. 'Don't you dare.'

Weaver took a deep breath and wiped away the tears that were soaking his cheeks.

'I'll tell you,' Weaver said, his voice a croak. 'But you have got to know that it was all him, all his idea.'

'What was?'

Weaver swallowed, rubbed his hands together, and said, 'DCI Hunter killed David Jex.'

Evans looked at Hunter, her mouth open.

There was movement, Hunter rushing at Weaver, a fist raised, shouting something unintelligible in raw fury. Sam got there first. He smashed his forearm into the side of Hunter's jaw, knocking him to the floor, blood splashing from his mouth onto the wall.

As Hunter lay stunned, groaning and wheezing, Sam turned to Weaver and said, 'You better start talking, and make it good.'

Sixty-two

Declan Farrell dragged Alice out of the hole. He pushed her back towards the cottage. She stumbled. He grabbed the rope round her wrists and pulled her, dragging her along the floor, her clothes getting muddier. He threw her against the wall once they were back inside.

He straightened, sweat sticking his shirt to his back, dirty trails across his forehead where he had wiped away the perspiration.

Alice drew her knees up to her chest, her feet blackened. She put her head down and shivered.

There was a small posy of flowers against the wall, just pansies in a small ribbon. He had left them there a couple of weeks earlier. They were dried out and the stalks were rotting, but it was still enough to invoke some memories, his mother's body buried not far beneath. She would never move from there, be transported around by the ever-shifting peat soil. The walls would keep her in.

He went over to Alice and pulled down her gag. She gasped and smacked her lips to try to get some moisture back into her mouth.

'Don't scream,' he said quietly, putting his finger to her lips, almost tenderly.

She recoiled and then nodded quickly, tears streaming down her face. She gulped and said, 'What are you going to do to me?' He didn't

423

answer straight away. 'I'm a mother. Please don't kill me. My babies shouldn't grow up without me.'

That stalled him. He looked back again at the dying flowers and for a moment his mind was flooded with memories. Her laughter, the feel of her cheap dress against his cheeks as she held him close to her, static dancing on his cheeks; swaying with her in front of the fire, his father glaring from the nearby chair. Her laugh was easy, happiness just one of the gifts life gave her. His father had to go looking for it, and was often found wanting.

For a moment, tears tickled his eyes, but then the memory of her cold hand as he helped his father bury her came back to him and pushed them away. His emotions retreated, like the slam of a door. Only the recall of his father's arms wheeling at the top of the stairs gave him any satisfaction.

It was the look in his eyes that stayed with him. Acceptance, and knowledge of what he had turned his son into.

Declan pushed her gag back over her mouth and stepped away. He went to the window and gazed out at the moonlight that cast a silver glow on the moors.

Hunter pulled himself up onto his haunches, pointing at Weaver, wiping the blood from his lips onto the sleeve of his jacket. 'You need to be quiet,' he shouted, and then to Sam, 'And you too. That's an assault. I should have you arrested.'

Weaver laughed, in derision at first, tears still streaming down his face, but then it got louder, more hysterical.

'Talk,' Evans said.

Weaver's hysteria disappeared as he said, 'Do you suspect me of being connected with the death of David Jex? So you have to arrest me, which means you can't ask me any more questions now if you want this ever to be mentioned in a court.'

Evans clenched her jaw.

'So this is just about finding Alice, right?'

'You bastard,' Sam said.

'Or I can shut up right now and not give you anything,' Weaver snapped back. 'Is that what you'd prefer?'

'Just talk,' Evans said.

Weaver put his head back and let his tears subside before saying, 'Declan Farrell killed Rebecca Scarfield, not Aidan Molloy. And we might have caught him if we had kept on looking, done a proper job on the cars we were looking at, except he was too hung up on Aidan Molloy.' And he jabbed his finger towards Hunter. 'That's all it was for him. Aidan or no one, because Aidan had been meddling in Rebecca's marriage, the assistant chief's little angel.'

'So when did you know?' Evans said.

'When Melissa Clarke went missing. David Jex was doing most of the work on that, and he had been with us when we looked at Rebecca, so he knew both cases. It was the library book group thing that did it. That was where Melissa went, and it was where Rebecca worked, and David became suspicious. He got a list of every dark red Ford Focus in the north-west and was working through it, trying to find a link with the library.'

'So Joe is right,' Sam said. 'The witness statements were false. You wrote them up to make them fit Aidan.'

'It wasn't as simple as that,' Weaver said, as if he was pleading for understanding. 'We spoke with the witnesses who saw the car, and Hunter thought they had got the car wrong, because he was certain it was Aidan Molloy, particularly when Aidan's mother changed her story. So he talked them into thinking that it was Aidan's car they had seen. Like he said at the time, if they had been so certain, they wouldn't have changed their story. And Aidan's mother had lied, Aidan too, and he had the motive as Rebecca was going back to her husband. We thought we had done the right thing. Yeah, we had twisted the evidence a bit, but for the right reason.'

'What about the spade in the boot, with peat soil on it?' Sam said.

Weaver looked down for a few seconds before saying, 'We bought it from a DIY shop and stuck it into the ground, and put it into Aidan's car when we took it away.'

Evans gasped. 'That goes way too far. Talking witnesses round is bad enough, but that? Planting evidence?'

'Oh come on,' Hunter said, making everyone look round. 'Who hasn't dropped some drugs in a house to justify a search or an arrest, or into someone's pocket? Padded out a statement to make it say what we needed? It's a matter of degree.'

'I haven't,' Sam said.

Hunter scowled in response.

'We were trying to put away Rebecca's killer,

426

that's all,' Weaver said. 'Why is it always us that have to play fair? We couldn't let Aidan just get away with it.'

'But he hadn't done anything,' Evans said, incredulous.

'Yeah, well, I know that now.'

'So tell us about David Jex.'

Weaver took a deep breath.

'David got panicky,' Weaver said. 'He realised that we were in trouble. He whittled it down to Declan Farrell and did some background checks on him. Farrell had form, a couple of assaults on ex-girlfriends, and had been arrested for a rape once but it hadn't gone anywhere. It was a married woman and she wouldn't go into any detail. She'd been found bloodied and sobbing, and she told a friend but wouldn't speak to us, in case her husband found out. When David went through Rebecca's case again, he found a connection to Farrell. She had gone away for the night once, told her husband that she was staying with a friend, but she had gone to a hotel. The bill showed up on her bank statement. When David went through Farrell's bank statements, he found a bar bill payment from the same night at the same hotel.' Weaver scoffed. 'Farrell didn't even have the decency to pay for the room, just a couple of drinks.'

'That might have been his leverage,' Evans said. 'Accumulate evidence that she is having an affair and she becomes scared; he's got something to use.'

'So David convinced us that Aidan hadn't done it, and that Farrell was the killer,' Weaver said, and glared at Hunter.

'So what did you decide to do?' Evans said.

'We need to get a move on,' Sam said, starting to pace. 'This is about Alice, not Weaver cleansing his soul.'

'We need the story,' Evans said. 'That's what he said.'

'David wanted to come clean,' Weaver said. 'If we got into trouble, that was just tough. We had done wrong, and we didn't have to admit to the spade or the wrong witness statements. All we had to do was pin it on Farrell and get Aidan out of jail. But that prick,' and Weaver pointed at Hunter, 'he thought it was too risky for us, that we might end up passing Aidan at the prison gate, with us on the way in for a while as he came out. So he decided to kill him.'

'What, David Jex?' Evans said, incredulous.

'No, Declan Farrell,' Weaver said, slamming his hand on the chair. 'He was a cold murdering bastard, we knew that because of Rebecca, and we had no idea where Melissa was, but she seemed dead to us. What loss would he be to humanity? None, that's what. So we waited for him after the book club, until everyone else had gone, and we lifted him. No one saw us, we knew that. Hunter drove. David and I wedged him in the back, and we were going to do to him what he was going to do to Rebecca.'

'Bury him on the moors,' Evans said.

Weaver looked down, rubbing his hands. 'David was quiet all the way. We had a spade in the boot and a lump hammer. We were going to hurt him first, just for what he had done to Rebecca, and then bury him. No one would ever find him, we were sure of that. We got away from the road so no one would see us, and just as we were going to start on him, David said we shouldn't.'

'It's conspiracy to murder,' Evans said.

'That's what David said, and that we shouldn't go through with it, and he got physical, tried to wrestle the hammer away, and that bastard...' And Weaver pointed at Hunter again. 'He started swinging that thing, the hammer.' He took a deep breath and looked up at Evans, and then to Sam. 'Have you ever heard a melon hit the ground? It's like a liquid crack, and that's what it sounded like when the hammer hit David on the side of the head. He went straight down and he didn't move. I touched his head and I could feel the fracture in the skull. It was a dent and the bone moved. I didn't think he was breathing. So we panicked. Farrell was gone by this time. He'd started running as soon as David went down, and he must know those moors well, because I tried to chase him and I just couldn't catch him. It was like the darkness just swallowed him up.'

'So you buried David Jex?' Sam said.

Weaver nodded. 'Hunter thought he'd killed him. What could we do? Say, *Oh, we meant to kill someone else?*'

'So you watched Lorna Jex grieve and sob for her husband, and you knew all along where he was?' Sam said.

'Yes, I suppose so.'

'You're a coward.'

'Yes again. And Declan Farrell had us. He wrote up everything that had happened, including the map reference as to where they could find David, and joined one of those online legacy sites. You know, where if you don't log in for sixty days, whatever you store there is sent to a nominated person, a way of passing on your crucial information if you die suddenly. Your passwords, things like that. He told us he had put Lorna's name in, and Rebecca's father, and Melissa's husband, Mary Molloy and two newspapers.'

'So if Declan Farrell died it would all come out?' Evans said.

'No, worse than that,' Sam said, stepping closer to Weaver. 'He can't log in from prison. So you two bastards had to keep Farrell free, or else it would all come out.'

Weaver nodded slowly.

'Call him,' Sam said to Evans. 'We've got the story now. Let's get Alice back.'

Sam and Evans had been focused on Weaver. They hadn't been aware of Hunter getting out of his chair until he made a run for the door.

Sam went after him, but Hunter slammed the door behind him, trapping Sam's hand in the jamb, the few moments of excruciating pain enough to allow Hunter to bolt along the corridor, already with his car key out.

Evans went to the door, but faltered, looking back at Weaver.

'Leave Hunter!' Sam shouted. 'Call Farrell. Get Alice back.'

'I'll go,' Joe said, as he made for the door.

'Where?' Evans said.

'I'm going to find Alice,' he said. 'And Hunter might just take us there.'

Sixty-three

Mary had waited in the car for Joe. She had seen Hunter rush out, his car racing away down the street. As Joe drove in the same direction, he told her the basics of what Weaver had said, that Aidan had been framed and that they had known Aidan was truly innocent for a few months. She had cried, more from anger than sorrow, before she turned to Joe and said, 'So Tyrone, sorry Declan, has her?'

Joe nodded grimly.

Mary put her hand to her mouth and tears appeared in her eyes. 'This is my fault,' she said, almost to herself.

'What do you mean?'

'He called me earlier. He asked about you at first, how you were getting on, but then I told him about Sam finding David Jex, the coincidence of it.' She looked across at Joe. 'I didn't know, Joe. I'm so sorry.'

'It's not your fault,' Joe said. 'You can help though.'

'How?'

'You might know Declan's secrets.'

'What do you mean? I don't know anything about him. I thought I did, but I don't.'

Joe glanced across and winced at the pain in her eyes. He gripped her hand for a moment. He tried to smile, but his worry for Alice kept it

431

away. 'He can't just take her somewhere new. He has to know where he is going or else he might be caught. You might have an idea.'

Mary looked at him, scared, confused. 'I don't understand.'

'He must have somewhere. A secret place, somewhere private, just for him.'

'Nothing he said was true, so how am I to know anything?'

'Because people like him want you to know, deep down. He told you a lie to get on your side. He used you to deflect attention from himself, to find out what you knew, but he would be unable to lie all the time. Convincing liars wrap the lies up in some truth. I've seen it with clients and witnesses, that provided you stay near enough to the truth it is harder to catch them out.'

Joe's phone rang. It was Sam. He answered.

'Where are you, Joe?'

'Trying to find Hunter and Alice. Have you heard anything else yet?'

'No, nothing.'

'So have you told Farrell what Weaver said?'

'Yes, a text. He hasn't texted back to tell me where she is.' Joe heard Sam gulp back the tears. 'I'm never going to find her, Joe.'

'We'll find her,' Joe said, and clicked off. He turned to Mary. 'He's on the moors somewhere, going from the picture of Alice. Did he ever take you there?'

'Only a few times, to where Rebecca was found,' Mary said. 'We ended up walking up there. He said it would help me, to see the location where Aidan's life changed, even if Aidan had nothing to do with it.'

Joe pulled up sharply at the side of the road. 'Did he say anything up there that might mean something else? Think.'

'I don't know. Yes, I suppose. He seemed different there, more human somehow. He'd talk about himself, get sort of nostalgic, talk about how his parents died and left him their house, and how he used to enjoy watching them dance together. They'd play records and drink and dance in front of the fire, and he told me that he liked to watch them, that it was when they seemed close, together somehow.' She shook her head. 'That must have been untrue as well. I used to think I was such a good judge of character – that I could read people, decide when I could trust them. It looks like I was wrong.'

'That's what Carl Jex saw,' Joe said, his voice getting faster. 'Peeping through the window, he saw a man and a woman slow-dancing in front of the fire. That must be his ritual. When they wanted to leave him, he got a promise of one last night. He recreated his parents' evenings in before he killed them. The woman Carl saw through the curtains when he was arrested? She will be the woman found dead on the moors. Tell me, how did he seem when he talked about them, when he was up there on the moors?'

'It was like he showed a bit more of himself. I thought at first it was because of what the location meant to me, the place that led to Aidan being locked up, but then I realised that the place itself made him different. It's the moors, I suppose. They do make you feel small somehow.'

'No, you're seeing it wrong,' Joe said, eager now. 'That location meant something to him, because it was where he was getting rid of Rebecca's body before he was caught. And what did everyone think Aidan was going to do?'

'Bury her.'

'Because of the spade in the boot of his car. It was seen as a one-off, a crime of passion, a way of getting rid of the body. And not a bad theory. She would never be found, but if the spade was planted then it was just a guess by whoever planted it. Except he was interrupted by that couple and he raced off, leaving Rebecca. But if he became different up there, more reflective, more human, was it something more practised than that?'

'What do you mean?'

'What would make him reflect up there? If he killed more than one person, was that place special because he was looking at his own personal graveyard, where he goes to remember?'

Mary put her hand over her mouth, her eyes wide.

'Burial seems important somehow,' Joe continued. 'Melissa wasn't killed. She disappeared. The mystery of the body's location is part of the torture, but he knows, and he can sit and reflect and look out over the ground, knowing what lies beneath. So we need to go to where Rebecca was found. Are you ready?'

She nodded, determination in her eyes. 'I'm ready.'

Declan Farrell looked out through the empty window frame.

He was stalling. Was he backing out because this was different? His previous visits here had either been to remember or to bury. This was just revenge, one final twist before he disappeared.

He felt it then, the emotion he had been looking for: anger, the slow bubble, the creeping heat. He was about to lose everything he had. Why shouldn't others? He was going to lose this – his place, his home. There would be nowhere left to get lost in the memories of his mother, now safe from harm under the soil. And those in the hills outside, too. Their passion, how they had submitted to him completely, and then how they had turned away from him. The moors were their resting place, and his hiding place – they would never be found. The moors were too vast, too open, the landscape too scarred.

Alice shivered and moaned behind her gag, dirty tears soaking her cheeks, soil staining her legs. He had wanted Sam to see her again – an image that would stay with him and haunt him, so that every day that he spent looking for her he would be reminded of her terror, be tormented by it, always trying to work out the location of the small square of land that would make up her grave.

He pulled up the collar of his jacket and pressed the power button on her phone. It was time for another picture.

The screen finally came to life, the software icons appearing at the top. The network signal, faltering to the occasional one bar, the time, the battery life. Then there was another, a small circle that pulsated.

He clicked on it, curious. He kept his phone use

simple, using cheap pay-as-you-go phones so that there was never a trail. No angry husbands to work out his name. No obligation to register a phone. Alice's phone was modern, sleek and black. His eyes flickered wide when he saw the letters GPS. He knew what that meant: her phone could be located.

The heat inside him changed, from anger to something hotter than that. It was fear. He scrolled through the icons on the screen until he found the picture folder. He brought up the picture he had sent before and worked out how to get the information about it. The view of the screen blurred as he saw it. There it was, the file-name for the picture, and the date and time, along with other things that didn't mean anything to him, but underneath all of it were digits. GPS coordinates. They would know where to find her.

He steadied himself against the wall. They would find this place. He would lose even this as a memory. He turned towards Alice. There was the blame.

He grabbed her by her arm and pulled her up. She shivered as she stood there, her arms still tied behind her back, her clothes sodden and filthy.

'We need to move,' he said.

Before they could go, there was something to his right. Lights, a sweeping beam, some of it reflecting along the narrow track that wound down from the road. Someone was coming. He wouldn't be able to drive away.

He grabbed Alice's arm and said, 'We've got to go,' before walking quickly out of the empty doorway of the cottage.

The lights were getting closer, the high beam spreading a bright fan that lit up the moorland ahead. There was the slow crunch of tyres on loose stones and the steady rumble of an engine.

He pulled at Alice, who yanked away from him, seeing rescue in the lights. She fell to the ground and started to scramble towards them, her eyes wide above the gag, the headlights getting brighter all the time.

He grabbed her hair, making her yelp, and pulled her to her feet before gripping her round her waist and propelling her forwards, down the grassy slope, and towards the slow meander of the stream and the grouse butts lining the valley.

They both landed in the water, Declan holding Alice down so that her clothes were drenched. The headlights crept around the final bend in the track and lit up the derelict cottage, his own car in front. The engine was turned off and someone stepped out, slowly and deliberately. Then he heard a voice he recognised.

'Farrell!' It was Hunter, shouting. 'Where are you?'

He had to think of a different plan. He grabbed Alice by the arm once more and set off down the valley.

Sixty-four

Sam paced, frantic, scared, his hands clasped behind his head, just about keeping everything together, but it was the impotence that was getting to him. Weaver was staring ahead, saying nothing. Sam turned on him.

'How could you do that?' Sam said.

Weaver looked up slowly. 'I didn't do anything,' he said. 'Hunter killed David Jex, not me.'

'He was alive when you covered him over,' Sam said, shouting now. 'Didn't you see the post mortem result? Or were you too busy trying to protect that murdering bastard? David Jex had soil in his lungs. You could have saved him.'

Weaver leaned forward and looked at the floor, his arms on his knees, as if he was going to vomit. 'I didn't mean for any of this to happen.'

'But it did, and you were happy for Aidan Molloy to rot away in prison to protect yourself, for David's wife never to know his fate, and, worst of all, to let Declan Farrell carry on doing what he has done. It all comes down to you, Weaver, and that prick Hunter. All you had to do was admit a mistake and lock away a bad guy, but no, you wanted to play vigilante and cover your own backside. Not only a coward, but a crooked coward, you piece of shit.'

Evans put her hand on Sam's arm. He had been getting closer to Weaver, so that he was standing over him, pointing, snarling.

'No, Sam, not now,' she said. 'Save this.'

He shrugged her off and pointed at Weaver. 'So where has Hunter gone?'

Weaver didn't respond.

'Come on, you must know. Hunter isn't just running. He's gone somewhere. So come on, where? How much do you know about Declan Farrell?'

Weaver glanced up and his eyes narrowed. He sat back and folded his arms. There were tears in his eyes, but behind them was the hard glare of defiance.

'What, so you can go after me with something else, as if I'm not in enough trouble.'

'This isn't about you.'

Weaver looked past Sam and at Evans, who was just behind him, still holding onto Sam's arm.

'Think of the Force,' Weaver said. 'It will do us a lot of harm. Hunter and I can retire, just fade away. The only winners will be the lawyers, looking to sue the Force for God knows how much. Hundreds of thousands for every dead body, and Aidan Molloy, and all of it taken from our budgets so that the people we try to lock up stay free. Is that what you want? And the public will never trust us again. All you have to do is let Farrell go, or at least let Hunter and me sort him out, our way. Where's the injustice in that?'

Sam shrugged off Evans's arm and gripped Weaver's throat. He pushed him backwards into his chair. Spittle flew into Weaver's face as Sam barked, 'Farrell has got my wife and still all you can think about is yourself?'

439

Hands gripped Sam, some uniformed officers running in from the corridor at Evan's shout. They helped her to pull Sam off Weaver and push him back against the wall.

Weaver spluttered and coughed. 'You see, we're not so different when anger takes over.'

Sam took deep breaths, barely hearing Evans in front of him as she tried to calm him down, speaking softly, reassuring him.

Weaver shook his head. 'If you won't help me, I'll do it myself. I'm finished, I know that now. You can do the rest. I'm not telling you anything. If you can't get my confession into court, you've got nothing, you know that. And you won't. It was an interview. You didn't caution me and you knew I was guilty. So I'll get sacked. At least I'll stay free.'

Evans pointed at one of the uniforms and then towards Weaver. 'Lock him up. Cuff him and find him a cell. He's under arrest for conspiracy to murder.'

The uniform looked uncertain until Evans shouted, 'Now!'

Weaver didn't say anything as the handcuffs clicked around his wrist, although his stare never left Sam as he was hoisted to his feet.

He pulled back and stopped by Sam as they drew level. 'If you'd have left it alone, Alice would be safe now.'

Evans closed her eyes and groaned as Sam's arm rushed past her and his fist caught Weaver flush on the jaw, making him crumple to the floor.

When she opened them she shook her head and said, 'You shouldn't have done that, but I'm glad you did.'

Sam headed for the door. He pointed at the other uniformed constable. 'Follow me.'

Evans didn't try to stop him.

Sam burst into the room where Gina was with Erin and Amy. She looked round, expectant.

'How's your driving?' Sam said.

'Advanced, according to my police certificates.'

'Good,' Sam said. He went to Erin and Amy and gave them both a hug and a kiss. 'I'm just going to find Mummy,' he whispered. 'This nice policeman will look after you.' And he pointed to the young officer in uniform.

'Come on,' he said to Gina. 'Let's go find Alice.'

'You can't,' Evans said, as he ran past her.

'You didn't authorise my overtime,' Sam said, as he headed for the exit. 'I've been off duty for hours. I can do what the hell I like.'

And then he was gone, banging through the door, Gina just behind.

Joe leaned forward as he drove, getting closer to the side of the road where Rebecca Scarfield had been left. 'Can you see anything?'

Mary shook her head. 'There's no one here.'

Joe pulled over, trying to brake gently, so that the crunch of tyres on the gravel wasn't too loud.

'We'll get out and walk down,' he said. 'If he's down there, I don't want to spook him.'

'Do you think he will be?'

'He'll be somewhere around. This is his place.'

They both stepped out of the car. He put his fingers to his lips and spoke in a whisper. 'We need to stay quiet, so we can listen out. Sound will travel, and I'd rather we heard him than the other way around. It might help us get a bearing.'

They were by an open gate.

'It was down here,' Mary whispered. 'This is where he brought me. I remember it now. We parked there,' and she pointed a few yards along the road, 'but then we walked down here, past where Rebecca was found. I remember the gate and a curving track.'

'Come on then,' Joe said, and he headed down the track, Mary following.

It was dark at the roadside. The moon helped, but the track seemed to swallow everything up. Joe pulled out his phone to illuminate the way, but only as a glow. He didn't want to announce his arrival. They used the dark outlines of the slopes as a guide to where the track was and the phone to work out the edges and trip hazards. It was a long steady slope down, with open moorland on either side. There were rustles in the grass and Mary reached out for his arm, gripping his sleeves tightly.

'Can you remember where he took you?' Joe said.

Mary peered forward, frowning as she tried to piece together memories to compare against the shadows ahead. 'It was at the end of this road. Keep going. Some kind of crumbling building.'

They tried to keep their footsteps light, but they were like loud cracks in the darkness. They couldn't see far ahead. The path curved to the left and downwards, swallowed up by the land with every step.

Something ran in front of them, making them

both jump, but it was just a rabbit, its dart caught in the glow. They laughed nervously, but then kept on going, Joe's focus returning to finding Alice. They rounded the bend and the moors spread in front of them, vast and brooding, except where stone outcrops made jagged lines of the horizon, blocking out the stars like rips across the sky.

They kept on walking, just Joe's phone lighting the way, until Mary pointed. 'There it is.'

Joe followed Mary's indication and saw it. A small stone cottage, but hollowed out, lit up by the moon. The roof had gone and the doorway and windows were empty, just a dark slit in the middle and two black holes on either side. Grass grew up the walls.

There was something else there too. Two cars.

'Is it him?' Mary said, her voice filled with bitterness, her lilt acquiring a tougher edge.

'That's Hunter's car,' Joe said, moving more quickly now, the thump of his footsteps drowning out the slow tick of Hunter's engine as it cooled down, the air heavy with the smell of warm oil.

'Hunter? What's he doing here?'

'I thought he was escaping. He's not. He's after Declan Farrell. He must have known Farrell's secrets all along. He could have stopped this.'

As they got closer, Joe recognised the other car. A dark red Ford Focus.

'He's here,' Joe said, turning to Mary, gripping her arm, her pale features gleaming against the dark sheen of her hair. 'Declan Farrell.' He pulled his phone from his pocket and called Sam. When he answered, Joe whispered urgently, 'I'm on the moors, a hundred yards from where Rebecca was found, at some kind of derelict cottage. Farrell is here. So is Hunter.'

'What about Alice?' Sam said.

'I've only seen the cars, but Farrell can't leave. Hunter is blocking him in. They must have headed for open country.'

Then there was something else, a noise. Joe turned round, trying to work out what it was. Then he heard it again. High-pitched, guttural, like a scream cut off quickly.

'She's here,' Joe said quickly. 'Get people here, now!'

Joe clicked off his phone and set off at a run towards the sounds. He didn't think about Mary, although he could hear the fast pat of her feet behind him as she tried to keep up, so that she wasn't left alone in the dark with Declan Farrell still out there, but it was Alice he was thinking about. He had to get to her, to save her. He had brought this about, his interest, his pursuit. For his brother, for Mary, for Alice, but also for himself, he had to bring it all to an end.

Sam threw the phone into the central console. 'Up on the moors,' he said. 'Where Rebecca Scarfield was found.'

Gina pressed hard on the accelerator. They had driven out that way, guessing that it would all end on the moors somewhere.

Sam had commandeered a patrol car and now he flicked the switch to turn on the flashing lights. The night turned into flickering blue. The houses became more spaced apart and the backdrop got darker. The engine strained as it headed upwards.

'Get on the radio,' Gina said. 'See if one of your helicopters is up there. Get it over the moors, looking for the white dots. We won't do it any other way.'

Sam reached for it and barked the order. After a few seconds, it was confirmed. It was ten miles away but it was heading over.

He looked out of the window and tried not to panic, but it was hard. Alice was tough, he knew that, but this was a whole different thing, more than just dealing with the pressures of every day but something wholly new, beyond anything she should have to contemplate. And he tried not to think about what Farrell might have done to her. He mustn't think about that.

He closed his eyes. His daughters came into his mind. They couldn't lose their mother. Just couldn't. They'd never recover from that. Even though they were young, their lives would be changed for ever by the loss of the woman they would be unable to remember when they got older. The knowledge that there was something missing, some joy they would never experience, of their mother's love.

He took a deep breath. He had to push that to one side, deal with it later. For now, it was all about finding Alice.

'Nearly there,' Gina said. 'I know where it is. He might be heading for the reservoir. It won't be as dangerous as going on the tops.'

Sam nodded. He was ready.

Declan hooked his arm under Alice's as they ran through the bed of the stream. He had to tread carefully. The stream was filled with large rocks that threatened to make him fall to the ground. She pulled back from him and slipped from his grasp, then scuttled away, splashing in the water.

'Get up,' he said, walking quickly to her, standing over her. She shrank back and collapsed. Exhausted, scared.

He took the tow-rope from his shoulder and made a loop at one end, before threading the rest of it through to make a noose. He dragged her by her T-shirt towards him and threaded the noose over her head. He pulled on one end tightly until it fastened around her neck and she gasped, her eyes wide.

'Come with me or I leave it tight and you'll die out here.'

Alice nodded vigorously, her heels banging on the ground.

He left it a few moments longer, just so that she got the message, and then let it slacken, just enough to let her suck in air. He gripped her cheeks with one hand, squeezing so that she pouted. 'All you have to do is keep up.'

He lifted her onto her feet and set off again along the bed of the stream. His shoes were slippery on the stones and Alice struggled to keep up, barefoot and cold, whimpering, crying, and now gasping as the rope stopped her from getting decent breaths.

'Farrell!'

It was Hunter again. He just needed to get out of sight and away from where the photograph had way they had worn smooth through the years. The tunnel sloped downwards and their splashes echoed as they went. Water dripped from the ceiling.

'Keep going,' he said, and tried to walk more quickly.

There was the sound of more water ahead. It was like something being emptied into the tunnel, a pipe spewing something out.

They kept going for another fifty yards, Declan always looking out for something to tether Alice to, when he saw it.

There was some light making it in from above, casting a weak shaft of silver moonlight against a stream of water cascading into the tunnel, like a direct fall. Caught in the faint gleam were the narrow rungs of a ladder.

As they got underneath it Declan saw that the ladder led up and out of the tunnel, the rungs tight against the wall and disappearing down into the water. Water streamed over it, another hilltop stream being diverted the quick way down the hill.

He took the rope from around Alice's neck and knelt down in the water. He tied it around the bottom rung as Alice stood and shivered, too exhausted and cold to run. He dragged her to her knees, then took the rope he had looped around the rung and threaded it through the one that bound her wrists. He pulled it tight so that it forced Alice backwards into the water.

Her eyes opened wide with shock as she fell onto her back and was lost in the fast flow of water through the tunnel as it headed down

been taken. There were no blue lights or sirens though.

The slope of the streambed got steeper and the sound of running water became louder. There was more water ahead as the slopes around him got higher, the tops marked out by rugged clusters of rocks. He had to keep heading downwards.

He tried to pick up the pace but Alice fell, crying out, muffled through her gag. It pulled the rope tight around her throat. He reached behind to slacken it. It wasn't her time, not yet. He might need her to trade. She sucked in air through the gag and coughed loudly.

He thumped her, his fist hard on her cheek. 'Shut up,' he hissed.

Alice curled up, cold and scared, the water running past her, soaking her, only the gag stopping her from wailing loudly. He'd hurt her.

He turned back. It was of no consequence. It would all end soon. Just not like this.

'Farrell, you sick fucker! Where are you?'

Hunter again.

Declan knew Hunter would keep going. Hunter knew all his secrets, where the bodies were buried, who they were. It was Declan's way of torturing him, the control, that Hunter could only stand and watch as Declan did his thing, because he had Hunter's secret. Now it was out and Hunter would want revenge. Declan understood revenge, but control was important. Hunter was angry and that would make him act rashly.

But Declan knew it was time to keep moving.

'Come on,' he said to Alice and pulled the rope tight again, so that it puckered the skin on her neck. He gripped her by her upper arm, her bone small in his grip, her arm weak.

He started running again, going downhill, skipping over the rocks, rugged and uneven, so that they both struggled to keep their feet. Alice was exhausted, and they had to keep stopping whenever she fell so that he could pull her back up again. The stream stopped winding and headed more directly downwards. The steady twist of grassy spurs opened out towards the silver gleam of water, lit up by the moon. Reservoirs. He wasn't thinking far ahead, lost in the moment, but he needed to get to the road below. He could flag down a car and deal with the occupant and get just enough miles away to hide.

Alice fell again.

Farrell stopped. He could leave Alice behind and make good his escape. Hunter would never catch him, but that was a happy ending. He had never done happy endings and Sam and Joe Parker didn't deserve one. They had brought this about. Alice wasn't going to walk away from it, not even with scars, visible or invisible.

But he would be caught if he kept her with him. She was slowing him down. He couldn't bury her, as his spade was back in the derelict cottage.

Then he remembered something.

The fast bubble of water was getting louder as they went. There was another valley joining, the two streams combining and falling into a concrete pool, held back by a weir. There was a tunnel, large and round, eight feet high, brick-lined, with green slime gathered at the entrance. It was a diversion for the stream, ensuring that the water

was collected rather than allowed to sink into the soft peat. It sent it through the hill and down to the reservoir, water coursing through it at knee-height.

They set off again, Alice struggling, his arm hooked under hers, almost dragging her on her knees. They slid together down a grassy bank, the noise of the water getting louder. Then he saw it.

The mouth of the tunnel gaped darkly, a black circle against the murky shadows elsewhere. Water gathered around the entrance, the tunnel narrower than the concrete pool in front of it, so that it rushed through. Access to it was gained by clambering over a stone wall and into the pool. He lifted Alice over first, losing his grip on the rope as she slid down and into the water. She went under the surface, unable to break her fall with her arms behind her back. He followed her over the wall and gasped as the cold water soaked him. He looked down at Alice as she struggled to get to her knees, her hair floating in the water. She pushed herself up eventually and coughed through her gag, but the sound was lost in the rush of the stream. She sucked in air through her nostrils, her eyes wide with fear and cold.

He reached for her and pulled her to her feet. She was shivering. He dragged her through the water, Alice slipping on the floor of the pool, until they entered the brick mouth of the tunnel.

The darkness enveloped them as they entered, the glow from the moon gone. The water was smoother, with no rocks or diversions to make it ripple, but it was moving more quickly. The bricks were treacherous from the wetness and the

towards the reservoir far below in the valley. Her hair thrashed around as she struggled to gain some balance, until she came bursting back to the surface, her teeth clenched around the gag.

Declan fastened the knot tightly around the rung and grabbed her hair, pulling her shoulders free of the surface. 'You won't last.' He had to shout to make himself heard above the water streaming down from above. 'Sam will always blame himself for not being quick enough.'

He kissed her on her forehead. 'Goodbye, Alice.'

With that, he threw her back into the stream and set off the way he had come, up the tunnel, splashing through the water. He paused for one last look along as he got to the exit. He couldn't see her. Just a long torrent heading into pitch blackness.

He ran out of the tunnel. He stopped and listened for Hunter but there was no sound. There was the faint flicker of a torch on a hill higher up the valley. He was searching up there.

Declan climbed back over the stone wall and was ready to run along the reservoir path when blue lights lit up the sky ahead. The police. They were heading his way, coming from below, not from behind, the way he had come.

Shit!

He turned around, trying to decide what to do. There was a shout from the hilltop further along. Hunter had seen him.

He looked up the high slope that towered over him, a steep climb to high rocky outcrops. Once on the top though, it was open moorland. That was his only escape.

He started running.

'Where are they?' Joe said.

They were at the cottage, looking around, turning, trying to see shapes in the darkness. There were just the high sides of the valley that made the reservoir below. The hills rose steeply in front of them, making all the noises bounce around, so that their sources were hard to pinpoint. There were flashes of colour lighting up the sky ahead, but he couldn't see how close they were.

Then Mary pointed and gripped his arm. 'There,' she said.

Joe followed her direction, squinting, and then he saw. There was some movement ahead, high on the moors, more than the slow ramble of a sheep. There was a light source, like a thin torch, but it bounced, just giving glimpses of the dark heather. It was someone moving quickly.

'Is that him, with Alice, or Hunter?' she said.

'I can't tell,' Joe said. 'We need to find another way. Whoever it is, they're too far ahead.' He pointed towards the valley. 'Down there.'

They both scrambled towards the rocky streambed, stumbling and moving as quickly as they could, the water cold, their shoes splashing loudly.

They lost sight of the light as they carried on downwards, swallowed up by the hills, but Joe wanted to be there when whoever was there came down from the moors; he couldn't stay up there for ever. It was too bleak and exposed.

The stream curved its way through the hills before the narrow valley opened out, the shine of water ahead. The flickering lights flashed brighter in the distance, bouncing between the valley sides far away.

Then Mary pointed upwards. 'Look!'

Joe followed her direction. There was someone else; a dark figure on the hillside, scrambling upwards, the hill steep and covered in black shadows, rocks and boulders, fallen down through the centuries. At the top, visible against the stars, were large outcrops, leaning out over the side; any fall from them would be too high to walk away from.

But there was only one person on the hillside. Whoever had the torch was still at the top.

'Where's Alice?' Joe said, looking around for any sign of her.

'I can't see her,' Mary said.

'Declan Farrell!' Joe shouted.

The figure paused, looked back, and then kept on upwards, faster this time.

'I'm going after him,' Joe said, starting to run.

'What about Alice?'

'Only he knows. I'm going to find out.'

And Joe set off for the hillside, scrambling over the rocks and jumping over a low wall, using his hands to help him as the slope got too steep. His lungs soon strained for air, the climb hard going, stumbling on loose stones and long grass, the top of the hill still far away, the overhanging boulders becoming more brooding with every step.

But he wasn't going to be stopped.

Sam strained forward as Gina steered the police car along a narrow lane, stone walls on either side, bracken peering over the top, just dark fronds under the canopy of the trees that ran to the reservoir in the distance. Their lights reflected from the hillsides, a coloured strobe highlighting the rocky tops. The strain of the engine echoed and Sam had to grip the door as the car bumped along.

'How far along?' he said, his voice fraught, checking his phone constantly for any news from Joe.

'Just around these reservoirs,' Gina shouted. 'Either he has to go back towards Joe or up onto the moors, but the helicopter will pick him out up there. Or else he will head this way, down the valley. We'll cut him off but hold on – it's going to be bouncy.'

She turned on the high beam and the way ahead was lit up brightly. A long expanse of water lay between hills that were high and steep. The narrow track opened out ahead but once again disappeared into trees.

'You keep a lookout,' she said and accelerated harder, so that the walls and nearby trees became a blur.

Sam scoured the path ahead, looking up the slopes, but there was nothing. The car slewed as it took a corner, throwing Sam towards Gina as she accelerated out of the slide, and headed along the reservoir banks. They rattled over a metal grid and their headlights caught the staring eyes of sheep that stood near the track, small spots of light in dirty bundles of white. One headed towards the car, but then thought better of it and scrambled back to the safety of the grass. Grouse scampered along a wall, a line of them.

Sam shouted as the car bottomed out when it hit a small dip. The wheels almost left the ground as they rose up again, the beam bouncing, and then into the space between the next cluster of trees.

It seemed like they were always on the verge of spinning off, the back end sliding on the loose stones, but Sam wasn't going to tell her to slow down. Instead, he gripped the door handle as they bumped and raced and followed the long curve of the reservoir.

Gina braked hard when the track turned into a rutted path that climbed upwards, as the reservoir came to an end and the hills and moors took over, the valley getting tighter and darker. Meant for hikers only, the car pitched and rolled as it struggled over small rocks and deep grooves.

Then Sam saw them.

'There,' he said, pointing towards dark figures scrambling up the hillside, caught in the beam.

Gina threw the car towards them, skidding it sideways, stopping quickly to avoid sending them into a ditch, her beam lighting up the hill.

It was Joe, and a woman some way behind, running and climbing towards a figure higher up. It must be Declan Farrell.

That didn't concern him. Only one thought was in his head. Where was Alice?

Alice fought against the water.

She was able to keep her head above the surface for a moment, the rope around her wrists stopping her getting to her feet. She put her back to the flow and it streamed over her shoulders, pushing her along so that her arms were forced up her back, restrained around the ladder.

She tried to stay upright against the fast flow, but she was pulled under. She couldn't see anything. The sound was gone, the constant rush of water replaced by a loud hum and the echoed shrieks she was able to make through her gag. She couldn't stop the water streaming in; it was soaking the gag so that it was hard to empty her mouth again whenever she got to the air. Her feet pushed against the slippery bricks, as she tried to get her head up so she could take one more deep breath through her nostrils.

It was so cold. It sapped her strength and her hunger to survive. For a moment, she thought of giving in, of letting the water stream over her and into her lungs so that it would all be over.

Then she thought of Erin and Amy. She had to stay alive for them.

One final push of her legs helped her raise her shoulders above the surface again, her teeth gritted around the gag as she tried to suck in air. The cold was her enemy, too. It had been hard to stay upright when she was marched away from the cottage, her footsteps laboured, so that she tripped and stumbled, and now she was losing feeling in her legs.

She tried to look back over her shoulder, but all she got was the faint glow of light as it reflected along the fast flow of the streams being funnelled down the hill, echoing, deafening, splashing against her shoulders, threatening to pull her back under. Ahead, it was just black and noisy.

She screeched as she started to slide again, the force of the water too strong. It became blurred ahead. Her breathing was quick and shallow, hard through the gag.

She gritted her teeth and thought of her children, to keep her mind sharp. She had to keep going for them. They were not growing up without a mother.

But it was getting too hard.

She closed her eyes and concentrated on keeping her head above the water. All she could do was focus and try to stay upright and wait to be found. Someone else had arrived. She had seen him on the moors, chasing. Others would follow. It was going to end, she knew it.

But she couldn't hold on for much longer.

Joe's shoes slipped on loose stones, sometimes stumbling on rocks that jutted out of the ground, but still he kept going. There was a bright light behind, and when he looked back, it was a police car, its blue lights flashing, the headlights bright and blinding. Mary was behind him, her hand sometimes on him as she sought grip and balance, both of them panting hard, Joe's legs stiff and aching.

He stopped and looked back. He recognised the person climbing out of the passenger seat.

'It's Sam, my brother,' he said. He looked down to shout, 'She's not up here.'

Sam didn't look like he could hear him.

Mary pushed him, breathless. 'Keep going.'

They both scrambled the rest of the way, finding a steep route through the outcrops that hung high over the slope. Joe couldn't look down again. A stumble would send him rolling down with only boulders to stop him. His legs ached and his lungs burned but he wasn't going to stop.

As they got to the top, they both leaned over, sucking in the night air. Joe went to his knees, feeling sick with effort, stars dancing in front of his eyes. When he looked up again, all ahead was complete darkness and silence. It was colder, the wind cutting through his suit. The long grasses swished and swayed in the moonlight, and with no trees to stop the wind it seemed to gather speed, Joe's hair sticking up, his ears aching from the chill. Mary shivered beside him. All there was for miles was rolling moorland, lost to the night, and blind crevices where the peat had resettled, opening up the grass like scars. He looked around. The lights from Manchester were visible now in the distance, a vast orange and yellow glow like a different country, bright and brash and noisy. The other way was just blackness.

'We can't find him up here,' Mary said, out of breath.

'We've no choice but to try,' Joe said, and set off at a brisk walk, wary of a fall if he ran, not wanting to risk a long cold wait with a twisted ankle as Declan Farrell disappeared into the darkness.

It was hard going. The darkness was complete, so that it was hard to see what was ahead. Joe was listening out. If Declan was hiding and ready to burst out, Joe wouldn't see him until it was too late. He was ready for the quick rumble of feet, tensed and alert. All he could hear was the thump and squeak of his shoes on the damp grass and the sharp draws of his breaths. His legs brushed against clumps of heather, snagging sometimes, all the time concealing hiding places.

There was another noise.

It was the sound of someone running, but not Declan Farrell. It was manic somehow, desperate, coming in bursts. Then Hunter's voice echoed across from somewhere on the other side of the moorland.

'Farrell, where are you?' His voice was plea more than threat, breathless, panicking.

Joe tried to work out the direction, the voice drifting across in the wind. Then he saw him. A small figure, just a black outline, moving slowly and turning, shouting again. The torch flickered, as if the batteries were about to give out.

'Let's go to him,' Joe said, and moved more slowly, almost creeping, so that his footfall became softer, feeling their way, always listening out for the sound of Alice or the sudden rush of Declan Farrell.

There was movement to his left, away from Hunter. Joe looked. Something dark moving quickly, framed against the glow coming from the city in the distance.

Declan Farrell.

'He's there,' Joe said. Mary gasped. Joe started to run, his feet fast thumps, trying to cover the ground, not knowing what was in front of him, no longer thinking of the danger of falling.

A shout from behind. Mary had stumbled and she cried out in shock as she went down.

The figure ahead stopped and looked Joe's way.

'Declan Farrell! It's me, Joe Parker.' He took deep breaths. 'You run if you want, I won't go after you. Just tell me where Alice is.'

His words echoed until the night fell still again.

Everyone was quiet, not moving, until Hunter shouted in frustration and started to run again.

Farrell turned to go the other way, away from both of them.

Joe ran again.

Farrell seemed to be heading back the way he had come, towards the edge, as if he didn't trust himself to go into the darkness. He was trying to find some way down, so he could somehow get away on a clear path.

As Joe got closer, Farrell stopped. He was thirty yards away and his whole body was framed against the stars in the distance, in silhouette against the beam from Sam's police car. The edges of the rocks that hung over the slope down were jagged and black.

Joe slowed down, sucking in air. 'What's going on, Declan?' he said cautiously. 'Or is it Tyrone?'

Mary appeared behind him, her hand on his arm, gripping tightly. 'You betrayed me!'

Joe put his arm across her. 'I just want to know where Alice is,' he said.

Declan stepped back. The edge was closer. Just a few feet. He looked back quickly. 'You're so gracious, Joe Parker. That's how you see yourself, is it, some kind of hero?'

'I don't care about you,' Joe said, stepping forward slowly. 'I don't mind if you get away. I just want Alice.'

'Maybe I prefer the suffering.'

Joe tried to stay calm. 'The police are down there,' he said. 'You can take your chances with them, but they'll lock you up for ever. Just tell me about Alice and I'll step aside, let you run past.'

Joe edged closer and Declan backed away.

Joe looked quickly along the edge. It was a slow curve marked out by large rocks that shone back the silver of the moonlight. He was coming in at Declan's right. Then he saw the flickering beam of Hunter's torch. It was on Declan's left, getting closer.

'Don't come any nearer,' Declan said.

'Just tell me where she is.'

Declan stepped backwards slowly. Joe moved forward, his arms out, trying to calm him down. If he went over the edge, they might never find her.

Below, Sam was shouting Alice's name, but nothing came back in response.

Mary stepped in front of Joe. 'You lied to me,' she said to Declan.

'I lied to a lot of people,' Declan said, and moved back further. He stopped and glanced over his shoulder. Everything behind him looked a long way down.

He backed onto the stones overlooking the drop and said, 'You all get away or else I go over, and then you'll never know.'

'Why?' Joe said. 'You won't get away if you do that.'

'What, you think I'm getting away at the moment?' And he laughed, shrill and loud. 'You'll let me walk past you all and slip away in the night?' He shook his head. 'This is the end, I know that.'

'So just make it easier for yourself.'

'No, you mean make it easier for you.'

Declan was on a rocky outcrop, his feet just a metre from the edge. There was no way forward except towards Joe and Mary.

Then there was a noise behind them. Joe looked round. It was Hunter. He was bent over, his hands on his knees, drawing in deep lungfuls of breath.

He straightened and glared at Declan.

'Farrell, you bastard.'

Sam turned around quickly, scanning the hills around, but once he was away from the headlight beam, all he could see was darkness.

'Where is she?' he said desperately.

Gina was alongside him. 'Try the cottage,' she said. 'It's up that way. Follow the stream.'

'No, Joe said she was with Farrell. He heard her scream.' He stared up at the dark outlines of the hills and shouted, 'Alice!' He waited. Nothing came back.

'We need that helicopter here,' Gina said. 'It might pick up her body heat if she's out there somewhere.'

Sam tried not to think of her alone up there, frightened and cold.

Gina ran to the wall in front of the police car. 'What about down here?'

Sam joined her and looked over. Pools of water, bordered by concrete, like a series of small over-flows. 'Not in the water, please.'

He scoured the surface for the trails of hair or some sign that she was there. Nothing. He ran along, trying to see into every dark corner, but it was pointless. He turned away and went as if to run towards the hills, but after a few steps away from the beam of the headlights the night enveloped him.

'Alice!'

Still nothing.

'Sam, look.'

It was Gina. Sam rushed back towards her, hoping she had found Alice, but instead she was pointing upwards. There was someone high up on the rocky outcrops, almost on the edge.

'DCI Hunter?' Declan said. 'Were you hoping it would be just me and you?'

'You bastard,' was all Hunter could muster.

Declan gestured towards him and then shouted to Mary, 'He's told you all about Aidan, hasn't he? That he guessed a while ago that your boy was innocent but lied to protect himself?'

'Yes, I know now,' she said, her voice low and angry.

'And I'm the only bad guy?' Declan said, in a mocking tone. 'I didn't put Aidan in prison. That was all Hunter's doing. He's got a problem now though. If he keeps me alive and I get arrested, I'm going to talk. I'll even get in the witness box, to make sure that he goes down for what he was going to do to me. What the hell have I got to lose?' He laughed again. 'But if I die? All those documents I've stored online get sent out and you're finished. So which is best, Hunter?'

'Or you give Alice up and I step aside,' Joe said. 'Ignore Hunter. You'll get past him, I'm sure, and Mary will let you go. There'll be other ways to prove it against Hunter. So you get Hunter and we get Alice. That's the trade.'

'No way!' Hunter spat. 'He's not leaving. No more deaths. He'll carry on and this time it will be blood on your hands, Parker.'

'Ignore him,' Joe said quietly, moving forward slowly, focused only on Declan Farrell. 'Send the documents anyway. You win both ways. You get Hunter and Alice comes home.'

Declan looked skywards and started to laugh again, wiping tears from his eyes.

'What's so funny?' Joe said.

When Declan looked back down, he said, 'There are no documents. No legacy account. Do you think I'm stupid? Computers leave traces, tiny tracks that can be pieced together to make the story whole again, the trail from start to finish. Warrants can be obtained. No, it was just to keep him and Weaver out of my hair, and guess what, it worked.' His voice became angrier, more contemptuous. 'They were so scared; it was like having police protection. Me, was I scared?' He shook his head. 'No, of course not. I had it all under control. I had Hunter and Weaver under my control. They could have stopped me at any point, but they didn't.'

Joe got closer so that Declan was just a lunge away. The view behind him was the landscape a long way below. The sheen of the water, the orange spread of Manchester in the distance but none of the city noise made it that far up. There was just the cruel whistle of the breeze mixing with the fast beat of his heart. Mary was quiet. Hunter was pacing behind him, audible from the thumps on the grass.

'Why do you think I left her there, sliced up where David Jex was buried?' Declan continued. 'He wasn't meant to be found. It was a warning to Hunter, that's all, a message that I could reveal everything. Carl changed things, so Hunter had to protect me. He could control the scene, divert attention, but good old Sam couldn't stop himself. Supercop. So he suffers.'

'Is that why you've gone for Alice?' Joe said, trying to control his anger. 'Just to hurt Sam?'

'Not the only reason,' he said. 'Because if they catch me, I'll tell them who told me where Sam lived.'

'Shut up!' Hunter shouted.

Joe looked round quickly, incredulous.

'That's right,' Declan said. 'Good old DCI Hunter gave me what I needed. My parting bit of hurt for him too. To make him the most reviled man in the Force.'

Joe took deep breaths to control himself. He had to keep his focus. 'All right, I get it, Hunter's the bad man,' he said quietly. 'But I don't care about him, or about you. I just care about Alice.'

'So there was never anything?' Hunter said, stepping closer, his voice was low and mean. 'No legacy site, no confessions to be sent out if you were arrested.'

Declan laughed. 'No. Not ever.'

'So I could have killed you and there would have been no loss.'

'Except to Aidan,' Mary snapped.

'Fuck Aidan,' Hunter said, starting to pace again. 'Collateral damage.'

Mary ran at Hunter, who tried to hold her off, her long dark hair thrashing as she rained punches on him.

'Stupid bitch!' Hunter seethed, and pushed her

away. She stumbled to the grass. As she went to scramble up, there was the glint of metal turning in the air. A knife landed on the grass near her. Declan had thrown it. The blade was long and jagged, a fisherman's knife.

Mary stopped, gulping down air.

Declan pointed towards the knife. 'Go ahead, Mary, take it. Kill him. See how it feels. They'll say it just runs in the family.'

'Mary, stay where you are,' Joe barked.

Hunter turned towards Joe but looked past him, at Declan.

'No!' Joe said. 'We need Alice.'

Declan laughed behind him, loud and mocking.

Joe whirled around. 'Declan, concentrate on me, not Hunter,' he said. 'Just give up Alice.'

Declan's laugh faded as he glanced over Joe's shoulder, just a momentary distraction, broken only by the sound of fast movement. Hunter screamed as he ran onto the rocky outcrop.

Declan stalled, unsure for a moment. Hunter flashed past Joe, moving quickly, lashing out with his fists. Declan moved his arm to defend himself and then grunted as he was punched on the chin. Hunter kept on, his arms going around Declan's midriff, his shoes slipping on the stone but still moving forward. A gasp of exertion and Declan was leaning backwards, towards the edge and the long drop to the rocks below.

Mary screamed. Joe shouted, 'No!'

Declan tried to push at Hunter's shoulders but Hunter's momentum was forward, going too fast to stop.

Declan twisted his body, striking out, punching

Hunter in the head. Hunter's grip slackened and Declan gave one final twist and slipped out of his grip. Hunter's momentum carried on, taking him forward, over the edge.

Hunter seemed suspended for a second, his heels still in contact with the rock, shouting with rage, arms wheeling. Then he was falling.

Joe gasped as Hunter screamed all the way down. There was the sodden thud of his body hitting the ground, before silence.

Declan tried to scramble away from the edge, but his shoes were wet and slippery on the rock, no grip in the leather soles.

Joe ran forward to grab him. He shouted, 'No!' but he didn't get there in time. Declan slipped, his ribs banging on the edge of the rock, a grunt of pain, and then he disappeared from view. There was no scream, no hard landing.

Joe threw himself to the floor and crawled to peer over the edge. Caught in the headlight beam, Hunter's body was splayed and broken. There was a shout, and the sound of someone panting. He looked down and Declan was hanging, a hundred-foot drop below him, his legs swinging, his hands clasped onto a sharp edge on the rock. He was whimpering with fear.

Joe reached down and grabbed the shoulder of his jacket. He shouted to Mary, 'Help me pull him up!'

Mary was paralysed for a second, and then she rushed forward, looking over the edge. Declan was gasping, struggling to hold on.

'Where is she?' Mary shouted at him. 'Where's Alice?'

Declan snarled and grabbed Joe's arm. He yanked Joe towards him, his upper body going over the edge.

Joe tried to pull himself backwards but Declan was determined, dragging him towards the edge.

Mary grabbed Joe round the waist. She tried to wrestle him back, grimacing with effort, but then she remembered the knife Declan had thrown.

She scrambled back for it, and when she had it in her hand, she lunged forward, sinking the blade into Declan's arm.

He screamed loudly, letting go of Joe, who crawled backwards quickly, breathing hard.

Declan was hanging by one hand, his legs swaying wildly, his injured arm hanging uselessly, blood dripping down. He glanced downwards and swallowed. He looked back to Mary and said, 'Pull me up, please,' desperate, pleading.

Mary stood and stared down at him. She gripped the knife in her hand, her lips set tightly in fury.

Joe reached out. 'No, Mary, don't.'

Declan looked up again, desperation in his eyes. The tension in his fingers was visible, clasped around the sharp edge on the rock, taking his weight, his right arm useless. 'Please,' he said.

Mary stared and didn't move.

His fingers started to slip, his mouth opening into a scream. Mary shook her head. She wasn't going to help him.

His fingers slid slowly over the sharp edge. He tried to strike out at the rock with his feet as if he could somehow support himself that way, but it was useless.

Declan screamed as he fell, his body launched into the glare of the headlight beam from below, his limbs splayed. The scream was short-lived, as breath was punched out of his body, his back catching a rock, broken over it.

Joe rushed forward and looked over the edge, sucking in deep breaths. Mary stayed still. She looked down, unmoved.

Joe turned onto his back and let the view of the stars roll over him for a few moments, exhausted and emotional, his arms stretched out, the rock cold on his hands.

Sam turned away and grimaced as Declan Farrell hit the rock, the still air broken by the sound of a loud crack. Then all he could think about was Alice.

He went to his haunches and fought the urge to vomit. He didn't know if he would ever find her.

Then Gina gripped his arm. 'There, Sam, look.'

He straightened and followed her gesture. The beam of her phone pointed towards something dark in the wall.

'There's some kind of tunnel,' she said.

Sam wasn't waiting to find out more. He scrambled over the wall and slid down, landing in the water with a gasp. It was up to his thighs, cold and murky. He started to stride through, slow and exhausting. There was a splash next to him and then a shout. It was Gina, nearly fully submerged, unable to manage her balance as she tried to keep her phone out of the water.

'Shit!' she said, as she stood up, and then they both began to wade towards the tunnel entrance.

The faint beam reflected off slimy bricks and the steady stream of water heading downhill. Sam tried to see inside.

'I can't see her,' he said, desperation in his voice. 'Alice!'

His shout echoed but was competing with the noise of the water. It was a smooth fast stream until further in, where it seemed to bubble up, as if there was some kind of obstruction.

Gina strode ahead of him, pointing the phone to illuminate the way. The tunnel didn't seem to have an end. She put her hand out to steady herself. The walls were wet and slimy.

'She's not in here,' she said. 'Farrell wouldn't bring her down here.'

'No, down there,' he said.

Gina shone her beam that way again. 'What is it?'

'There's something in the water, I'm sure of it.' He started to wade forward again. Gina kept up with him, so that his shadow didn't block out the light.

'She can't be this far down,' Gina shouted above the roar of the water. 'We need to get out.'

'No, I saw something.' Then he shouted, 'There!'

There was something there, being tossed around as water poured into the tunnel from a different direction.

'Alice!'

He started to run, the best he could manage, his movement slowed down. He needed to go faster.

He was crying out, shouting her name. He was going to be too late.

Alice couldn't see anything. It was too dark. The sound of the rushing water filled her head, her fear just muffled gasps as she fought to breathe through the gag. A few seconds with her head above the water, before the force of it rushing over her shoulders forced her back under, until she was able to find the surface again. Her gag was soaked and kept her mouth from closing properly, so that she coughed up water every time she found some air.

The pain from the cold was subsiding though. She felt warmer inside, but it was unreal, too good, as if she wanted to relax with it.

There wasn't just the noise of the water with her now. The laughter of her children was loud in her head, the sound of bathtime, splashing and fun. Their smiles, innocent joy, and she could kneel down for them, to kiss them on their foreheads, to say goodnight.

She went under again and the noises became muffled. There was comfort in it somehow, that it would end her terror. She couldn't find the surface this time but she stopped trying. She let the torrent buffer her and pressed her tongue against the gag to keep out the water. She couldn't hold on. It seemed almost silent under the surface and she thought of her children one last time. She wanted to say sorry that they would grow up without her. It was getting tighter in her chest, the need for air getting too strong, but she didn't have the strength to try to reach for it.

She opened her mouth.

The water rushed in past the gag. She coughed

as it filled her lungs, but more followed. Her chest pushed outwards but it was no use. This was how it was going to be, but it felt right, natural, euphoric.

She didn't feel lonely any more. Sam was calling her name, memories fooling her, but she was glad she was with him as she was thrown about by the water, her lungs aching for air. She couldn't say goodbye without Sam, and he was there, like always. His arms were round her, hugging her, lifting her up, pulling at the gag, his breath in her ear. She was cold, the air freezing as she broke the surface.

Then she coughed, water spewing out. She coughed again as she took a breath, long and painful.

It was over. She was safe.

Sixty-five

Joe smiled to himself as he drove along one of the roads around Dublin, making his way from the airport, just a stop-start journey of small retail parks and then past housing estates, the homes small and grey. Mary was sitting next to him, Aidan in the back.

Mary looked intently out of the window, sometimes turning round to look at something that had changed. Aidan was more relaxed, just enjoying his freedom and getting over the shock of his release, granted bail pending his appeal,

472

although the appeal was a formality, everyone knew it. He'd emerged onto the street to the flash of camera bulbs, which was so different to when he went into prison, leaning forward in the small cubicle in the prison van, the image that was used in the papers the following day, the lucky shot of a photographer who had picked the right tinted window to jam his camera against.

Weaver had been dismissed from the Force but had escaped prosecution for conspiring to murder Declan Farrell. The only evidence had come from what amounted to questioning when under suspicion, and he hadn't been cautioned. He'd made no comment in his police interview and the only other two people who had known about the plot were both silent. Hunter was dead, and as for Declan Farrell himself, a rock broke his fall but his back too, his head taking the rest of the force. He survived, if you could call it that. He couldn't move or talk, and would spend the rest of his life breathing and eating through tubes.

Even though the court didn't get hold of Weaver, the employment tribunal did, where the interview rules didn't apply. He lost everything when he was dismissed. His pension. His wife. His friends. It wasn't the plot to kill Declan Farrell that cost him. No one cared about Declan Farrell and Weaver would have secretly been a hero to many, if he had killed him. No, it was the way that he had helped to bury a seemingly dead colleague and let his widow grieve over his disappearance without knowing the truth.

It became too much for Weaver one night, when he was at the wrong end of a whisky bottle, which was overturned on the floor next to his body and the shotgun that he had jammed into his mouth. He had been dead for more than a month before he was discovered. People didn't visit him any more.

For Joe, it was all about a new start. His gamble had worked. He had addressed the media with the firm's name on a board behind him. Honeywells had become the firm to go to when there was a fight to be won. The day-to-day routine stuff still made up his diary, but Joe was receiving a stream of letters from prisons around the country, from people wanting help in being released. Gina was vetting them. Some were hopeless, but others were from prisoners whose campaigns had long since run out of energy. Joe was deciding which ones he would try to bring back to life.

'It hasn't changed much around here,' Mary said, her voice quiet as they entered greener areas and into Raheny, the last major suburb before Dublin slowly petered out towards the small fishing towns like Howth and Portmarnock. Joe noticed that her accent had become a shade stronger ever since he had collected her from the airport. He'd been making a short holiday of it before Mary and Aidan arrived.

'It's nice, I like it,' Joe said.

Mary put her hand on her stomach. 'I'm so nervous.' She turned to Aidan, just before Joe made a right turn. 'That's where I met your father, in that pub.' And she pointed at a small building with a black front and gold lettering in the middle of a parade of shops. 'It was called the Green Dolphin back then, but I bet it has hardly changed.' She smiled. 'My daddy used to come and visit me sometimes when I was working, and sit at the front of the pub with the other old guys and watch the horses.'

She went quiet, and Joe didn't have to look across to know that Mary was trying not to get emotional.

They turned into a road that ran gently towards the sea, a calm blue strip against stretches of green. Houses lined both sides at first, some rendered in concrete and painted pale colours, others with their vivid red brickwork highlighted by thick light mortar. When the houses stopped, the light got brighter and the view ahead opened out into green school fields, the fields that fronted the boys' school on one side, the girls' convent school on the other. Mary pointed things out to Aidan as they went – how the old girls' school had given up some of its field to housing and how some of the old corporation housing had been smartened up.

She stopped talking, though, when they got nearer the sea, driving slowly past stretches of water on either side of the road, where the tide swept in behind the island ahead and where birds floated lazily, towards the slow undulation of grass-covered sand dunes that bordered Dollymount Beach.

Dublin felt far away as Joe turned towards the beach. It was suddenly tranquil, and the steady hum of his tyres was silenced when they drove onto the sand, the slow tumble of the tide just a few yards away. It was just as Mary had described it: an escape, an unexpected oasis on the edge of a capital city.

The beach was quiet. Large rocks lined up along it, placed deliberately to make a breakwater and a small car park. The sea rolled gently onto the sand, a long peaceful strip that fronted the entire island, a three-mile stretch of grass and rolling dunes, with Dublin visible to the south and the gentle rise of the hill over Howth to the north. The thin chimneys of a power station and the high cranes of Dublin port spoilt the view southwards, but it was easy to ignore them and instead feel the gentle coolness of the tide. A man walked a small terrier in the distance, a lone figure against the gentle sway of the water and the hills on the other side of the bay.

The soft breeze blew Joe's hair as he climbed out of the car, Mary with him. There were tears on her cheeks.

She wiped her face. 'I spent so much of my childhood down here,' she said softly. 'My parents brought us here and we'd play in the dunes, chase each other and fly kites and just enjoy the salt in our eyes.' She looked around. 'I miss the sea. I'd forgotten how much it meant to be close by it. I couldn't think much about it, as memories of this place brought back other memories too. Painful ones.' Then a glint appeared in her eye. 'And perhaps some not so painful...' And she laughed as she blushed.

'Let's walk,' Joe said, grinning, and set off along the beach. Mary was animated as they went, her hands in her coat pockets, turning and looking around, smiling.

'It's a nice place,' Joe said to her. 'I wouldn't have expected something like this so close to the city.'

'Dublin is full of surprises,' Mary said. 'It's not all about the craic.' She stopped and put her hand on Joe's arm. 'Thank you for everything, Joe. I appreciate it, I really do. We both do.' And she looked towards Aidan, who had walked ahead, his hands in his pockets, his shoulders hunched, as if he was still getting used to the open spaces again.

'So what now for you?' he said.

'I don't know. I feel a bit lost now that my fight for Aidan is nearly over.'

'Why don't you move home?' Joe said. 'Rediscover Mary Molloy, the woman you were before you had to fight for everything.'

'It's not as easy as that,' she said. 'There's a lot of history here for me. Personal stuff.'

A car pulled onto the beach behind them, next to Joe's car. No one got out. Then Joe's phone buzzed in his pocket. When he read the message, he turned round.

Someone was getting out of the car. A man. Tall and grey, hunched over in a faded checked shirt and loose slacks. There were other people inside.

Joe put his hand on Mary's. 'I came here early for a reason,' he said, his voice soft. 'I wanted to be here when you arrived because you coming back here felt like it completed the story. Except it isn't fully finished, not with things as they are.'

'What do you mean?'

Joe sighed. 'I wanted to make it right with your family, build some bridges.' He put his hands up, palms outwards. 'Don't be angry with me, Mary. I just wanted to make it right. You're a proud woman, and I didn't want that to get in the way.'

Mary swallowed, and a tear ran down her cheek.

Her chin quivered. 'You spoke to my family?'

Joe nodded.

'What did they say?' she said, her voice a croak.

Joe turned and pointed to the car. 'There they are, Mary. They're here for you. They want to bring you home.'

Mary looked past and her hand went to her mouth. 'It's my daddy,' she whispered.

'He misses you. They all do. Too many things were said. Now is the time to try to make it right.'

She nodded slowly and let out a sob, before stepping past Joe.

Mary walked back along the beach, her hair blowing gently. Aidan had stopped further along and was looking back, confused.

Mary's father started walking towards her, his arms out, and she started running, her sobs drifting up on the breeze.

As she threw herself into her father's arms, she buried her head in his chest. He kissed her head and then lost his face in her hair. Everyone else got out of the car, and soon they were in a huddle, kissing Mary, hugging her.

Joe turned around. Go to them, Aidan,' he said. 'It's your family.'

As Aidan went past, slowly, nervousness on his face, Joe smiled, his eyes glistening.

It's done, he thought. This was why he did it. It wasn't for him, or for the law. It was for this, the right thing.

He nodded to himself, satisfied. He'd done the right thing.

The publishers hope that this book has given you enjoyable reading. Large Print Books are especially designed to be as easy to see and hold as possible. If you wish a complete list of our books please ask at your local library or write directly to:

Magna Large Print Books
Magna House, Long Preston,
Skipton, North Yorkshire.
BD23 4ND

This Large Print Book for the partially sighted, who cannot read normal print, is published under the auspices of

THE ULVERSCROFT FOUNDATION